Strands of My V

Book Fou. .. ...
Elizabeth of England Chronicles

By G. Lawrence

This book is dedicated with thanks to Terry Tyler
And to Susan Cooper-Bridgewater
Two fine, bold, and talented women,
without whose support, I would not be an author today

"Think you that I could love my winding sheet, when, as examples show, Princes cannot even love their children that are to succeed them?"

**Elizabeth I to Scottish Ambassador,
William Maitland, Laird of Lethington, 1561**

Prologue

Richmond Palace
February 1603

Death has ceased to dance.

He lifts the hand of His partner, Amy Dudley, to kiss. Her ghostly skirts billow as she curtseys to Death. She draws back into the darkness and I hear her soft chuckle on the wind that creeps under the tapestry and into my old bones. She joins the other ghosts left there waiting... waiting for me.

In the dim shadows, eyes shine. They are watching me.

Death turns to gaze at me through the cowl of His hood. It is strange to look into such deep darkness and yet feel no fear. I do not fear Him, not now, not as I once did. There was a time when all about me seemed to talk only of my demise and what it would bring to England. But at that time, as all talked of my death, it was others who fell to His power. I feared Death then, for His power, for His talent for thievery. But I found ways to thwart Him. I found ways to escape Him, to stand tall, to face Him... Now, I welcome His presence for Death is my old friend.

But then... Ah, then it was so different. There comes a time in life when the people we love rush to leave us... A time when it seems life has become more about loss than about gain. I had lost people in my youth, but they had fallen to the changing whims of politics and power... events I believed I could change, and control when I became Queen. But there are some circumstances which do not alter, even under the hand of such mortal power as mine... Disease, plague, illness... These events I cannot change. These events I cannot control.

But He can.

Death glances back into the gloom. I know who waits there, watching over me. There are many shades waiting to come forth. They are waiting for me to join them. Shadows of ones I loved; ghosts of those who loved me. My words, my tale will bring them forth. This is what happens when one tells a story; the past and its people are brought to life again... Just as they are, too, brought once more to die.

We weavers of tales, we tellers of stories, we have the power to make the dead live again. Through our stories we see their faces once more dappled with the light of the sun. We can recall their lives, and the events they shaped. We can smell the scent of their skin, and feel the warmth of their eyes. We can call them to us, but we cannot change how their stories end. That is Death's power. Death is the true story-teller, for He alone decides when our stories end.

My words have the power to draw those I have loved and lost from the darkness behind Death. And there is one, one amongst all the others, one I am not sure I can bear to see, even now. Even though the time draws close when I will join the ghosts of my past in eternal rest, I do not know if I can look on those eyes again and know myself separated from this one person still, if only for a short while.

Oh shade! Oh beloved ghost... I see you. I wish you had not left me. Oh shade... wait for me.

My tale is not yet done.

Chapter One

The Old Provost's Lodge
The Garden of Kirk O'Field
Edinburgh
Scotland

9th February 1567

The explosion came at two o' clock in the morning.

The settled night was spread dark and deep over the lands of Scotland. The air was bitterly cold and snow tumbled from the skies. As the stars stood high and proud in the velvet black of the skies, slumberous people twitched in dreams they would not recall when the dawn emerged. In the muted shadows of the trees and in town alleyways, creatures of the night roamed, gathering food, seeing off rivals… claiming this murky world as their own. It had been a normal day. The sun had risen. Snow had fallen. People had gone about their business; gathering wood, tending livestock, cooking, trading and buying at market. There was nothing to suggest strange events were lurking as the light drained from the skies. It was the feast of *Quinquagesima*; the Sunday before Ash Wednesday and the beginning of Lent; a time of fasting and prayer. That Sunday, my cousin Mary, Queen of Scots, had attended a wedding. Bastian Pages, one of her valets, and Christina Hogg, one of her favourite gentlewomen had been married that morning in the chapel of Holyrood Palace. My cousin had presented the bridal gown to her lady and witnessed the celebration of what she believed would be a happy marriage.

Happier than her own had turned out, she hoped…

By mid-afternoon, my cousin had left the wedding to attend a feast given in honour of the Duke of Savoy's ambassador who was leaving for his homeland. Leaving this engagement at seven, Mary returned to the small house in the garden of Kirk O'Field, where her husband was celebrating his return to health. Many, knowing well Lord Darnley's voracious appetites, suspected he had been struck down with syphilis. He had healed under the tender care of his wife and they were newly reconciled after months of tension, and treason. That night it seemed their troubles were behind them.

By eight o' clock, Mary was at her husband's side. As they sat and ate together, Darnley became amorous. Kissing and touching his wife, he asked her to spend the night with him. Mary smiled, and gently reminded him that she had promised to return to the marriage celebrations of her beloved servants. They had all the time in the world to be together, she said, now that they were reconciled. Petulant at being refused, Darnley sulked, consuming vast quantities of wine. When she left the house at eleven of the clock, Mary took a ring from her finger and slid it upon his, promising to lie with him the following night. As Mary left the hall and walked into the outside courtyard, she saw that one of her servants, Nicholas Hubert, had a mightily dirty face. By the flickering orange light of the torches held by the riders, Mary peered at Hubert, who was often called 'French Paris' saying, "*Jesu*, Paris, how begrimed you are!" and was baffled when the man flushed deep crimson. Putting this slight incident from her mind, Mary rode to Holyrood where the bedding ceremony was about to take place. Taking the lead role in Christina's chambers, Mary took part in the raucous ritual. A little after midnight, tired, but in good spirits, the Queen of Scots retired to her own room.

Darnley stayed up, drinking, as was his habit. Slurring commands to his men to have his horse ready so he could join his wife at Holyrood the next day, he staggered to his bed. His servants, Thomas Nelson and Edward Simmons, slept in the gallery adjoining his chamber. They had a page with them also, named Andrew McCaig and perhaps another half dozen servants were in rooms below. The house fell to silence, as the hours rolled on and all within it slept.

The chapel clock struck one… then two…

A brilliant flash lit the skies. For a moment, the cobalt blue of night flushed as bright as noon, and just as sudden, the light vanished. Immediately after the light came the noise. A mighty crack ripped the skies and shook the ground. In the town, men and women sat bolt upright from their warm beds. There were shouts of alarm and then strained whispers, calling for silence. Thinking it was cannon fire, and believing the English were invading, many grabbed at dagger, sword, scythe or musket, and raced out into the chilled air, still buttoning jerkins and tying on belts. Candles were lit with shaking hands. Wide eyes flashed white in the flickering gloom as dogs barked, racing about in panic. Crowds formed, full of shouting, worried, people. They pointed to the house of Kirk O'Field on the hill. Billowing plumes of smoke rose in the darkness and drifted white against the starlit skies. The scent of gunpowder was heavy on the wind and the sound of creaking masonry and breaking wood groaned like men close to death. The townspeople ran to the house. Men shouted to their wives to stay and guard the children. As they reached the shattered building, clouds of dust danced in the air, mingling with snowflakes. Cinders floated like butterflies. Splinters of wood, chunks of masonry, and large pieces of timber lay strewn around the gardens… Black burnt wood shining bright against the deep white snow.

The Old Provost's Lodge, where Lord Darnley had been sleeping, was razed to the ground.

Rubble lay everywhere. People picked through it, searching for survivors. Men kept their weapons close, wary of attack. Shouts of "Who goes there?" sounded as groups of searchers glimpsed each other in the light of their blazing torches. The scent of terror rose, mingling with the stench of burning wood and gunpowder. Wild rumours rippled through the crowds. The eerie shadows of those searching the grounds loomed wide and tall, and then shrank small. By candlelight, everything looks like a foe. Every movement in the dark made them leap with fright. Every creak and crack of moaning masonry unnerved them. Many feared for their Queen. They knew she had been here this night with her husband and rumours grew that their Queen had been slain by English assassins, or had been carried off to be ransomed.

And then, a stiff, harsh cry shouted for help. Searchers had come upon two bodies. Lying under a tree in nothing but their nightshirts, two men were discovered. They were dead. The tree was forty feet from the house, in a garden on the far side of Thieves' Row. The bodies were on the opposite side of the wall about the grounds of Kirk O'Field. Evidently, these men had clambered over the wall, escaping the blast, for close to the bodies was a chair, a rope and a furred cloak. A dagger lay in the grass, but when this was found it only caused more bafflement, for there were no scorch marks on the nightshirts of the corpses, no burns upon their pale skin. There were no bloody stab wounds, no evidence of musket shot. There was not a mark on the bodies to show how they died.

It was as though they had scaled the wall, sat down next to the tree, and simply died.

It did not take long to identify one of the bodies as Henry Stewart, Lord Darnley. The second was William Taylor, one of Darnley's servants. The body of Andrew McCraig was found near his master, under some rubble on a path leading to the wall. Of Darnley's remaining servants, Nelson and Simmons were found alive. One of the servants sleeping downstairs had been killed in the blast, but the others were found alive, yet none of them could say what had happened, or who was responsible. Many people had managed to survive the explosion, but their master, Lord Darnley, had made it from the house, had escaped the blast, but was dead... by means unknown.

In Holyrood, Mary had been woken by the explosion. Sending her great supporter, Lord Bothwell, along with her captain of the guard to investigate, she dressed quickly, fearing a plot on her life. When she heard what had happened, she was amazed. Mary said Darnley and his servants must have been thrown from the building by the explosion, but others objected. If that was so, then where were the marks on their clothes? The dirt? The burns from being hit by the blast? The corpses were unburned, unharmed... Over the days that passed, other theories started to emerge, many of them dangerous to the Queen and her men.

I received a missive from Mary, written two days after the event. After I read this ill news, I walked to my window and stood there staring, seeing nothing. I felt as though part of my story had taken flight and joined hers. As though a strand of my tale had come loose from the past; billowing in the winds of fate, its frayed ends had touched her life. Its untold ending found a home in her story instead of mine. Echoes of Amy Dudley's death washed over me. I shivered.

A sudden and mysterious death... no marks on the body... a couple who all knew were no longer in love, and another husband waiting in the wings... There were too many echoes of Amy's death, of the situation I had faced only a few years before, for me to ignore. I stared from that window not seeing the present. I saw only the past.

I did not want to think of the future for I feared what it would bring.

Chapter Two

Windsor Castle
Autumn 1560

Seven Years Earlier...

"Your Majesty *must* eat," Kat insisted. Her tone was scandalised. I glanced back at her from my window seat. Kat's good, honest face was twisted with concern. Her eyes were bright with anxiety. She did not like that my appetite had deserted me in these recent, troubled times.

"I am not hungry, Kat. I have no appetite," I murmured, as my eyes fell back to the river. The lapping waters were grey and dull, reflecting storm clouds drifting above. England sensed my mood, and had mirrored it in her skies, in her rivers and in the air around us. There had been no rain, yet the air was thick with its heralds. Clouds with blackened edges hung over us. The wind was picking up pace. I could hear it calling to me as it keened about the grey stone walls of the castle, as it flew over the battlements... as it crept through the chamber, making the tapestry which hung along the walls billow as though ghosts waited behind it. The winds had been calling to me for months and I had ignored them. But, finally, I had heard, I had listened. I had obeyed.

I had made the choice I *had* to make; for me, for Robin, for England... and yet although I knew it was right, it felt nothing other than wrong. I had chosen not to marry, and never to marry Robin. I could not marry the man I loved. His wife had died in mysterious circumstances and to marry him now, or in the future, would only confirm to my enemies and to my people that he had murdered Amy, and I had been complicit in that barbarous act. He would remain at my side, as my servant, and yet I knew myself separated from him forever. This was a special torture fate had invented for me. My spirits were low. I did not want to eat and sleep ran from me. Kat was not the only one who worried for my health, but she was the most outspoken.

My eyes roamed over the slippery banks and water of the Thames. The swans were gathering; their grey and white feathered cygnets swimming between them. They hooted and hissed as boats navigated around them, their wings like fierce, arched sails. Some rose up, beating their wings, making rivulets and waves in the slate-grey depths. The river moved as though an old maid were knitting under its surface, making criss-cross patterns through the water with her needles. The swans would soon fly from England. I wished I could do the same and leave my troubles far behind me.

"What has *appetite* to do with eating?" Kat scolded, picking up plates of roasted capon and venison pie from the table. I had received the meal without interest, toyed with the dishes and then left without eating to stare restlessly from the window. "You need to *eat*, Majesty, or else you will die. This is not a matter of appetite, but one of survival."

"I have long known how to survive, Kat. Allow me to know what is required to achieve that aim."

"*Elizabeth*!" Kat's patience broke. Her voice clipped through the air like the clopping of hooves on a frost-covered courtyard. I turned and stared dully at her. She glowered back, her eyes bright with defiance, her cheeks pink with anger. "Enough of this!" she exclaimed, striding towards me with a chunk of marchpane in her hand. She thrust it at me, stood back and folded her arms. Kat's stare would have cowered nations. "Eat!"

Obediently, I put the sweet marzipan into my mouth and chewed. Kat glared, trying to find further reason to be angry, and then her face tumbled. She dropped her hands and sat beside me. "You are skin and bones, Elizabeth." She nudged me with her shoulder. There was a catch in her voice.

I swallowed the last of the sugary marchpane. "I have just not felt like eating, Kat. It will pass, as all things do."

Kat sighed. "I know these past months have been hard for you, my love." Her tone turned gentle. "But you cannot let yourself waste away. You are the *Queen*, Elizabeth."

"I know well enough who and what I am, Kat, as I have proved. Have I not given up much for the good of my country?"

Kat paused. There was compassion in her eyes, but she agreed with my choice. "Well," Kat went on, not wanting to pursue a line of conversation we both knew could go nowhere. "*I* know that queens, like everyone else, fall down and die if they don't eat. So from now on, think on mealtimes as part of your duties to the realm, Your Majesty."

I reached out and touched her face. There were traces of grey in her brown hair, and lines at the corners of her eyes, but to me she would always be beautiful and young. "I will think of *you*, Kat." I ran my long fingers down the curve of her jaw. "And I will eat."

"That will do well enough." Kat's face puckered. She opened her arms and I sank into them. I had no tears left now. I had cried for so long when first I knew Robin was lost to me that I believed I had used up all my tears. I was dry, parched inside… My heart had shrivelled like a dried walnut. It was torn and raw, dry and sore, and riddled with stinging, acid guilt. I had told Robin there may still be hope for us to marry, once the scandal of his wife's death died down. It was not so. I knew there was no path I could take that would lead me to Robin now. That time of dreaming was done. But I loved him. My heart would never, in truth, let go of him. I had lied, seeking to keep him; a craven act, born from my instinct for survival, for I could not do without him.

"Master Cecil asks for admittance," Kat said. "Shall I let him in?"

"Cecil believes I have let my responsibilities to the kingdom drift away, whilst I concentrated on pleasures." My tone was bitter, but my most able advisor had a point.

"We all make mistakes, my love," Kat consoled. "God made us human, not divine. Even the angels made mistakes."

"I am no angel, Kat." I lifted my head and smiled. "And I am far from divine."

"We all have to make choices in life, my love." She put her hands into mine; they were warm against the coolness of my flesh. The scent of lavender rose from her skin. It was an old, familiar scent, one that reminded me of childhood, of nights when she lay in my bed, singing me to sleep. "And for you, being Queen, your choices are harder than those of others."

I inclined my head. "What news is there from about court?"

Kat lifted her shoulders. "Much the same, my lady... All still speak of Lord Robin and the death of his wife. Many believe you will marry him now that he is free. Others say you will not." She lifted a finger and whirled it slowly in the air. "And so the world goes on, my love, as ever it did before."

"And I must re-join it."

"And you must re-join it," she agreed. "But first, you must eat, or they will say there is not a queen who rules over England, but a wraith."

"Bring me some bread and quince jelly." I gave in. "And I will eat. Then, Cecil may come in."

"It is sometimes better, my lady, to concentrate on work when you are at a loss in life."

I pulled her to me. "My wise old hen," I whispered. "What would I do without you?"

"You will never have to find that out, Elizabeth."

I released her. Kat made for the table to cut thick slices of quince jelly and slathered it on fine, white bread with yellow butter. Although I normally loved such sweet fare, the smell made my stomach curl. But, for Kat, I lifted the bread to my mouth and ate. It did not taste sweet but strange and foreign. Everything tasted bitter these days. The sourness in my heart was consuming me. I was sad. I felt lost. I had to find a way to stop my resentment devouring me. Kat was right. I should work. That was how I would lose this feeling. That was how I would put my foolish dreams behind me.

"Send for Cecil," I said, washing my sticky fingers in a silver bowl of perfumed water. I took a linen cloth from her hands and dried my own. "If I have denied myself one marriage, I still have another to maintain," I murmured, "with England."

*

"I *did* say that the plan was not without risk, Majesty." Cecil leaned back in his chair, tapping his quill against his customary pile of parchment on the table. I had begun to wonder if Cecil was always accompanied by a mound of papers. Was he able to sleep at night without the scratching sound of parchment rustling and the plopping clink of a quill entering an ink pot?

"You did, *Spirit*, and it was noted at the time, as it is now," I agreed, to set his mind at rest. "Have you taken all the ornaments that once decorated my sister's chapel?"

He nodded, narrowing his eyes at his list and running the feather end of his quill down it. "There are perhaps... eight thousand ounces of gold and silver from your sister's papist chapel, Majesty," he informed me. "From crosses, cruets, pyxes, incense boats, bells and other sundries." He glanced up, a wary smile on his face. "We have *plundered* your royal chapel, my lady."

"Plunder away, *Spirit*. I require nothing more than the candlesticks, the prayer books and the three crosses I asked to be retained. The coinage needs that wealth more than my chapel does."

"Although all such items smack of popery, Majesty, it was still a generous sacrifice."

"I am sure my sister's grave is restless this day, Cecil." I waved a hand at Katherine Knollys to bring me a cup of small ale. "But I will bear the outpouring of her ghost's grief when we meet in the light of God."

Cecil chuckled at my jest, but I am sure he did not believe my sister would be in Heaven waiting for me. Despite his reverence for the monarchy, my sister's ardent Catholicism and zealous persecution of Protestants in her reign were reasons he believed she might be excluded from Heaven. I did not think this was the case. For all the ill my sister did, I did not believe God would reject her soul. And on the day she and I met once more, I would have to explain why I had melted down the items she had loved so dear from her royal chapel.

During the last years of my father's reign, and those of my brother and sister, the coinage of England had been debased. Reducing the amount of silver or gold in each coin had helped my predecessors boost royal revenues, but a country can only go so long debasing its coinage before troubles arise. Debasing coins devalues their worth and decreases the spending power of the people. It was time to restore the coinage before it was permanently de-valued in the eyes of the world. It was something I was determined to set right, but this restoration came at a price. I had to sacrifice gold and silver plate from the royal collection to underwrite the cost, and a large portion had come from the once-glorious chapel of my sister, Mary. Although I believed God requires no wealth and ornamentation in His house, the sacrifice was still a wrench. I had loved and admired many of the superb ornaments of my sister's chapel. But much like my recent sacrifice to give up the man I loved, for the country I ruled, I was required to do the same with many glorious items in the royal collection. This was another personal sacrifice for the England I wished to see emerge from the shadows of her troubled past.

"We still do not know if it will work *entirely*, Majesty," Cecil noted, his nose almost brushing the parchment as he checked his figures. "But I believe we *should* have enough to revalue the coinage."

"Good, I want England's coin trusted once more." I ran a finger over my lips and felt scaly skin. Despite the mixture of goose fat and cochineal I was wearing, my lips were rough and dry. Kat had told me, clucking in her fretful way, that this was due to my not eating enough. Every ill, apparently, was due to my lack of appetite these days. Katherine Knollys handed me the small ale, watered just the way I liked it and I smiled in thanks, putting it to my lips. As I drank, the cracks in my lips stung. I set the goblet down.

"There is word from France, too, Majesty," Cecil continued.

I lifted my carefully plucked eyebrows. "If it is another report from Throckmorton on the unmatched loveliness of my cousin, the Queen, I can do without hearing it, *Spirit*," I retorted waspishly. "If the man were any more in love with Mary Stewart he would sail into the clouds on tiny wings sprouted from his back, and play a harp unto Venus."

Cecil smiled. "It is true Throckmorton appears much taken with Queen Mary," he agreed. "But he writes to counsel you, Majesty, about Lord Robert Dudley."

"Telling me not to marry Lord Robin, am I right?" Cecil inclined his head and I heaved a sigh. "I have already said I will not marry Robin, Cecil," I said. "How many times must I say the same thing?" Every time I had to state I was not going to marry Robin the sharp blade of sorrow thrust through wounds raw and bleeding in my heart. "I am not of a mind to marry *anyone*." I tapped my fingers on the table. "And that includes Lord Robin Dudley. Tell Throckmorton to cease to pester me on the matter. I am done with it."

"I fear, Majesty, we may never be done with it." Cecil gazed at me with sympathy.

"Aye... That would seem to be the case, *Spirit*, for none will let the matter rest."

"Perhaps if your Majesty would distance yourself from Dudley, for a time, it may be easier for your people to grasp the idea that you are not intending to wed him."

"Robin will not place a ring on my finger, Cecil, but he has my trust and my friendship. I will not abandon him, and certainly not now, as he stands with the eyes of the world gazing at him with suspicion. I am no flighty friend, or fanciful soul. He has little protection but I, *Spirit*, and I will not serve him to his enemies trussed up like a winter hog with an apple in his mouth." I shook my head. "No... I do not desert friends, Cecil. England is a demanding mistress. I have sacrificed much for her already, let that be enough." Cecil allowed the subject to drop, but I had no doubt I would find it sneaking back soon enough. "Is there any other news?" I asked.

"Ambassador de Quadra is keen for an interview, madam. He is most distressed you have ignored him of late."

I sniffed. "And my days were *so* peaceful without him, what does he want of me now?"

"What else, my lady? To marry you to a Hapsburg."

"Bring him in to see me tomorrow, Cecil, but ensure the meeting is brief. I am in no humour to listen to de Quadra's whining."

"I will make certain the ambassador understands."

"Excellent, and any other news?"

"Only that Lady Douglas Howard, or Lady Sheffield, I should say now, since she is married, has sent some good mutton for Your Majesty's table from her husband's lands since she knows you are fond of it. Also, Viscount Hereford and his new wife send their thanks for the gifts you sent on their wedding day," Cecil went on. "Walter Devereux is quite delighted with his new wife."

"Whether she feels quite the same remains to be seen," I noted dryly, thinking of my intoxicating cousin, Lettice, and her new husband. It had been a good match, and a healthy rise in status for my Boleyn-blood cousin, but I had suspicions her true fancy ran in another direction. In fact, the wandering of Lettice's hazel-green eyes over the body of Robin had been reason enough to hurry along her match with Devereux … She was far too tempting a woman to leave unwed and loose about the court.

"Well, I hope they will be happy together," I said. "Devereux is a good man."

"As Lettice is a good woman?" Cecil's moustache rustled with amusement.

I chuckled. "Perhaps, Cecil... that too remains to be seen, doesn't it?"

Chapter Three

Hampton Court
Winter 1560

"How are you, Robin? With all that is going on at court of late?" I spoke awkwardly to my Master of Horse, and cursed my voice for betraying me. I had tried to avoid further talk about marriage, trying to conceal my lie in silence. Robin sensed my unease. We had parried about each other for weeks and were stilted, ill at ease with each other. There was a distance between us. I wanted to remedy this, but knew not how. Robin was more than my friend. He was a part of my very soul. This strange, strained friendship we had entered was not to my liking.

Robin shrugged. "The rumours continue, but all see that I have your support, Majesty, and that settles the matter in some minds. In others, it does not."

"I wish they could all trust in you and be satisfied. The case has been heard, the truth has been told." I sighed. "If they could look into your heart, Robin, they would know there was no cause to suspect you."

"Some would rather judge me without knowing me, Majesty. It is easier that way."

"True enough, Robin," I agreed. "Many people judge on rumour and gossip alone. They do not welcome the truth, especially if it is less exciting than their fantasies."

We wandered through Hampton Court's icy gardens. The paths were white, sparkling silver serpents wending their way into the distance. England was beautiful in her winter clothes. Hoary frost sparkled on bare tree branches. Ice shone like diamonds on plants still bearing leaves. Fragile and brittle, those last leaves fought on, clinging to their branches and twigs, defying the cold wind. The skies were streaked blue and grey, silver and bright white. There was a taste of iron on the wind, promising snow soon to come. My eyes shied from the dazzling light of the sun on the frost, even as they were attracted by its unearthly beauty. Winter is so stark, and yet so glorious. I marvelled at the beauty of the year's death. I thought about the coming of the spring, and new life. More than usual, I needed to believe in the resurgence of life. Death sparkled about us, but He would not rule forever. Spring would come, banishing Him. There was hope in such thoughts.

"I wondered if Your Majesty had taken time to think about my suit." My heart leapt with panic as Robin spoke. I had no wish to speak of this again. I wanted to leave the matter, to forget, to simply be together as we had been; free and easy in our love, without the pressure of marriage. Guilt gnawed at me, whispering that I should tell him the truth. And yet I did not dare. *He will leave you and find another to love,* murmured my traitorous heart. *Do not reveal the truth. We must keep him for ourselves.*

Robin must have sensed my nervousness, for he did not look at me. He gazed at the river, where boats shipped passengers back and forth. Behind us my ladies walked, chatting to my guards about preparations for winter progress, and the entertainments to be held this season at court. Their voices were merry, carefree. I wished my heart were as light as theirs.

"It is too soon, Robin," I said in a low tone. "Your wife's death is still fresh in the mind and on the lips of England. Whilst the scandal lives, nothing more will be said on the subject."

"You do still love me, Elizabeth, do you not?" Still he did not look at me. He was afraid of my answer.

"I do," I murmured, and those words at least were honest. "But you must understand the situation, Robin. I cannot gamble with the love of my people. You do see that, don't you? We must wait."

He breathed in sharply, betraying his frustration. Clearly, he did not see. Robin believed that I, as Queen, could do as I wished no matter what people thought or said. I knew differently. I would lose my people's love if I married him, and Robin would earn their hatred. I could not bring war to England, in seeking love for myself. It was never going to be, but I could not tell him that. I could not bear the thought of losing him. For another woman to sleep in his bed, rest her head upon his naked shoulder, talk with him through the night... It pained me to play him false, but I was caught up in fear. It made me a coward.

I had lied many times, for survival. This was but survival of another kind. That was what I told myself then, as I lied to the man I loved. I fed Robin false hope; a broth that begins with such heady flavour and ends in a bitter aftertaste.

"We will talk of it again in the summer, Robin." We rounded a corner and walked towards the palace. Hampton's red bricks glimmered with frost and melting ice, glorious against the grey, imposing skies. Snow started to fall, and there would be deeper showers that night. But by then we would all be tucked safe and warm inside, dancing, as outside the world frosted and froze.

"In the summer." Robin's voice was flat. I hated to hear that tone. I wanted to return to the time before we spoke of marriage, where all was exciting and amusing, when we had flirted and danced... Now, everything was different. We were frozen like the gardens. We had become the ice-covered twigs on the trees, waiting for spring's thaw. We talked no more, but left the chilled grounds. Snow floated down, landing on the short grass and silver paths, settling and sparkling against the falling light. I shook my head as I entered my apartments. I had bought time from Robin, I hoped. But Time is a slippery creature. Sometimes he creeps, sometimes he races. And sometimes he flies by so fast that we have only to blink, to find our world has altered beyond all comprehension.

Chapter Four

Greenwich Palace
Winter 1560

That winter came in with bitter winds and driving storms. The coast was lashed by the sea, and rain fell from the skies in endless, stinging showers. Great waves crested, spiked against blackened skies. Tempests of hail and snow followed in their wake, freezing the sodden land and making the earth sparkle. Shivering rooks held council in the bare trees, as finches and magpies hopped along the ground seeking hidden seeds or tasty flesh of frost-slain beasts. Under the snow, primroses and violet shoots hid, waiting for the thaw. The wild wind brayed at night, flouncing about the palace walls and creeping in through crack and nook. Fires blazed in every hearth, their golden light trying to hold back the chill. Even in the palaces and castles, we could feel the wrath of that winter.

I had decided to take a winter progress; we had visited Whitehall, my lovely *warm box*, as I called it, then Greenwich and from here we would make for Eltham Palace. There was a fine park in its vast lands, with good hunting, and it was the place where my siblings and I had been sent to live together when we were young. Perhaps it was sentimental, but I felt their spirits beside me in ancient Eltham. My father's presence was strong there, too. The walls were filled with his maps, and corridors clicked and ticked with clocks he had collected and loved. Sometimes it was strange to me that a man of such rampant energy as my father could have loved something as steady and regular as a clock. But perhaps his enthusiasm was born from a lack of such steadiness in his life. Perhaps he had needed to place his hand upon the regular, sound, ticking pulse of life, and feel constancy reverberate in his blood and bone.

Cecil loved Eltham. It gave him a chance to indulge one of his favourite pastimes; maps. Oftentimes, I would find Cecil with his nose stuck so deep in a map I believed he might emerge with whole continents stuck up his nostrils. My father's collection was particularly fascinating, and since much of this was housed at Eltham, Eltham was where I often lost Cecil. It was amusing to see him, for once, restless in Council meetings, eager to be released so he could lose himself in those maps. I did not mind. It was pleasing to have at least a few hours each day, whilst Cecil pored over his beloved charts, to escape into the wilds of England.

This time, we were to make for Eltham primarily because Robin wanted to put on an entertainment for me there. There was to be a feast, a dance, and days of hunting. Robin was seeking to demonstrate he could be a fine husband, a great consort... if only I would agree to wed him. He did not know all such efforts were useless.

On the day we were to leave, Mistress Jane Seymour requested to speak with me. I liked Jane. She was the sister of Edward Seymour, Lord Hertford, and daughter of the late Protector Seymour who had been executed in the reign of my brother. Whilst I liked Jane, I was never sure about the company she chose to keep. Jane was friends with my cousin, Lady Katherine Grey, now one of my ladies of the Privy Chamber. Katherine Grey was popular at court and many, including Cecil, believed she was the natural choice for my heir. She was a female, which was not in her favour, but she was Protestant, which was. And she was English, making her instantly preferable to my cousin of Scots to many in England. Although some might view Katherine as a worthy choice for the throne, I did not. The girl was of much diluted royal blood, hailed from a traitorous family, and she was a halfwit! What good would it do England to have a queen such as her?

Despite the many voices which called me to do so, I was not about to name an heir. I had lived that position when I was a princess, and was only too aware of how dangerous it was. The heir to the throne can become a force, a focal point, for any who oppose the current sovereign. I had no wish to offer a figurehead to foes who desired my downfall.

I had made Katherine one of my highest ranking attendants, but I despised the girl. I had only promoted her because Ambassador de Quadra and his Spanish master, King Phillip of Spain, were noted taking too vested an interest in her. Last year, a plot had emerged. Phillip and his cronies were intending on kidnapping Katherine so they could marry her off to Phillip's unhinged son, Don Carlos. Once they had Katherine, they could stake a claim to my throne and there had been rumours of invasion, and assassination. I doubted Katherine had had much to do with the plot, if she had even known of it, but it had unnerved me enough to pull her close. I disliked having to do this, for spending time each day with one whom many believed should succeed to my throne when I was dead was like walking about with a sword at my throat. I did not want to be reminded of my mortality, who would? And besides, the girl was infuriatingly dense...

Jane, however, was different to her friend. She was pale of face and hair, but bright of spirit. She always had a ready smile and a titbit of gossip to share, and despite her delicate health, she was always merry. I liked such qualities. Being around miserable people is wearisome after a while. I preferred to associate with those who found joy in life. God only knows, I needed some happiness. So when she came to me with an unusually worried expression quivering on her brow, I gave her my attention.

"What is it, Jane?" I asked, watching Kat and Blanche fold and pack my gowns into oaken chests, working together to ensure my gorgeous wardrobe was not damaged en route to Eltham. They sprinkled dried lavender and the preserved heads of yellow-flowered ladies bedstraw into the trunks to ward off fleas and hungry moths. Packing to go on progress was like preparing to march an army to war; the organization often dictates the outcome.

"It is Lady Katherine, Majesty," said Jane, standing from her curtsey. "She is unwell, and asks permission to remain behind."

"What is wrong with my cousin?"

"A grievous pain in her teeth and jaw, Majesty, and her face has swollen up. She fears the cold air of the journey to Eltham will only make her sicker."

"Why did Katherine not come herself and ask permission to remain behind?" I watched as Katherine Knollys and Lady Bess St Loe walked in behind servants heaving a chest of slippers and shoes over to join the main packing efforts. Bess Parr appeared behind them with a pile of linen over her arm. I glanced at Bess with concern. She had been ill of late, and whilst she seemed hale enough today, I knew she had concerns about a lump in her breast and a pain in her arm. I had sent her my doctors, who prescribed a change in her diet and bled her to restore her humours, but their ministrations had not rid her of the pain, nor the growth. We all knew such cankers could be dangerous and I hoped that, in time, the efforts of my doctors would see her restored to health.

"Katherine feared if her ailment was catching, Majesty, she might place you in danger," Jane said, drawing my attention back to her.

I doubted whether my falling ill would upset Katherine. When I first elevated her, I had treated her as though she were my own daughter to ensure Phillip of Spain understood I was watching her closely. Of late, however, it appeared Katherine had deduced my affections were but a show. If she had realised this, it would have been the first indication that I could credit her with for intelligence. I waved my hand at

Jane. "Very well," I said. "Tell her that she can remain behind."

"May I stay and care for her, Majesty?"

"If you must," I agreed with grudging reluctance. "But when she is well I want the two of you back in my chambers. Positions in my household are few and precious, as well you know, Jane. Give me no cause to consider granting them to others instead of you."

"Of course, Majesty," Jane said, looking aghast. "I would never wish to lose my place at your side, not for *anything* in the world."

"Well," I said, feeling a little mollified. She appeared genuine. "Have done then, Jane."

"I hope you have a lovely visit, Majesty." She bobbed a curtsey and strode out.

Kat walked past and I stopped her, putting a hand on her sleeve. "Did you notice Katherine Grey in any pain recently, Kat?"

Kat stared up at the decorated gilt ceiling as she thought. "She *was* holding her face yesterday, Majesty, and groaned through Mass in the morning. She was making a bit of a show of it, if you ask me."

"She has asked to stay behind because of a pain in her teeth and jaw."

"It may be that is the truth," Kat said, pursing her lips. "I thought her a little over the top, but then some are skilled at handling pain and others are not."

I nodded. "Well, let us get on." I gazed about at the spectacular mess which always seemed to somehow knit itself into order through the ministrations of Kat and Blanche whenever we moved. "I want to be at Eltham in good time." I thought no more on the absence of Katherine Grey and Jane Seymour as the chests were packed onto the wagons and our horses clattered along the roads and out of the city.

There came a time, a little later, when I would curse my lack of inquisitiveness that day.

Chapter Five

Eltham Palace
Winter 1560

On a crisp morning in late November, we rode out into Eltham's park. At my side were Katherine Knollys, Kat, Blanche and Mary Grey, their cheeks flushed with the cold air and the excitement of the day. Robin led my huntsmen and noblemen, taking us to marshy fields where we would fly the fine hawks and falcons of my royal mews.

My falconers were superstitious men. They had a great many small, strange rituals, and spoke prayers over their birds before hunting. I did not reprimand them for these rituals, which to many spoke of popery; of times past, when we English were consumed by the need to sanctify everything with superstitious rites. Although I doubted God was ever so freed from all His tasks that He would intervene to aid me in the hunt, I allowed my men their rituals. What harm did it do? Besides, I liked to hear them mumble prayers in Latin over my falcons. My father had always done the same before he went hunting. He had been a superstitious man.

We rode through ice-blanketed fields, past small patches of woodland, reaching the marshy ground where my falcons could fly best, and where wild ducks would be plentiful. Frost clung, poised on the edges of leaves as it melted, dripping in the pale sunlight. The skies were bright and cold. The frozen earth under my horse's hooves cracked and splintered as his weight broke through the lining of frozen water. Spaniels, their long, pink tongues steaming in the cold air, valiantly attempted to stand still, and failed. Their legs, restless with anticipation, bounced upon the frozen ground willing us to begin, so they could charge over the fields and through the shrubs, to retrieve our kills. As the Master of Hounds told them to sit and wait, the sound of their tails wagging, thumping on the wet earth, rose up like a drum-beat through the silver-streaked skies.

Beaters, their numbers swollen with local children keen to earn a coin for a morning's work, walked towards the bushes. Long sticks in their hands, they would flush game from the undergrowth. At their side was my Moorish drummer, Peter, newly arrived from Spain. Thumping a steady, ringing refrain on his skin drum, he set the pace. I took up my falcon, a fine black, grey and almost blue-feathered bird. Stroking his head, as he pranced on my thick leather glove, I glanced at the Master Falconer. "Shall we let fly together, Master Osbern?" I asked. The man bowed, sensible of the honour. The beaters entered the reeds as we lifted our hands, releasing the birds simultaneously into the air, up and into the clouds.

As the beaters continued, swiping through reed-bed and grass, mallards flapped out with raucous shouts of alarm. They flew up, heading straight into the path of the swift falcons. I saw mine swoop, his blue-grey feathers shadowy against the sky as he plummeted down upon a fleeing duck. Talons outstretched, a scream of triumph shrieking from his beak, he plunged and caught a fine, fat duck. The duck cried out, helplessly, as it fell and was pinned to the ground by my falcon. The kill was met with a heavy burst of applause from those around me, and as I looked up again, I saw the Master Falconer's bird swoop, her brown-gold feathers glittering as she stretched her talons wide and pierced deep into living flesh.

Robin pulled his horse close to mine as I complimented Osbern. "A fine strike, Majesty," he observed. I noticed creases around his eyes I had not seen before. I suppose we were all growing older. I was twenty-seven now, and Robin was the same age, but I knew that the strain he had suffered after his wife's death was also to blame.

"Think you, my lord, that you can beat my score this day?" A smile hovered at my lips, but I remained staring at the skies, as though I were impervious to his presence. Nothing could have been further from the truth. When Robin was near me, I was alive.

"A challenge!" he exclaimed, sitting upright on his saddle. "I'll wager the finest hawk in my own mews, Majesty, against that of yours, should I best you this day."

Grinning, I twisted in my saddle and held out my hand in its decorated leather glove. Etched deep into its brown-black covering were the badges of the Tudor rose, and my mother's crowned white falcon emblem. Robin took my hand, and a jolt passed through me at his touch, like the cracking spit of coal dust in the air above a fire's flames. "Done, Rob," I agreed. I waved him forward, along with Mary Grey. "Time to try your luck, my lord," I teased.

Robin's face was ruddy with excitement as he and Mary flew their birds. We continued on through the morning, watching each fly their bird, and counting the spoils of our hunt. When the final count came, I had won. "Ill-luck, my lord," I commiserated without sympathy, grinning wolfishly.

"Ill-luck is my constant companion at the moment," Robin said. "But I have hope, Majesty, that one day this will alter."

"Nothing stays the same, Robin," I observed. "Except for me. *Semper Eadem*... It has ever been my motto, just as it was once my mother's."

"In some matters, Majesty." Robin's tone grew more pressing. "I would you could consider the virtues of *sometimes* changing your mind."

"And perhaps I will, someday," I agreed. Wishing to head Robin off before he could speak of marriage, I turned to the falconers. They were collecting the game into bags, twisting the necks of still-living birds, and counting the falcons and hawks. "Any lost, this day, gentlemen?" I asked. Losing birds during the hunt was always a problem. No matter how well-trained they were, oftentimes a saker, or a hawk would catch sight of something and fly for it, causing my men to spend hours recovering them.

"Two, Majesty," replied Master Osbern. "I have sent lads to find them, but the birds wear the royal jesses and bells. If they are found by common folk they will be returned for the standard reward."

"Good enough." I nodded. "We make for the palace. You will bring the game to the kitchens?"

Osbern bowed, his hands holding a flopping, dead mallard. "Of course, Majesty."

I glanced sideways at Robin. "Are you tired of wagers, my lord?" I asked. "Or shall we bet which of us will reach Eltham first?"

He narrowed his eyes at the terrain ahead, and then cast them over my horse, evaluating both mounts and the weights they carried. "I am always ready to *win*, Majesty. It is a foolish man who gives up when he does not at first succeed. To my mind, the only true failure lies in not trying for what we want in life."

I sighed inwardly. It was another point, made with such careless ease, to let me know he was not about to give up. As I had done so many times of late, I decided to ignore Robin. It was easier, in some ways, but such pretence was not helping the friction between us. With a great cry, I urged my horse on, digging my heels into his sides. He needed little encouragement. As I tore through the fields, back to Eltham, I could hear the panting of Robin's horse hard behind me. We rode like creatures possessed. He beat me back to Eltham, and I gave him my best falcon. It was the least I could do, since I could not give him what he truly desired.

*

When I arrived back from the hunt, my cheeks cherry-pink from racing, Cecil relayed the message that Master Robert Jones, secretary of Ambassador Throckmorton in France, had arrived at court. He had already been to Cecil to give his news, and now sought an audience with me. As my ladies stripped my riding clothes from me, I wished I could avoid meeting with Jones. Throckmorton sent endless missives from the French Court, all warning me about marriage with Robin, that was, when they were not dripping with slavish adoration for my cousin, Mary Stewart, Queen of France. I had no doubt Jones had been sent with more of the same. There are only so many times that one can hear the twitter of an unwelcome bird without wanting to wring its neck. That was how I felt about my ambassador in France. If I had to listen to one more warning, or another lecture on the apparently never-ending parade of virtues possessed by the Queen of France, I believed I might lose my mind. But I had small choice in the matter. Rulers may be the masters of their people, but they are subject to them as well.

"Allow Jones into the Privy Chamber." Kat was making final adjustments to my gown of gold and red velvet. Her mouth full of pins, she narrowed her eyes critically at the set of the dress, making sure it was perfect. "But have some route ready for me, Kat, in case I need to escape the man."

Her mouth twitched at my plaintive tone and she removed the pins from between her lips. "I will have a *most* urgent emergency ready for you to attend to, Your Majesty," she agreed solemnly. Her voice fell to a whisper as she leaned in. "Fear not, my lady, I have your back."

I put my fingers against each other and cracked them back to the knuckles, making Kat wince. She said the noise made her bones shudder. "Send him in," I commanded, taking my place on my chair.

In walked Robert Jones. A man of average height and below-average intelligence, I had often thought. He served Throckmorton in France ably enough, but was not a man of much imagination. Perhaps that served my ambassador well, for he always sent Jones as his mouthpiece. Throckmorton was an intelligent and able man, but often spoke, and wrote, in a patronising manner I resented. No one, especially a queen, enjoys being looked down upon. Throckmorton had never got over the idea that his sovereign was a woman, and an unmarried one at that. Mary Stewart had his undying admiration because, in his mind, she was everything a queen should be; beautiful, powerful, yet obedient to her husband, gracious, modest and sweet. He did not understand me. He thought of me as an infant, requiring constant guidance. It was vexing. At times I wanted to order him home just so I could box his ears. But he *was* a useful ambassador, skilled in finding out all the gossip and information I wanted from the French.

"Your Majesty." Jones bowed low and as he did, one foot faltered, making him stumble. *Not the most auspicious of beginnings*, I thought.

"Master Jones." I played with a bright pin that had come loose from my gown, twirling it in my fingertips. "You have news for me?"

"My master sends his love and undying respect and adoration, Your Majesty," Jones said, in such a flat tone I wondered he even made the effort to speak. "And he sends me with *important* news, of a most delicate nature."

His pomposity made me want to chuckle, but I restrained myself. "Indeed?" I asked coolly. "Then do relay all to me, Master Jones. I am quite *breathless* with anticipation, as you see." Jones stared up with a startled expression, hearing sardonic acid thick upon my tongue. I waved a hand. "Do get on with it, Jones!" I commanded. "We have much to prepare before the feast arranged by Lord Dudley this evening. With your dithering, I shall miss out on my evening meal entirely."

"It is of Lord Dudley, madam, that I have come to speak," Jones replied stiffly.

"*What* a surprise," I murmured to myself and then raised my voice. "What does my ambassador have to say *this* time? I would have thought, with all the missives I have had from Throckmorton about Lord Robin Dudley, I would have heard all there was to know… You should advise Throckmorton to write a book on his favourite topic, Master Jones, for he appears to be a true authority on Robin Dudley." Jones coughed and shuffled his foot. "God's Blood! Do get on with it!" I swore, handing the stray pin to Kat. "My time is a precious commodity and you are carelessly throwing it to the winds."

Jones stepped forward with a piece of rolled parchment in his hands. Offering the scroll to Kat, who handed it to me, Jones finally got to the point. "The Queen of France was speaking about the recent death of Lord Robin's wife, Majesty," he said. "And made a comment of which my master believed you should know."

I glanced at the parchment. It said that Mary Stewart had exclaimed, whilst laughing, that "the Queen's Majesty would marry her *horse master*." Although irritating, and insulting, it was not the first time the little Scots strumpet had said such words. It was hardly news at all. I rolled up the parchment. "And?" I asked, frowning.

Jones blinked with surprise. "And… my master thought you would want to know… Majesty. Spanish and Venetian ambassadors are spreading rumours at the French Court that you will marry Robert Dudley."

"And?" I asked again. Not waiting for an answer I continued. "Ambassadors spread rumour, Master Jones. That is what they are sent to foreign courts to do… to gather information, and to gossip like old men in the ale house." I frowned deeper. "By my troth, I believed this was why Throckmorton had sent you, but it would have been better to keep you in France!" I laughed suddenly at this ridiculousness. To send a man all the way from France only to tell me what I already knew? What a high estimation Throckmorton had of his opinion! Jones stared at me as though I had taken leave of my senses; obviously his *dire* warnings were being lost on such simple a creature as I…

"But, there *is* danger here, madam," Jones went on, the colour of his cheeks and throat rising as he grew angry at my inability to take him seriously. "There are many accusations against your favourite, Majesty, both abroad and at home. Dudley's sudden rise at your court… the mysterious death of his wife and the rumours that you will marry him…"

Anger flared within me. I held up a hand and Jones stumbled to a halt. "I have heard all this before," I said. "And I am not so dull of wits, Master Jones, that I require it repeating. You might remind your master that his job is to discover *new* news for me, not to repeat the old until my ears bleed."

"But…" Jones lurched on, causing me to lift an eyebrow at his audacity. "My master's concern for Your Majesty is so deep, he feels bound by the reins of duty to inform you of anything which might threaten you." Jones burbled on like a brook swollen by the spring thaw. "And to tell you about these rumours in person, rather than leaving them to seep unheeded into the minds and mouths of your people."

"I am grateful to have such a diligent servant," I said coldly. "But once more, Master Jones, try to understand I have a *mind* within this skull, and do not require being told a piece of information more than once to understand it. Lord Dudley is my friend. That is all. His wife's death was a terrible accident, as has now been proved, and the court, and our country has sorrowed with him."

"But… Your Majesty tarries with him so long and often that it causes much scandal!" Jones continued, his eyes black and agitated like a nervous hen. "And his past and family history only adds to such rumours and troubles, Majesty. He is twice descended from traitors! Why, during your brother's reign, Dudley's father, Northumberland, hated *you* even more than he did your sister!"

Angry though I was, that made me laugh. What a thought, indeed! For someone to hate *me* more than my poor sister? Perish the notion! Such bizarre arguments my people resorted to, to try to make me abandon Robin. What would Northumberland's feelings, the feelings of a dead traitor, mean to me now? Seeing Jones's face contort with amazement only made me want to laugh harder. I twisted my face away from him, trying to hide my mirth behind my hand and a handkerchief. Kat and Blanche, standing just behind me, both had tears welling in their eyes as they tried not to splutter with amusement. As Jones's face grew darker, I thought my sides might tear in two. It never does to try to deny mirth; he will only tickle you more if you try to resist him.

Finally I turned to Jones and wiped my eyes. "The matter has been tried, Master Jones, and found to be contrary to what was suspected. Lord Robin is innocent, he was then at court and had nothing to do with the attempt at his wife's house."

"*Attempt*… Majesty?" Jones asked, his eyes widening.

All mirth disappeared in a trice. "Accident," I quickly corrected. "I misspoke, Master Jones. It is not usual that I use the wrong word, but I did here." It was not really the wrong word though. The inquiry had found that Amy had died accidentally, but I did not believe it. I knew not who was behind her death, but I was sure it had been done on purpose, either to ensure that I could never marry Robin, or so that if I did marry him, it would make my people rise against me, and bring about my destruction.

The word, "attempt" had slipped out, but it was what I believed had happened. Not an accident, but an attempt on Amy's life, and one which had succeeded. As for who had really killed her? They had covered themselves too well, and who would believe the truth if they were found? If I produced a murderer now, all would say I had created him to pin the blame on another so I could marry Robin. Sometimes it does not matter who is guilty and who is innocent... Sometimes the truth is decided in people's minds, and they will never believe otherwise. The only way I could prove our innocence, was to never wed Robin. He was the only man I had ever considered marrying. I had no wish to hand my power to another, to promise to obey a husband, and lose my control over England, and over my life. Robin was the only one I had believed I could trust not to abuse the rights of a husband. If I could not marry him, I would never marry at all.

Jones was watching me with his wary, chicken-eyes. I cursed the slip of my tongue. "Tell your master I am aware of the danger," I said, my tone dull and flat. "These rumours are false and will not become truer the more they are repeated. Time will prove me right on this score. You will tell your master I deny all such rumours that I am to wed Lord Dudley, and have no mind to marry at all unless there is a worthy suitor presented who will have England and her best interests in his heart, as I do." I breathed in deeply through my nose. "Now," I said. "Tell me of the rumours spread by the ambassadors, and I will give you answer for each. Then you must be away, Jones."

With a face still ruddy with shock, anger and confusion, Jones told me the rumours about Robin and me. Each one was worse than the last. According to gossip, I was a murderous strumpet, and Robin was a demon-lord sent to seduce me into sin and England into ruination. By the time I sent Jones away so I could dress for the feast, all humour had left me.

"Will this never end, Kat?" I asked as my ladies dressed me. They stripped me of the red and gold gown and started to pin me into my costume for the feast. My gown was new, made of gold and silver cloth combined with white silk and velvet, lined with green silk and embroidered with serpents and doves. These beasts and birds symbolised wisdom and kindness. Two qualities I wanted to possess, and wondered if I did. I did not feel I was being wise or kind towards Robin at the moment.

"It has only been a matter of months, Majesty," Kat consoled. "In time, it will all be forgot."

"It feels as though eons have passed."

"Pleasures cause time to pass fleetingly, as troubles make it stagnant," said my poetic Blanche, ducking under my arm to attach my new sleeves. "But as Mistress Ashley says, Majesty, it will pass."

"You are telling me to be patient," I grumbled. "It seems that is the advice you have been offering me since I was a child."

Blanche smiled. "It was the advice *you* more often offered us, my lady," she said. "Remember? When we were in danger from your sister? Watch and wait, you said… and all will be well."

"I am not sure I ever said all would be *well*, Blanche." I patted her cheek. "But perhaps there is something in what you say."

I stared at the fire, blazing away, consuming the dark sea coal in its belly. "*Patience*," I mouthed at my reflection in the large copper mirror over the fireplace. "Patience, Elizabeth…"

Chapter Six

Eltham Palace
Winter 1560

That night, we gathered for Robin's entertainment in the great hall. The ornately carved ceiling of dark wood hung over our heads, and outside was the still calm which settles after a fresh fall of snow. The stars were bright in the heavens, and the air in the hall was thick with warmth and the smell of good food.

As I entered the great hall, with my cousin, Margaret Clifford, now Lady Strange, at my side, I breathed in the savoury scents and felt the heated air seep into my bones. I smiled at Margaret. Unlike my other cousin of the same name, Margaret Lennox, I held affection for Lady Strange. She was a great-granddaughter of Henry VII, and her grandparents had been Charles Brandon and Mary Tudor. Placed in the succession after the Greys, Margaret was a more obscure heir to the throne, and perhaps her distance from my throne made me feel safer in her company than in the presence of other cousins. Although she had pushed for recognition of her title during the reign of my sister, under my rule Lady Strange seemed content to remain as she was; a high-ranking and noble lady of the royal bloodline, but without aspirations for the throne... unlike our Grey and Lennox cousins. There were many Protestants who wanted Katherine Grey named as my heir, and Margaret Lennox, who would have loved to push her suit forwards for the same position, was favoured by Catholics. I was glad, therefore, that at least one cousin of royal blood was not as demonstrative as these other women, or their supporters.

Lady Strange and Kat accompanied me to the head of the great hall, where I took welcome rest upon a purple cushion on my grand chair as Robin called on his troop of players to produce a short piece for us. When their comedy ended, there came musicians, their flutes, drums and pipes filling the great hall with the sound of glorious music. Eltham, being an older palace, had a hall the like of which the ancient kings of England would have known. Although such chambers were dying out of fashion, there was something grand and proud about Eltham's great hall. The voices of my ancestors echoed here… Once they would have gathered on tables set about a huge, central fire, gazing over their thanes and barons, wondering which was set on murdering them for possession of the throne. Whilst I did not worry *too* much, on a day to day basis, about being slain by my own men, I wondered how much had really changed. The position of monarch is a slippery post we of the blood royal scramble upon; sliding down, clambering up… never quite managing to remain in one position. It was staying upon the pole, however, which mattered.

Robin came to me before the feast began, and I told him of my meeting with Jones. "The man was quite impertinent," I said. "I wonder that Throckmorton holds him in such esteem, for I would not keep such a servant."

Robin's face was still, but his eyes were sharp with anger. "And the Queen of France, Majesty, called me your *horse master*?"

I put a hand on his russet sleeve. "She seeks to insult me by insulting you, Rob." I spoke with care, for Robin's pride was fragile. "Do not pay heed. Mary Stewart has always wanted to be Queen of England, and thinks she might gain my throne by dishonouring me. It was a slur made for politics, and not something to be taken to heart."

Although there was only a slight difference in the terms *horse master*, and *Master of Horse*, there was a vast disparity in meaning. To be a Master of Horse was a position of authority, nobility, favour and power. A horse master was little better than a vagabond. My cousin was more than aware of the distinction. She had not made a slip in her speech. Her words were *intended* to insult. Mary Stewart believed I was a bastard, and she was the true Queen of England. I was happy enough to acknowledge she was my cousin, and was descended, as I was, from Henry VII, but Queen of England she was not, nor ever would be, if I had anything to do with it. My words of comfort, however, did not make any impression on Robin's sour expression.

I patted his arm. "We are gathered here for *celebration*, my lord," I reminded him. "And I see you must be of a mind with me on this, for you are no longer in widower's weeds." Robin was wearing a new tunic of russet silk lined with silver cloth, and matching velvet breeches with ribbons of silver. His hose were tight, showing his legs' fine shape, and his tunic was snug against his muscular chest. I gazed on him, wondering if there could ever be another man as handsome as my Robin.

"I thought it was time," he murmured, staring down at his new clothes with a downcast expression. It pained me to see his merriment had been stolen by my foolish cousin. "To let Amy go... to let all this be a thing of the past." He looked up, his eyes dull. "But I wonder if that will ever be possible, Majesty."

"We must allow time for people to forget. None have true cause to doubt you, Robin," I assured him. "And if they do then such suspicion is based on jealousy, not on the truth. Now, fret not, my *bear*." I made reference to his family's heraldic emblems of the bear and ragged staff as I teased him. "For bears are made for dancing, not for worrying."

"And for *baiting*, Majesty," Robin replied smoothly, his old mischief creeping back into his eyes. "Something you never fail to do to me."

"Then ask for my hand for the first dance, Robin, and I will cease to bait you."

"When the feast is done, Majesty, I will claim you."

I chuckled as I watched him go to check on his preparations. Robin had taken over Eltham in his enthusiasm to put on a good show for me and the court. Many nobles thought Robin overstepped his boundaries, but I indulged him for I wanted everyone to see he had my trust. As the servers began to bring out the feast, I saw Arundel was sitting with Norfolk and Pembroke. What a combination! The three most disaffected men of court all sat together; a sure recipe for a disastrous meal. Arundel had been unhappy since last year, when I had politely turned down his marriage proposal. Norfolk just plain detested Robin, mainly out of jealousy... And Pembroke? He was increasingly thick with both Arundel and Norfolk, but I liked Pembroke. He was a hardy, hot-headed man, but he had a great deal of charm. I was less pleased, however, with the company he chose to keep.

The feast began to emerge from behind the screen which sheltered the passageway to the kitchen blocks. Since this was the last feast before the fast of Advent began, Robin was determined we would remember it. Row by row of servers, their tunics green and white for the colours of the Tudor dynasty, entered the hall. Marching in twos, their hands were full of delicious smelling food. There were steaming pottages of venison in bruet with frumenty, rich stews of mallard, goose and pigeon, as well as eel pottage, and hippocras jelly. Roasted pheasant, venison, mutton, capon, and peacock in ginger sauce were brought out next. Mortress of fish with piles of boiled crayfish emerged, along with shrimp, tiny crabs and succulent fried whiting. Boiled onions, buttered worts, and brawn with nutmeg, peppercorns, and white wine jostled for position on the tables. Then came smothered rabbit covered with raisins and cabbage, and leek doused with cinnamon. Cheese tarts, saffron tarts, egg tarts, apple tarts and great pies stuffed with close-clustered songbirds, decorated with falcons, lions, hounds and Tudor roses were sliced into hefty portions.

Robin had paid particular attention to the banquet of sweets after, for he knew this was my favourite part of any meal. There were pippin fritters, glistening with fat and sparkling with sprinkled sugar powder. Golden tarts of preserved strawberries, apricots, plums and peaches came along with prunes swimming in claret syrup. Succades of sharp-sweet lemon, quince jelly with crisp wafer biscuits, kissing comfits and white gingerbread were eagerly pounced upon. To much applause, sticks made of cinnamon and sugar, made for dipping into wine and crafted to look like the bare branches of trees were brought out, finishing the sweet course.

Although my appetite had been spare lately, I indulged in the banquet of sweets. I had to eat enough so that people would not notice my abstinence and think it an insult to Robin. Besides, he had always known how to best appeal to my senses. Sweet delicacies tempted me that night where many other dishes could not. I ate well enough, although not enough to appease Kat. I could almost hear her disgruntled thoughts as she cleared my plates away. I was going to receive another lecture that night, I could sense it.

But the beggars will eat well this night, even if their Queen did not, I thought, knowing what food remained at the end of the feast would go to poor people who came begging at the palace gates.

At the end of the banquet, Robin stood and lifted a hand; four servants entered, carrying the largest work in sugar I had ever seen. It was a traditional end to any court feast, to have a clever sugar-work paraded before the company. Even though I had seen many such creations in my life, I could not help but gasp as they brought this one out. It was St Paul's Cathedral. I walked around it, marvelling at the tiny details. It must have taken weeks to construct, and so much care and attention that it seemed a shame to eat it. Such artistry, for such a swift-passing pleasure. Robin was watching me carefully. I knew he was pleased by the wonder in my eyes.

"It is a work of beauty, Robin," I said. "You must tell me which of your servants has such an eye, and then I will steal him from you." People around me tittered, but I was serious. Like my father before me, I was a keen thief of useful servants.

"I will bring him to you, Majesty." Robin was beaming, pleased with himself. "And I will grant his service to you as part of my New Year's gift, along with these…" Robin took a parcel wrapped in dark green velvet from a servant hovering behind him. It was tied with a blood-red ribbon. I walked over to him. Although the hall was filled with people, we might have been alone for all the attention I paid to anyone else.

I touched the cloth. "But it is not New Year's yet, my lord."

"I thought you might want these for the Christmas celebrations, my lady, and I have something else to offer at the New Year."

I took the parcel and sat down with it. Opening it I found a pair of stockings, made of sheer, exquisite black silk. The finest I had ever seen. Stockings of this kind were not made in England, and they cost more than twenty times the price of the normal stockings that even I, as Queen, wore. I ran my fingertips over the smooth, cool silk. It whispered against my skin. "They are *stunning*, Robin," I breathed. "Even more than the last pair you found for me."

"These are of even better quality and workmanship, Majesty," he boasted, leaning towards me, his voice dropping to a murmur. "The finest I could have made for your pretty legs."

I flushed. "You are always thinking of me, Robin," I said. My guilty heart shuddered. I wished I could be honest with him.

"Never think that it goes unnoticed." I looked up, realising the whole hall was staring at us. "Command the servants to clear the hall and prepare to dance, my lord." I smiled at him. "For I remember a bear promising to dance the first with me this night."

Robin bowed. "I am yours, Majesty, always…"

Chapter Seven

Westminster Palace
Winter 1560

As Christmas approached, the men of my court seemed determined to introduce chaos and trouble where there should only have been peace and goodwill. Thinking the matters Jones had brought up were done with, I was unpleasantly surprised to find Robin had decided otherwise. At a meal held at the Scottish ambassador's residence, Robin left early, only to send a message back that he wanted to talk with Jones, who was still at the table with the ambassador and Cecil. Cecil did not allow talk of state and business at the dinner table, preferring to speak of merry and light matters when he was in company, and also so that he did not inadvertently become embroiled in giving away state secrets. Outside the chamber, Robin confronted Jones about Mary Stewart's insult. Barely able to contain his annoyance at the derogatory title of *horse master*, Robin peppered Jones with questions. Cornered, and not wishing to further insult Robin, Jones resorted to lying, pretending he had never said such a thing. Robin did not believe him. Eventually Robin let Jones go, but asked Jones not to inform Cecil that he had accosted him. Not wishing to become caught up in a struggle between Robin and Cecil, Jones promised he would not. He then had the audacity to write to Throckmorton, and accuse *me* of having set Robin on him, as I learned when Cecil intercepted his letters.

"Why does Robin suspect you, Cecil?" I asked my Secretary of State. "I thought the two of you were friends now?"

Cecil was wearing a baffled, slightly pained expression. "I know not, Majesty," he admitted. "I had thought my recent support for Lord Dudley in the matter of his wife's death would mean something, but it would seem…"

"It would seem Robin still does not trust you entirely, *Spirit*," I finished for him. "He must have some reason to not want Jones to tell you about their conversation."

"Will you warn Lord Dudley against these little infractions, Majesty?"

"Lord Dudley is at liberty to talk with whomsoever he wishes, Cecil," I said. "But I *will* ask him to be more moderate." I glanced up as Kat entered to inform us Sir Thomas Parry was waiting. "Send Parry in, Kat, there is nothing said here that he may not hear." I looked at Cecil. "I will speak to Robin, but you must do your part, too, Cecil. If Robin does not trust you perhaps there is still work to be done in your friendship."

"For the sake of peace, Majesty, I will do all that I can."

Parry entered. I noted with dissatisfaction that his face was pale. He had lost more weight over the winter, and his doublet hung off him. "You are still unwell, Parry," I scolded, wondering when my voice had begun to sound so like Kat's whenever I berated someone. Perhaps it is only natural that we begin to sound like those who raised us. "You are taking the pills and potions my doctors prescribed for you?"

Parry smiled at my chiding. "Your Majesty's concern is the best tonic," he said. "But I promise, I have taken their advice *and* taken all the foul things they have inflicted on me. My appetite is better, and I assure you, my wife scolds me whenever my Queen does not. I am well looked after."

I laughed. "It is a good thing when women scold men, Parry, for then you know we love you."

"Then I must be the best loved man in the whole kingdom of England," Parry replied dryly. "And I thank the Lord for such, I assure you."

"You were ever a sensible man," I said. "What have you brought me?"

"Just the latest dispatches from Sweden, Majesty. King Erik is still as much in love with you as ever, and has written to me to ask that I intervene on his behalf."

"And does he offer you coin to do so?"

Parry dipped his head. "An offer of a pension, which I shall refuse, if you wish, Majesty."

"Take the money, Parry, if you will. I know you will deal with me honestly and not become Erik's creature for the sake of a few coins."

"I will always be *your* man, my lady."

"Good, Parry, for I still have much for you to do... Now, gentlemen, let us attend to the business of the day."

*

One afternoon, a few days later, as mushy sleet fell slopping from the clouds above, I was wandering the halls with my ladies. I had wanted to go for a ride, but the weather was being uncooperative. Robin had gone to the stables, and I had found sitting in my chambers dull. The usual battalion of guards trooped behind us, swords at their sides and eyes alert for danger. Cecil, and my captain of the guard, William St Loe, never allowed me to go anywhere unless it was with a company of well-armed men. There had been many plots against my life uncovered in the short years I had been on the throne. I had many enemies. My conversion of England to a Protestant state meant Catholic leaders in Europe regarded me with suspicion and even hatred. Phillip of Spain was one. He claimed to be my friend and good brother, but I knew he would dearly love to see me stumble into an early grave. And there were many more who believed I had no right to the throne; either because of my sex, or because of the still-questioned legality of my parents' marriage. It would be easy to fall into thinking every shadow was an assassin, and every noise was a killer come to get me, but I ignored the threats to my life on a daily basis, thrusting them resolutely to one side. One cannot enjoy life with Death perpetually hanging over one's shoulder, after all.

Although I allowed my men to do all they wished to protect me, I often became irritable with my guards. It was not their fault, of course, but I resented giving up so much of my already sparse freedom, simply for the bluster of my enemies.

I came across Bess, Lady St Loe, standing alone. Her eyes were locked on one of the portraits which hung in this part of the palace. She was lost in her thoughts and hardly noticed my approach. Suddenly realising I was there, Bess dropped to an elegant curtsey. I was fond of Bess, now the wife of Sir William St Loe. I had approved their marriage the year before, and looked with satisfaction on it ever since, for they were a happy couple, much devoted to one another. St Loe was a favourite of mine. A quiet giant of a man, he had been with me for a long time, and served me well and loyally. I had rewarded the couple, upon their marriage, by giving Bess one of the few, coveted positions in my Royal Bedchamber. I found her a pleasant spirit, more than able to carry out her tasks with ease and offer lively company.

"What has you so captivated, Lady St Loe?" I asked, looking up to see what she had been staring at. It was my coronation portrait. I had many copies of the original, which hung in places of prominence in my palaces. It was beneficial to remind my subjects of my constant presence in their lives. My father had once ordered little people to be carved of wood and placed in the eaves at Hampton Court. These 'eavesdroppers', as they came to be called, were there to remind courtiers that all they did was watched over and heard. A warning, if you will. For the same reason, my portraits lined the walls of my palaces, reminding my subjects that whatever they got up to, I had my eye on them.

I gazed up into the stylised face. The portrait was done in an antiquated style, and was not, in fact, a true representation of my face. It held similarities, of course, but it was not like gazing into a mirror. There I sat, with the crown on my head, my red hair loose and flowing over my shoulders, the sceptre in my right hand, and the orb in my left. The ermine-lined robe of cloth of gold I wore swept about over my lap on the left side. My waist was thin, and my hips had been enlarged by the artist, so that I looked like a most elegant, royal wasp. I wondered why Bess was so taken with it, for surely, she had seen it before?

"Majesty…" She turned her eyes to another portrait on the other side of the corridor. My ladies walked on. "It was just… I had never noted how similar your portrait here is, Majesty, to that of King Richard II." Bess pointed to the portrait which hung opposite. "Am I wrong, Majesty? Is there not a similarity?"

"You have keen eyes, Bess. It was done on purpose. I asked for my coronation portrait to be modelled on that of Richard II. It was no accident."

I glanced over at Richard. He was seated in his portrait, wearing the robes of estate gathered and lying over his lap, just as I did in my portrait. His right hand held the sceptre and his left, the orb, creating a perfect mirror image of my coronation portrait. Although his clothing, under the robes, was different to mine, his fingers were shown as long and tapering, just as mine were. Even our faces were similar. I knew all the portraits of my ancestors, of course I did, for I had grown up with them staring down on me. It was a deliberate act on my part to order that my coronation portrait should echo Richard's, for I had reasons for believing we were similar souls.

"He was the last of his house to hold an unquestioned, God-given right to the throne," I said. "He lived a chaste life, never lying with the queens he was granted in marriage. He wished for peace, even though peace was not always possible, and sought to end war between France and England."

"And that is why Your Majesty styled your own portrait in his image?"

"I feel I have a simpatico with him," I agreed. "He came to his throne young, Bess, just as I did, and made his court a place of art, culture and music. He walked away from the war-like machinations of his forebears and crossed his arms with the emblems of Edward the Confessor to show his love of peace. He set aside the joys that children might have brought, and instead united himself with his country in marriage. He was a celibate monarch, Bess, a chaste prince of peace; something I have long believed I was also destined to be."

"But eventually, Majesty, was he not betrayed and deposed?" she asked in a cautious whisper. Bess did not want to insult me, but she was curious. I was not displeased. Too many people are surprisingly un-curious, and therefore learn little. To be curious is to invite learning, and hopefully wisdom, into one's mind.

"A warning, to myself, perhaps," I agreed. "No sovereign can allow themselves to become complacent. There is always danger..." I gestured to the guards behind me. "... As your beloved husband is more than aware, and therefore sends me *everywhere* surrounded by his men." I turned back to her and smiled, and then my brow creased at her uneasy expression. "I was only teasing," I said quickly. "I did not mean to worry you, Bess. Be assured I am well looked after by my good St Loe. I could not do without him."

"Oh!" she exclaimed. "I am sorry, Your Majesty, but it was not that I was thinking about."

"What was it then?"

Bess glanced around in a covert manner. "Your Majesty, do you remember when I fell ill earlier in the year?"

I nodded. "Of course, you were absent from court and I missed your company."

"At one point, Majesty, it was quite serious. Had I not been given an emetic, the physicians believed I might have died."

"I did not know it was so severe, Bess," I consoled, wondering where this was going. Was Bess still sick?

"There have been difficulties, Majesty, between my husband and his brother. When I fell ill, my beloved started to investigate and found a certain Master Draper, named Hugh, who owned an inn in Bristol. He was a known associate of my brother-in-law, Edward St Loe. Draper was arrested recently, Majesty... and charged with necromancy. He was trying to conjure my death."

"Bess!" I exclaimed, horrified. "You should have told me this sooner!"

"You have had your own troubles of late, Majesty." There was pity in her eyes. "I had no wish to burden you with mine."

"Has anything further happened? Has the man been questioned?"

She stepped closer. "Draper was committed to the Tower, Majesty, and is held there still as the investigation goes on..." Bess paused as though she did not want to say something and yet could not stop herself, "... But then I had a letter from William's mother, wherein she called her own son, Edward, a *devil*, and insinuated he was behind the attempt on my life. My beloved husband is working with your officers to find anyone involved, Majesty. And others have been found, but…"

"But what, Bess?"

"All who have been arrested thus far, Majesty… they are *all* associates of my brother-in-law. I fear that as my husband searches for those responsible, he will find himself looking into a face most familiar." Bess leaned back. Her eyes were troubled, but steady.

"You suspect your brother-in-law poisoned you?" I asked. "But why? What gain is there to be had from such evil? Does he hate you, Bess?"

"On the night I fell ill, Majesty, William and I were *both* at our London house," she whispered. "He was called away, on an errand for you, shortly before dinner and told me not to wait for him. Had he been there that night, and not with you, Majesty, he may have fallen ill as well."

I gasped. "You think the intent was to murder both of you?" Such an act would certainly make more sense than poisoning Bess alone.

She nodded her head slowly. "For William's estates and money," she said. "That, I believe was the motive, madam; money. My husband is the elder brother and holds all rights to the St Loe lands and wealth. His brother is a strange and devious man, and if his own mother suspects him…" She trailed off, and I stared at her with grave eyes.

"And all this was going on this past year, and neither you nor St Loe told me?"

Bess's lips puckered. "William had no wish to burden you, Majesty," she confessed. "And the investigation goes on, with help from your officers. William is held in high regard and many have rushed to help us. Please do not be angry that we did not tell you. We discussed it, but both of us believed there was nothing more you could do for us, and we were getting all the aid we needed from your men."

"But still, you are troubled, Bess. I see it." I put my hand to her soft, plump cheek. Many women faced with such a situation would have laid down and wept with helpless fright, but Bess was made of a different mettle. Troubled, concerned and worried she was, yes... but she was also active and alert, energetic and wary. She was a woman after my own heart; a fighter, a survivor.

"The events have pressed upon us, I will not deny it, Majesty," she admitted, running a hand over her gown of rich crimson velvet. "William grows worried if he does not hear from me often when we are apart." She smiled. "He is very protective, but I have taken steps to assure our safety. I have gone through all our servants and dismissed those I had reason to doubt. I am careful with my food, as William is now, and have told all my children to do the same, even though I do not think they are in danger, for none are of William's line and therefore cannot inherit since they are all the children of my second husband."

"When you are at court, Bess, your meals will be made in my personal kitchens," I said on impulse. "And those of St Loe, too. I will order it this day and extend it to all ladies of the Bedchamber and my chief guardsmen. Then it will not attract attention. As long as you are at court, I will have you protected."

Bess fell to one knee. "Majesty, you are most generous... I was not expecting such an offer when I spoke to you..."

"I know that, Bess." I put a hand on her shoulder and tapped for her to rise. "But I insist that you keep me advised about this. If there is any evidence found to implicate Edward St

Loe, I assure you, I will make sure the full weight of the law falls on his head."

"*That* would be the greatest gift of all, Majesty," Bess said with a hungry grin that made me want to laugh. Bess was a rare creature with the courage of a warrior inside the body of a delectable woman.

"Tell me of other things, Bess," I said, indicating for her to walk with me. "How goes your building work at Chatsworth? St Loe tells me you are redesigning the whole building. He groans often about the costs."

Bess chuckled, falling into step with me. "My beloved exaggerates, Majesty, as men are prone to do."

"They do, don't they?" I mused. "It is strange that oftentimes they accuse our sex of being the one to give in to histrionics and embellishment when they are so often taken with the urge for exaggeration."

"A common mistake, madam. So often we see flaws in others before recognising them in ourselves."

"Wise words, Bess." I stopped by a portrait of my father at the end of the hall. Done in his youth, it showed him at his most vibrant and handsome. It was easy to see why so many had swooned over him. We stood there for a while until I continued. "You will keep me apprised on these matters, Bess?" I asked. "I am fond, both of you and of William, and if there is anything I can do to help, please ask. Although, unlike Cecil, I do not believe that every person in this world is out to poison me, I am well aware there are many of my enemies who might try. You may even say, Bess, we are in the same position. Let us foil our enemies by surviving." I took her hands. "But if there is anything I can do…"

"I am honoured, Majesty," she said. "But we are in good hands. We will be safe. We will be careful, and cautious." She beamed at me suddenly. "We follow your example, Majesty," she went on. "Many times when you were a girl you faced danger and survived, as you do now, too. So as you follow the example of your ancestor, Richard, we shall emulate our courageous Queen."

"How you flatter me!" I put my arm through hers. "Come, enough of this miserable talk. Let us dispel the troubles we face with a game of cards in my chambers. You shall play me, Bess, and as I rob you of your good coin, you will tell me of all your plans for Chatsworth."

Chapter Eight

Westminster Palace
Winter 1560

It was a season of death and deceit.

Death was plain to see. Deceit, as ever, was cloaked.

In early December news arrived from France. The young King, François II, had died. Although we had received word from Throckmorton that François was taken ill early that winter with a series of fainting fits, we had not thought he was in peril of his life. The King was in Orleans when he began to suffer from a pain in the ear, leading to his royal physician, Ambrose Pare, wanting to perform the invasive and controversial procedure of drilling a hole into the King's skull to relieve the pressure on his brain. The dangerous procedure, unsurprisingly, was not allowed by François's mother, Catherine de Medici. Writhing in pain and slipping in and out of consciousness, the young King died on the 6th of December. There were immediate rumours of poison. Many suspected leading Huguenots in France, as the King had been opposed to the rise of Protestantism. But this was never proven.

François had been only seventeen months on his throne, and was but sixteen years old when Death took him.

There had been much trouble in his reign, even though it was so short. He maintained an unpopular, repressive attitude towards Protestants, which had led to an attempted coup against François and the house of Guise, Mary Stewart's uncles. With intervention from his mother, Catherine de Medici, talks had opened with Huguenot leaders, but small local revolts appeared all over France in response to François's increasingly controlling methods.

This had led, much to our benefit in England, to the French being unable to send more men to Scotland to support the Regent, Mary of Guise, when her nobles had risen against her. Since this had been to our advantage then, I had not been unhappy that François was having difficulties.

The main problem for his rule, however, came not from those of my faith, but from the Guise. Although their sister had ruled as Regent in Scotland, and their niece sat upon the throne of France, many viewed the staunchly Catholic Guise as interlopers. They were power-hungry, grasping and had controlled the young King and his wife like little puppets. Antoine, King of Navarre, was seen by those opposed to the Guise as the true choice for François' chief advisor, since he was a Prince of the Blood, and a descendant of Louis IX, but the crafty Guise had maintained their sway over the court and King.

In terms of finance, France had been weakened. Decades of war against the Hapsburgs and Imperial Spain had led to massive debts. The Guise, in their roles as advisors, imposed harsh austerity upon France to try to rectify this... something which was clearly never going to make them more popular. The Guise delayed payments to the military, to officials and to merchants who supplied the court, causing endless problems. They also reduced the size of France's standing army and many ex-soldiers became beggars, adding to existing tensions within the realm.

The past year had seen many arrests, searches of houses and confiscation of property from suspected Huguenots. Many in France wanted the Protestant religion to be recognised and a decree for freedom of worship to be allowed, but the Guise furiously opposed this. This had led to the failed coup, and many whispered that the rebels had the secret support of Louis, Prince de Conde, the younger brother of Antoine, King of Navarre.

With whispers of conspiracy in her ears, the Dowager Queen, Catherine de Medici, had offered concessions to French Huguenots and amnesty was granted, but it was too late to stop revolt. Rebels tried to move against their King, leading to a great spilling of blood on both sides. The Dowager decided that persecuting Protestants only made matters worse, and so the royal Council offered clemency to the Huguenots, in return for peace. Public assemblies of Protestant worshippers were still banned, but the prisoners of religion were set free and an edict had been signed forbidding harm against a person for their faith. There were indications that, one day, freedom of conscience would prevail in matters of religion. It did not legalize Protestantism, but was enough to rattle the Guise and encourage Huguenots. Gaspard II, the Admiral de Coligny, had read a petition from Huguenots of Normandy before a much amazed court, asking for *full* freedom of religion. It was not granted, but it was increasingly clear that France was divided on the matter of religion.

Encouraged by the boldness of their leaders, Huguenots in France had begun to congregate openly for religious services. Law officials intervened to disperse them, and to arrest ringleaders, but the sheer size of some of the gatherings, over a thousand souls in some cases, made it impossible to detain all of them. Riots and acts of civil disobedience had increased in France, and armed Huguenot militia attempted to overrun the city of Lyon. The King had responded with violence. There were arrests and executions as the heavy hand of the King pressed upon his subject's throats. Peace had been restored by force, but Huguenot anger lay barely concealed under the skin of France. When the French lost control of Scotland, with the death of Mary of Guise, the Guise had signed the Treaty of Edinburgh with England, which brought an end to French occupation of Scotland. My cousin of Scots had been unwell when this treaty was signed on her behalf, and was horrified when she discovered its terms. It promised that she would cease to use the arms of England as her own, and would stop styling herself Queen of England. Mary remained adamant she would never ratify it.

And now, with his country simmering in half-revolt and beset with religious upheaval, the young King had died. He had no children and his throne passed to his younger brother, Charles... a boy who was just ten years old. Catherine de Medici hastily stepped forward to become Regent, and many believed this spelled the end of the Guise. Catherine had hated their influence over François and would not allow them to exert the same power over Charles. I did not believe we had seen the last of the Guise. They were still powerful, rich and ambitious. Such creatures do not set their dreams aside. Even as I read about the hysterical grief of my cousin over her husband's demise, I knew her uncles would have a part to play still in the destiny of France.

There were consequences for England from this death. It became apparent, early on, that Catherine de Medici did not want Mary Stewart to remain in France. Perhaps it was just that then there would be one too many Dowager Queens, or perhaps this much-overlooked Queen had finally seen a chance to secure true power, but for whatever reason, Catherine de Medici did not want her daughter-in-law in France. The grieving widow would be sent back to Scotland. Mary Stewart, that arrogant young woman who had already given me so much trouble, was about to become my neighbour. She was eighteen when François died; a young, fresh damsel with much charm and beauty. I was not best pleased to hear she would be returning to the land of her birth.

Upon hearing of François's death, my cousin Margaret, Countess of Lennox, sent her eldest son, Henry Stewart, Lord Darnley, to France. Although it was reported that Darnley, an oafish, feckless young man, was sent to comfort his cousin Mary, I was sure Margaret had sent him to propose marriage. Margaret had always aimed above her station, and saw a chance to make her darling son a king.

She did not consult me before she sent Darnley to France, knowing I would not have allowed it. But what Margaret clearly did not know was that Cecil had men planted in her household. When I heard of her plans, I had her placed under house arrest, and Darnley too, upon his return.

Darnley was of royal blood. His mother was the daughter of my aunt, Margaret Tudor, from her second marriage to Archibald Douglas, the sixth Earl of Douglas. Darnley's father, Henry Stewart, Count of Lennox, held ties to the crown of Scotland and had once attempted to woo Marie of Guise in an effort to become the King of Scots himself. Darnley therefore had the blood of two royal houses in his veins. His mother had been born in England, whilst her mother, Margaret Tudor, had been on the run from enemies in Scotland. Since she had been born an English subject, many Catholics considered Margaret to be my true heir, even though my father had excluded the heirs of his eldest sister from the succession. Brought up as a princess at my father's court, and a firm friend of my now-dead sister, Margaret Lennox had thought my sister would name her Queen upon her death. She had been *awfully* disappointed to find that, despite all our differences, my sister held the claims of royal blood in greater esteem than that of noble.

However diluted Darnley's royal blood was, it was for *me* to decide whom he would marry, not his mother. Margaret Lennox despised me as a bastard and believed she had a better claim to my throne. This led to her often flirting with danger to defy me. Fortunately, Mary of Scots believed it was too soon to consider a new husband, as Throckmorton told me when he wrote of her great grief and sorrow at the loss of her husband.

"Although there is often a false habit for royal couples to claim great and endless love for one another," he wrote. *"In this case, of the Dowager Queen and her beloved, there was only truth in all reports. They loved each other from the time they first met as children, and it is the greatest sadness to*

the Dowager of France that she was never able to bear children for her sweet lord. We should, all of us, look on such elegance of feeling, and honour it. For a woman to know such devotion to her duty, and also to her lord husband, is a thing to be praised and extolled in this world."

I screwed up the parchment and threw it far across my chamber. Throckmorton was admonishing me for my single state, and extolling Mary's worth by comparing her virtues to my apparent lack of them. *God's Bloody Cross!* I fumed. *Does Throckmorton think he is subtle?* I wanted to slap Throckmorton, and slap him hard. I had to make do with kicking a cushion across the floor.

Just as I was recovering from this latest news, trouble broke out at court. On St Andrew's Day, an argument occurred between Robin's supporters and men from the retinue of the Earl of Pembroke. Long in cahoots with Arundel and Norfolk, Pembroke had been setting himself up in opposition to Robin and the tension from this alliance was spilling out and infecting their men. One of Robin's supporters had brushed against a man of Pembroke's causing an affray to break out, with blows exchanged as well as insults. I ordered the men involved arrested, and fines were charged for causing disorder at court, but there was little I could do about the wrath within their hearts. I brought Robin to me, and asked him to make peace with his enemies.

"You are too *proud*, Robin," I said. "It does nothing to aid you. Pembroke, Arundel and Norfolk… they are becoming your enemies, and I will have no more of this unruly behaviour at my court!"

"*I* was not involved in the fight, Majesty." Robin spread his hands as though he were entirely innocent. "As I am sure you have been informed."

"And yet you *were* involved!" I cried, throwing my hands into the air. "As well you know, Robin." It was hard to take him to task, for his enemies hated him because I loved him. Taking his arm, we walked about the chamber. "I can do much, as Queen, but I cannot alter men's hearts. That is something *you* must take responsibility for, Robin. Make peace, for my sake, as well as for yours. Moderate your boldness and in time they will accept you as a friend."

"I will try, Majesty," he agreed and then his hand pressed on mine. "Have you thought about our matter, Elizabeth?" he whispered. "Enough time has passed now since my wife died, and you said you would consider my offer of marriage." We ceased to walk. My heart stopped along with my feet.

"It is too soon to consider anything of the sort," I said quietly. "Still people talk of Amy's death, Robin, and still they accuse you, as I have already told you of late." I shook my head. "It is too soon." My heart started beating again. I hoped I had put him off.

"I feared you would feel that way. But my desire to marry you grows only stronger by the day, Elizabeth. I *love* you. I am desperate to know myself separated from you, even as I stand daily by your side."

His voice was low, but passionate, and every word stung my raw heart. I swallowed my truths, and offered him more lies. "In time, Robin," I said. "Give me time."

"Do you still love me?" His voice was at once shy and bold.

"I will never love another, as I love you, Robin." His face brightened, and I was made miserable to see it. We walked on.

Just as we were turning to come about the chamber again, a white-faced boy arrived with a message. "It is urgent, my lady," he said to Kat. Kat opened the parchment. As she read, her face drained.

"What is it, Kat?" I asked, thinking it was a missive from Cecil with further news from France.

She stared at me, her face drawn. Her skin was bloodless. "It is Parry... my lady."

"What of Parry?"

Kat stared at me, her face ghostly. "He... he is dead."

Chapter Nine

Westminster Palace
Winter 1560

I stared with blank and unseeing eyes at Kat.

The air had gone from my lungs. I could not form words. My head spun and I thought I might fall. Parry... *Parry*? How could Parry be dead? He had been ill of late but he had assured me it was nothing serious. I had seen him only days ago. How could this be? My knees buckled. I staggered and thought for a moment I might faint, but Robin caught me. He held me up, leading me to a chair. I sat down with a great thump, as though I were a sack of grain and stared up at Kat with bleak eyes. "Dead?" The word croaked from my throat. "How? When?" There was not enough air. I pulled at the ruff about my neck. My gown was too tight. Black spots danced before my eyes.

Kat tried to read the missive, but her eyes swam with tears, blinding her. Silently, Robin took the parchment from her. "This morning, of the fifteenth of December 1560..." Robin read aloud. His words warped and distorted in my ears. I had to concentrate to hear him... to understand. "... Sir Thomas Parry was taken with a convulsion of the limbs and a fell pain in his arm. He was taken to his bed in his London house and nursed by his wife, but after an hour, he received the last rites and left this life for God's Kingdom." Robin ducked to one knee, his face clouded with concern. "Majesty, are you alright?"

There was no blood in my face. My hands trembled. I shook my head and it drooped upon my neck, my eyes staring impotently at my lap. Parry, *dead*? How could this come so swift, so sudden? How could a man of such strength fall so fast? This man who had endured torture for my sake... This good man who had followed my footsteps into captivity in Woodstock... This man who had become my eyes and ears about England when my sister held me prisoner? Parry had raised an army of supporters to aid me then... How could a man of such vital energy simply die? Parry had been with me since I was a girl and had supported me in all events, and in all matters. He had been the only one, before the death of Amy Dudley, to tell me he would support me, should I choose to marry Robin. He had at all times, and in all matters been *my* man, my true servant... my good friend.

I put my hands to my face and buried my eyes there. Shock and disbelief resounded through my belly, through my heart. Kat's arms reached around me, but I did not, could not, move into her embrace. I was frozen by the sudden shock. I bowed my head over my legs, tears running down the paint on my face, running in rivulets through the powder of alabaster. I sought to gather my breath. I tried to find my thoughts, but they had all abandoned me, save one. Abruptly I stood, making everyone start, stand back and stare at me; their Queen, her face a ruptured mask of tears and powder and paint.

"Order my horse." My words shook as they dropped from my lips.

"Majesty?" Robin asked. "You are not well, you should rest."

"You are my Master of Horse!" I shouted. I hated being told what to do. "Do as I say! Order my horse, assemble my guard and come with me."

"To where, Majesty?" Robin's face was grey with concern. Clearly he thought I had lost my senses with grief.

"To the house of Mistress Parry," I said. "I have to visit with her... I have to tell her... tell her what her husband meant to me. I have to tell her Parry was a good man. I have to tell her that I loved him." I knew I was making little sense, but I had to go to Parry's widow. I had to share her grief and join it to mine. If I could not ever again tell Parry what he had meant to me, I had to tell her. "I have to go, *now*, Robin. Assemble my guards and bring my horse."

He hurried away, knowing it was no use arguing with me when I had set my mind to something. I pressed Kat's hand. "Will you come?" I whispered. Kat nodded, lacing her fingers through mine.

"I will be with you, Elizabeth," she whispered. "For as long as you need me."

Tears dripped from my eyes. My face was dirty with mottled cosmetics and grief. "Wipe this off me," I said quietly. "I cannot go to Parry's widow with anything but my own face at such a time."

I rode out that hour to Parry's house in town. When my men knocked on the door, a surprised servant escorted me into the small courtyard, and there I met Anne, Parry's wife. She went to curtsey, but I grasped her hands and roughly pulled her to me. Against my shoulder she broke into tears. I held her to me, so tight I thought we both might cease to breathe.

"I will make sure you have all that you need, Anne," I whispered. "*All* that you and your family need... You will want for nothing, for the love I had for your husband. Parry was my good man, Anne... He... " Words failed me. All the noble sentiments I had wanted to say to Anne washed away. Fresh tears tumbled from my eyes and I buried my face into her dark gown.

"He loved you, Majesty," she said against my shoulder. "He loved you so much. You were his every care, and hope. He admired you greatly. There was none he spoke of higher. He was ever *your* man, and devoted servant."

"I loved him too, Anne." I could say no more, but drew back, and took her hand. We two women, bound together in grief, gazed at each other. In that moment, we both knew there was nothing more to say. Loss cannot be expressed in words. It can only be felt. "Can I see him?" I asked.

Anne nodded. "He did not suffer, Majesty," she said. "If that brings you consolation... It was quick."

I cast my eyes away and swallowed hard. I squeezed her fingers and nodded by way of an answer. Parry's eldest son, a young man of only nineteen, named Thomas for his father, led me up the creaking stairs of their smart townhouse and into Parry's room. Parry had been laid out, his face and body washed. He had been dressed in a simple gown of white linen.

"Can I sit with him, alone, for a moment?" I asked Thomas.

"Of course, Your Majesty." The young man left. I heard his footsteps creak down the stairs. In the silence of this house of death, the sound of his steps was a groan of pain.

I sat at Parry's side and gazed on his face. Until this moment I had wanted to believe that all of this was a trick, a lie, or a falsehood. I had wanted someone to spring out to announce it was all a jest... That I had not lost Parry... That life was still within his breast... But when one looks into the face of Death, there is no denying His power. I reached out and clutched his cold hand. Parry had been so warm. He had always been the first to remove a cloak even when others shivered, and it was not only his flesh that had been warm; his humour, his wit, his love of life... But now his skin was cold, damp; like the flesh of a toad.

I entwined my fingers into his stiff, cold ones and felt my chin and jaw contract. "Parry..." I whispered. "This is not how it was supposed to be, old friend. You should have told me, sent word that you were ill, and I would have moved heaven and earth to save you… Did you not know that? Did you not know how important you were to me? Did I never show it as I should have done?"

I blinked. Tears fell upon my skirts; blossoming, wet flowers of grief. "You were my good servant, Parry, were you not? You were my master of spies… The cunning fox in the shadows. You swore to be ever at my side, Parry. I am not yet done with my need for you."

I put my head to his hand and kissed it. "In the face of Death all my powers are proved useless." I did not want to stop talking and leave, for then, somehow, he truly would be dead. "I can no longer command you to rise. I can no longer command you to protect me, watch over me, advise me. What will I do without you?"

There was no answer, and there never would be. I had lost my friend.

"Go with God, good Master Parry," I whispered to his corpse. "And when you reach Heaven, tell God that you served your Queen well and faithfully. That she listened ever to your counsel, even when she had not the wit to take it. That you had a place in her heart which will never be filled again… Tell Him that you were not only her servant but her dear friend. That she will never cease to sorrow that you chose to go on ahead, to see the lie of the land."

I shook my head. "You always were one step ahead of me, Parry… Make sure that the path is good, and the chests are packed, old friend, for one day I will join you. Together, we will sit under the light of God and talk of the old days… The days at Woodstock, Parry, do you remember? When we made old Bedingfield dance for us? The days when you spun a web of secrecy about me? The days when Bedingfield suspected us, and searched even fish sent for my dinner for clues and codes?"

I smiled, despite myself and then my smile fell, taking the corners of my mouth downwards, into a twisted grimace. "This was not how it was meant to be, old friend," I whispered again. "You have left too soon." I slid my fingers tight into his, wanting to feel his skin against mine, if only for a short while longer. I ceased to talk. I put my head upon the bed, and laid it there for some time, allowing my tears to fall upon his cold skin.

My friend was gone.

Chapter Ten

Richmond Palace
February 1603

Subtle trickster: Death.

You steal so soft and silent into the halls of life. You rob us of friends. You prance into the light of day and bring the deep dark of night into our hearts. You come when we have had no time to prepare. You attack us when we have our guard down.

Are any of us ever prepared to hear that one we love has died? Even in long-suffering sickness, even under the shroud of old age, we are never prepared. Death is the most cunning of all thieves.

There is nothing like losing one we love. The air becomes too thin to breathe, the light too bright to see. We feel our hearts contract as they shrink within us, withered by the acid of loss. Our souls become broken like the backs of old gossips. Our bellies know hunger no more, for in hunger and thirst there are the wants of life. Death steals this from us. It is not only the life of the deceased Death takes when He comes to call…

How can it be He still takes us by surprise? When all men know they are mortal… When we all know we have but limited time with those we love? The secret is, because we hide this truth from ourselves. In order to live, in order to love, we hide the fact that we are mortal. We do not care to look upon Death as we live, and so He ever comes as a shock.

He lifts His hand, and takes the souls of those we love. And with them, a small shard of our spirit is broken off, too. It takes flight with the soul of the dead, leaving us with an empty space in our hearts.

Subtle trickster: Death.

You stole much from me that day.

Chapter Eleven

Westminster Palace
Winter 1560

Sir Thomas Parry was buried in Westminster Abbey with full honours accorded to his rank. I paid for his funeral myself, and made provision for his widow and children. I offered Anne a post in my household, as a lady-in-waiting, and made sure that Parry's two sons and two daughters were taken care of as well. I gave Parry's post of Master of the Wards to Cecil. Robin had wanted the post, but I offered it to my *Spirit* instead.

"Remuneration for your losses in Scotland, *Spirit*," I murmured. Putting together the Treaty of Edinburgh had cost Cecil dear from his own pocket for lodgings and food. This was a way to repair some of the damage.

Cecil glanced up with sad eyes. "I would rather that I still had my old friend, Majesty," he said. "But I thank you for thinking of me."

"I miss him too, Cecil." My voice broke over the words like waves crashing over rocks in the sea. "He was the best of men."

"I find myself looking about, thinking I have lost something," Cecil said. "And then realising the reason I feel this is because I can no longer find Parry... No more shake his hand, or call at his house to share a cup of ale with him at his fire."

"*Please*, Cecil." Fresh tears sprang to my eyes. They were already sore and angry from crying. "I can think no more on this... it brings me too much pain."

Cecil crossed the room and put his hand on my shoulder. "He would not want you to grieve, Majesty," he said. "Parry was committed to you and to England. One day, we will all meet again. Parry was one of the faithful. He will be waiting for us in Heaven."

"I know it, *Spirit*," I blinked back my tears. "It is just that I have the rest of this life to go through, without him in it. My heart is torn and my soul is heavy. It is as though Parry took all the lightness and happiness with him as he left us."

Days passed. The court was in mourning for Parry and yet from outside my chambers I could hear young people talking and laughing. I bristled to hear sounds of joy in my time of misery… but then, they had not known Parry. They had not lost a friend. Should I wish for all happiness to leave the world, because of the grief in my soul? I struggled with my sorrow. I went about my business like a lost child. Sometimes, when I could not sleep, I would lie in bed thinking of him, missing him.

As I struggled on, we had further news from France. Mary had passed into the traditional period of isolation for royal French widows, into a private chamber, lit only by candles, where none were allowed to visit. For two weeks Mary was removed from the court, and during that time Catherine de Medici rose and was confirmed as Regent. Mary's uncles, the Guise, fell back. Some suggested Mary should marry her ten year-old brother-in-law, the new King, Charles, but that idea did not find favour with his mother. Catherine also rebuffed a proposal to wed Mary to Don Carlos, the insane son of Phillip of Spain. Catherine knew that if Mary was raised to fresh power, then the Guise would rise with her. Catherine did not want the Guise holding such power again, anywhere, through their niece. Catherine wanted Mary gone, and made open remarks that her daughter-in-law was to return to Scotland.

What my cousin heard or thought of this, I know not. I believe it was likely to come as a shock. Mary had not seen the land of her birth for many years, having left Scotland's shores when she was five years old. France was the only home she had known, but Scotland was still her kingdom, and despite the rise of the Protestant nobles who governed there under a Regency Council, she was still Queen. We had reports that feelings in Scotland were mixed about her return. Some wanted their Queen back, but many feared Mary for her faith, and worried that she might try to impose Catholicism on her people. Not all her Protestant subjects were opposed to her return, however; if men such as the influential Calvinist preacher, John Knox, were unenthused, there were others willing to see how she would fare as Queen before proclaiming her to be a sprite bent on leading them astray.

Her illegitimate brother, Lord James Stewart, arranged to go to France to meet her, and secure terms for her homecoming. For me, the return of Mary to Scotland was far from ideal. Although I believed the throne of Scotland was hers by God-given right, I had small wish to have her so close to my borders. Another queen, another ruler, and a Catholic one so close to me was likely to bring me little rest, especially if Mary retained the belief that she should be Queen of England instead of me... There was also the worrying fact that every man she met seemed to fall instantly in love with her. This was an annoyance in any case, as no woman wishes to be outmatched by another, but I little needed the men of England falling for the charms of a younger, and most beautiful queen. They might start to have ideas about replacing their old plaything with a new, shiny toy...

As Christmas drew near, however, it was not only fears about my cousin of Scots which were gnawing at my nerves. It was Robin. I was becoming more than a little annoyed with my Master of Horse. Quite apart from the fact that he would not set aside talk of marriage, even though I had told him it was too soon *many* times, he had been badgering me to elevate him as a sign of my trust. Robin wanted advancement. He wanted to be an earl, or even better, a duke. It was natural for him to want this, but I was not sure this was the right time. Robin already had enemies at court, and my love for him was a large part of the reason they despised him, although his pride and arrogance did not help either. I worried my people would not look favourably on such an act so soon after the mysterious death of his wife. I believed this request might place him in greater danger than he was already in, and it might endanger my people's love for me.

But Robin did not see as I did. His vision had become limited. He saw only what might bring him closer to his goal to marry me. He attended upon me daily, and managed to slip his request into every conversation. It was wearying, and grating. Robin was also oblivious to my sorrow. Once Parry was buried, Robin appeared to think I had forgotten about him. He did not see my heart hanging, bloody and torn within my frail chest. He did not note the dullness of my spirits. Robin was becoming blind to all but his ambitions. Once, he would have seen this change in me in an instant, and sought to cheer or console me. Now, he did not. I was hurt by Robin's lack of empathy and felt this constant insistence on being made an earl was unfeeling. He knew only his own troubles, and had ceased to care for mine. I did not say so to Robin for I hoped he might notice by himself. A fool's hope, as it transpired.

"It would show the people that you had the utmost regard for my talents and skills, Majesty," he said as we played cards one wet afternoon. I glanced up at him and arched an eyebrow without speaking. He had already raised the subject earlier that day and I had already told him I would think on it.

What had happened to my Robin? Was this where his ambition would take him? To lose all the sweetness and kindness I had loved, and to replace those qualities with ruthlessness, selfishness and greed? At such times he did not appear at all like the man I loved. He was a stranger, and one I was not best pleased to keep company with. Was this what his thirst for the throne would do to him? Was this what he might have become, even faster, had I agreed to marry him? When I saw the ugliness his character was capable of I had no regrets about my decision. In some ways, I was relieved to have refused him.

Eventually, noting my silence, Robin glanced up from his cards and chuckled at my baleful expression. "Am I becoming annoying, Majesty?"

"You are, my lord," I agreed. "And it would better suit your purpose to still your lips long enough to allow me to think. It is a bold request, my lord, no matter how dear you are to me… No other lord would dare to ask, and ask so often, for their monarch to elevate them. It is supposed to be something for the monarch to decide themselves."

"But in such times as these when I have enemies crowding about me and rumours at my back…" Robin rearranged his cards, as though he was even slightly interested in the game, which I knew he was not, for his mind was afire with this new plan. "… It would show your trust in me."

"As you have said, several times today already, Robin." My tone grew fractious. I was on the verge of losing my temper. I needed no parrot to repeat the same words over and over and over. What I needed was my friend. "I grow weary and annoyed when people repeat themselves. I have enough of that on the matter of my marriage, and on the succession, from my own Council. Cecil talks about Katherine Grey as though she is the only hope for the future of England. I don't need you to bleat at me continuously too."

"Then I will still my tongue."

"Do."

We played on, and he said nothing further, but the subject was brought up often in my chambers, and not always by Robin. Although I loved Robin, and knew he had many good qualities, he was often not the most subtle of men. Clearly he had drawn his sister into his plan to scuttle me into granting him an earldom, for soon enough, it was all of which Mary Sidney could talk.

"*God's Death!*" I swore at her after she 'happened' to mention that more lords who were entirely loyal to me would be a fine thing for England. "What business is it of yours, Lady Sidney, if there is not *one* Duke or Earl who loves their Queen as they should? Are you the captain of the guards? Have you become my minister for security of the realm? Or should I call you not Mary Sidney today, but Mary *Dudley*? For it is clear that today your loyalties are firmly with your brother!" I walked out, leaving Mary white-faced and stunned.

"They all want to push me and pull me until I am naught but their puppet!" I announced to Kat as I stormed into the Bedchamber, not bothering to explain the history of my outburst.

Kat handed me a cup of small ale. "Then you must cut the strings, Majesty."

"Hah!" I exclaimed and then sipped at the ale. It was refreshing and favoured with herbs; rich rosemary and fragrant thyme. "If I could do that, Kat, I would be running free by now!" I beckoned her closer. "What would you say if I told you Robin was asking to be made an earl?"

Kat cocked her head to one side. "I would say it is for Your Majesty to decide on whomsoever *you* believe to be suited to a post or title, rather than for someone to ask for it."

I nodded in agreement. "My thoughts were the same, but I do not wish to make it appear as though I do not trust him, Kat. It is important for Robin to have my support at the moment."

"Your Majesty *has* given him your support," Kat protested. "Did you not welcome him at court immediately after the investigation into Lady Dudley's death? Did you not make all efforts possible on his behalf? You allowed him to keep his positions, and made no secret of your belief in his innocence. You *have* been a good friend to Robin Dudley." Kat crossed her arms over her generous bosom, her brow dark with disapproval. "Surely, that should be enough for any man, should it not?"

"Sometimes I think too much is not enough for most men, Kat."

"I believe, Majesty, Lord Robin would be better suited, at this time, to offer friendship and comfort to you rather than begging for favours, especially in light of the great loss you have endured."

"He will not talk on another subject. I find myself dreading his step upon my chamber floor."

Kat's nostrils flared with anger. Of all the things that riled her, someone mistreating me was the worst of all offences. "Rather than seeking to advance his own ambitions, Lord Dudley should be thinking of *you*, Majesty... He should be returning the many kindnesses you have showed him. I know that he is close to you, Majesty, but I must question the depth of his friendship if he does not offer consolation to you in *your* time of need. Should he not wish to reciprocate? Friendship is not a street where carts pass only one way, Majesty. Friends are there when they are needed. They should *want* to be there. It should be their first thought... to put an arm about their friend when they are felled by sorrow, and offer solace. To my mind, Lord Robin needs to remember what his duties are as a *friend* and now more so than ever."

Kat echoed my own thoughts. Robin *should* be acting as a friend. Had I not, only recently, done all I could to aid him, to protect him? Perhaps Robin had become too used to being the one who *received* rather than *gave* in our relationship. But Kat was right. He was not doing his part. Was my friendship with Robin, was his love for me, *not* true, then? His behaviour was giving me cause to question him, and this increased the sorrow within me... making me feel isolated and alone.

Despite my annoyance at Robin and all the members of his family he trooped out to cheer on his cause, I decided I would still consider his elevation as promised. I spoke with some of my ladies-in-waiting, to allow the information to leak out into the court. I would test the reaction of the nobles, and of my people, and weigh up what dangers elevating Robin might create. The reactions were not favourable. Norfolk, in particular, was incensed at the idea.

That night, I went to my private chapel, and said a prayer for Parry. I did not believe, as Catholics did, that Parry had need of my prayers to help him into Heaven. Such a man as he would be welcomed by God with open arms. I just wanted Parry to know I was thinking of him, missing him, as the world continued on in such a blithe and unconcerned manner, after he had left it.

"You would have supported Robin, would you not, old friend?" I whispered into the incense-filled dim light of the chapel as I rested on my knees. "And perhaps you would have been right to think he should be elevated. He has done much for me in the past. I just wish he could look into my heart, as once he did with such ease, and see there is little there but the space you have left."

As I rose to leave, I kissed my fingers and laid them on the altar. "Rest well, Parry," I murmured. "You have earned it, for ever did you serve me well."

Chapter Twelve

Greenwich Palace
Christmas 1560

As Advent drew to a close, and the traditional period of fasting ended, everyone was looking forward to the great feast of Christmas Day. After a last austere meal on Christmas Eve, where no eggs, milk, cheese, or meat were allowed, to finish the fast of Advent, all at court were ready for a fine meal, and a good dance. I had not found the fast a trial this year. I was not averse to a period where I was *expected* to refrain from food. It gave me excuses to offer to Kat and Blanche when they tried to feed me. Kat was most displeased at my frail appetite. She worried for this habit, which grew only stronger over the years, to abstain from food in times of trial. But it was not a conscious choice, not exactly. It was just how I reacted to pain, strife and trouble.

On Christmas Eve, my servants went out into the parks and cut boughs of green box, laurel and scented yew, along with bushels of shining holly, clambering ivy and clustered mistletoe to decorate the halls of court. Yule logs were brought in for the fires. On Christmas morning, a piece of last year's fire, saved for this purpose, would be put under the Yule log, so the coming year was kindled from the flames of the year past.

Around the city, and throughout the towns of England, Christmas Eve was a night for wandering players and performers to roam, seeking a coin or an offering of food from the houses and doorways where they performed. The sound of voices rose, singing, from the dark streets of snow-bound London. On the air, too, were the scents of roasting meat, spices sizzling in butter, and the smell of baking bread. All over the country, farmers and yeomen offered more fodder to their animals on Christmas Eve, in part because it was traditional, and we cling to our traditions, and in part to save them from having to attend to their beasts in their stables much the next day, when they wanted to be in their homes, celebrating with their families. There was a long-held belief that as Christmas Eve turned to Christmas morn, cattle and sheep would lift their heads and cry out to mark the birth of Jesus Christ. Perhaps, seeing as their ancestors had been amongst the first to see the coming of the Christ child, this was only to be expected.

Before the fire, in my chambers on Christmas Eve, I gathered with my ladies, each of us clasping full cups of wine, or small ale, listening to the stories of old. Although my Privy Council and many of my more zealous Protestant subjects did not approve of such pagan practices, I loved to hear the ancient tales. They are a link to our past, to our ancestors, through the power of stories. Kat and Blanche were masters at this sport. Tales of fairies, witches, hobgoblins and the Devil Himself dripped from their lips to terrify and enthral my household.

Their backs to the bright fire, Kat and Blanche would tell a tale together, each playing different parts of the story. Their faces twisted into the fearsome visage of demons, and drooped into the idiotic faces of fools. They held us spellbound. They told the tale of St Nicholas, saving sweet virgin sisters from marriage to boorish old men; they spoke of fairies who stole children in the dead of night and replaced them with changelings; they told of ghosts, souls who haunted the places of their deaths, in times of evil men and evil deeds. As Kat and Blanche danced about each other, their faces shadowed, then illuminated by the crackling flames, the eyes of my young maids would grow wild and white. My ladies leant forward, their breath caught in their throats, as Kat and Blanche reached the climax of a tale.

"And then..." Blanche leaned forward, folding her back like an old, broken witch, creeping towards my ladies with her hands outstretched like claws. "...They opened their door..."

Blanche paused, her hands reaching slowly forwards, close to the faces of the youngest maids who cringed from her. Blanche's face was bound in shadow. There was not a sound, as we all held our breath. Her voice fell to a whisper. "The door creaked open... slowly... slowly... they stepped outside..."

"And the Devil swooped upon them and carried them all to *hell!*" shrieked Kat, leaping in front of the fire from her hiding place in the corner. My women jumped, screeched loud with terror, and then dissolved into uncontrollable giggles, leaning against one another, holding their sides in pain.

"Enough!" I announced when I had recovered the strength to speak. I had not laughed so hard since Parry had died. "Enough, you wicked sirens! Or my Yeomen will break down the doors, thinking we are under attack!"

We made for our beds, the sound of laughter trickling along the hallways as my maids departed for their shared rooms. I asked Kat and Blanche to sleep in my bed that night. I always had at least one lady with me, and often several on pallet beds on the floor, but there was something about Christmas Eve which told me to gather family about me. Kat and Blanche were the closest I had to family. In many ways, since they had raised me in the absence of my mother, they were closer to me than my own kin had ever been. Perhaps such a thought should have been sorrowful, but I did not think of it in this way. If I was unfortunate to have lost my mother so young, I was equally as fortunate to have her replaced with such good, loving women.

At least I have them, I thought. *There are many in this world who have no one.*

We lay in the bed that night, under the scented bed sheets and thick covers of good English wool. I listened to Kat's gentle snores, and Blanche's steady breathing. I smelled Kat's soft perfume of lavender rising from the warmth of her body and I felt at peace. It was true that my life was far from perfect. The humblest man may look at a queen and believe she has all she would ever need; all the wealth, all the freedom, all the privilege he does not... and whilst much of this is true, it is also true that I was more bound, less free, and less able to do with my life as I wanted than the poorest man of my stables.

But at times such as this, I understood I *was* fortunate. I had friends, and they loved me. Such gifts, when we remember to be grateful for them, count as the best of blessings.

*

As Christmas Day peeked over the pink and blue striped dawn skies, I rose, danced six galliards with my ladies and then walked the paths of my gardens, hearing thin ice crack under my feet and the ringing of bells pealing all over London, calling people to Mass. William St Loe walked quietly behind me. His presence was reassuring, familiar, and made me feel safe. I returned refreshed. Before the fire, where juniper wood burnt, releasing a heavenly scent into the chamber, my ladies washed and dressed me.

I bathed regularly, much more so than many of my court, for I could not stand ill smells, especially upon my own skin. Myrrh-scented water was poured over my hands, and I used Spanish soap, a mixture of salted wood ash, oil and scents, to cleanse my skin. Upon my clean skin were placed undergarments of linen, and over them, a stiff whalebone farthingale to hold up my skirts. I liked farthingales for they made my waist appear even slimmer than it was by accentuating my hips. Kat rolled silk stockings up my legs, the ones Robin had bought me. About my neck was a small ruff of white lace, starched with the sap of a wild plant. That plant had earned a new name amongst the common people as the ruff became popular at court. The plant was now called *Lords and Ladies* for it was only nobility who could afford such pretty, useless and high-maintenance items of dress such as a ruff. My gown and sleeves were embroidered with patterns of roses, honeysuckle, and snakes, for my lineage, purity and wisdom. Pearls clung to the edges of the gown along my chest, glimmering against the clear skin of my breasts.

A mixture of egg white and alum was spread lightly upon my face, and then powdered over with alabaster, so that my skin shone and sparkled. I did not like to paint myself too heavily, but a little embellishment does no harm. My cheeks and lips were painted delicately with colouring made from crushed red rose petals. My long, elegant fingers were afire with rings of gold, bearing stones of emerald and sapphire. Since the sapphire was supposed to hold the power to dispel discord, I thought it might be appropriate for court that season... for it seemed that Arundel and Norfolk were determined to make war upon Robin.

In the evening, before the feast and dancing began, courtiers played Hoodman's Bluff in the halls. Robin and Thomas Heneage were blinded by lengths of red velvet. They staggered and grabbed at thin air, trying to catch my giggling ladies as they danced out of their grasp. Heneage was a year younger than me, and a handsome man. He hailed from Essex. His father had been a member of my father's Privy Council and his uncle had once been Groom of the Stool, a most important and trusted position, since it was the Groom's job to attend to the King as he emptied his bowels in the privy... Although Heneage did not hold a position at court, he was a Member of Parliament and I had high hopes for him in the future. An affable, witty soul, he had the dark looks I admired in men, and was a fine dancer. He enjoyed riddles and jests, and when at court there was always a merry band about him. Robin and he were good friends, and Heneage was often with us when we rode out or walked in the gardens.

"Have a care, Master Heneage!" I cried as the young man, rendered sightless by his thick blindfold, mistook me for one of the ladies in the game and grasped hold of my waist as I passed. "Unhand your Queen, sir!"

Heneage dropped his hands and a deep flush emerged under the blindfold, but I laughed merrily. "You have a fine pair of hands there, Master Heneage," I praised. "There are few men indeed, other than my father, who could say they have managed to hold on to me!"

"Then I am most fortunate of all men," Heneage announced, bowing to an empty space beside me since he could not see where I was. Mirth fluttered through the crowds. "To have known what it is to touch the most radiant of all women."

Did I not say he had great promise? What sweet flattery!

"Have a care with my ladies, Heneage," I said, tapping my lace fan on his bowed shoulder as I passed. "I want all of them returned in one piece!" Walking on, I smiled with affection at the wild antics of my courtiers. Christmas had stolen inside them, made them gay with childlike enjoyment.

Mummers had come calling at the palace gates in the days before Christmas, and now they came to perform traditional pieces for us. In some parts of the town, women would go from house to house, visiting, offering a good-luck cup of drink to each of their neighbours. Others took the wassail cup out to the trees in their orchards, or to hives on their lands, singing to the bees and the trees to make them fruitful. I did not mind these traditions. I celebrated many of them myself. The more puritanical of my Protestant subjects disapproved, wanting to remove all the joys of life along with popish superstition, but this I did not agree with. If God created anything, He was certainly responsible for joy. Could the Devil have made such a sweet blessing? I think not. Joy and laughter, love and friendship are God's works. To deny them is to deny God. Even Jesus was known to jest at times, using sardonic wit to make a point. Why should we not follow in his footsteps?

We danced that night for hours. Silk and velvet whispered against the rush-covered floors, leather boots and soft slippers slipped and tripped through galliards, voltas and *basse dances*. Ladies were thrown into the air, and men leapt like proud stags. When the time came for the feast, we were pink of cheek and rumbling of belly, eager for food. The servers carried their wares from the kitchens. Dough balls stuffed with spiced pork and currants were served in a winter herb broth and leeks cooked in white wine dripped upon toasted slices of plump, white bread. Gourdes and cowcumber were cooked in pottage of sweet, gingered broth. Jellied soup of mutton and hens came boiled in almond milk with cubebs and mace, and tarts thick with eggs and cheese, spiced with cinnamon and cloves shone under the light of the tallow candles.

Roasted goose, golden and sizzling arrived on beds of purple carrot glistening with oil and salt. Skinned peacocks, roasted whole and then re-dressed with their feathers were brought out to great cheers of admiration. Fish, surrounded by jelly, moulded to look like the waves of the sea, melted gently on the tables and rabbits cooked in wine syrup, heavy with ginger, sugar and pepper, stared out with sightless, brown-crisped eyes. Fat-breasted turkey, an import just beginning to be bred in England, stood proud next to whole haunches of roasted and carved venison on frumenty. Hare pie, white pudding, duck in mustard and honey, and boiled larks in verjuice and butter were dished out from the shared platters.

To a grand cheer, the wild boar was brought in. The roasted head, cleaved from the body, was served to my table and sweet slices of his cheeks and tongue were offered to me. Boiled quail on beds of sweet cabbage, and capon with roasted, blackened slices of lemon and orange made the tables gay. Baked pheasant, crane and bustard came then, accompanied by pink-boiled shrimps and piles of muscles clicking in their shells, slathered in garlic and herbs.

Sturgeon swam in sweet vinegar. Pickled mushrooms, stuffed eggs, piles of baked onions, heaps of tan-coloured, roasted garlic, and fried, shredded, turnips joined this nation of foods. Herring pies, eels, carp and trout were delivered to the already overstuffed tables. Pages took up knives to impress their lords with their carving skills, cheered on in their efforts by the hungry, waiting hordes.

The traditional pie made of minced mutton meat and dried fruits, rich with thirteen spices, was brought out and shared; thirteen spices were used to honour the Apostles. Then there was soft, tangy, new cheese, pear pies with sugar and cloves, baked quinces, preserved oranges in syrup, apple pies and possets of cream, sugar and cinnamon. Clotted cream was smeared on dainty wafers. Newly imported sweet potatoes in rose and orange syrup, apple fritters, walnut comfits, and pottage of bright red-purple cherries on sugar-fried toast arrived to end the meal.

The wassail bowl was filled with gallons of steaming hot ale, spices and sugar. At the bottom was a crust of bread, and, when all the ale was drunk, the crust was put upon a platter of gold and brought to me to eat. I have to say I found it delicious; sweet and spiced, soft and warm, it held a delicious sour tang from the ale.

After the feast, as many sat looking green, clutching their over-stuffed bellies in pain, singers came forth to lull our senses. They sang of the Nativity, of God and hope and peace and charity. Some fanatical subjects wanted no singing at Christmas, but I believed that God wanted us to celebrate the birth of His son, and how better to celebrate, than to lift one's voice to the Almighty and sing?

That night we went to beds with bellies and hearts that were full. As the twelve days of Christmas celebrations continued, I was feeling sated, and calm, as though with the coming of the Christmas season, all was made well with my world. I wished Parry had been here to see this glorious Christmas, but the space he had left in my heart was starting to mend. I was not healed, but certainly this time of kindness and joy had done much to bring peace to me.

I was shortly to come to regret being lulled into such calmness.

Chapter Thirteen

Greenwich Palace
Winter 1560-1561

Even as we celebrated through the twelve days of Christmas, many small and seemingly inconsequential matters occurred in my household which niggled at the edge of my consciousness. I did not pay them the attention they deserved. Although, later, I would curse myself for this, I was a busy soul at this time. News from France, and the impending arrival of my rival, Mary Stewart stole my attention. There was the organisation of festivities for Christmas, the usual everyday business of my Privy Council and country and Robin was making me wish I could twist my own ears off by endlessly pressing about his ennoblement. My head had never been as full, and my days never as busy.

During Christmas, I had believed I had left my grief behind me. Amongst the celebrations, I had found both excitement and peace, but as the season passed, grief crept back to my side. He had been disguised for a while, but as normal life resumed, he returned.

Grief is a cruel companion. You would think that he would come and remain at your side when a loved one dies, and for the first few weeks this is indeed the case. You grow used to him. You wake with him and go about your day in his company. You climb into bed and he is there. Then, time passes, and he seems to step away. You believe yourself safe. You have whole moments where you do not recall your loss and start to laugh and smile again. Life goes on... It is then that grief becomes the most unwelcome of surprise guests. He is a malicious visitor, arriving unannounced and unexpected. It can be the slightest of things which calls him to you; the scent of a particular dish, the sight of the setting sun, a familiar object which brings forth memories. Everyday things. Things to which we normally pay no heed. This is where grief hides, waiting to spring his trap. He leaps; bringing back your loss fresh, raw and new. Your heart falls again. Your sorrows crash upon your shoulders. Grief is a cruel fool; an evil jester who takes delight in stealing happiness. He is never satisfied. He always wants more.

That was how I felt, then. Grief would allow me to forget my loss for blissful moments, only to rush at me anew. He stole my energy, and feasted on my sadness. It would have been good for me to have Robin, my *old* Robin, at my side. But my friend was nowhere to be seen. Someone had taken his place. A stranger who could not see his friend was slowly being eroded by sorrow. When I had the energy, I was angry. When grief stole my spirit, I merely plodded along, listening to Robin's increasingly frequent and insistent 'requests' to be elevated. So when Katherine Grey was absent from her duties more often than she was present for them, I hardly noticed, until it became increasingly obvious.

"Your friend, Katherine..." I said to Jane Seymour as she tied a silver ribbon on my new shoes of black velvet; a gift from the King of Spain. No matter how often he and I were in disagreement, it could not be denied Phillip of Spain had excellent taste in presents. The shoes were very pretty, and they made my feet look tiny and elegant. "... She was supposed to be in my chambers today, was she not?" Jane's usually pale cheeks infused with a hint of pink. She did not lift her eyes to my face but busied herself with the ribbon. I gazed down with growing suspicion. "Where is she?" I went on, keeping my tone light.

Jane finally looked up. "She is ill, Majesty," she said, and then promptly flushed crimson across her chest and throat. There are many reasons a young lady might blush, but to my mind there was only one in this case. I was being lied to, by one of my own women, *about* one of my own women. What was Katherine up to?

"Indeed?" I asked slowly, fixing my eyes on my new slippers, turning my foot this way and that to admire the effect. "She seems to be sick an awful lot of late. I will send my physician. Will you escort him to her, Jane?"

The girl looked utterly mortified. "Of course, Majesty," she agreed. "Shall… shall I go ahead and make sure she is decently dressed before he arrives?"

"Oh, I think not… My doctors have seen many a young maid or old woman whilst in her bed, Jane. They are professionals." I glanced backwards and waggled my fingers at Kat, bringing her to join us. "Mistress Ashley will accompany you, Jane, in case any message needs to be sent to me, for I am *most* concerned about the constant poor health of my kinswoman." Jane's red face was growing pale as Kat stepped forwards. As they were about to leave, I leant in to Kat's ear. "Go with Jane and see what the matter with Katherine Grey is, *if* there is anything the matter at all," I murmured. "And if the girl is not where she is supposed to be, then I want to know of it. Immediately."

When Kat arrived back perhaps an hour later, she came straight to me. "Well?" I asked.

"Katherine Grey *was* in bed, Majesty, and appeared to be running a fever, so thought your doctor."

"So… it was true?" I drummed my fingers on the side of my chair and then stopped as I saw Kat's dubious expression. "What is it?"

Kat stepped closer, keeping her voice low. "The girl was flushed and hot, Majesty, and although the doctor prescribed her some salts and a potion, as well as bleeding her, I would say there are reasons why a young lady might be flushed in the face other than with fever…"

"You think she was not ill."

"I think she was well enough to race from wherever it was she was *not* supposed to be to where she was *supposed* to be, and pretend she had been there all along," Kat whispered. "I have tended many a fever, Majesty. I know the signs of sickness. Katherine's eyes were bright, not glassy, and her cheeks were ruddy, rather than fever-flushed. I can prove nothing, but I think she was somewhere she should not have been, and someone warned her you were about to check on her."

"Jane?" I asked. "Did she leave your sight?"

Kat shook her head. "Not for one moment. But Katherine has many friends amongst the maids, *and* a sister here in your chambers. Perhaps one of them managed to sneak out and told Katherine you were looking for her."

"Do you think she was meeting with Hertford?"

Katherine had long been making eyes at Edward Seymour, Lord Hertford. She knew I did not approve. A union between Katherine and Hertford was potentially dangerous. He was a direct descendant of Edward III and had been cousin to my royal brother. If Katherine married him then her slim claim to the throne would be enhanced and I had no wish to see that happen. There were many who might think on the union of a Grey, and a Seymour as more legitimate than my own claim. Plotting minds might think to place the descendants of Edward III and Princess Mary Tudor on the throne of England, over me. I had no objection to Katherine marrying, just not to Hertford.

Kat lifted her shoulders. "I can think of no other reason why she would play such a dangerous game, putting her position in your chambers at risk, if not for love, Majesty."

"Then it is time we separated them," I said angrily. "Katherine knows well enough my feelings on the marriage once proposed between Hertford and her. It is within my power to say whom she will marry, not hers! She is a Grey rather than a Tudor, it is true, but she is still a descendant of my grandsire. Her blood is diluted, but still royal and therefore she is under my power to marry, or *not* marry, according to my wishes." I glowered at nothing in particular. Had the girl been neglecting her duties for a chance to run off and meet Hertford? If so she would come to regret it!

"I believe we need another representative in France," I said. "Young Hertford should be tested as a dignitary. His father had great skill in the art of persuasion. I will send him to France and we will see if Lady Grey suddenly becomes more interested in her post in my household..."

*

That New Year's I was given the oddest present anyone gave me when Sir Humphrey Radcliffe offered me his daughter, Mary, as a gift. Radcliffe had just been presented, and had only brought a small gift for me. Perhaps realising how insignificant his present looked in comparison to those my other nobles carried, he made a graceful bow, and offered me his daughter, when she came of age, to serve in my household. I laughed, at first thinking it a jest, but he was serious. "Do you usually go about handing out your children at New Year, my lord?" I asked. "If so, then I hope you have plenty of them, *and* a forgiving wife at home!"

"You are a unique case, of course, Your Majesty," Radcliffe said with a broad grin. "For you, there must be something special. I assure you, my daughter is a good girl. She is humble, meek but with a ready wit and a keen mind and will serve you well."

"And how old is she?" I asked. "How long must I wait for this gift to arrive?"

"She is but ten, at the moment, Majesty, but will mature in good course."

I pursed my lips. It was a flagrant way to gain an appointment for his daughter. Everyone knew how precious the positions in my household were. I wondered if he had not brought a small gift on purpose, and had used this to engineer his offer. But I warmed to Radcliffe. He had presented his 'gift' in such a clever way I decided it was worth rewarding. "I accept your gift, my lord," I said, shaking my head at his audacity even as I smiled at his cleverness. "But I must ask that you do not give out any more children as presents. I might become bombarded with gifts of daughters, as others ape you."

*

After the audiences on New Year's Day, I held a feast. It was easily as grand as the one at Christmas, and we supped on steaming herb pottage, boiled pink shrimp in wine sauce, oysters in lemon and oil, roasted goose, duck and venison and finished the meal with kissing comfits, almond milk with rose petals, apple sauce slathered over buttery biscuits and tarts of egg, cheese, cinnamon, and cardamom. At the end of the feast, a marchpane work was brought out; a chessboard, with all the pieces arranged ready to play, all worked in sugar paste and marzipan.

Robin presented me with imported galingale, an aromatic root from Italy for making sweet gingerbread from, something of which I was most fond. Robin also gave me two pounds of my favourite quinces and other banqueting items, such as goblets, silver spoons and sucket knives. I was delighted with this collection of gifts, for they demonstrated attention to my personal tastes. He knew I loved sweet things. No one could find presents which pleased me as those of Robin did. *He is attentive to my needs and wants*, I thought with affection, wondering if my feelings towards him of late had been ungenerous. Perhaps I had been transplanting my feelings of loneliness in the wake of Parry's death too roundly on Robin's broad shoulders? A moment later, Robin demonstrated this was not the case.

"I have been thinking, Majesty, about trading houses with my cousin, Lord Dudley," Robin mentioned idly. "I would like to reclaim my family's ancestral seat, Dudley Castle, which as you know was granted to my cousin upon the fall of my father."

It was all said in such an apparent careless manner... as though he were simply voicing thoughts aloud. And yet there was something artificial in his nonchalance; something that caused me to look on his gifts with less liking than before. In all times past, I had seen Robin's gifts as presents given to please me. Now, I felt as though he was trying to *buy* my favour. I expected this from others but had not thought to expect it of him. The sheen suddenly slipped from his gifts. "And why would you chance upon this idea, *now*, Robin?" I asked, as we stood watching the dancers trip and prance through a volta.

"Perhaps it is just an urge I have, Majesty," he said, his eyes wide with innocence. "To take back the ancient seat of my forebears."

He was lying, and not doing a very good job of it. Robin had been relentless in his pestering about the earldom. I am sure he believed it was a done deal, even though I had not, as yet, said yes. For many weeks I had been of two minds. On the one hand I wanted to support Robin. Before I came to the throne, he had supported me with men and money. I had promised his offerings would come back to him threefold, and I intended to reward him still for past loyalty. But there were other considerations. The suspicion surrounding him was not yet dead and the reaction from my leaking the notion to the court had been unfavourable. My people might think I was elevating him to marry him, which would test their love for me... But above all these considerations, there was his late behaviour. I did not like this creature Robin had become. I did not like his lack of care, his endless whining and demanding, or the high pride with which he sauntered through court.

This idea to gain back his family seat was but a part of his grand plan, I was sure. It smacked of arrogance growing within my beloved that I liked not. He had grown lazy in my love. Over-confidence made Robin act as though I was something that could be picked up and put down when he felt like it. Was this how he had treated his wife? Suddenly I pitied Amy Dudley. Had she been treated carelessly, too, because he had been assured of her love? Was this how Robin treated love? With such reckless, heedless flippancy? He seemed to think he was the one in charge of me, rather than the other way around.

There were other issues which troubled me too. The Duke of Holstein had recently written me a letter. The Duke had long been a supporter and ally of mine, and we had exchanged letters and honours over the years. But of late, ill reports of me were gathering at his door. The first part of his letter commiserated on my late poor health. I was not actually ill. I was just still not eating a great deal. The court had secretly been commenting on how ill and wasted I looked. In alarm that they might begin to question my strength, and this might lead to my being pestered on marriage and the succession, or more seriously, that it might encourage my heirs or enemies to think of removing me, I had taken steps. I had ordered more cosmetics to be used to conceal my tired skin and ordered a gorgeous array of fine wigs to use. At the Christmas celebrations I danced with great vigour, so ambassadors could report to their masters how hale the Queen of England was. All well and good, but the second part of the Duke's letter spoke with great alarm about rumours he had heard questioning my honour. There was gossip that I was intending to marry Robin as well as rumour we were already lovers. I had written back to the Duke, telling him I was not interested in marriage at all at this time, and asking him to try to believe the best of me.

The Duke's letter and my growing concerns about Robin's behaviour brought about my decision. It was not going to be one Robin would like, but he was overstepping his authority, and challenging mine. No Tudor has ever liked being told what to do and I was no exception. I made up my mind and decided to teach Robin a lesson. It was time for Robin to know what it was like to slip, just a little, from favour. If he were made less sure of his footing, perhaps he would have more care in considering the path he walked.

*

Plough Monday arrived, and with it came the end of the Christmas celebrations. People returned to work, readying the fields for the sowing of crops in a few months. The tradition of taking ploughs about local parishes to be blessed had been lately banned, since many thought it a rather heathen ritual. This did not stop the common people marking the event by dressing as fools, or with men dressing as women, and collecting money for the Church, or for the poor. Some of my Council wanted this banned too, but I allowed it to continue. It was but jesting and play and if it raised money for the poor, where was the harm? Plough plays went on and I allowed some to be performed at court, to demonstrate my support. My people loved this. There were some old customs I was moved to ban by my Council and Parliament, but in keeping parts of them alive, my people believed I was on their side. Of course, I wanted my people to be happy, but it is often beneficial for a queen to play both sides of a game... Then, she cannot lose.

Later that month, there was a meeting of the Privy Council, where the ceremony of investment for Robin was to be held. Although it may appear cruel, I had decided to make my point here, both to my people and to Robin. I sat before my Council with Robin beside me. He looked far too pleased with himself, too self-assured, too arrogant. I did not like this change of tunic; the scarlet of superiority did not become him. I had to bring him down, just a little. I had to teach him any advancement came from *me*, and therefore he should take more care of our friendship.

The matter of his ennoblement arose. Before the Council, I held the papers aloft, took my eating knife from my belt, and pierced the parchment where Robin's ennoblement was laid out. Slowly, I ripped the blade downwards, tearing Robin's dreams asunder. There was stunned silence.

"I love the house of Lords too well, my lords," I said, staring coldly at Robin. "To have another Dudley placed there, since three generations have proved themselves traitors to my line."

Robin stared at me, astonished and angry. "I would that you would not… censure me so, Majesty," he stuttered. "In front of my lords and noble gentlemen." His face was amazed, not only at my rejection of his request, but at my hard words. Never had I spoken of him in such a way before. I had always defended him about his family's traitorous past. He stared, gaping like a herring, and then tore his eyes away from mine, glowering at the table as though he wished he could smash it to splinters. I watched him, seeing the heat on his cheeks and the shame on his face. I was sorry for causing him pain, but he had to understand that *I* was the one with the power here, not him. He had to understand he had failed in his duty to me. That he had hurt me. All the same, I reached out and touched his cheek.

"The bear and ragged staff are not so soon overthrown," I said. And then lower, I whispered, "this is not the time, Robin."

Robin did not dare snatch his face from my hand, but his eyes burned with malice. I dismissed the Council, allowing Robin to flee and lick his wounds in private. Rumours spread through court. Many believed I would abandon him entirely, but they were wrong. I had hurt him, shamed him in public. I could not allow him to continue as he was, but I was not about to give up on him. I hoped he would learn his lesson.

For his own good, I told myself, he needs to drop some of the high arrogance and pride which he carries upon those broad shoulders. Robin was gaining enemies faster than a greyhound races over heath and heather. This is for his own good, I told myself. And when he has had time to calm down, he will see his errors. He will come back and all will be as it was before.

I did not see Robin for some days. When I called him to attend upon me, he sent a messenger back saying that he was taken ill. I did not believe this was the truth. Robin was hurt. Perhaps he did not understand my reasons for disgracing him so publicly, but Robin needed to understand that he was not the master here… I was.

Give him time, Elizabeth, I counselled. *Time to remember all you have done for him. Time to remember how a good friend should act.* I assured myself he would think on these matters and be struck with how badly he had behaved.

I assured myself in vain.

Chapter Fourteen

Greenwich Palace
Winter 1561

"I hear *much* whispering in my chambers of late, Kat," I said as she helped me prepare for bed. Handing me a pot of chickweed balm to preserve my skin, Kat lifted her eyebrows. "Do you know what the whispers say?" I asked, smoothing the lotion onto my arms and rubbing it in. I required more and more potions and lotions these days to make myself appear as I had when first I came to the throne. Was it only four years ago? It was as though a lifetime had passed.

"You speak of Katherine Grey and her friend Jane?" Kat took the pot from me and started to smooth olive oil over my legs, *tsking* at my dry skin.

"Of whom else? They should learn to be more covert. Glancing around and scuttling off into corners is easily noted after a while. They will never be employed by Cecil at this rate."

Kat's hands moved up and down, massaging the oil into my skin. Her touch was gentle yet firm. It was soothing. "I will keep an ear out, my lady, but I suspect it is nothing more than another conversation on the *many* virtues of young Hertford's fine legs."

"Mmmm," I muttered, unconvinced. "They seem rather animated in their discussions, Kat... Katherine and Jane." I pulled a disgruntled face. "Although it is understandable, I do so wish the Seymour line would cease to name their daughters *Jane*... Although I loved my brother, his mother displaced my own. It seems unfitting I should have to go about my court with her ghost following me, reminding me at every step that even the highest and most powerful of queens can tumble from grace at any moment."

As if I am not reminded of that enough by my Council, every day, I thought.

"Perhaps a royal decree, my lady?" Kat's face was a blank mask of mock-seriousness as she glanced up at me, her hands slick with oil. "A proclamation banning all Seymours from naming their children after the most prodigious daughter of their house?"

"Perhaps I shall consider such an act indeed, Kat, and have it sent through Parliament, too. I shall have them all name their daughters Elizabeth, or Anne, and see how they like that!" We chuckled at the notion.

I breathed in. "Just keep an eye on them, will you? Ever since I elevated Katherine to the Privy Chamber she believes she will be named my heir. I don't want anyone supposing I will do such a thing. The girl may well have little between her ears, but others have sought to use her for their own purposes. Remember de Quadra thinking of kidnapping her and marrying her to Don Carlos?" Kat nodded, wiping her hands on a cloth. "So I want to know what all this whispering is about. If she wants to be made heir, and is plotting to make it so, I need to know. If they are making plans with Jane's brother, Hertford, I want to know that, too. Those two are far too close… and the way she simpers at him makes me want to stick my head in the privy until I pass out… If Katherine is up to anything with Jane, Spain, *or* with Hertford, I need to know."

"I will ask Blanche to help," said Kat. "She spent time with Dr. John Dee before he left for his travels, Majesty, and he instructed her in the mysteries of palm reading."

"What has that to do with this?"

Kat smirked like a cunning weasel. "Perhaps I can persuade Blanche to carry out a *special* reading for Katherine, warning her of the perils of going against the wishes of her Queen."

I chuckled. "Kat, you are a canny minx... And think you Katherine will fall for such a reading?"

"The girl is *entirely* credulous, my lady, and Blanche can be awfully convincing when she puts her mind to it."

"As I well remember from Christmas. My chambers still echo with the screams of my ladies after you two terrorized them."

Kat spoke to Blanche, and the plan went ahead. At a gathering in my chambers, Blanche read the palms of the other ladies for sport, promising them long lives, many children and, of course, handsome husbands. Eager to hear her fate, Katherine put her hand under the gaze of my oldest servant. Blanche stared at the lily-white palm for a moment. She leaned in, and narrowed her eyes. Then she drew back sharply with a shocked gasp as though she had seen something terrible. Lady Clinton, Katherine Knollys and Kat all leant in, inspecting Katherine's palm. "What is it?" Katherine asked, bringing her hand swiftly up to her face to examine it, trying to glean what awful destiny Blanche had seen there.

Blanche paused, put her hand to her breast and regarded Katherine with grave eyes. "The lines say, madam, that if you ever marry without the Queen's consent, you and your husband will be undone, and suffer a fate worse than that of your poor sister, Lady Jane Grey!"

Katherine was most upset by this fortune. She put a hand to her belly as though Blanche's words had made her nauseous, but then seemed to right herself and shook her head. "I would *never* do such a thing," she breathed. "The Queen knows of my love and respect for her. I would never seek to marry below me."

"*Or* without her permission," Mary Grey promptly added from behind Katherine, reminding her sister of the actual point of the prophesy.

"Or without permission." Katherine's words sounded strangled.

From the corner, where I sat playing two of my Besses at cards, I smiled. Looking at Bess St Loe, and Bess Parr, I caught them viewing my grin with confused faces. I beamed and tossed another coin gamely into the mounting pile. "I raise the stakes," I said as the coin tinkled against those it joined. "For I believe I have the winning hand."

Let that be a warning to you, cousin, I thought.

Chapter Fifteen

Greenwich Palace
Winter 1561

"Kat!" I shrieked, my voice high, shrill, and filled with anger as I marched into my Bedchamber. I was furious. As if I did not have enough to deal with, now there was another matter come to confront me!

"Madam?" Kat emerged from one of the side rooms, her face confused.

"Your husband has been banished from my court!" I narrowed my eyes, daring her to defend him. Kat was amazed for she knew how fond of John I was.

"What has John done to offend you, Majesty?" she asked carefully.

"Spoken many rude and ill words to Robin Dudley," I said. "Insults said openly to his face, Kat! In front of the court! I will not tolerate such behaviour!"

Robin had come to me only moments before. At first I believed he wished to make things right between us, but instead this argument between him and John had emerged. I was angrier than I should have been. Fury, which had been directed at Robin, leeched out and spilled over John. Although I recognised it not at the time, I was also angry at myself for not putting matters right with Robin, leading me to overcompensate in my defence of him. John Ashley, Kat's husband, had confronted Robin in public, and had made his feelings about my favourite clear as day for all the court to hear. This kind of public quarrel always annoyed me, for nobles and courtiers had dignity to maintain and an example to set... But today, hearing of this, I was wild with wrath.

"Overseeing court is like governing a gaggle of unruly goslings at the best of times!" I exclaimed, rounding on Kat and glaring at her as though she were responsible for her husband's actions. "I will have no more of it. John is banished, and let that be a lesson to him and to any others who think they can do as they will!" I yanked my shawl from my aching shoulders. The cold wind had made its way into my muscles and made them sore. The pain was not helping my temper or patience.

"Majesty… If you would allow me to talk to my husband? It must be a misunderstanding…"

"It is nothing of the sort!" I threw my hands out, wrenching my shoulder. The sudden burst of pain made me grimace, but since my face was already soured by anger, Kat did not notice. "I am surrounded by people who all believe *they* should make the rules rather than I! I have banished John, and I will not forgive him for the insults he has thrown at Robin." I put a hand to my shoulder and pulled against it; red-hot pain protested against the motion.

Kat's face assumed that expression all women recognise; a kind of weary annoyance, which comes of knowing and loving a husband only too well, and often being called to answer for them. "I know not what has occurred, Majesty, but John has always been your loyal supporter and friend. Perhaps you should call him here, to talk?"

"I have heard quite enough of John Ashley this day." My tone was ominous. "Think yourself lucky that I do not banish *you* along with your unruly, ill-mannered husband!" I left for the privy gardens, leaving Kat staring after me in bewilderment. I was too far gone in rage to listen to Kat, and too irritated to remain in her presence.

As I stalked through the misty rain, reaching up to pull at my aching shoulder, Katherine Knollys and Lady Clinton trailed warily far behind me. I thought on John Ashley. Robin and John had exchanged harsh words about my favour for Robin. John had at first attempted to impress upon my favourite that my affection for him was standing in the way of my making a match with any other man, but this had descended, over a short space of time, to infantile name-calling and remarks of a derogatory nature on Robin's heritage.

The insults about his family are your fault, Elizabeth, I told myself. Had I not, after all, recently questioned Robin's loyalty because of his lineage? The thought that I had allowed others, such as John, the means to insult Robin was uncomfortable. Guilt had prompted me to banish John. I had not elevated Robin, but that did not mean anyone was allowed to cause disruption at my court, nor insult my friends! It seemed everyone about me believed they knew better than I did on what to do with my life, my court, and my country. I was going to set them all straight on that matter! I tugged viciously at a rosemary bush, trying to pluck a stalk, and succeeded in slicing my finger open. Cursing, and sucking my rosemary-flavoured blood, I marched on. My shoulder ached, my finger hurt now too... Robin and I were still not right with each other, and even my loyal servants were acting against my wishes. Oh... I was in a foul temper that day!

I was not keen to talk with Kat, but when she came to me, a few days later, she was wearing an expression I recognised. She knew something she was not supposed to. "What is it?" I asked waspishly, my ill-temper still obvious.

"I overheard something, Majesty," she replied, twisting her hands awkwardly. Kat knew my temper. She did not want to bring me further ill news.

"What?"

She breathed in. "Majesty, Lord Robin has sent his brother-in-law, Henry Sidney, to meet with ambassador de Quadra."

"For what purpose?"

"To gain the support of Phillip of Spain." Her eyes were guarded as she tried to gauge my mood.

"In what matter?"

"In the matter, Majesty… of your marriage to Robin Dudley."

I stared at Kat, hearing her words clink through my mind. "There *is* no matter of marriage between Robin and me," I said slowly. "And certainly no matter between us that would concern Spain or de Quadra." I did not like the direction this conversation was heading. What was Robin up to?

"But Lord Robert believes there may be hope, if he can gain support from a foreign prince, Your Majesty," Kat explained. "I heard Dudley and Sidney talking in whispers near the stables. I went to talk to Lord Dudley to ask him to intercede with you for John, but found him with Sidney…" she paused, her eyes steady upon mine. "And, there is more, Majesty."

"More I will not like, given your obvious reluctance to tell me."

She inclined her head in agreement. "I heard Sidney ask Robin why Phillip of Spain should support him. What gain was there for the Hapsburgs if Robin should marry the Queen?"

"And?"

"And Lord Robert said the offering would be the restoration of the *faith* in England, Majesty." Kat held up her hands as my eyebrows shot up. "I would not lie about this, Majesty, no matter what troubles there are between my John and

Dudley. I would not try to deceive you. Dudley told Sidney he would *serve and obey* the King of Spain, in return for Phillip's support. And saying he would work to restore the *faith*… that can only mean one thing, surely." Kat sighed, her face miserable. She knew she had made me unhappy. "I thought you should know, Majesty… There is something ill growing here, and Lord Robin is right in its rotten core."

I felt nauseous. My Robin, my friend, the man I loved, was willing to offer his *fealty* and *fidelity* to another monarch in order to gain the crown? He was willing to make promises to restore the Catholic faith? To go against my decrees, my plans for England, which had been so hard fought, and which I was still perfecting even to this day? Robin was willing to betray me, and become vassal to another king? And not just any king, but Phillip, the man who, when I was a princess, would have had me kidnapped and forcibly wed to one of his minions, had I not tricked him into believing I would give him my hand in marriage? No matter *what* Robin wanted, this was unacceptable. In many ways, it was treason.

Men had died for less.

It struck me then how far Robin and I had grown apart. There was a time when all he thought of was my happiness, and now he was working against me, playing games in the shadows. Robin must indeed be desperate, and desperation makes men do strange and foolish things. He was gambling with my love and affection; gambling in the hope of winning a crown. Was the throne more important to him than I was? Before, I would have been sure the answer would have been no… Now, I was not sure of anything.

By the faith, I was alone in that moment. I felt I knew my love not at all.

In my father's day, Robin's actions would have been quite enough to ensure his head parted company with his shoulders. Although anger caused me to linger over this possibility for a moment, I knew I could not go through with it. I could not kill Robin, although I was sorely tempted by the idea of having him arrested. But to do so would mean he would lose his post, and I would lose him. Had I already lost him? Lost him to ambition? I knew not. *Damn* the fool! What was he thinking? That if Phillip of Spain offered support, I would forget all that was stacked against this match and fall, fainting, into Robin's open arms with a sigh? Did he think this attempt to hoodwink me, by working with my enemies, was *romantic*? Did he think flaunting my laws, forgetting his loyalty, and conspiring to trick me was a sure way to secure my heart?

Halfwit! Pernicious, insidious wretch! Traitorous, wily serpent nestled at my breast! *And* Robin had proved himself even more foolish by allowing himself to be overheard. I remembered the remorse I had felt when I cut up his patents of nobility... I should have burned them and thrown him in my prisons instead!

But then, even as rage threatened to envelop me, I wondered how much of this was as it seemed. I had no doubt Kat had overheard this, but were Robin's promises to de Quadra true or were they simply a ruse to get the Spanish to support him as my suitor? Was he *really* promising to serve Phillip? Robin had been long at my side. Had he noted how I toyed with ambassadors and my Council, confusing and bamboozling each side by promising a great deal, delivering little, evading much and thereby usually getting my own way? Perhaps Robin was using de Quadra to get Phillip's support, but had no intention of fulfilling any promises made. Whether Robin was seeking to play de Quadra and Phillip, or if he sought to play all three of us, I was not happy. I liked better the idea that he was fooling de Quadra and Phillip, for then at least Robin was not *actually* a traitor, but simply a liar.

Whether he was a true traitor, or a reckless liar, I was enraged. Robin had learnt nothing. He had not looked inside himself for fault when I refused to ennoble him. Rather than trying to restore our friendship, he sought instead to trick me! Robin was not done with his schooling. Since he played now in the dark shadows and dim light of subterfuge, my next lesson would be taught there. I had tried open censure and that had not worked, but if Robin wanted to play games, he would find me an able opponent. Had I not been trained in this sport since I was a child? He would regret this; that I swore. I would not kill him. I would not take his head, but my heart was bitter with spite. He was not going to get away with this.

"And you are *sure* all this is true?" I asked. I did not truly doubt Kat. She was not about to bring me false tales. She was not fool enough to try to play me, as Robin, it seemed, was. But I *wanted* this to be false. I did not want to believe the worst of Robin, even though I knew he was capable of such. The Dudleys had all been like that. Whenever a Dudley thought something, he strove to try and make it so, often flouting the monarch he was supposed to serve. Arrogance was in their blood. I had believed Robin would never do such to me, because he loved me. Apparently I was mistaken. *Damn* him!

"I swear, Majesty, this is what I heard."

I swallowed. "And I believe you, Kat."

"What will you do?"

I ran a finger over my lips. "I will let this unfold and see the truth as it is laid bare to me," I said, and then smiled without humour. "Besides, no matter if they are to be disappointed in the end, it never hurts to have Spain and the Hapsburgs flirting with the idea of alliance, and this offer of Robin's, if it goes ahead, will pull them closer to us." I gazed steadily at

Kat. "You will tell no one of this, Kat," I instructed. "*I* will deal with Robin."

"Of course, Majesty." Kat looked relieved to be excused. I sat on my chair, my mind flooded with desire for revenge.

As for you, Robin, my voice was low and dangerous in my mind. *You will find me prepared… You have not learnt your lesson yet, my lord? Allow me to become your tutor once again.*

Chapter Sixteen

Richmond Palace
Winter 1561

It transpired that Robin had indeed sent his brother-in-law, Henry Sidney, to de Quadra. Paying a man in de Quadra's household for information, I discovered all.

Robin sent Sidney to promise many things to the Spanish ambassador: Robin would work to restore the *faith* in England; he would secure an invitation for the papal nuncio, Abbot Martinego, to come to England and give me an invitation to the Council of Trent; Robin would *do service* to Phillip as one of his *vassals*, and would do all he could to keep peace and friendship between England and Spain should his suit be supported by Phillip. All of this was deeply disturbing. The Council of Trent was one of the Catholic Church's most important councils. They had started to meet in 1545, in response to the rise of Protestantism, and worked to bring about counter-reformation of all states that were now Protestant in an effort to stamp out heresy, as they saw it. Getting me, the leader of the Church of England, a heretic queen and rebel daughter of a rebel king, to attend the Council would be most advantageous for them. They believed if they could get me there, they could persuade me to return England to the Catholic fold, or could threaten me with papal-endorsed invasion should I resist. I had no intention of resisting, as I had no intention of ever attending the Council of Trent, or allowing any of my men to do so. If I never attended, I could avoid conflict with the Catholic Church.

I also had no wish for this nuncio to come to England. If he did not arrive here, I did not have to insult the Bishop of Rome by refusing to attend. If Robin, by his scheming, brought this Martinego to England, then England could be put in jeopardy. England was surrounded by Catholic nations. We could not afford to transform them from wary allies into hostile foes.

I seethed against Robin. He would risk the safety of England for his ambition? Even if he had no intention of following through with these promises, he was still playing with fire, *and* putting me in a most awkward political position. I was only more resolved never to marry Robin when I heard this. Had I not always said I would only marry one who put England above all other considerations? And here he was, using her as a pawn in his game!

Fortunately for Robin, I discovered that neither Robin nor Sidney had expressly said they would work to restore the *Catholic* faith, only the *faith*. The implication was still obvious, but at least Robin had had the sense to be ambiguous so he could wriggle out of his promises when the time came. Sending Sidney was clever too. Perhaps borrowing the idea from me, when I had sent Mary Sidney to de Quadra to pretend interest in the Archduke Charles as a suitor, Robin had sent Sidney. This meant Robin had the option to deny that any of this had been his idea, and blame Sidney for it. I wondered if Sidney was aware Robin's mind might be tending this way.

It consoled me somewhat to know Robin was seeking to play the Hapsburgs. This, at least, meant there was a chance he did not intend to go through with any of these promises. What did not please me, however, was everything else.

"Apparently, you were blamed, *Spirit*," I said to Cecil. He stood near the fire, his face grim, after listening to all I had uncovered. "Sidney informed de Quadra I was tired of your *tyranny*, and wanted to move back to a form of religion where my heart truly rested."

"I am well-known for my tyrannical ways, of course, Majesty," Cecil said with a perfectly blank face which made me chuckle. My humour did not last long.

"Robin promised to serve Phillip of Spain *'as one of his own vassals'*," I said bitterly. That part had been the hardest to swallow.

Cecil let out a long whistle. "You could have him arrested, Majesty," he suggested and then shook his head. "But I know you would not want that."

"I am well aware of the seriousness of the situation, Cecil," I said. "I never thought that Robin would go so far as this... To offer his loyalty to another king? To promise I would accept a papal envoy? To promise to restore the Catholic faith? He has betrayed me. What would make him turn from me so?"

"He loves you, Majesty," Cecil replied. "But he also loves his ambition, and the two together do not make for a man who is honestly deliberating on his actions. I believe he is reacting, as a man may do when he sees fire in his house. He is not thinking, just *acting*." Cecil rolled his eyes. "He probably thinks himself clever."

"If he loves me, Cecil, he should not be betraying me, nor be attempting to *trick* me into marriage. I do not believe he will truly do any of the things he has promised de Quadra. But all the same, Robin has gone too far, he forgets himself. He seeks to *use* me, use me against my own self! I will not stand for such."

"I say, again, Majesty, you could have him arrested. His actions are treasonous. Your father would not have hesitated."

"Unless it was a thing unknown to me, Cecil, my father did not love Robin Dudley."

"Your father understood there comes a time when even those we love can be dangerous to us," Cecil said. I stared at him until he realised he had just vindicated the execution of my mother. Cecil flushed. "But perhaps, there are other ways of dealing with such a situation."

I breathed in, long and deep, trying to centre my thoughts. "And we will find them, Cecil. I will not make my heart a graveyard as my father's became." I rubbed at my forehead. This situation had brought on headaches which had made a home in my head. Little gnawing worms rummaged through my brain and it was not only my head which hurt. My feelings for Robin were affected, it could not be denied. Although I knew that deep within me I still loved him, I did not know if I trusted him. I had lied to him, but did that excuse his actions? I thought not. I would not take his head, or send him to the Tower. I would not reproach him in public, or take his lands, but I would have my revenge.

I was hurt too, about other comments I had heard from de Quadra's servant. Henry Sidney had told de Quadra that England was in a state of flux in terms of religion, and my 'experiment' in making a settlement which accommodated all was not working. Was this really what people thought? That the middle path I had made, that the moderate way I had approached religion, was not successful? There had been no burnings of the kind seen in my sister's reign, none of the mass destruction of religious idols and churches in my brother's time. I had worked so hard to make my way work for my people. To hear Robin, who should have been one of my greatest supporters, use another to spout vile words about my efforts, and even seek to speak *for* me, was unbearable. I had ever been a touch vain about my intelligence as it was something I prided myself on. Robin clearly believed I was a dullard. He added insult to betrayal.

"Can we use this, Cecil?" I asked eventually.

Cecil inspected a fingernail. "The Hapsburgs have been distant of late, Majesty," he said. "Since the last round of discussions about marriage to the Archduke Charles faltered. Perhaps, if you were willing to play along, then this may bring them back into talks with us? We may be able to gain something from Lord Dudley's plotting."

"I will talk to de Quadra," I agreed. "And pretend I know nothing of Robin's plans with him. I will find out how deep Robin is into this mess. And *you* will find a way to prevent me getting an invitation to the Council of Trent, Cecil. If we receive an invitation, with no way to refuse it without insult, England will be placed in danger. The Pope has been conciliatory towards England and me. I hardly want him to change his attitude and demand restoration of the Catholic faith. He could sanction Catholic nations to invade England, or force hidden Catholics in my realm to choose between their Queen and their faith. I believe secret Catholics can be loyal to me, but not if the Pope issues an ultimatum, or excommunication." I sighed. "Find a way to stop this, Cecil, in secret, and I will deal with de Quadra and Spain."

"And Robin Dudley, my lady?"

I glowered at the wall. "Robert Dudley will learn who is sovereign and who is servant," I said and then grinned at Cecil. "He thinks to play me. I will show him who is master of this game."

The anger within me turned to relish at the thought of the pleasure I would gain when my arrogant favourite found his plans thwarted. There was great spite within my heart towards Robin, I do not deny it. Spite is not a healthy emotion, and yet it can bring such pleasure. The game was begun. Robin had made the first move and it was up to me now to counter him.

De Quadra was brought to me later that day. I had never liked him. Slippery and slimy, oily, duplicitous, and often foolish, he possessed all the traits I disliked in large measures. He liked me about as much as I did him, so our meetings were often interesting. De Quadra had been often in close contact with my cousin, Margaret Lennox, and I knew he considered her, a Catholic, to have a better claim to the throne than me... and now he was including Robin in his plans. Since we had learned of his connections to the Lennoxes, Margaret's house had been infiltrated by Cecil's men. But now it seemed de Quadra had moved on from merely conspiring with my troublesome cousin, and had aspirations to corrupt my favourite as well.

"My master's greetings and love to Your Majesty." De Quadra bowed shortly, so short it was almost an insult. The stinking pole-cat!

"And my love and best wishes to my beloved brother, Phillip of Spain," I replied, dipping my head ever so slightly, to return the slight. De Quadra's face was displeased, which amused me. "I have heard you have requested to see me, Your Eminence. What brings the Hapsburg ambassador to delight dull hours in my Presence Chamber?"

"My master wishes to inform Your Majesty that you have *all* his support for your marriage," de Quadra said. "As I hear the matter is now, at last, under the fullest discussion. Ever be assured, Majesty, whatever choice you make, your loving brother of Spain will stand at your side in support."

"Even if I marry with a Protestant prince, say... of Sweden, Your Eminence?"

De Quadra looked taken aback. "I had understood there was another suitor Your Majesty was considering," he replied, his eyes searching mine. "I *had* believed, Majesty, perhaps in error, that you were thinking of wedding Lord Robin Dudley." De Quadra's eyes snapped to Sidney who stood in the crowds of the Presence Chamber. I saw Sidney nod to the ambassador to encourage him. Malicious anticipation leapt into my heart. I would raise Robin's expectations, and when the time came to trip him, my foot would be in just the right place…

I sighed with dramatic effect. "I would confess to you, as a man of the cloth, Eminence, that I am no angel. It is true that I have affection for Lord Dudley, for his many noble qualities, as well as the years of good service he has shown to me," I said, running a fingernail down my gown, tracing the pattern of fern fronds embroidered in gold. "But I have not made up my mind to marry Lord Robin or anyone else, even though I daily see the necessity of marrying for my country, and my people. I come to believe my people will accept no foreign husband at my side, and will only be satisfied with a man born of English stock." I smiled at de Quadra. "After all, my lord ambassador, who loves England more than the English? Who would relish her stormy skies and enjoy talking about her ever-present rain more than a true Englishman?"

An affectionate chuckle rose from the Presence Chamber. Again, de Quadra's eyes slipped to Sidney. I could read triumph there. De Quadra did not want me to marry Robin for my own happiness, and he was not, either, giving his support because of Robin's promises. De Quadra knew, as I did, that marrying Robin would bring neither riches nor power to England, and may well incur the wrath of my people. The Spanish ambassador liked the idea of de-stabilising England. De Quadra had his own games to play; he thought this was a hand he could not lose.

"What would the Emperor think," I continued, running a ribbon through my fingers as if lost in thought. "If I married with one of my servitors, as the Duchess of Suffolk and the Duchess of Somerset have done in the past? Would my brother of Spain not look down on me, for marrying one of my own men?"

"My master is a loving brother to you, Majesty. He would be happy if *you* were happy." De Quadra smoothed the front of his habitual black tunic, offering up his serpent smile. "But, I believe my master would be only *more* content to hear of the advancement of Lord Dudley, for all know of the deep affection between you. My master remembers him from his time in England and always speaks highly of him, as you do, too, Majesty."

I allowed a soggy smile to briefly flit over my lips, to make de Quadra believe this was what I wanted to hear. "I will think about what you have said, my lord ambassador," I promised. "Please tell your master I am overcome by his support. Please thank my good brother, for the sweet hope he offers me."

I knew de Quadra would go to Robin and tell him what had occurred. Robin would be pleased, thinking I was giving public indication that I might, at last, marry him. But it would not happen. I would not be hoodwinked into a church or shackled to an altar.

The games are begun, Lord Dudley, I thought as I watched de Quadra exit the chambers and a new petitioner was brought forth. *Let us see how well you play, boy, against a partner who has been winning such games her whole life.*

Chapter Seventeen

Whitehall Palace
Spring 1561

As the songbirds returned to warble in the skies, I relented and allowed John Ashley to return to court. Kat had gone to Robin, asking him to intercede for John with me, but really, and with all that had gone on of late, there was no need. Perhaps John had even been *right* to attack Robin for his arrogance, even though he should not have done so before the court. The more this situation went on with de Quadra and the Council of Trent, the more I looked on Robin with an eye of disfavour. Soon enough though, there was something which came to steal my thoughts from Robin.

Death came for a visit.

On the 29th of March, aged but nineteen, little Jane Seymour died. She had grown ill with a cough, which led to her bringing up blood. She weakened by the day and died, falling from life with such ease it was as though she welcomed Death. She had never been a physically strong creature, but her death, at such a young age, was still a shock. As a descendant of Edward III, and blood-kin of my long-dead brother, I had Jane buried in Westminster Abbey. Her coffin was borne on a chariot, in a procession where the whole of my royal choir followed, their voices lifted in mournful song. Katherine Grey was the chief mourner, for I could not attend funerals in case it caused my people to think of my death, and in doing so, commit treason. I was told that Katherine stood sobbing, rendered voiceless, as she watched Jane laid to rest in St Edmund's Chapel, beside Frances Grey, Katherine's mother. Jane's brother, Hertford, ordered a wall monument made for her in alabaster, with gilded letters proclaiming her name and lineage.

I missed Jane. It was not a loss as Parry's death had been, the pain of which I still carried, but it was still a loss. Jane's death compounded my feelings of lowness and depression. In the aftermath of Robin's betrayal, I flickered between wrath and spite, and then melancholy and dejection. Jane had been a bright spark in my chambers, and all my women missed her, none more than her friend Katherine Grey.

*

That spring, catkins danced in the wind. Their yellow pollen flew on the breeze as chestnut buds broke open, releasing sticky brown scales to join the dance of the skies. The fickle beginning of spring washed in with days both bold and cold and surprising days of sunshine and warmth followed in their wake. One never knew what to expect in spring. Skies as clear as pond-ice one day and the next would arrive with winds chasing driving rain across the storm-stirred heavens. Birds began to return from journeys to other lands and the green of England returned from under the dissipating thaw of snow and ice. The fields awoke and were filled with people tending crops. Thrushes began to build nests and jays and magpies watched for tasty eggs to steal. In the woodland the ground grew thick and brilliant green with tangy wood sorrel, as daisies and primroses shone yellow and white against the dark, damp earth. Cowslips and violets sprang up alongside celandine and on the skyline, their silhouettes dancing and boxing, long-legged hares raced, jumping, twisting, and fencing as females held off amorous suitors with claw and paw.

It was not only doe hares who sought to ward off suitors. That spring I sought to separate two would-be lovers. I told Hertford I was to send him to France, firstly to travel with Cecil's son, Thomas, and then to train under Throckmorton and eventually take over from him. I could not stand any more dispatches from Throckmorton on the many *marvellous* qualities of my cousin. And, with Mary set to leave for Scotland, I believed it was time to have a fresh face at the French Court, and one not so associated with my cousin.

The Dowager, Catherine de Medici, who was now using the unusual title of *'Mother of the King'*, obviously disliked my cousin. To have an ambassador, who was stained by his noticeable infatuation for Mary Stewart, was not to England's advantage. Hertford was charming and attractive. I had no doubt he would charm the Italian snake who slithered at the side of Charles IX, but I had other reasons for sending him. Well, one other reason; Katherine Grey.

For too long had those two been making eyes at each other, and there were even rumours about court that Katherine was Hertford's mistress. Although I did not believe the girl would be so dim-witted as to forget her station, honour and standing and become Hertford's jade, I wanted to head off such an event before it occurred. I made the announcement, and it created mixed reactions.

Katherine went about court with red eyes for a week, ready to burst into tears at every word spoken to her. Hertford, however, made preparations for his trip to France in obvious high spirits, elated by the position he had been offered and my trust in his abilities. It was, indeed, an advantageous appointment for a young man. France and the city of Paris in particular were, and are, exciting places for men with a heavy purse, a witty tongue and a handsome face. I had no doubt that, along with his diplomatic endeavours, there would be a great deal young Seymour would find to amuse himself with as he represented his country.

I did feel sorry for Katherine; having so lately lost her friend she was already low, but I could not allow Hertford to stay. There was too much peril in such a plan. I little needed her to make a match with Hertford, a lord with his own royal connections, which would increase Katherine's potential for the throne, and that of any children she might bear in the future.

Think me unkind if you will, or believe I had transformed into my sister, who spent much of her reign trying to control me, but I could not risk Katherine with Hertford. I would let her marry, of course, just not to someone who would make her more of a threat. If Katherine had been a sensible woman, which she was not, she might have chosen to make a match which would allow her to increase her standing, without becoming a constant thorn in my skull.

Another potential heir, Mary Stewart, was having a few problems of her own, quite aside from her recent widowhood. Protestant Scottish lords did not want their Catholic queen back if she was going to cause them problems with religion. Due to past English intervention in Scotland, on behalf of the Protestant rebels, I was seen by some there as the champion of the Protestant faith. It was not a role I had ever looked for, nor wanted. I had never been at ease with inciting rebels against their sovereign. I believed my cousin of Scots *was* the rightful ruler of that kingdom, and understood when one encourages sedition in one area, it spreads only too quickly. I wanted none of that kind of trouble in my own lands. I had sent troops against Marie of Guise, yes, but responding to Protestant lords against their rightful sovereign would be another matter entirely. They had not asked for aid, but Cecil and others were sure it would come with Mary's return. If she was foolish enough to try to alter the religion of her realm there were many on my Council willing to sanction an invasion.

I was further ill at ease because Mary would not ratify the Treaty of Edinburgh. The treaty replaced the 'Auld-Alliance' with France in favour of England. Mary refused to give her consent to the treaty, leaving it hanging like a ragged length of wool caught on a fence in the breeze. She believed that the wording was prejudicial to her future claim on the throne of England and would exclude her from the succession if I died. Mary wanted the treaty to be revised with her claim in mind, but I would not allow it. Since her widowhood had left her in a precarious position, she *had* agreed to stop styling herself the Queen of England, but it was not official, and when promises are not written down, people have a habit of forgetting them.

I could understand her exasperation that others had made decisions for her realm. But the treaty was agreed, and I was not willing to alter its terms, not when they were so beneficial to England. Had I not been generous? I had not taken Mary's country. I had not left a military presence in her realm. However much I disliked my Scottish cousin, she was the rightful Queen of Scotland and I was not about to usurp her throne. God had chosen me to rule England, not Scotland, and I would not go against His plans. Considering all this, I found her hesitation annoying. If Mary had not been present to talk about the treaty at the time it was agreed, that was her fault. Many times *I* had been forced to set aside my own grief and strife and concentrate on what was best for England. Let the Queen of Scotland do the same for her country!

Since her widowhood, and change in station, however, Mary had become more placating. Her letters, which once had been high-handed and arrogant, had become conciliatory. She was aware of the rift she had made by daring to claim my throne, and she was also aware I was a much greater threat to her now, since we were about to become neighbours.

Not so easy to act the part of the defiant heroine now, cousin? I thought when Throckmorton sent glowing reports, protesting that Mary had simply been *unaware* she was insulting me by using England's arms, and now wished to make amends. I was not fooled. Mary was unsure of herself, perhaps for the first time in her life. Raised in France, coddled, spoilt and pampered, she had never had to face the dangers I had both before and after coming to my throne. Now, she was starting to understand what it was to be a single, unwed Queen of a small and potentially hostile country. She was beginning to understand it would be of great benefit to have me as a friend. Mary must have hoped my memory was failing, and I would forget her previous insults. Not a thing likely to happen. I was willing to forgive, if she would sign the treaty, but Mary held out. Saying she needed to take advice on the matter from the nobles of Scotland, Mary sent word to me, in a more humble tone than she had ever used before, asking me to understand her delay, and informing me she only *"wanted to live in peace and harmony with her good sister and tender cousin."*

"Good sister!" I snorted contemptuously as I read her missive. *"Hah*! A different tone, indeed, to previous dispatches! Good sister indeed! Was she not my good *enemy* only a month before the death of her husband? Not so bold now, cousin... without a husband to hide behind?"

"Majesty?" Kat's voice emerged from the next chamber. I had been caught talking to myself.

"It is nothing, Kat," I called. I scowled at my cousin's unruly handwriting. Mary was playing for time. She wanted time to wriggle out of this treaty, time to hoodwink me into an agreement more pleasing to her. Another one trying to dupe me! Was I surrounded by people who thought me a cretin? With that in mind, I turned my attention to two others who thought me dim-witted...

In April, I granted new apartments at Greenwich to de Quadra as a show of friendship between England and the Hapsburgs, and to make him believe I desired Phillip's support to marry Robin. De Quadra was delighted; as well he might be, for those chambers cost enough to fit out in furniture and cloth. At the same time, I expanded Robin's chambers. I wanted to lull him into the belief I was intending to accept him. When I moved against him, it would make his failure more satisfying. Robin was *ever* so pleased. Thinking me entirely unaware of his plotting, Robin went about court like a handsome cockerel, his chest puffed out with pride. But there is that trouble with pride, isn't there? What does it always come before?

Perhaps it is always this complicated, when those who love each other and yet cannot be together enter a stage of limbo, as we had. About each other, we two spiders spun our webs, and all the while, the court and country were gossiping about us, noting my favour increasing towards him, and asking what would happen next.

De Quadra was eager to push for the papal nuncio to come to England. I, obviously, was not. I had asked Cecil to find a way to stop this from happening, and had trusted him to find some method of delay. Cecil's choice of distraction, however, was not to my liking when it unfolded.

Father John Coxe, a Catholic priest and chaplain to Sir Edward Waldegrave, a noble who had been popular at my sister's court, was arrested and interrogated by my port officials. He had been travelling to Flanders, and was detained for carrying a now-banned rosary. The rosary was enough to allow a search of his bags, and he was discovered with money and letters for Catholics living abroad. Even though I had been lenient with those of the Catholic faith, there had been some who had chosen to go abroad to follow their faith publicly. Whilst it irritated me that they could not simply attend the public Protestant ceremony and keep their own faith in their hearts, I had not attempted to stop them, nor captured their estates as my sister would have done. I was attempting to demonstrate that the faith of England was one of moderation and peace. Yet the events of that April were to test my patience and resolve, with *both* sides of the religious divide.

When this priest was seized, it was found that amongst his papers were messages written in cipher, messages that were alarming and dangerous. The cipher, when broken by Cecil's men, talked of ensuring a Catholic succession through sorcery worked by Catholic priests. It also stated Catholics had conjured how long I would live, which, according to them, was not going to be long. This, in itself, was treason. Speculating about the death of the monarch had been outlawed for many generations, for obvious reasons. Coxe confessed he had performed the Catholic Mass for Waldegrave's household many times, which was also against the law, although this discovery worried me less than the other accusations.

I was well aware there were Catholics in England hiding priests in their houses and hearing Mass. It mattered not to me as long as they attended the Protestant service in public and remained loyal to me. My Privy Council wanted to root out all such priests and punish the families hiding them. I did not see the need for this, unless those hiding priests were too open, too obvious, and therefore demonstrated open defiance of my laws. I had never been enamoured with the idea of persecuting Catholics. It too closely echoed my sister's actions for comfort. I believed that to gradually allow Catholicism to die out was the better plan. That way created less martyrs, and less fury in Catholic hearts, and would lead to less resistance in the future.

Waldegrave and his priest, however, had been discovered acting in open defiance of my laws and I had little choice but to order their arrests. Waldegrave's household, including his wife, were brought to London for questioning. Their house was searched. A letter was found in Waldegrave's chests, which held information about the imminent arrival of the papal envoy. It voiced hope that greater freedom for Catholics would come from the visit of Ambassador Martinego, but also held details which suggested it was not based on mere rumour. Cecil was absolutely assured this was all part of a plot to remove me, restore Catholicism, and place Mary of Scots, or Phillip of Spain upon my throne. He also believed de Quadra was involved.

"But why do you suspect de Quadra so?" I asked Cecil. "You must know I cannot move against Phillip's ambassador unless there is overwhelming evidence against him?"

"And such evidence I do not have, Majesty," Cecil admitted, folding his hands behind his back and swaying on his heels. "But it seems strange that the writer of this missive would be *so* well informed about the nuncio and the Council of Trent. Hardly anyone in England should even be aware of it. The information in this letter suggests it came from the court itself. My first guess would be de Quadra. You know he has been in contact with leading Catholics in England, Margaret of Lennox not least amongst them, and I believe he is plotting with them. Your cousin is set to return to Scotland, Majesty, and it is but a slight distance from her borders to those of England. Spain would like to see a Catholic on your throne, and since there have been suggestions that your cousin should marry Don Carlos of Spain, they could take back their power over this country through Mary Stewart and a union with Spain."

I could not deny Cecil had a point, but I wondered if this plot was as well-developed as he seemed to believe it was. It is all too easy to slide from speculation to paranoia. "I will allow that it is indeed strange the author of this letter is so well informed, but there is nothing firm enough for me to act on here, Cecil."

I looked out of the window with a heavy heart. Rain was pelting the glass and the skies were grey. Although nothing had been said in this letter which *directly* spoke of my death, the implication in achieving a Catholic succession was that I would have to be removed... That I would have to die. There were those in England who wanted me dead. I had known this before, of course... but to read it implied here was another matter. My heart tore with loneliness. To feel the hatred of others, at a time when you have lost a person, or two people in my case, that you loved dearly, is most painful. I had lost Parry to Death. I feared I had lost Robin to ambition.

"On the basis of this, I will put it to the Privy Council that we cannot allow the papal nuncio into England," I said.

"Although this is the result I wanted, this is not how I wanted it to come about... Waldegrave! What an ass! Why could the man not take care? I will have to detain him, and that will stir up anti-Catholic feeling, *and* rile ardent Catholics. I wage peace, whilst others stir war!"

"You should be thankful that we caught Coxe when we did, Majesty." Cecil bobbed up and down on his feet. His expression was grave, but I could tell he was pleased with himself. "Worse could have transpired if these letters had been allowed out into the world."

I narrowed my eyes at Cecil. That little jig he was doing made me vastly suspicious. "And was it *just* chance, then Cecil? That this man was arrested *just* now, *just* as I required a way out of allowing Rome's ambassador into England?"

"I did not set him up, Majesty," Cecil replied smoothly. "If that is what you are implying. The papers were found on the priest and that led us to Waldegrave. That is how it happened, but I will not deny the exclusion of the Bishop of Rome and his envoys from this country are in England's interests, as well as yours."

"And I suppose you *just* happened to have men who *just* happened to pick this man to search? Come, Cecil, I have enough men about me who take me for a dolt. You knew this man was a Catholic priest, just as you knew he was carrying something inflammatory before you had him searched."

"We *have* been watching certain households, Majesty," Cecil confessed. "Those who pose a possible danger to you, and to England. But we plant nothing, and we interfere not if they keep the peace and act within the law, as you have commanded, Majesty. If they chose to do neither of these things it is not our fault."

"Guilty until proven innocent…" I said thoughtfully. "It goes against common law, Cecil. It is a treacherous road to take. The most moderate of men can become a danger if he feels himself watched and hunted. Do not force my people into cages forged of their own beliefs, Cecil; you will make them my enemies."

"*Ei incumbit probatio qui dicit, non qui negat,* the burden of proof lies upon him who affirms, not he who denies," Cecil said. "And I *will* have proof against any I move against, I assure you, madam." Cecil spread his hands. "And, as you see here, Majesty, the priest and his master *were* both working against you. They flouted the law, and were speaking of your death, not only in passing, but in planning. And… you *asked* for a way out of meeting with the nuncio, Majesty, and I have given you one."

I lifted my eyebrows. "Be sure to run your plans past me in future, Cecil." I sighed. "Waldegrave must go to the Tower for having the Catholic Mass said at his house, and for his priest and those letters… But I will not order his execution, Cecil. Hopefully, in time, he will learn that I mean to be generous and will leave the Tower wiser than he entered it. Hopefully, also, it will allow secret Catholics in England to see that I mean to deal fairly with them, and will encourage them to keep the peace."

"Although I will not contradict you, Majesty," Cecil said. "But I doubt that will happen. Waldegrave was imprisoned once before, as I am sure you remember, by your brother for refusing to carry out the King's wishes by stopping your sister from hearing the Catholic Mass at her house."

"But he served my sister well and loyal, Cecil."

"Because *she* was a Catholic, my lady," Cecil said gently. "And you are not. He will not serve you. He will only cause more trouble. Such men as he, they serve their faith, not their sovereign."

"I will not take his head, Cecil." I stood and walked to the fireplace, putting my hand on the ornately carved surface, running my fingertips over the pale, cool marble. "He will go to prison, but he will not be treated harshly. I want that rightly understood."

The Privy Council duly refused entry to the papal ambassador, Martinego, and all negotiations for an English presence at the Council of Trent were broken off. This was what I had wanted, but the manner of achieving this aim was not as I would have wished. Although I had not executed Waldegrave, his arrest and confinement in the Tower were much talked about. I did not wish to stir up people within my realm against one another. I had a feeling that this affair would do this. I had to limit the damage.

I released a report of the incident, to tell the facts of the matter, and to show I had generously allowed Waldegrave to live despite his crimes. I hoped this would help my people to understand that if they lived within my laws, and did not try my patience, we could all live together in peace. Waldegrave was taken to the Tower and given rooms there, but the rooms for noble prisoners in the Tower were comfortable. He was given servants to attend him, as befitted his station, and was made aware I did not intend to execute him, so that the shadow of Death did not hang over him. His wife and family were released after questioning, and allowed to visit him under supervision. I had hope that, given time, he would be released and would choose to live more wisely than he had done before. My hopes were in vain, for some months later, Waldegrave died in the Tower. I had his death investigated, and was told he had been unwell for some time, and his passing was natural. Many Catholics did not believe this, of course, which only made my task harder.

Robin was deflated. His plans with de Quadra had gone awry. If he could not ensure this first promise and get England to attend the Council of Trent, what good were his others? Robin was no closer to getting me to the altar, and the Hapsburgs were no doubt displeased that his influence over me was not as strong as he had boasted. I marvelled that Robin did not wonder, as I had, just how *impeccable* the timing of Coxe's arrest had been. Perhaps Robin did suspect that I had something to do with it, for he was aloof with me. Our recent troubles had now led to both of us now being wounded. Our injuries could only be healed by talking, by coming out into the open. Neither of us, however, was ready to reveal our dark and secret doings. I, because I feared driving him away, and he, because if he confessed all he had been up to with de Quadra, I might well lose my ever-changeable temper, and arrest him for treason.

I watched Robin's downcast face with satisfaction... for a while. Then I pitied him. I came to think his present sorrow was enough to satisfy me. Perhaps I did not need to go further.

Mayhap he has learnt his lesson now, I thought, *and will cease to plot when it is clear he has not the skill for it.*

As ever, when it came to Robin, I was blind.

Chapter Eighteen

Whitehall Palace
Spring 1561

Later that season the Earl of Sussex returned from his post in Ireland. No doubt encouraged by my favourite, who was more than willing to bribe men to act for him, Sussex proposed that the Order of the Garter should unite with one voice, and petition me to marry Robin.

Arundel, Norfolk and Lord Montague swiftly stepped in and altered the proposal to say that the Queen *should* marry, but did not state to *whom*. They had no desire for Robin to rise above them. Word got out and people started laying vast wagers that I would marry Robin before the year was out. The rumours were so intense I came to believe my favourite was conspiring again, although in a less dangerous manner, by stoking the flames of gossip. I had small time to worry on this, as I was preparing for the pleasurable task of deflating that pompous old pig's bladder, de Quadra.

I had called de Quadra to me to go over the reasons for the refusal of the papal nuncio, and also to let him know, in an obvious, yet careful way, that he was suspected of having dealings with Waldegrave. If the ambassador of Spain was found to be in league with traitors, we could end up in a serious and embarrassing situation. I was not about to insult Spain and risk war by revealing de Quadra's plotting, but I was not going to let de Quadra get away with all he had been up to, either. Cecil had discovered further links between de Quadra and Catholic zealots in England, and indications which suggested de Quadra had indeed been in contact with Waldegrave. I had no evidence; all I had were shadows and suspicions. But I was sure he was involved, and if de Quadra was involved there was a fine chance Phillip of Spain was, too.

For the sake of peace, I wanted to warn de Quadra off before he did something I would be unable to ignore. After all, the man was about as subtle as a hungry bear in a pigpen. England had not the men or resources to face Spain in all-out conflict. I wanted de Quadra stopped before he did something obvious and stupid, but I was also ready to have a little diversion too. The past months had been hard, painful and distressing. And there was nothing, *nothing* more pleasurable than pulling the carpet from under the feet of the Spanish Ambassador and watching him stumble...

I informed de Quadra of Waldegrave's arrest, noting with satisfaction as a greyish sheen appeared on his cheeks as I spoke. How close had he been to this plot? Too close, I believed. I went on to tell de Quadra that an English presence at the Council of Trent was not to be, and the nuncio would not be allowed into England. "It is *most* unfortunate, my lord ambassador," I said evenly. "But with such events, with men willing to flout my laws, and follow those of Rome instead, I cannot continue with this meeting, nor would England's presence at the Council be advisable at this time. My men are greatly worried for my safety, as many of the intercepted letters spoke of Catholic sorcery and witchcraft used against me. I could not allow an English envoy to attend the Council, if this is the general attitude of Catholics towards their most peaceful Protestant neighbour, and I certainly cannot allow an envoy to come to my court under such circumstances."

I paused and fixed my eyes on him, watching a tiny bead of sweat work its way from his vile, ragged beard to his rubbery neck. "And it would appear that something was leaked from discussions *at court* into the public sphere," I continued. "For some of the imprisoned bishops and papists in London were going about saying I have promised to restore Catholicism in England at the insistence of Lord Robin." I stared into his eyes. "Some say they heard this from your household, my lord ambassador. Whilst I have a mind to believe such a *scandalous* accusation could not possibly be true, I must, in good conscience, put this to you and hear your answer."

De Quadra swallowed. The bead of sweat leapt from his Adam's apple and down onto his dark doublet where it vanished. That is the benefit of black fabric, if one stands in the right light it can hide even the deepest sweat brought on by exercise or ill-ease... A fine colour, therefore, for an ambassador up to no good. But even the darkest of fabrics cannot mask the whiff of fear. I could smell de Quadra. Smell him squirming.

"This is pure malice on the part of Protestants who despise me and any other Catholic, Majesty," de Quadra at last managed to splutter.

"*I* am sure of your innocence, ambassador, of course," I purred. "But we had this tale not from Protestants, but from those who uphold the Catholic faith still in their hearts." He went to answer and I held up a hand, a gesture that always annoyed him. I continued, trying not to chuckle at his fear and frustration. "However, I am sure such rumours are false. I do hope our continued difference in religion will never affect your master's feelings for me, for always have I had peace and love in my heart towards my good brother."

"The Emperor has ever loved his dear sister, and would never think badly of her for being... of a different mind to him." De Quadra had begun to relax, thinking we would exchange polite platitudes and end the conversation here.

It was time to startle him again.

"Is it true, my lord ambassador, that your master promised Lord Robin Dudley his friendship and support if the Catholic faith was restored in England?" I looked at my gown, shaking it of imaginary dirt as though what I had said was of small importance.

De Quadra's eyes flashed wide. His pale cheeks caught fire. Somehow I kept my face straight. "His Majesty has promised nothing to Lord Robert, nor has he asked any conditions from him," De Quadra lied smoothly, although he spoke just a touch too fast to be truly convincing. "But hearing, by my letters, of the goodwill Lord Robert professed to the restoration of religion, His Majesty ordered me to thank Lord Robert and praise his good intention, whilst promoting a continuation of the favour his Majesty has always shown him."

"I do not think Lord Robert has ever promised you that the *Catholic* faith would be restored here in England," I insisted. I wanted to know if those words had passed from Robin's lips. I wanted to know if he had only *insinuated* this, or if he had *actually* said it. To insinuate was one thing. To actually *say* he would restore the Catholic faith was another. I needed to know how far Robin had been willing to go.

"Yes he has," de Quadra protested. "If you would send for him, Majesty, I believe he will confess as much in your presence, as you yourself have promised exactly the same thing."

"Only on certain conditions, and never absolutely," I replied. It was true I had toyed with de Quadra on the issue of the Catholic faith, and had often enough said there was but small difference in the Christian faiths, which I did believe. But I had never said I *would* restore Catholicism. That was in de Quadra's head.

Quadra smiled; a greasy expression crept up his lips like oil rising to the surface of water. "I do not remember conditions, Majesty," he said, "but perhaps my memory is at fault."

Or your ears, I thought with annoyance. *Perhaps you should trim the lank hair which wriggles from them, to better hear me, ambassador?*

"I would urge you, Majesty, not to miss this opportunity, granted by God, to pacify and tranquilise your country for good," de Quadra went on. "The restoration of the Catholic faith would win you many friends in Europe, Majesty, and restore your own people's love to you."

"I have ever been assured of the love of my people, and it will be for me to know my people's hearts, my lord ambassador, and do what is good for them. Such is my God-given right as Queen. This interview is at an end. You can go, Your Eminence, but as you seek to counsel me, I would urge *you* to be more guarded with your words and choice of company, if you wish to remain in this post and at my court, that is."

De Quadra stared at me, aghast. What a pleasure it was to see him so uncomfortable! "Although I am sure that no action you have taken was done with malicious intent, there are others who might use your words against you," I continued. "We are done here, ambassador." I waved at Kat to lead him out. When she returned, I allowed myself to laugh.

"What a pompous old fool that man is, Kat!" I chuckled. "He always enters as though he is the Emperor of the world."

"And leaves like a failed jester, booted from the door!" Kat finished for me.

"More fool him for thinking he could best me in a battle of wits," I said, shaking my head. "More fool *anyone* who thinks thus."

Cecil was delighted at the outcome. De Quadra was admonished, the nuncio was banned, and Robin had failed. Robin went about, unsure how much I had discovered of his scheming, and unsure of himself. This also pleased Cecil. My emotions were more complicated. Although I could find no evidence that Waldegrave and his priest had been set up,

Cecil's willingness to use my Catholic subjects in such a way was troubling. I was also saddened by Robin's betrayal, although I have to admit I had somewhat enjoyed the game against him, particularly since I had won this match.

And still the rumours continued that I would marry Robin, even though the thought of giving myself to a man who was willing to work against me for his own ambition was becoming not only impossible to me, but distasteful as well. It goes to show how people will look on a situation from the outside and believe they know all that is going on underneath. It is like gazing on a river, believing you can see all the life within it from a cursory glance over the ripples on the top of the water. You do not see the milling shoals of fish, the brown billowing weed floating in the water's tide… You do not see the little shrimp that bobs along the sandy bottom, nor the bright kingfisher as he flashes through the water in hunt of prey. People believed they knew all that was between Robin and me, but they did not. They could not see the sorrow he had carved into my soul or the pain and distrust I now carried.

But I loved him. Of course I did. No one can hurt another so keenly unless there is love between them. I decided I had hurt him enough. His plans had failed and he was downcast. I felt the urge no more to move against him. I simply wanted us to be reconciled, but I knew not how to go about this.

We had replaced open love with secret war. And the games were not yet over.

Chapter Nineteen

Whitehall Palace
Spring 1561

I had been rather preoccupied with all that had gone on of late, so when Katherine Grey began behaving oddly again, at first I barely noted it. It was only as she became increasingly clumsy and started to stare off into empty space, when I began to take note.

"What *is* wrong with the girl?" I murmured to Kat after Katherine upset a tray of kissing comfits all over the floor. Although they were retrieved quickly by Katherine and her sister, Mary, the accident left small lumps of sticky sweetness upon my expensive carpet which the maids were now attempting to remove with damp bread. "Is it the death of her friend which causes such clumsiness?"

"She is distracted recently," Kat agreed. "I believe she is pining for Hertford, Your Majesty, and of course she grieves for Jane, as we all do."

"I have many sorrows in my own life, of late, Kat, and I do not spend my time staring off into space and throwing sweets all over the chamber of my mistress!"

"*You* have no mistress, madam," Kat replied with a grin. "I was on the path to delve more deeply into Katherine's doings, and then the troubles with John and Lord Robin arose… I admit I have let my duties to you slip, Majesty."

"It is understandable, Kat," I said, putting my hand to her arm. "With so much on your mind."

"You just said the opposite about Katherine, my lady," Kat pointed out, her wry smile spreading up her face.

"Whatever is troubling the girl it is hardly life and death, is it?" I asked. We allowed the conversation to end, as I was due at a meeting of my Privy Council, but as it would later appear, I was not entirely right in my last criticism of my cousin Katherine.

*

As Easter approached, I undertook a sacred and ancient right of English kings and took part in the Maundy ceremonies. It was traditional for the kings of England to take on the role once assumed by Christ, with his disciples, and wash the feet of common people. It was an imitation of the humility of Christ, which was why I did it. But to Catholics, who had long held the ritual dear, it was also a sign, especially important in light of the late troubles with Waldegrave, that I was not unsympathetic to the practices of the Catholic faith.

On the Thursday before Good Friday, I entered the great hall at Whitehall, where poor women had been gathered for me to wash their feet. I knelt before them, washing their feet in a silver bowl, using silver goblets to pour water over their skin. I drank to each of them in turn, offering them my blessing. Each was given one of my old gowns, and the cup I had used to anoint their feet, as well as a gift of money. In the afternoon, at St James's Palace, I stood before crowds of thousands as my women distributed smaller gifts of money to them in my name. Whether Catholic or Protestant, my people cheered on this act of generosity. It was not, however, so popular at court.

Many in my Council, Cecil in particular, did not like my participation in such rituals, which kept alive the kind of superstitious rites they were trying to move England away from. But to me, it was another way of keeping the peace. Whilst I could not allow all people to do as they willed in England in terms of faith, there was still room for their Queen to demonstrate she was sympathetic to the ancient ways her people adored. There needed to be a continuation of the old, within the new, in order to persuade some into the light of the English Church, and not make my Catholic, or more traditional subjects, desperate, and therefore rebellious. By moving carefully, respecting people's devotion to events such as the Maundy Day ceremony, I was placating those who still harboured the Catholic faith. English Catholics were my subjects as much as the Protestants and I wanted them both to love me. I was accused of hesitancy and indecision for keeping some of the old ways alive, but it was not so. I wanted both sides of the Christian faiths to understand that they could live in peace here in England.

Perhaps the most important part of this moderate, middle way was that despite numerous urgings from my Privy Council, I had not made the nobility of England swear the Oath of Supremacy. Perhaps that sounds insane, for all bishops, priests and public servants had to swear, along with scholars and tutors, if they wanted to keep their posts, but it was a calculated move on my part. If I did not make my nobles swear, then those who were still Catholic in their hearts would not be forced to choose between me and Rome. My belief was that if nobles were not forced to choose, then I could have no rebel lords, with men and money at their disposal, feeling themselves forced to take up arms against me for their faith.

I was a pragmatist. I wanted peace, for peace is more productive than war. Religion had brought much strife, division and bloodshed over the years. I wanted this to end in my reign. I would give the Catholics some of the rites they had loved and honoured, amongst the new light of the Protestant faith.

I was determined to be lenient, and whilst there came a time, later on, when I could not afford such grace, at that time I still had hope that we could live side by side, and worship God together, as a united people.

Chapter Twenty

Greenwich Palace
Summer 1561

That summer, we prepared to go on progress. Despite my troubles of late, or perhaps because of them, I was more eager than usual to leave and tour England. Quite apart from the need to cleanse London's palaces, which after lengthy stays of the court became unpleasant, dirty and defiantly odious, it was a time to see my people and allow myself to be seen. I have learned that people are much more likely to think well of you, when gossip breaks, if they have met you.

Rumours continued that I would marry Robin, and in public we were as we ever had been, but in private, we were distant. There was a voice within me which whispered I had always known that any man I chose to wed would attempt to control my political power, and my personal choices. That was my greatest fear about the state of marriage, and Robin was proving me correct.

Before we left, I made plans and heard petitions of where to visit on progress from various lords and towns. Nils Goransson Gyllenstierna, Lord Chancellor of Sweden and ambassador to King Erik of Sweden arrived at court to try to woo me for his master... again. With relations a trifle chilly between Spain and England, after de Quadra's suspected meddling in Catholic plots, many were eager to put forward Protestant Sweden as a suitor for my hand. The fact that I had already refused Erik countless times did not deter the young man. He believed he and I would make the perfect couple, and would forge a new, Protestant future between us for Europe. I have to admit, his poetic efforts *were* getting better, but there were times I still winced as I read one of his outbursts of love in poor verse.

Nils was a pleasant man. He was cultured and eager to make friends. He had a fine wit, dark hair and warm brown eyes. I had greatly enjoyed the company of Johan, Duke of Finland, when he had visited court too, and began to wonder whether I was drawn to the men of Sweden. They seemed ever-ready with a jape and happy to enjoy all that life offered. Idly remarking this to my women set off a volley of rumour that I was seriously interested in Erik, and even led, a little later that summer, to merchants making wedding souvenirs; sweet little medallions with my face and Erik's on either side, in anticipation of a royal wedding soon to take place.

This was of benefit to me, and I encouraged the rumours, for I heard Erik had lately been glancing in the direction of my widowed cousin, Mary. I had no wish to lose a possible ally to her, although I doubted the match would ever take place. Mary wanted a Catholic husband, but there was always a possibility she might accept, and so I stole back Erik's attention. He responded with enthusiasm. England was the bigger, richer country, and the better prize, no matter if my cousin was younger than me, and apparently breathtaking in her beauty. Marriage is so often not about love, as leverage, when made between royalty.

Just before progress, Robin put on an entertainment for the court; a feast, followed by a moonlit ride on barges along the River Thames. Although disappointed that his scheme with de Quadra had failed, Robin had not given up hope entirely and hoped to prove himself to me and to the court as a good prospect for marriage. After the feast, we made our way down to the waterfront at Greenwich. Soft-shuffling parties giggled in the velvet darkness, jostling together, chattering with excitement. This was an unusual entertainment. Trust Robin to come up with something new for the court! I was feeling warm towards him that night. He had not sought to bring up the subject of marriage once during the feast, or the dance which followed. I was looking forward to a night free of troubles as my party emerged from the palace and started to wander through the shadowy grounds of Greenwich.

The paths were lit with hundreds of glowing torches and shone with the hoary light of the moon. Ponds burned under the refection of the orange blaze of the torches. Flowers, now thick in the borders and gardens, bobbed in the night breeze and fluttered their pretty petals under the sparkling stars. Decorated boats waited to take us out onto the water. There was to be a display of fireworks, and barges carrying choirs would sing as our boats floated on the water.

Stepping onto my barge, I was discomforted to find Bishop de Quadra aboard. It would have been pleasant to have a night free of the man. I wondered if it was an oversight on Robin's part, for he knew I detested de Quadra, but then I wondered if it was not. Even if they did not really like each other as friends, they had become allies. I wondered if Robin had brought him here for some purpose. I sighed inwardly. *Still,* I thought, *if Robin is about to make a new move, then it will be good to know what it is. Does he think to move his Bishop against me? He shall find a Queen poised to counterattack…*

Our boats headed out into the water. Bright coloured sails flapped and billowed in the breeze. I went to one end of the boat and sat on plump velvet cushions, watching the burning torches along the edges of the river illuminating the colours of the sails. Flashes of green, white, blue and red flickered past. The voices of the choirs rose over the noise of the city. As the fireworks began over the dark waters, shots of blue, yellow and green were reflected against the black depths our boats travelled upon. Robin came to sit beside me.

"You are enjoying the entertainment, Majesty?" he asked, handing me some hot wine. I sipped. It was watered and sweetened with honey and spice. Nutmeg and cinnamon quivered on my tongue along with flavours of blackberry and earth. On the barge was a coal brazier, to keep the wine warm. The air had an edge of sharp coldness, so the steaming cup was welcome.

"Indeed, my lord," I agreed, glancing up as an explosion of light darted through the sky. The sound of sweet voices singing floated over the water and I could hear people laughing, joking and talking. Fireworks flashed bright and bold in the sky. Along the river, crowds of Londoners had gathered to watch. Children, sat upon the shoulders of their parents, pointed at the lights with tiny fingers, letting out squeals of surprise, delight and fear at the noise and the sights. It had the potential to be a good night, one of the most memorable entertainments at my court. "There have been other times in my life, Robin, when a ride in a boat was not such a party of pleasures. It is sweet to put aside such memories and replace them with new ones." I smiled gently at my favourite, lifting the cup to my lips once more.

"De Quadra does not appear so happy," Robin observed. He pulled a dour face, so like that of the ambassador, I had to take the goblet away from my mouth as I chortled.

"*Hush*, Robin, he will hear you." I gazed with open affection at Robin. He was so handsome in the dappled light of the boat's torches, with his dark hair set against the night's sky. His eyes were lit with the flashes of brilliance in the skies above, and there was that naughty, mischievous look upon his features which I remembered well of old. When we were apart it was easier to be angry at him. But when he was with me... Ah, then, such resolutions were harder. It was difficult now to believe he could act as he had. It was tempting to gaze into those striking eyes and believe I would be the happiest woman in the world, if I married him.

"Perhaps we can enliven the ambassador, Majesty." Robin sipped thoughtfully from his goblet. "What would cheer his spirits, do you think?"

"My immediate removal from the throne and sudden, gruesome death?" I suggested. Robin guffawed and snorted wine from his nose, making me giggle. Laughing together, like this... it was as though I had my friend back. My spirits lifted and my heart sang. It felt like the old days. De Quadra must have heard us, for he glanced over, and caught us staring at him. His face darkened, and he turned away.

"I don't think it is possible to cheer the ambassador," I whispered naughtily to Robin. "Perhaps this was the thirteenth labour of Hercules, never fulfilled; to discover the secret hiding place of de Quadra's sense of humour."

Robin reached into my sleeve and removed my handkerchief to wipe his face; an almost unconscious gesture of familiarity and one I did not mind at all. I was ready to forgive all, then. "Perhaps," he said, wiping his chin clean of wine. He stood up abruptly, making me start.

"What are you doing?" I pulled at his doublet, trying to get him to sit down.

"I will ask de Quadra to *marry* us, Majesty." Robin's eyes were sparkling with mischief, but there was something else there too. I smiled at his jest, but I was uncomfortable. *Here we are again*, I thought. *Just as I had been lulled into such sweet happiness...* And with that thought all pleasure fell from me in an ungainly thump. Had Robin been *attempting* to lull me into this happy, friendly state? Had he been *playing* the good, merry and trusted friend, in order to spring this on me? Merriment slipped from my soul and my heart felt suddenly heavy and old. Had I ripped my heart from my chest in that moment and thrown it overboard, I believe it would have sunk to the murky bottom of the river.

"Your Eminence!" Robin cried. The noise carried not only over our barge, but to those of others as well. On another boat, I saw Cecil look up from the conversation he was having with Master Francis Walsingham, a new arrival at court. Cecil frowned and muttered something to his companion. They chuckled softly; clearly Cecil believed Robin was drunk. I was not sure how much wine Robin had consumed, but he was swaying a little on his feet. *Was* he intoxicated, and this was why he was acting the fool? Was this also why he could not see the unhappiness in my strained smile?

Robin stood unsteadily, grinning wide at de Quadra. "My lord?" asked the ambassador.

"My Queen was pondering on how to best make you happy, Your Eminence, and I suggested it might please you to officiate at the marriage of her Majesty, for such an honour, no bishop would wish to pass over, is it not so?"

"I am not sure that the good bishop knows enough English to perform such a ceremony, Robin," I said, rising and walking with my fixed smile frozen on my face. I stood a little away from him. The *old* Robin would have understood I wanted this discussion to end. This stranger wearing Robin's face, however, did not.

"Your Majesty, should you ever be desirous of my services, then I would be happy to learn," de Quadra said.

"My thanks, my lord ambassador, but there is no need…" I was replying, even as Robin cut me off.

"Marry us here!" he cried, sweeping out the hand which held his wine, slopping it all over the deck. I believed then he was drunk indeed. "Marry me to the Queen *now*, my lord, and make me the happiest of men and my Queen the happiest of women!"

This Queen was *hardly* the happiest of women. There was something in Robin's eyes I did not like. There was a wildness about him that night, a desperation. I could see how reckless he was becoming.

"Were Your Majesty to rid yourself of your Protestant advisors, and restore the Catholic faith to England, then I would be the happy to perform the ceremony." De Quadra bowed, with a smirk on his lips as he eyed Robin.

"Then I must disappoint you twice, my lord ambassador." I turned to de Quadra with my eerie smile. I had become one of my own portraits. Underneath that petrified smile I felt deeply uncomfortable and alone. The evening, which had started so beautifully, was now utterly soiled. I was repulsed by Robin. I had never felt that way before. "I will never send away men who have a *use* for me and my kingdom, lord ambassador," I said to de Quadra. With a pointed glance at Robin, I made for the end of the barge where Kat and my ladies stood watching the explosions still resounding in the skies.

"I have a headache," I announced. It was true as much as it was an excuse. The ache had grown as I talked to Robin and de Quadra. Robin was, quite literally, making me sick. "I wish to go to my bed."

The other boats carried on along the river, but I ordered mine to return. Without another word to Robin, I left. My ladies were disappointed to leave earlier than expected, even though it was still past one of the morning, but I had to get away from Robin.

This was not the way to win my heart. This was the way to drive me away.

Chapter Twenty-One

Greenwich Palace
Summer 1561

"The Queen of Scots will receive *no* safe passage through my kingdom until she has ratified the Treaty of Edinburgh!" I announced to the shocked faces of my Council. Many of them looked taken aback that I should be so harsh in not offering safe conduct for Mary through England as she returned to Scotland, but in view of the fact that she would not complete our treaty, I could not allow her request.

"Make my royal cousin well aware, when you send word of this, that her refusal to ratify the treaty stands in the way of us ever becoming good friends, and sisters, as she professes she *so* wishes to be in all her letters," I went on, my fingers taking up an unsteady refrain upon the armrest of my chair. "But as soon as she *is* willing to ratify the treaty, and shows goodwill to our nation and to me as her kinswoman, she shall find in me the very best of friends, allies, and sisters."

Pembroke leaned forward, about to argue with me. "I have said all I will say on the matter, my lord," I warned. "And now, to other business." My Council did not look happy. My order was an insult, but in my eyes, Mary had insulted me by her stubborn refusal to complete the treaty.

"There is talk, madam, of a match between my son, Henry, Lord Herbert, and Lady Katherine Grey," said Pembroke, sensibly abandoning the idea of talking with me about Mary. "Before anything is discussed further, I wanted to know your thoughts. Since Lady Grey is a ward of the crown, you are in essence her father, madam, and so it is from you I must gain permission for my son's suit. I have no wish to offend, should the idea not be to your liking."

My fingers drummed haphazardly on the table, making many of my men twitch. "Were they not once married before, my lord?"

Pembroke nodded. "When the lady's sister, Jane Grey, married Guildford Dudley, my son was contracted to Katherine Grey," Pembroke said. "But later, as times and politics changed, the contract was broken off. Since the marriage had not been consummated, both parties being too young, their union was annulled."

I considered the idea. I liked Pembroke. Although he was a bit of a hot-head at times, and kept company with lords opposed to Robin, he was almost family, having once been married to Anne Parr, sister of my beloved stepmother, Katherine. Anne had died some years ago, but the bond remained. Pembroke had been one of my brother's guardians, and Edward had liked him, and although Pembroke had supported Northumberland and Lady Jane Grey against my sister, hence his son's brief marriage to Katherine Grey, I had a lot of affection for the man. Pembroke had proved he was politically canny by changing with the times, annulling the marriage of his son to Katherine Grey, and fighting for my sister Mary against the Wyatt rebellion. You might think this would not endear me to Pembroke, seeing as I had been imprisoned in the Tower for suspected involvement in that same rebellion, and had come close to losing my head, but this was not the case. Pembroke had offered me his loyalty when I came to the throne, and had not yet disappointed me. He had served my brother well, and my sister, and could be a good servant, when pointed in the right direction.

He was a strange member of my Council, for he could not read nor write, and signed his documents with a stamp, but he was not a simpleton. Pembroke had a ready wit, a keen mind, and was a creature of the outdoors. He had a small hound which went with him everywhere at court. Whenever he came to meet me, I allowed him to bring his dog, which often caused great disruption in my chambers. There were a growing number of beasts who lived there, including an ape; all presents from various dignitaries and nobles. The ape took delight in taunting Pembroke's hound. My ape, named Gardiner, had a wicked, often fiendish, idea of enjoyment, which was why I had named him after my greatest enemy in my sister's reign. Gardiner, the man, had delighted in causing misery just as Gardiner the ape did, so I thought it a fitting name. What made these encounters all the more amusing was that Pembroke's hound was always so well-behaved, and never retaliated even when the ape crept upon him and plucked hair from his tail. His only response was to gaze up at his master with mournful eyes, as if to say "can't *you* do something?"

And now Pembroke wanted to marry, or rather re-marry, his son to Katherine. I liked the plan. Firstly, the couple had been married before, and so perhaps they were meant to be joined in the eyes of God. Second, Pembroke was descended from an illegitimate line. His father had been born of a liaison between the first Earl of Pembroke and his mistress. The first Earl had produced no legitimate offspring when he died, and so the title had been granted to his bastard son. The family hailed from Wales, and as far as I was aware, there was no royal blood closely mingled within theirs.

This would be a much preferable match for my cousin. By marrying Pembroke's heir, Herbert, Katherine would take no further royal blood into her line, and yet have a husband whose titles and worthiness would eventually increase her own. The match would allow her to advance, yet not advance too far, and the pair were already acquainted and liked each other, I believed. It was about time the girl was married. Katherine was too pretty and far too silly to leave wandering about court for the likes of de Quadra to get ideas about kidnap and forced marriage. Marriage to Herbert would pacify the danger she presented to me and allow her to concentrate on raising a family, which I knew she wanted. Perhaps, in marrying her off to Pembroke's heir, I could at last look upon Katherine without hearing my own death dirge playing in my mind… Yes, I liked this plan. It made me far less nervous than the idea of her marrying Hertford

"I support the idea." My fingers bounced off the table, then stopped as I rapped my knuckles on the surface, my thoughts reaching a conclusion. "It would allow my cousin to marry into a title and bloodline worthy of her. I give you leave to continue with the suit, Pembroke. You will have to get the goodwill of the lady, but I seem to remember they were fond of each other, in the short time they were married?"

"She knows and likes my son, Majesty," replied Pembroke, looking mightily pleased, and relieved. "She was devastated when their match was annulled. I am sure she will wish to return to the union."

"Even better." I meant it, truly. I did not want the girl to be forced into a marriage she did not want. Since I had been often enough in the same position, I found the notion repulsive. But if Katherine liked Herbert then much good could come of this.

The ones we fall for in the flush of first love are often not as suitable as the ones we love later in life, I thought. Imagine if I had been married off to the first man who made my heart race! What a thought! That now I might be joined to Thomas Seymour, that man who had hunted me in the house of my stepmother when I was but a child? That such a man might now be King? Long years and experience had shown me Thomas Seymour had been immoral to treat me as he had when I was a girl. But I could not deny that amongst the revulsion and horror he had woken in me, there had been fascination too. That had been part of his power. I had never known which man I was to meet; the loving lord I adored in my girlish inexperience, or the fearsome predator who terrified me. Power is never so complete as when it has the ability to confuse. If I had married him, Thomas Seymour would rule England now rather than me. What a horrific notion… to reward an abuser for their abuse.

Katherine was young enough to set aside her first love just as I had done, and, in time, I hoped she would think well of it. I left the Council meeting that day with a skip in my step. One of the potential threats to my throne was about to be dissolved.

*

A few days before we left London, a box of bracelets arrived from France; presents for me and my ladies. They were gifts from Hertford. He had not, however, sent anything special for Katherine. She received a bracelet, just like my other ladies. Her face fell when the parcel was opened and the glittering trinkets were distributed. It seemed Hertford, who could not as yet have heard of the proposed match between Katherine and Herbert, was demonstrating Katherine was a part of his past. Although Katherine was sad for several days, she soon rallied and poured all her energies into the match with Herbert. He had begun to send her tokens and letters, all stating he was desirous of resuming their union. Katherine brightly told my ladies she had always considered their marriage valid and went about showing his letters, poems and costly gifts to any who had the patience to listen.

"With such ease do the young set their first loves aside, and find others to adore, eh?" I murmured to Blanche and Kat as we watched Katherine show off a rather lovely necklace of gold and pearls to Mary Sidney; another gift from Herbert. I was warming to the girl. Katherine had welcomed the match with Herbert so enthusiastically that I had began to think I had misjudged her. *Perhaps I have been too harsh,* I thought, watching her almost skip about my chambers. *I have placed my fears about the succession upon her. In truth, perhaps she is just a girl… in love with the notion of being in love.*

I had regarded Katherine's relationship with Hertford as a threat to my authority and position. I had wondered many times if her choice of Hertford was *intended* to threaten me... if she thought to set herself up as my rival. I had feared Katherine because many saw her as my replacement, but had the girl ever wanted such a role? Possibly not. Seeing her happiness about Herbert erased much of my suspicion. *Perhaps I have transplanted my fears into her,* I thought ruefully. *I have become as suspicious as they say my grandsire was, as my father was in the last years of his life...*

"I think she will be happy with Pembroke's boy," said Kat. "Perhaps it will bring her some steadiness. She will have a family again. Since their mother's death, the two Grey girls have seemed like lost souls to me."

"And perhaps she will cease to be a focus for all who would put her in my place," I muttered dryly.

"Which, I believe, may make her happier still, Majesty," Kat interjected. "I doubt Katherine ever desired to be set up against you. She has not the wit to be the focus of rebellion." Kat ruffled her shoulders and nodded with satisfaction. "With this match, she has a chance to live a simple, normal life. To become a wife and mother, and you know how often she chatters about children. She will make an affectionate and able mother. I can see that in her."

"Pembroke is a good man, and a good *Welsh* man," Blanche said. Good Welshmen were above all others in her estimation. I considered mentioning that I believed Pembroke's blood was English in origin, and then thought better of it; I did not wish to dispel Blanche's dreams. "When Katherine marries his son, and goes to their seat in Wales, she will be surrounded by the unsurpassed beauty of Wales and it will calm her soul."

"I think if she were any more placid in spirit, Blanche, we might not rouse her at all in the morn!" I jested, but I was pleased with myself. My one concern had been that Katherine would refuse Herbert, but since the girl was so happy, there was no obstacle. Deciding I had been too hard on Katherine, I took time to converse with her, and found that if we discussed hunting, clothing or dancing, we had plenty in common. *Perhaps we might even be friends, one day,* I thought, amazing myself with the notion. A bare month ago, it would have seemed impossible.

As we set out for the summer progress, with scores of baggage wagons rolling behind us, I was cheerful. My spirits lifted, giving me new energy. I was determined to leave behind all my troubles and concentrate on the future. I would give Robin another chance to redeem himself. I would spend more time with my Grey cousins. I even sent word that I would allow Mary of Scots safe passage through England, although my missive arrived too late for her to take up the offer. I was feeling generous, happier than I had done for a long time. We left for a summer of enjoyment, and I felt young again, merry.

I did not realise, that as with all things, this was soon to change.

Chapter Twenty-Two

Richmond Palace
February 1603

Happiness makes time move fast, just as sorrow seems to slow it down. I have often found this to be the case. When sorrow comes, time stills and slows, creeping past us, making us feel aged by its sluggish passage. When happiness arrives, time races, speeding along, enlivening our spirits and making us feel young.

It is all an illusion, of course, but we humans, we are creatures of illusion. The notions we hold dear; love, peace, happiness, virtue, justice, mercy... all these are illusions we create and maintain for the betterment of life. All our ills are illusions too; hatred, discord, jealousy, envy, wrath... They are all made by us, brought to life by our minds.

We invent such things because we cannot help it. We are creatures made for story-telling. Stories define our lives, guide our choices, and make our world. We cannot hold love in our hands and show it to another. We cannot cut a slice from justice and demonstrate that it is real. These values and virtues, these sins and evils; we create them all.

We are story-tellers. We are the creators of worlds, of lands, of visions of perfection and imperfection in our souls. And if we know how to control the stories, we can change the world.

I was happy then, captured by a new story. The tale of two cousins who had been parted in affection by the gossip of others, yet who could come to be friends as a new strand of our story was lifted into the loom of life. I wanted to trust Katherine Grey. I wanted there to be a time when I would not hear her step and think on her with dread. I rode out for progress that year and I was happy. Time sped by... My heart felt freer than it had in months.

But all too soon, the thread of another story, an older one, came back. This story had not been resolved, and stories cannot rest, cannot leave if they have not been completed.

We are story-tellers, yes, but sometimes we do not control the stories; they control us.

Chapter Twenty-Three

Pirgo House
Havering
Summer 1561

Katherine Grey was drawing glances.

We had arrived at the house of her uncle, Lord John Grey, and were welcomed with a great feast in his hall, with mummers, tumblers and musicians to amuse us. Grey's lands had been turned into an encampment for my court. An endless sea of tents was spread over his grounds, their sides flapping and snapping in the wind, growing sodden with the light, falling rain of summer. There were bonfires, players to entertain us, and a fine bedchamber, newly decorated for my visit, in which I was to sleep. Grey had gone to much trouble, but even as we made merry in his halls, eyes were drawn not to our host, or to me, but to his niece, Katherine.

The first stages of the engagement between Katherine and Herbert had gone well, but rapidly, the potential groom appeared to be waning in his affections. Many of us were puzzled about this, none more so than Katherine. And there was a curious side-effect to this as well; Katherine was putting on weight. Usually a slight and small creature, Katherine was growing portly. It had caused the women of the court to glance upon her with great suspicion, but I could not believe she would have been so forgetful of her honour as to become a man's mistress. But still, her rounded belly was suspect.

"Is she with child?" I whispered to Kat, watching Katherine go about her duties in an ungainly fashion. "Or is she simply overeating because of her unhappiness about Herbert?"

Kat pursed her lips. "The lump *is* suspicious, Majesty, but remember your sister? Queen Mary grew a lump in the belly that was filled with sickness, rather than a child. Perhaps Katherine is ill. I cannot believe she would have been so foolish over Hertford to have allowed him into her bed."

"You don't think she could be Hertford's mistress, or Herbert's?"

"I would hope not, Majesty. I keep a close eye on the unwed ladies, especially at night. She and her sister share rooms, and I always check they are in them at night."

"I am sure, Kat, that whatever is going on with Katherine, there is no blame attached to you." Kat looked mollified, and I went on, "but there is something going on. Herbert seems to have removed his affections, and with the loss of Hertford too... Perhaps she is low in spirits and this affects her appetite?"

"Troubles always make you cease to eat, Majesty." Kat's voice hummed with disapproval. "But people *are* different, I suppose."

"I will ask my physicians to examine her," I said. "When we return to London. If she is indeed ill then perhaps they can help her, and I would much rather that was the case! If that girl is with child, by Herbert, Hertford, or any other, it brings disgrace upon the royal house!"

We left the company of John Grey and made for Beaulieu Palace. Katherine ceased to wear the necklace Herbert had given her as a token of affection. When I asked her sister about it, Mary Grey's cheeks turned crimson. "Herbert has asked for his tokens back, Majesty," she confessed. "He no longer wishes to marry my sister, although Katherine is at a loss to know why. She is most distressed, Majesty. She eats walnut comfits and sweetmeats all the time, trying to find the sweetness she lacks in life, in such treats."

I nodded. At least this was an explanation, and a reasonable one. Whilst I lost all desire to eat when beset by troubles, I had seen it could have the opposite effect on others. But I was still disturbed. Why would Herbert so suddenly remove his affections? The plan to marry Herbert to Katherine was dissolving, and I could not get a straight answer from anyone as to why. Pembroke was at a loss, and promised to talk to his son. Katherine could offer no explanation, and was close to tears when I confronted her about it. It was puzzling... Most puzzling.

*

The summer turned hot and uncomfortable at Beaulieu. We fled the stuffy air of the palace and sought cool shade under grand oaks and ash trees in the parks. As we rode out before the dawn, the air was cool and still, but there was warmth on the breeze from the rising sun. Mountains of cushions were brought out on carts, along with chairs, stools and rugs. Whilst we rode through the parks, my servants would make a fire to cook our kills, arrange the furniture and cushions, and set up musicians to play for us. When we arrived, hungry, thirsty and happy, there was a chamber constructed for us under the dappled shade of the trees. We ate outdoors, feasting on tender, fresh meat, roasted over open fires, and falling from the bone like melted butter. Bread came slathered with fresh new cheese, topped with shaved, hot, horseradish root gathered from the hedges, teetering on generous amounts of salty, yellow butter. Willow herb fluttered by the edge of pools and marshes where my servants buried jugs of ale to keep them cool for our meals. We would eat, talk and converse, watching the glory of England in summer unfold about us.

The parks were green and lush. Water trickled harmoniously down tiny sparkling steams. Barley and wheat were ripening in the fields. Stoats roamed through their golden and green stalks making sudden rushes through the undergrowth as they hunted mouse and vole. Fresh fruit was plentiful, and ripe, crisp pippins, sweet strawberries and delectable plump cherries were regular attendants at our picnics. Stewed into sauces, or baked in the palace kitchens and presented as pies, they were brought to us outside. The taste of summer fruits upon our pink tongues was fresh, sweet and delicious. Flowers were turning into fluffy seed heads, and winged seeds flew on the breeze. Although Katherine gave me reason to ponder on her with concern, we were a bright party that season.

At least, most of the time…

"Summer is here, Majesty," said Robin one day as we sat under the shade of a giant oak, listening to musicians play. We had eaten well, and now the hot sunshine was affecting our senses. Many of our party had fallen asleep in the shade, propped up on cushions of white, purple and green velvet. Kat was snoring gently, her head on John's lap as he stroked the hair that had tumbled from her riding cap. Even Blanche was nodding. Younger courtiers were playing dice and laughing quietly as Heneage entertained them with japes and riddles. Until Robin spoke, I had been quite content, my mind wandering pleasantly over nothing; free of all worry and thought. But peace, it seemed, was not to be found that day.

I glanced about me and opened my eyes wide. "You are right, my lord," I exclaimed. "*How* observant of you!"

"You did say that when summer was here, there was a matter for us to speak on."

Curse you, Robin! I thought. *Can you go not a day without pestering me?*

"I remember no such matter, my lord," I said evenly, flapping a fan to ward off a flying bug bent on drinking my blood. "Perhaps there is too much chatter in my ears of late. People say the same things over and over, so I no longer hear their words." His expression became unhappy. It pained me to see Robin thus, but what was I to do? Did he really think I would rush to marry him after all he had done?

"Do you love me no more?" Robin's eyes were wounded. He looked like Pembroke's mournful hound when Gardiner plucked hair from his tail. But I would not be moved.

"I love those who *deserve* my love, my lord. Just as I turn my face from those who try to force my hand and rule me." I rose and called to my servants to start packing up. Kat lifted her head from John's lap, rubbing her eyes. Blanche started at my call, and then tried to pretend she had not been asleep, throwing herself into giving such sudden orders to the younger courtiers that they all knew she had been nodding into slumber. For a while, I ignored Robin's eyes burning into my back, but when we were ready to leave, I looked back.

He stood under the oak tree, his face dark in the shadows. His hands were listless at his sides. His shoulders drooped and his face was sad, and angry. As I looked at him, he turned away and made himself busy with the horses. There was a part of me that pitied him, but there was a still stronger element which told me this was all he deserved.

*

We left Beaulieu three days later, heading for Colchester, and the air turned hot and sticky. There was an ominous feel to the skies; they were close and charged. I knew the signs of a summer storm. We had not many miles to travel, and I was glad of it, for I had no wish for my gowns and bed, as well as all my chests of clothes, linen and other, precious sundries, to be ruined by inclement weather. We rode out, past fields where the first hay was being cut. There is nothing like the smell of fresh cut hay… Rich and swollen on the breeze, the sultry scent flooded through my nostrils and filled my chest. I went to grin at Robin and then remembered

I was displeased with him. I stared at the road ahead instead.

We rode past orchards of cherry trees and heard the bright songs of the maids who harvested fruit. Butterflies were abundant in the air, and I saw many brooks and ponds running low of water as the echoes of the streams that had fed them dried to dust under the hot sun. Starlings whistled on rooftops, and house sparrows clustered about flowers where the insects were thick. The crops in the fields were growing golden, and the crackle and creak of their ripening stalks could be heard when one listened closely. As we rode on, the sun grew hotter and the air became closer. Beads of sweat broke out on my forehead, and the horses started to sigh, their eyes glancing about them, for they too knew what the charged air heralded. A storm was coming. The air became humid and static and the countryside fell quiet. The hot air closed in on me. I dabbed at my throat and face with a handkerchief until a breath of cold wind ripped through the close air, bringing relief, but also warning.

We were almost at our next stop when the wind began to pick up pace, keening through ripe crop stalks. People we passed on the road gazed watchfully, warily, at the skies and hurried on their way once their bows and curtseys were made. Farmers started to harry their workers, sensing the storm was upon us. We made it to the house of St Osythe just as the storm broke. It started with large drops of rain falling from the warm sky, and then a rumble of thunder sounded from far over the hills. The rain fell faster and faster, changing from huge, lazy drops to pelting, tiny ones. We rode hard for the gates of St Osythe, screaming with both horror and delight. As we reached the house and dismounted, Robin threw a cloak over my head and bundled me inside. Not the most ceremonious entrance for a queen... We stood in the doorway, laughing at our close escape, as the rest of our party dismounted and ran for cover. Rain poured from the skies, running through the courtyard and paths in swift-moving streams. The glorious smell of baked earth flushed with new moisture rose from the ground.

"Thank you for the cloak, my lord." I handed it back to Robin. "Although you saved me from the rain, I don't believe you aided my appearance." My hair was coming loose from its pins, my riding hood was crooked and my damp dress clung unpleasantly to my skin.

"You only look more beautiful to me, Your Majesty, when you are in slight disarray," Robin replied. "Then, you are more like the girl I remember, than the fearsome and intractable Queen."

"I will always be that girl at heart, Robin." I touched his face with affection, feeling my previous anger dissolve. It was ever so. Was there any man who could make me as warm as he? And yet, was there any man who could make me burn with rage as Robin could? "But I will ever, too, be the Queen, Robin. I cannot be one without the other."

His face grew as sullen as the skies. "I must see to the horses," he said, bowing low and heading for the stables.

"And I must see to my hair," I said to our host, who chuckled.

The whole court was not housed here. St Osythe was a small manor, and many had to seek accommodation in local towns and villages, in rafter, barn and attic. I enjoyed having more intimate company from time to time on progress. It was as close to privacy as I ever got. I danced that night with Robin as thunder roared and lightning crashed. Our joined hands clasped as, about us, the storm raged. He sought no more to talk on the odious subject of marriage, and so I was given a chance to enjoy his company, rather than thinking on him as one of the pesky insects that had bitten my skin that day.

"Lord Robin looks well this evening," Kat noted as I paused from dancing and allowed Robin to partner Bess Parr. Bess looked well and hale; laughing and dancing. She had said little of her canker. I hoped it had left her in peace.

"He always looks well," I breathed, feeling the wine in my blood fire my passion for him. Robin danced like Dionysus.

"And yet does not always act well, towards you, Majesty," Kat reminded me primly.

"Give him a chance, Kat," I urged, wanting to be generous. "A chance to be my friend once more."

"Sometimes I think he has had enough chances, madam," she said, taking her husband's hand to dance. It was not enough to ruin that wild and eerie night, but I admit Kat's words pulled my spirits down. I went to my bed late and lay awake, listening to the crashing of the winds and the pelting rain upon the slate roof tiles.

When I slept, my dreams were filled with water, with the sea. Great waves rose and fell over me as I lay, tempest-tossed, helpless; carried by the power of the oceans to distant shores.

*

By morning, the storm had passed. The skies were bright and the earth damp. There was that fresh, wonderful smell, as the scent of wet earth rides upon waves of sunlight. The world smelt new and good; clean and inviting. We rode on for Ipswich, with much merry jesting and conversation on the way.

Reaching Ipswich, however, I found myself less pleased. This was an area where many ardent Protestants had settled, and it was abundantly clear to me that they had forgotten many of my decrees on religion. I saw priests in churches not wearing surplices, and many were married with children. I had allowed priests to marry, but with reluctance for I believed they served God better without distractions. Even though I had allowed this, however, I did not want women living in churches with their husbands, or co-habiting in colleges. Wives and families of priests were supposed to find lodgings elsewhere, so they did not interfere with their husband's duties. I did not allow nobles to house their wives at court, just for the sake of them being there, so why should I alter this policy with regards to *my* Church? Seeing my disapproval, Cecil pressed a firm hand to my arm, quietly assuring me he would deal with the issues with all speed. Thinking I might banish the wives and families I saw, or revoke the right for my priests to marry entirely, he tried to head off my temper before it broke.

"They could at least *pretend* they are following my restrictions, Cecil!" I cried as I entered my chambers. He scampered behind me trying to keep up. "All I ask of my people is if they have a mind to disobey me in their hearts, that they make *public* demonstration of obedience. The same is true for Protestants as for Catholics."

"I will remind them of their duties, Majesty," poor Cecil agreed. "By the morning, you will find much altered, I assure you."

I breathed in and let it out as I cursed. "By the faith! How much do I ask, *Spirit*? How *little* do I ask? Outward obedience, that is all, to keep the peace! Oh, have done with you." I waved him away, vexed by his anxious face. "Send Kat and Blanche in. I will eat in my chambers. I am in no mood for company"

And it was this night, as I raged in my chambers about the cheek of my clergy, that a visit was paid to one of my ladies.

I did not know of this for some days, but when the news came, another storm broke, and I was no mere observer anymore. I became the lightning and the thunder. I was the fire in the skies. I was the tempest breaking over the head of my cousin, Katherine Grey.

Chapter Twenty-Four

Richmond Palace
February 1603

Let me tell you now of events I did not see, but were later revealed to me. Imagine I have become a speck of coal dust, floating in the hallways of our Ipswich lodgings that summer night in 1561. Imagine I drift from room to room, freed from the prison of my hearth, a light sparkle of white carried on the breeze, sped along by warm draughts. I will show you much. I will be your eyes.

It was late. Members of the court had eaten in the hall, their Queen absent as she raged in her chambers. Courtiers played at cards and dice as night fell, and many made for their rooms early, seeking welcome rest, after weeks of travel along the bumpy roads of England. Down the dark halls, a figure walked. She moved with haste, her hands bunching restlessly into fists, and then splaying out into rigid-fingered spikes. She made for the rooms of Lady St Loe and she was nervous. The bulk she carried on her front was becoming more noticeable every day. The pleated inlays of her gown, which had concealed her secret for months, were becoming increasingly obvious. She had small time left before everyone would know her secret. The secret of the child she carried. But this was not the only secret in the heart of Lady Katherine Grey. She had much hidden that was about to become known. Her breath puffed from her lips, sour with the tang of fear. Katherine had been frightened for a long time. She had hidden it under bright gaiety and had striven not to think on her woes, but there comes a time when even the strongest fantasy cannot conceal reality. Katherine Grey needed help.

Knocking at the door, Katherine waited, her heart pounding loudly in the empty silence of the corridor. When the call came to enter, Katherine rushed in, her spirits almost deserting her. She had chosen to reveal her secrets to Lady St Loe, for Bess had been brought up in the household of Katherine's mother and Katherine hoped she was confiding in a friend. She found Bess sitting alone, reading. Bess got up and made a curtsey. "Lady Grey, what brings you here at this time of night?"

Katherine swallowed hard. She had to say something before she lost her courage. "I am in trouble, Bess," she admitted, her voice scarce louder than a whisper. "And I need help." She gazed up at Bess, meeting brown eyes that had begun to narrow in suspicion. Bess's gaze was drawn to the lump on Katherine's front and Katherine placed her hand there. It was an unconscious, protective gesture which, to a mother of so many, as Bess was, revealed Katherine's secret.

"You are with child," Bess said. Katherine nodded silently, her eyes filling with tears.

"I do not know what to do, Bess."

"Who is the father?" asked Bess, her mind afire with all the trouble this would cause, for although many had suspected, there had also been a rumour that Katherine was ill. Bess had preferred to believe this rather than think the young maid had let her virtue slip.

"My *husband* is the father."

"Your *husband*..." Bess repeated weakly. "Herbert?" she asked with desperate hope. There was slim chance he could be father to a babe clearly so long in the making. There was no answer. Katherine shook her head and bit her lip. Bess stared at her pale face. "Oh, Katherine, what have you done?"

Katherine walked to the fireplace and stood staring into the flames. Then she faced Bess with a defiant expression. "I have done nothing other than lie with my husband, as I promised when we were married."

"When you were married *without* the Queen's permission," Bess interjected. Katherine nodded again. "You are married to Hertford," Bess said. It was not a question but a statement of fact. Katherine nodded again and Bess walked to her, taking hold of her shoulders and shaking the girl. "Do not nod and nod at me as though you are some simpleton, Katherine Grey! Do you have any idea what you have done? You have gone against the express wishes of the Queen! You have married a man you *know* she did not approve for you, and have lain with him and got a child in your belly! Do you have any idea what the Queen will do when she finds out?"

"That is why I have come to *you*!" Katherine clung to Bess's hands, starting to weep. "I could not be without him, Bess! I could not! I love him! And he swore he had never loved another as he loved me. Ned would not be satisfied until I was his wife."

"When?" Bess asked. "When did this happen?"

"Last December, whilst the Queen was on winter progress. It was Jane's idea... She was the one who told me to pretend illness so I could be left behind. Jane brought the priest to us in London and arranged a room for us that afternoon... She was the witness."

Bess released Katherine. "Jane... Seymour?" she asked. "Jane... who is now dead?" She stared at Katherine, a horrible fear slinking in her gut. "Katherine... Tell me there were witnesses besides Jane." Katherine merely stared back with tears dripping from her eyes onto her gown of blue silk. "Tell me that you know the priest's name, and that he was one of the Queen's proper clergy," Bess demanded.

"I think he may have been Catholic," Katherine sobbed. "We never found out his name… But it matters not, does it? We were married, and that must be recognised!"

Bess tried to collect her thoughts. "And what about Herbert?" she asked, searching Katherine's eyes. "Why were you so bent on marrying him, if you were already wed to Hertford?" Bess's eyes were drawn to the lump and she put her hand to her mouth. "Oh, Katherine… you were going to pass Hertford's babe off as Herbert's, weren't you?"

"I thought if we were married quickly enough then I could say the baby was born early." Katherine wrung her hands.

"You would have married bigamously and passed another man's child off as your husband's?" Bess shook her head in amazement. "By God's holy cross, Katherine! Did you not think Herbert would be suspicious on your wedding night, when he lifted your nightgown to take your maidenhead, only to find a life already swelling there? And even if you had managed to trick him, it might do credit to your cleverness, but it adds nothing to your honour!"

"I did not know what else to do!" Katherine wiped her eyes furiously. "Ned was sent to France. I found I was with child. I could not tell the Queen. I thought… If I could just secure another match, then I could…"

"*Lie*, and make your unfortunate, bigamous husband a cuckold?" Bess's tone was scathing. "Do you have no honour, Katherine? No shame? Herbert deserves better than to be played for a fool, or be made a sinner by your tricks!"

"I am hardly the first woman to have done such a thing." Katherine's lips wobbled.

"Just because others do something that does not make it right, Katherine."

"He discovered the rumours about my belly in any case," Katherine said dejectedly. "And suspected the child was Ned's. Now he has abandoned me, I am lost. What shall I do?"

"You must tell the Queen," Bess said shortly, her tone cold. "And fall on her mercy."

"Can *you* not tell the Queen for me?" Katherine pulled a handkerchief from her pocket and blew her nose noisily. Her normally pretty face was ugly with tears. "You are close to her, Bess. She loves you. She does not love me. Most of the time I think she hates me, yet I have never done a thing to deserve it!"

Bess blinked. "You can be so bold as to say that, when you stand here, great with child, having told me you have secretly married Hertford?" Bess asked, her tone incredulous. "That you went behind the Queen's back, that you betrayed her... You do know that if a royal ward marries without permission it can be considered *treason*, do you, Katherine? And you cannot be unaware that the Queen would see this rebellious act as a direct threat to her position... You say the Queen has never loved you, but perhaps you should look to your actions before judging hers! She elevated you to one of the best positions in her household, shows you obvious favour about court and you repay her thus? With treason, lies and betrayal! And not a word to say you regret your actions!" Bess stood back and glowered at Katherine. "I feel as though I do not know you anymore, Katherine."

Katherine stuck her chin in the air. "My sister was Queen of England, and my grandmother the Queen of France. My blood is royal! I have as much right to claim my own life, to make my own choices, as they did."

"Your grandmother was Queen of France for five minutes and your sister was executed as a usurper!" Bess retaliated.

"Your father was a traitorous fool, and your mother married scandalously beneath her after his death. You and your sister were lucky that Queen Mary and then her sister took pity on you! They could have locked you up in the Tower with your sister, Jane, and left you there to rot!"

Bess bit the inside of her cheek so hard she tasted blood. "One day, Katherine, you are going to have to realise that the world you were born into and the world you live in now are two different places. Your family *were* high born, higher than many, but they fell lower than most as well. Look around and you will see others who have families such as yours, with noble loved ones who fell from grace, and yet whose sons and daughters have been welcomed back by the Queen and given a chance to prove their loyalty. That was the chance she was offering you, you... *simpleton!*" Bess threw her hands up. "And you have taken that chance and done just about the worst thing possible with it! You have defied the Queen. You have taken a husband of royal blood. She could take your head for this, or that of your beloved Ned."

"I have done no wrong," Katherine repeated, her lips quivering and her chin trembling. "Ned is my husband, in the eyes of God and according to the law of the land."

"Then go to the Queen and tell her that yourself, Katherine, since you are so bold and courageous, since you are so sure you are right."

Katherine faltered. "I... fear her temper."

"As well you should," Bess replied in a grim voice. "But I am not about to go to the Queen with this and implicate myself along with you. Certainly not when you have the audacity to stand there and proclaim you have done nothing wrong! No..." Bess lifted her hands and walked backwards. "You have done much wrong here, Katherine. I will not be your champion, my lady... You must be your own knight. This mess is your doing, and so must the consequences be. I advise you to do something you have never done before; consider your actions and own up to them. Repent for your sins, not only against poor Herbert, but against the Queen as well. I wash my hands of you."

Katherine stood still as Bess walked to her chair, and then fled from the rooms in tears.

The next day Katherine attended Mass with members of the Privy Council and the court. Afterwards, all were commenting not only on her swollen red eyes, but on her swollen belly as well. That evening, still unwilling to face her cousin alone, Katherine went to Robin Dudley and revealed her secrets to him. Although horrified to be involved in a matter which was going to anger the Queen, Dudley listened as a weeping Katherine spilled her secrets, and wondered if this news might help him… With the woman who most considered to be the rightful heir to the throne pregnant, in such a disastrous and ignoble fashion, the Queen would need another heir. Perhaps this might convince Elizabeth, finally, to marry him in order to get one.

Chapter Twenty-Five

Ipswich
Summer 1561

When Robin came to my quarters with a dour face, asked me to dismiss my ladies, and told me about Katherine, I felt I had stepped into another world. Although I had suspected that the girl was with child, I *had* hoped Katherine would not have been so foolish. But I had no idea that she would have flaunted my will so completely by marrying Hertford. For a moment, I just stared blankly at Robin, seeing his watchful eyes flicker over my face. I hoped he was about to tell me that he had made this up. But he did not.

"She is married to Hertford?" I asked, although I hardly wanted it repeating. "And is carrying his child?" Robin coughed and nodded his head. "And the sole witness to this supposed marriage is Lady Jane Seymour, who is dead?"

"Indeed, Majesty, although I did wonder…"

"Wonder what?"

Robin was nervous. He was trying to work out if he was about to incur the wrath he could see growing within me. "If Cecil had helped the pair, Majesty," he continued, his eyes wary. "For he has often spoken in support of Katherine being your heir and…"

Robin did not get to finish.

"*That girl is not my heir*!" I shrieked. My wrath exploded. My pale cheeks ignited with fire. "And *never* will she be with a bastard in her belly!"

"She claims that she is married, and the child is Hertford's legitimate heir," Robin said carefully, taking an involuntary step backwards.

"She may *claim* all she wishes!" I snarled. "But claims from a liar mean nothing. How do I know she did not play the whore, and the babe sleeping under her treacherous heart is not a bastard?" Robin's eyes could give no further answer and he spread his hands helplessly. "And what about Herbert?" I cried. "He must have discovered she was pregnant! That must be why he called off the engagement! Oh, suddenly all becomes clear!"

I began to pace about the chamber, my anger consuming me. Katherine Grey married to Hertford! And pregnant! She had chosen a mate with royal blood, and the child she carried was a descendant not only of my own grandfather, but of Edward III too. *If* this was true… *Why*, I thought, *she could have lain with anyone! And* Hertford was not here to confirm nor deny her story! *And* what of the reading of the banns, and the priest who had joined them? Her one witness was dead, and the other was an unnamed priest who had vanished into thin air! A Catholic priest! She had defied my laws of religion as well. "I want Hertford recalled from France, *this very day*," I spat. "If he corroborates Katherine's story, they will both be condemned for treason. If he does not support her claim, I will have her under house arrest for the rest of her life for playing the whore about court! How dare she? *How dare she*?"

I frowned at Robin. There was a look on his face as though he were wondering whether to say something or not. His wavering chipped at my shattered nerves. I had just thought this girl was no longer a threat to me, and now this! She had made herself a greater threat than ever, and I did not know if she was clever for doing so, or if she had wandered blithe and heedless into this situation. Either way, I was ready to take her head that day.

"Go and get Cecil," I said to Robin. I could not stand him hovering there like a hesitant mouse. Robin left. It was a wise move. Even my ladies tried to avoid me. Their heads down, their eyes on the floor, they carried out my commands swiftly and silently. By the time Cecil arrived I was almost ready to find an axe and go after Katherine myself.

"You have heard?" I demanded as he entered. His face was troubled and chary. "Did you know anything about this, Cecil?"

"Nothing, Majesty, although I along with others had, of course, noted her growing belly." He ran a hand through his beard. "Perhaps it is a sign from God that the lady is not worthy of the place some thought she should hold."

"Such as *you*, Cecil. *You* thought she should be named my heir! Are you not going to admit that now?"

Cecil was not fool enough to admit any such thing given my current mood. "Should we return the court to London, Majesty?"

"Progress continues," I insisted coldly. "I will not be altered in my purpose by the nefarious actions of this unruly girl. Lady St Loe and Katherine will be taken back to London under armed guard. *Both* will be taken to the Tower and questioned. Hertford will be called home from France, and when he arrives, he can join Katherine in the Tower!"

"Majesty, she is with child…" Cecil objected.

"She will enter good apartments, Cecil." Speaking through gritted teeth, I was finding, was a challenging task. "I am not about to throw her in a dungeon, but neither am I going to leave a traitor loose and roaming my halls. See to it this is done, and if she cannot ride in her condition then send her in a litter. But it *will* be done, Cecil, and done today. For once that girl is going to learn there are consequences to her actions. And by the faith! Katherine Grey is going to face some consequences!"

I glowered at Cecil. My voice became low and threatening. "My father had Lord Thomas Howard condemned as a traitor by Act of Attainder for becoming engaged to Margaret Douglas without permission. Howard died of ague, but my father could have taken his head, and hers."

"Majesty," Cecil said weakly. "Consider that Katherine Grey is your cousin. Remember how your sister regretted executing Lady Jane Grey…"

"I forget nothing, Cecil." I marched to the window. I tried to control myself. "I will make no decision on this until Hertford returns."

There was a clause in the Act of Succession that might have allowed me to indeed condemn Hertford and Katherine as traitors. When my Lennox cousin, Margaret, had dared to attempt a love match with Lord Howard, my father had included a new stipulation into the Act; that if any man took it upon himself to offer marriage, sex, or *did* marry, a sister, niece, child, or aunt of the monarch without the monarch's consent, then they could be judged and executed as a traitor, and the woman in question would incur the same punishment. Unfortunately, the Act did not stipulate cousins… *but*, I thought, *laws can be amended…*

Cecil ordered Bess and a tearful Katherine to be taken by litter to the Tower and placed in the chambers reserved for noble prisoners. Hertford was commanded to return to England.

Everyone but Kat ran from me, trying to escape my anger.

*

We lingered in Ipswich for a few days after Katherine and Bess were taken to the Tower. I hardly came from my rooms and when I did everyone scurried from my path like terrified bank voles seeing the approach of a battle-hardened tom cat. When I had a moment to think, I marvelled how like my father I had become. When he had been angry, thunder clouds and rain squalls had seemed to hover over his palaces. When he was merry, it was as though the first warmth of spring had sprung. I had inherited this talent, if that was what it was. Born from the darkness of my temper, a storm raged over the heads of my courtiers.

Hot, heavy days turned fast to tempest and storm by night. Rain battered down on the fields and the forests and the skies turned black. Progress went on and we continued to travel from house to house. I tried to conceal my rage, but it was clear to all hosts we stayed with that their Queen was in a foul temper. I was not only angry, I was afraid. Whilst Katherine was in disgrace now, she had a babe in her belly who many would view as a likely heir to my throne. If she produced a boy, this would only be intensified. I knew people would overlook the stained character of the mother, if the child turned out to be a son. An English boy with Tudor blood... Such a child could be a focus for rebellion. There were many ambitious souls who might prefer an infant on the throne. If they could be a part of a regency council, or gain the title of Lord Protector, they could rule England through the child. There was no denying it; Katherine had put me in danger.

As I stormed and sulked my way through progress, Mary Stewart arrived in Scotland. I found myself thinking about Mary often as we heard her ships had left France. I could see Mary becoming another standard behind which others of her faith might gather if they became disaffected. In my present mood, as I thought on all the dangers Katherine posed to me, I could not think well on Mary of Scots, either.

All these cousins. My thoughts grumbled, growing paranoid and suspicious. *All these cousins who men would seek to replace me with… They bring nothing but trouble.*

Mary's ship took a surprisingly short space of time to travel from France to Leith; just five days. When her ship was sighted, those who were supposed to greet Mary were taken by surprise. They had not expected her for another week, so unsurprisingly there was no welcome party, and no crowds gathered to cheer her to the shore. They say Leith was swathed in thick mist that day, through which light rain fell. The skies were grey and low as she stepped from the boat. Mary stayed at a local house to wash and rest, no doubt wondering what kind of a country she had returned to.

Her illegitimate brothers, Lord James, and Lord Robert, rushed out to greet her and took their half-sister to Holyrood Palace. I imagine the palace must have been rather bleak and unwelcoming to a woman used to the spectacular grandeur of the French Court. The palace was undergoing work to make it ready for use, which had not been completed upon her arrival. The palace furniture was in storage, and the ships carrying her personal items had not yet arrived. Although it might have felt bleak, alien, in many ways, there were elements at Holyrood to comfort the Queen. The palace had been remodelled by Mary's father, and based on the chateau of Chambord in the Loire Valley, so perhaps there was a ghost of comfort in her stark homecoming. By the evening, however, guns were firing to herald her welcome, and celebrations had begun. Perhaps, by then, Mary was not feeling as lost as she may have when first she stepped onto Scotland's shores.

Mary's household was French, aside from her *Maries*, as they were called. Her *Maries* were four women who had been with her since she was a child, they were around the same age as her, and all called Mary; Mary Seaton, Beaton, Livingstone and Fleming. I often thought *I* had a problem with the amount of Catherines and Besses in my household, but at least I was not attended by four women bearing the same name as me. Mary called her women by their surnames, which is just as well; imagine the general daily confusion caused otherwise…

It was reported to us that Mary got straight to work, named her Privy Council, and gave her bastard brothers prominent places on it. Seven of the twelve men she picked were Protestant, making a majority, and giving lie to the idea that she would only honour and support those of her faith. Lord James, who had acted as regent, was her chief advisor; her Cecil, if you will.

Lord James wrote to Cecil. He knew Mary would never agree to ratify the Treaty of Edinburgh in its present state. James asked for talks to open to amend the treaty, saying it was a mistake on the part of his Queen to have ever styled herself as Queen of England, and was only done because of the wicked influence of her Guise uncles. He opened with a compromise; if Mary Stewart was named heir to the English throne, she would renounce her immediate claim. Although we had already rejected this idea when Mary was in France, we knew her return to Scotland was going to open such matters again. It was agreed that she would send one of her Council, William Maitland, to try to find a "middle way" between us. Since the middle way had always been my preference, I agreed, but I was not about to name Mary my heir. I was hardly in a mood to coddle my cousins.

"If she wants to be my good sister, Cecil, *she* must make the first move," I said. "I am not about to make concessions to this imp who so lately styled herself Queen of England."

"Nor should you, Majesty," Cecil agreed.

"But I will not reject her offers of friendship," I went on. "She is, after all, my only cousin of true *royal* blood."

"But was struck from the succession by your father's will, and by the recognition of her foreign status," Cecil interjected hastily. He did not like the notion that Mary might be recognised as my successor. As she was a Catholic, he suspected her of much.

"Even so, she is a worthier candidate than some whom *others* have supported." I glared at him.

"In terms of blood, Majesty, certainly... but not in terms of sex or religion."

"Do you find me wanting, for my sex, Cecil?" I asked, rounding on him. "Do you find my judgement impaired by the breasts upon my chest, or my mind decreased in intelligence for the lack of a shaft between my legs?"

Cecil coughed. "Of course not, Your Majesty. But not all women are created equal."

"Neither are all men, Cecil. Would you wish instead of me, a fool such as Henry Darnley, my cousin of Lennox's heir, on the throne? *He* is a man, and holds a trace of royal blood in his veins. Would you wish then for him, over me, simply because he is a man and I a woman?" Henry Darnley was a fop and a fool. After his return from France and house arrest, I had had him installed at court so I could keep an eye on him and his mother. Many were the times I regretted having to do so. The boy was arrogant, spoilt, often drunk, and brawled with other young men at court.

"Of course not, Majesty. Henry Darnley is a dalcop."

"Then cease to talk about Mary of Scots' sex as though it has anything to do with the matter," I commanded. I disliked his stance on Katherine Grey, and this made me defiant in promoting my cousin of Scots over Katherine, even though I had no reason to trust Mary. "Let us see what there is inside Mary Stewart's mind, Cecil, rather than concentrating on the contents of her skirts. Now she is separated from the Guise and that Medici snake, there may be more to her than previously thought. We will keep a close eye on my cousin,

Cecil. I will not name an heir, but I will not discount the possibility that she may succeed me. She is the only one of all my cousins who is royal and has been chosen to rule Scotland by God Himself. Let us see how she does."

I gazed from the window. "She has not, in truth, ever had the chance to prove herself as a queen," I said. "In France she was manipulated by her relatives. Now, she stands alone, much as I do, so now, we will see what kind of a ruler she is."

Cecil agreed with me, since he was a pragmatic man and did not want to further rile my fury, but I knew he did not believe Mary of Scots was suitable. I was starting to think differently, however. There was no denying Mary had caused me trouble; she had claimed my throne, she had insulted Robin and used the arms of England where she had no right... I had reasons aplenty to distrust her. But now, she was a Queen in her own right, it occurred to me we had much in common.

My fear and anger about Katherine Grey moved something within me. I began to consider Mary Stewart not as an upstart chit, but as my potential successor. We would have to see what unfolded in Scotland, of course, but perhaps Mary, unlike the polluted Grey line, would prove herself worthy. I ordered an envoy to go to her court and welcome her home, and started to take close interest in all dispatches from Scotland. I wanted an alternative to Katherine Grey. I wanted to know Mary better.

Chapter Twenty-Six

Ipswich
Summer's End 1561

News did not take long to arrive from Scotland, and the first wave was on the issue of religion. Mary had been promised freedom to worship as a Catholic as long as she did not try to impose her faith on her Protestant country, but at Mary's first Mass in Scotland, Protestant protestors tried to break into her chapel and disrupt the Mass. Her brother, Lord James, kept the troublemakers at bay and the next day, Mary issued a proclamation stating that religious changes in Scotland were forbidden. I read this dispatch with cautious satisfaction. It seemed Mary was not about to interfere with her country's faith, as many had feared she might. She had arrived home to an uncertain Scotland; uncertain in its trust in her and how she intended to rule. Mary was setting aside her personal beliefs and acting for her country. It was a pleasant surprise.

Perhaps the most difficult rock in her road ahead was the preacher, John Knox. He was a zealous Calvinist, and had no love for my cousin. After her first private Mass, he preached publicly against idolatry and superstition. All knew he was talking of the Queen and her faith. This may have troubled Mary for Knox was a formidable opponent, and was popular with her people, but Knox, however influential, did not represent *all* people in Scotland. Whilst many of the nobles were Protestant, many other Scots still clung to the Catholic faith. But, even so, Knox was a problem. He was opposed to Mary not only on the basis that she was Catholic, but also because she was a female ruler. To Knox, there was no greater evil. To him, having a woman in power, holding authority over men, over a whole country, was an abomination, an unnatural, abhorrent occurrence. He was also not overly fond of me, at that time, but I, at least, was

Protestant, which made up for some of my *failings* in being born a woman.

When he preached his first sermon before Mary, blasting the evils of Catholicism, she invited him to a meeting. Our envoys reported that Mary asked him why he was apparently inciting her subjects to rebellion by speaking out so passionately against her. "Can we all not live in peace, together?" she asked him. "Can you not be content under my rule?"

"I shall be as well content to live under Your Grace as St Paul was to live under Nero," Knox said, insultingly. Had such been said to me, it would have earned the man a sharp slap about his cheeks. They argued over the Scriptures, and Knox further made the case that if a ruler was unsuitable, tyrannical, or possessed with a fury then his people might rise against him in good conscience. It was a warning. Should Mary try to interfere with religion, Knox would provoke rebellion. I doubt whether my cousin had ever heard such blatant insubordination from a subject, *and* known he was going to get away with it. She could not start her reign by imprisoning the man many saw as the leader of Protestant faith in Scotland. It would have gone against her agreement not to interfere, and incited revolt. Their interview ended when Mary was called to dine. Her last words to Knox were, "I perceive that my subjects shall obey you, and not me, and shall do what they like and not what I command. And so must *I* be subject to *them*, and not they to me."

It was a clever response, for as much as a prince is ruler over his people, so his people rule him as well. Knox left shaking his head. My ambassador reported that when she reached her private quarters, my royal cousin had burst into tears of frustration and anger. I could sympathise with Mary. There had often been times when I had felt the same. I, however, did not allow any but my ladies and intimates to see outbursts of weeping. My cousin needed to understand she was no longer a woman, nor was she a man. She was a prince, no matter her sex, and princes must be seen to be powerful, in control, and collected when before their people. True enough, I had not always controlled my anger, but to erupt with rage is often more respected by men than are outpourings of tears.

Knox wrote to Cecil, a figure of whom he approved, seeing he was a man and of the correct faith. *"Her whole proceedings do declare that the Guise Cardinal's lessons are so deeply imprinted in her heart that the substance and quality are likely to perish together!"* Knox wrote.

"Or, in other words, Cecil, my cousin was Knox's equal in this argument!" I crowed, daring him to contradict me.

"Perhaps so, Majesty," Cecil agreed. "Knox values an argument, and it would seem he has found an ongoing one with his Queen."

Mary could not afford to arrest Knox, although I am sure she would have loved the idea. She had to bide her time, play nicely with the man, and attempt to hide her disdain. But no matter her first troubles, my cousin rallied and took herself on a progress about Scotland It was a wise move, and I applauded it. Apparently taken aback by the obvious poverty of her people, Mary was found often in tears on her first progress. Her habit of showing her emotions so openly both drew people to her, and made them nervous. It was put down to her sex, but I began to wonder if it was a tactic, for it had advantages. It made men protective and engendered the sympathy of women. *Perhaps there is a great deal more to my cousin than meets the eye*, I thought as I read the dispatches detailing her progress.

I was growing more interested in Mary every day. When she was in France I had thought of her as but part of a larger annoyance; as though there was one great tick in France, and she was one of its twitchy black legs. Now, however, I needed to understand her better. We were neighbours and likely to be so for a long time. My father had battled Scotland on numerous occasions, and peace had never been easy between our nations, even though our royal houses carried shared blood. And there were similarities between me and my cousin which I could not deny. Even though she appeared immature in comparison, perhaps because she had not encountered the dangers that I had survived in my youth, there were yet elements binding us. We were both women. We both ruled as single, unwed sovereigns. We shared blood and we both had differences in religion in our kingdoms. Yes... I found myself curious about Mary, and only more so after Katherine Grey's disgrace. I would not name an heir, believing it would cause trouble, but eventually there must be one if I had no children. Mary Stewart, for all that had passed between us, was royal and was the rightful heir to my throne, in my mind at least.

But to openly voice such an opinion would not be popular with many of my people, my Privy Council, or Cecil. Protestants saw her religion as a barrier. They did not see, as I did, that a crown was a right passed on through a royal bloodline by God. It was God who had chosen my grandfather to win at Bosworth. It was God who decided the crown should pass to Edward and then to Mary, no matter their differences in religion, and God had picked me for the role I performed now. The Greys, the Lennoxes, and all other noble contenders for the throne were not royalty, and therefore they were not of God's chosen line. But my cousin was. If I were to die, which someday I must, I wanted my England in safe hands, in royal hands, but I also wanted England to have a wise and just ruler. I did not know yet if this ruler I envisioned was Mary, but I was willing to believe there was a chance she could be.

There was, however, still much about her to make me nervous. The question of her marriage was of pressing concern. Unlike me, Mary had no objection to the wedded state, and there had already been talks of Mary marrying the unhinged Spanish prince, Don Carlos. Many of her own lords were opposed to this on the basis of religion, but I was opposed to it on the grounds it would give Spain a foothold in Scotland, which was far too close to England for comfort. I did not want my cousin to wed a foreign, Catholic power who might threaten England. There were many who might seek to use religion as an excuse to invade England. Fortunately, thus far, the Pope had been more of a mind to attempt to *persuade* me to rejoin the Catholic fold, rather than sanction invasion, but I still had no wish to allow a Catholic power to enter Scotland.

I was determined to have a say in who Mary would marry. She had no wish to irritate me, being now so close to my borders. In fact, since she wished to be named my heir, she had many reasons to be polite and deferential. My cousin of Scots was eager to play nicely with her "good sister" of England, so I believed there was a true chance I could dictate her choice in her husband.

I was to be proved perhaps half-right…

Chapter Twenty-Seven

Hertford Castle
Autumn 1561

As I was still simmering with fury over the illicit marriage of my kinswoman, and thinking on the matter of my newly returned cousin to Scotland, another event came to try my strained emotions. A scandalous text had been printed in France and was circulating not only at the French Court, but in the streets of Paris and beyond. It was not unusual for salacious texts to become popular in France, but this one was different, for me at least.

It was about my mother.

Written by a man named Gabriel de Sacconay, this defamatory book condemned my mother as a heretical whore. It said she had led England's King, my father, astray and *"stolen the light"* of the Catholic faith from the people of England. Denounced as a *"Jezebel"* and compared to the wives of Solomon for heretically persuading my father to turn his back on the 'true' Church, it said *"their foul matrimony"* was a result only of lust. The text ended by rejoicing that, in her fall and bloody death, my mother had met a just reward from God. I can hardly describe how I felt when I heard about this book. Some emotions are hard to put into words for they are myriads and mazes of different thoughts and emotions bound together. Old wounds tore. I became nauseous, and heated as though I had a fever, but more than anything else, I felt sorrow and anger.

Had her fall, her disgrace, the ending of her life in such a brutal public display of ignominy and humiliation not been *enough*? Why must they continue to attack her? Why must they use her as a weapon against me? Slander upon myself

I could handle with practised ease, but to attack my mother, who could not defend herself, was unforgivable.

My poor mother... Would she never be allowed to rest in peace?

As it transpired, Cecil had known of the text for some time before I was informed of its existence by Throckmorton. Cecil had been afraid to tell me about it, not least because I had spent most of the summer enraged at my cousin Katherine. Although I talked little of my mother with any but my closest friends, Cecil was aware I loved her, much like I did all my close kin. Like the box I kept hidden with all the keepsakes I had gathered of them over the years, my love for my family was deeply personal. It was not a simple love. My feelings for them were crowded with many emotions, yet my love was strong. Cecil understood this news would hurt me, and had been waiting for the right time to tell me, so he said when he admitted knowledge of the book. I realised he had been attempting to protect me, but his dithering had allowed hundreds of copies of this work to be published and circulated. I could not allow this to continue.

"You will tell Throckmorton to go *directly* to the Dowager Queen, or the Mother of the King... or whatever that Medici *snake* is calling herself, and demand the books be seized and the printer and author imprisoned!" I shouted at Cecil. I had thought when I heard of Katherine Grey that I could know no greater anger. I was wrong.

Throckmorton duly went to the Dowager, but although Catherine de Medici expressed disgust, she did not order an immediate seizure of the book, nor its author, or printer. In fact, she brought *further* copies into the French Court, and read them with her eleven-year-old son. What a nurturing mother! I had no doubt that the sly Medici had already read the text, and was simply looking for a way to elongate the time it had in circulation to further humiliate me. Catherine de Medici had never liked me.

I grew weak and ill. All that had happened of late was too much. Although sometimes sustained by the power of my anger, I was eating little, and sleeping less. Demons chased me in my dreams and my ghostly mother whispered pleas to me to save her from this shame. I started to dread sleep, for there my fear and guilt found me. At night I lay awake listening to the sounds of the creaking castle. I thought on my troubles with Robin, with Katherine, with France, and I became despondent, listless. Each day, I used more cosmetics to cover the exhaustion plain upon my skin. Each morning, as I sat with my ladies plastering paint and powder on my face, I tried not to think of how similar I looked to my sister Mary when she had been Queen. Was this my fate? To turn into my sister? Perhaps it was just a delusion born of stress and weariness, but at times I thought I saw Mary in my mirror. Her haunted face stared back at me with a kind of knowing sympathy, mingled with spiteful triumph, which seemed to say *"see? Being Queen is not as easy as it looks, is it, little sister?"*

Kat and Blanche united to save me. I ate enough to keep from fainting, but I was not a well woman. I had ceased to dance my six galliards of a morning, something which had never happened before, for I found I had neither energy nor spirit for such exercise. Robin was distant with me and the affair with the book dragged on, compounding my misery. Eventually an order went out for Sacconay to *"alter the offensive passages"* in his text, but I demanded that the books be seized, destroyed, and the author punished. Finally, this happened, but the damage was done. I was furious with Catherine de Medici and with France. When the French ambassador commented that I should send a note of thanks to King Charles and his mother, I walked straight past him without answer or acknowledgement, causing high offence. I cared not. They had been trying to hurt me. If I could retaliate, I would.

One night, when I was sat in my chambers, filled with gnawing loneliness, I asked Kat to call for my jewel-maker. I ordered a new ring. One made of gold and mother of pearl with my initials *ER* on the front. But the ring held a secret, which I asked my jewel-maker and Kat to keep. The ring was crafted so that the front opened to reveal two portraits hidden inside. One was of me, and the other was based on the few likenesses of my mother I had. After her fall my father had purged the palaces of her portraits. The one I used was brought from Hever Castle to be copied. When the ring was finished, I opened the front and gazed upon the beautiful face of my mother. She looked so young, so striking. Her dark hair covered by a French hood and tiny pearls glimmering against her white skin. I remembered the last day I had seen her alive, when she had held me out to my father as though I could protect her from all the horror that was to follow. I remembered her soft hands and the scent of rose perfume which rose from her warm skin. I wept over my new treasure, but the ring brought me courage. My mother would always be here, upon my hand, as I ruled. It made me feel less alone to know I could open the ring and see her face whenever I had need of her... Need of her memory... Need of her strength... Need of her love.

She had been slandered and defamed but she would be with me now every day, in the highest position I could grant her at my court. For if to be at the side or in the company of the Queen is a place of honour, then to be upon her very skin is the highest of all positions. I could not honour my mother publicly for my enemies would use her against me. I had not the power to restore her reputation, nor could I ever make amends for the horrors she had faced, but I would honour her in my heart, in my soul, and carry her memory with me, always.

*

That autumn, Mary's ambassador, William Maitland, arrived. He came with a clear brief from his Queen; to get me to name Mary as my heir, and bring about peace between our nations. With all that had been happening lately I welcomed the idea of peace, although I was not about to agree to the other request.

I was still not hale. I suffered constant headaches and was low and despondent. Much as it had fallen out when Amy Dudley died, my hair resumed its desire to part company with my head. I had taken to wearing false sections of hair, yet another action which reminded me troublingly of my sister. When I watched hair falling from my head with every stroke of Kat's ivory comb, I wanted to cry. My hair had been something I was proud of and loved to display. I knew well enough that I was striking rather than beautiful, but my hair had made me more attractive, and now it was leaving me. I wore wigs to cover my thinning hair, but this was not the only suffering I endured.

My doctors pressed me with bitter herbs to rouse my appetite and potions to make me sleep, but sleep I could not find and I simply did not want to eat. It was not as though I was not hungry. The urge to eat was there in my belly, but its commands did not travel to my mind. There was something within me which called out for control… Control over my own body, if I could not control what was going on about me. It was this impulse which spoke to my stomach, telling it that it needed no sustenance to survive. I found roasted meat repulsive, and vegetables disgusted me. I picked at comfits, quince jelly and bread, but ate only to appease my ladies. I felt I was losing control of everyone and everything in my life. I think I was lost. For the first time in my life, I had lost my sense of myself.

Hertford arrived back in England and I had him taken to the Tower. He supported Katherine's story, which meant that my cousin was not a jade, but both of them *were* traitors for marrying without my knowledge or permission. They were also conflicted and unsure on many questions regarding their marriage. Neither could remember the date on which this happy event had occurred, Hertford could not remember what money he had assigned to Katherine as her dower, and Katherine seemed to frequently be at a loss to remember anything at all. Hertford confessed that they had lain together many times, whereas Katherine maintained they had been together as man and wife only once, on the first day they were married. Katherine said she had received no letters from Hertford, whereas the young man declared he had sent several during his time in France. The inconsistencies went on and on and on, and I became doubtful that either was telling the truth about anything.

I toyed with the idea of condemning them by Act of Attainder, but was unsure of public reaction. I wanted an investigation into the marriage, and I wanted the priest found, for if the priest had indeed performed a Catholic ceremony then Katherine would soon discover she was *not* in fact legally married to Hertford and the child she was close to delivering was a bastard! I had no intention of releasing either one of them, although I had allowed Bess St Loe to leave the Tower after a few days. Although I was convinced Bess was innocent, and had merely had the unfortunate fate of being the first Katherine took her ill news to, I was disappointed Bess had not come to me with this information. I had to trust those about me, my women most of all. I removed Bess from her posts, although I assured her husband that, in time, I would let her return. If I was convinced of Bess's innocence, however, I was not at all convinced of Hertford's or Katherine's. The investigation into their marriage began.

When Ambassador William Maitland arrived, therefore, he found me in a frame of mind that switched easily from paranoid fury to pensive contemplation. But he also found a woman who was willing to open talks with her nearest royal relative. I was in need of friends. Mary had been my enemy in the past, but I was starting to believe, to hope, that she might be a future ally. I also wanted to offer her reassurance that I was not about to recognise Katherine's unborn babe as my heir. Mary Stewart was a far greater threat to England than Katherine Grey was. I scarcely needed my Scots cousin taking offence if another was recognised in her place as the heir to England's crown.

Ambassador Maitland had a long face which made him look rather like a handsome horse. He wore a pointed beard and a long moustache. There was a lazy look to his features, as though he was half-asleep, but he was no dullard. He was Secretary of State in Scotland, a reformist, and seemed to be a man who was ever standing in the middle of all parties, never forming firm alliance with any but his Queen. Loyal to Mary, Maitland was no great friend to Knox and his puritanical followers, but gave the impression that should changing sides suit him, then he might. He was a political pragmatist. It was rumoured that he was in love with one of Mary's *Maries*, the one named Fleming, but her devotion to her mistress was such that she was uninterested in marriage, at least for now. I was envious to learn this, for amongst my ladies only my beloved Blanche was as determined as me to remain unwed. Besides, I had had enough trouble of late with the state of matrimony…

Maitland wasted no time in getting down to the principal reason for his visit. I listened to him politely as he put his case forward, and then responded with disappointment heavy in my tone. "I had looked, my lord, for a message of friendship from the Queen, your sovereign, and an agreement to ratify this treaty left to tarry so long between our peoples," I said with frustration. "And I tell you now; I will not meddle with the succession. When I am dead, they shall succeed that have the most right. That person shall be decided on not only by the men of England, but by God. If the Queen, your sovereign, be that person, then I would be satisfied."

"So you recognise, Majesty, my Queen is the most worthy person to be chosen as heir for the English throne?" Maitland asked in his rather lulling, pleasing Scot's accent, trying to press me into a firm answer.

"Your mistress is a better choice than those of my blood in England," I spat bitterly, meaning the Greys. "*Some* of them have made declaration to the world that they are more worthy of the throne than my cousin, or myself, by demonstrating that they are not barren. However all of those who claim such have been excluded from the succession due to their father's treason and their sister's usurpation of *my* sister's throne." There was muttering from the crowded Presence Chamber as I spoke. Not a great deal had been said publicly about Katherine and what her recent actions had done to her claim.

"I have noted," I continued. "That you have said your Queen is descended of the royal blood of England and I am obliged to love her as being nearest to me in blood than any other… all of which I confess to be true. I here protest to you, in the presence of God, that for my part, I know of no better claimant to be my heir. I myself would prefer her to any other." The muttering grew to rumbling. Shocked faces stared at each other. I had never openly approved of an heir before. This was no formal declaration, but I wanted everyone to understand Katherine Grey was not an option.

Maitland looked pleased and I held up a hand. "But," I continued. "I must avoid a formal declaration, as it could prejudice my security and that of my realm, since *plures adorant solem orientem quam occidentem*, my lord, *more people worship the rising than the setting sun*. If your mistress would take from me as a personal, rather than official declaration, and be satisfied with that, then I would have no objection in saying I believe her worthy to become my successor. The terms of my father's will and the Act of Succession may, however, impede me from making even *private* promise to my fair cousin. A*nd* any claim made by the Queen of Scots would have to be debated in my Parliament."

Maitland appeared bemused, as I had intended. If I could offer hope to my cousin, and keep talks with her ongoing, then I lost nothing, and would not have to commit myself to anything, either. I didn't want Mary getting it into her head that the English throne was hers. There were concessions I wanted from her, and my position would be stronger if she was left unsure, but hopeful.

"It would perhaps be better for your mistress to attempt first to try to win the love of the English by showing herself a generous and friendly neighbour, rather than make immediate demands of me," I said. "If my people come to see her as a gracious mistress, one given to peace and charity, then they may become more open to the idea of her becoming my heir." I smiled at him. "Did not your mistress say that she would be ruled by her people?" Maitland nodded, "and so you see, lord ambassador, the same is true for me."

"But it is also true, Your Majesty, that where a sovereign leads, her people follow," Maitland said. "And if example was set by you, Majesty, then perhaps your people would come to know affection for my mistress and honour her claim."

I gazed at him with steady eyes. "The desire is without example, my lord... to require me, in my own life, to set my winding sheet before my eyes. Think you that I could love my own death shroud? Princes cannot like their own children that are to succeed them. How then, shall I like my cousin, if she is declared my heir apparent? And what danger it may bring... For in assuring her of the succession, we might put our present state in doubt." I breathed in. "I have good experience of being, myself, in the position of the heir in my sister's time. How desirous men were then that I should be in place, and how earnest to set me up as heir! And how eager others were to use me against my sister, and cause trouble between us. It is hard to bind princes by any security when hope is offered of a kingdom. If it ever became certainly known in the world who was to succeed me, I would never again think myself safe, or secure."

I beckoned Kat over and rose to leave. "I am willing to be a friend to your mistress, and will consider all you say, *as and when* the Treaty of Edinburgh is ratified by her," I said. "I will send a letter to my cousin this very night, and I will praise your polite efforts on her behalf, my lord. We will talk again."

As I walked out with Kat beside me, I started to mutter under my breath. "My cousin demands her rights, and yet forgets they are only rights if *I* decide they are!"

"When you have eaten, Majesty, I will offer my opinion," Kat said briskly, reaching out to brush a speck of coal dust from my sleeve.

"You seek to force me to do your will by withholding your counsel, Kat?"

She grinned wolfishly. "I learned the trick from my own Queen, Majesty. If I keep back what others want, they are more likely to do as I please."

Chapter Twenty-Eight

Islington
Autumn 1561

In September, to my utmost irritation, my cousin Katherine Grey gave birth to a healthy baby boy. The girl was apparently doing all she could to vex me! Although it was irrational, and obviously I *knew* Katherine had no control over the sex of her babe, I was flung into fresh wrath and terror. To many, this child was England's long-awaited Protestant male heir. To many, this was the answer for which they had been praying. This boy born of a traitor! For days I went about like a roaming thunder cloud.

The autumn came in flush with golden browns and brilliant reds. The dusk skies were striped cherry pink and brilliant blue. In the woodlands animals gorged themselves on last feasts of fruits and seeds. Spiderlings flew in the air, released from sacks of white silk spun by their mothers, and carried on the breeze to begin new lives. My kitchens stewed quinces, apples, pears and cherries into preserves, making the air sweet with the scent of sugar and spice. In the evenings, the long trailing hoots of owls sounded in the darkness as they floated through the air like ghosts. Rooks cursed at sudden blasts of high winds, and jays shrieked like witches in the trees. Swallows winged above, swooping and diving, heading for warmer climes. England's storehouses bulged with produce and weary farmers nodded by their hearths at night; warm in the knowledge they were prepared for winter. Wasps, angry and dozy, descended on unwary walkers in the palace grounds, and sent people flying away from autumn picnics. Large black and orange bumblebee queens buzzed from the nests of their birth searching for burrows where they could sleep until winter retreated. I only wished that *this* Queen, like the bees, could put her head down and sleep until her troubles had passed.

Katherine named her boy Edward, after his father, and whilst I did not want to offer the pair any reward, I did allow Hertford to see his child once, under supervision, and sent a wet nurse to aid Katherine. By the faith, though! How I would have liked to leave them apart and with no help! But to act spitefully would only set people against me. There was already too much sympathy for Katherine. It was infuriating, but people *warmed* to this story of these traitors; two lovers separated, and with the princess held in a Tower no less... To many, I was the evil Queen of this fairytale. Their separation and imprisonment was lamented. Since they had dared treason for love *that* was different, apparently, than defying me for ambition, for religion, or for wealth... Not so in my mind.

Katherine's son, little Lord Beauchamp, was baptised in the chapel at the Tower two days after his birth, only a few feet away from the graves of his family members executed during my siblings' reigns. There was his grandfather, the Protector Seymour; his great uncle, Thomas Seymour; his infamous aunt, Lady Jane Grey, and yet another grandfather, that great fool Henry Grey. What a collection of traitors to be baptised next to! And what a feat for this new Seymour to be born *already* under arrest... Lord Beauchamp had surpassed his forbears, indeed.

Throckmorton wrote to defend Hertford, saying the young man had proven himself in France as a diplomat, and was a credit to me. At the same time, Hertford's mother, the Duchess of Somerset wrote to distance herself from the *"wildness of my unruly child,"* as she put it, and to apologise in most dramatic terms for Hertford's actions, of which the Duchess protested she had known nothing, writing *"neither for child nor friend would I willingly neglect the duty of a faithful servant to her mistress."*

Cecil was finding it hard, given his previous support for Katherine, to distance himself from her scandal, and Robin kept assuring me that my Secretary must have known something. Arundel exchanged hard words with Robin, about this and other issues, and stormed from court, saying he would not return whilst Robin was there.

Trouble and strife had become my constant companions.

About me there was a conscious effort, particularly on the part of my Protestant advisors, to free Katherine and set her and her son up as my heirs. Disturbed by my refusal to exclude Mary of Scots from the succession, and emboldened by the arrival of a male in a Protestant branch of the Tudor line, they pressed me to forgive Katherine and accept her son. But I would not. I could not even bear the thought. *Reward* the girl for her treason and insolence? The thought was not to be borne.

It was in this irritated frame of mind that I wrote to my cousin in Scotland and demanded she ratify the treaty. I admit, it was not the most polite letter I had ever penned, but I was feeling increasingly alone, frightened and imposed upon by others. If only my cousin would ratify this damned treaty, then something would be going well for me! But when Maitland heard of the letter, he came to me in a hostile frame of mind. "If my Queen is not named heir to your throne, Majesty, then she may consider acting with force where words do not prevail," he said, his droopy eyes bright with defiance.

"Are you threatening me with invasion, my lord ambassador?" I asked, lifting my eyebrows.

"Although your Majesty takes your claim to be lawful," the sneaky Scot went on. "Yet you are not always recognised so in the world."

Usually, such a stark and bold threat would have brought forth a furious response from me, but I was exhausted in mind and body, and growing increasingly afraid of

Katherine's boy. Maitland's words were true enough; there *were* many who did not recognise my claim. I could not afford the threat of war. "I will consider reviewing the terms of the treaty," I replied, miserable to have been brought to such a low state by the Greys and Hertford.

"We should not review or change a single clause!" Cecil exploded later. The treaty had, after all, been his work. "Your Majesty should have stood firm!"

"Lift your voice just one more octave, Cecil, and you will not like the reaction you will get," I warned and then exhaled noisily. "I know, *Spirit*, I know... But what am I to do? Mary demands her rights, as she sees them, and I cannot risk war by refusing. What is to be done when everyone demands that I name this one or that one my heir and I have said I will not name one in my lifetime?"

"*Name* an heir, Majesty," Cecil replied. "And have done with the matter."

"And you would have me name a traitor held in my own prison? Or her bastard babe, perhaps?"

Cecil was silent, but I believed this was what he wanted. Although he disapproved of Katherine and her illicit pregnancy, she had improved in his eyes by bearing a son. No matter Cecil's loyalties to me, he believed much the same as my other men; that the world was meant to be ruled by men. The prospect of a Protestant, male, heir for England was worth putting up with an unsuitable mother, in his mind, and in the thoughts of many others.

That night, I stared listlessly into my mirror as Kat combed my hair. As more hair fell from my head, as I gazed upon my wasted face, and my hoary skin, I felt as though I was staring into a looking glass where my own death was foretold. I shivered and looked away.

Perhaps it was all this talk of the succession, talk which although was ever politic and polite, was talk of my demise. Everyone was thinking about it, and concentrating more on what would happen when I was dead, than on what I might do whilst still alive.

I felt cold, ill, alone and old.

I was only twenty-eight years old, but the strands of my winding cloth were already gathering about me, clinging to my skin, leeching the life from me, whilst I still lived.

Chapter Twenty-Nine

St James's Palace
London
Autumn 1561

In September, the court arrived back in London and made for St James's Palace. When I arrived, with my mind on other matters, it made my heart sing to find ten thousand Londoners had turned out to welcome me home. The streets were full; their heated cobbles beaten upon by the thump of thousands of shoes and boots and slippers. As I rode up on my palfrey, with Robin at my side, I paused for a moment, looking upon the crowds. My heart swelled within me and my spirit soared. As the crowds caught sight of me they exploded into rampant cheering. They surged forwards, and were only held back from crushing me with their love by my guards. Happy faces beamed up at me and shouts of welcome rang through the air. I had not expected this. My people, the good people of England, had heard the sorrowful cries of my heart upon the wind, and had rushed to console me. I stopped my horse often to talk to people, or to take the small gifts they offered. I was overcome.

"Your people adore you, Majesty," Robin said, shaking his head with amazement at the sheer number of people gathered.

"As I love them." How had they known? How had they known how much I needed them?

"I thank you, good people, for coming to welcome me home," I called to them, turning my horse to face the milling masses. "There is no prince, in all the world, as fortunate as I. For I am blessed by you. No other ruler has subjects like the loyal, loving people of England and in return for the sweet blessing of your love I will ever strive to make myself worthy of your affections."

A wild cry rose from the ten thousand people gathered. Flowers were thrown to mark my path to the palace. Wagons trailing behind me were stuffed full of gifts of freshly baked bread, cakes, posies, small lengths of silk, ribbon and wool, and mounds of flowers. I slept better that night than I had done for months, years perhaps. I was rocked into slumber by the warmth of my people and lulled into happiness by the outpouring of their love. I woke refreshed, and began to think that my dark thoughts of death, of being replaced, were groundless. My Council, my advisors might be looking at the future, might be thinking about my death, but my people were not. They, like me, preferred to live in the present. My people reminded me that day I was not alone. As long as I had their love, I had all the company I needed.

*

My happiness managed to last several days before something arrived to cut it short. And when it came, I was flung once more into thoughts of my own death. Never a subject to cheer someone's spirits...

Throckmorton wrote of a plot to assassinate me. An Italian called Jean Baptista Beltran had informed Throckmorton that a Greek named Maniola de Corfeu had been instructed to come to England and poison me. Ambassador de Quadra was implicated. It was suggested, but never confirmed, that the assassin was to gain access to my person through de Quadra. Beltran offered to intercept the would-be assassin in France, come to England with him, and turn him over to my men. If caught within my kingdom, the assassin would be subject to English law, and could therefore be punished accordingly. Although Throckmorton had told Beltran to go ahead with the plan, the assassin, Corfeu, left secretly and was spotted heading for Dieppe to gain passage to England. Cecil sent men to all ports with the description we had of Corfeu, but he was not discovered. Cecil informed me he was going to place more men and women to spy for us in de Quadra's household, as well as increasing my guards.

"Any more men walking at my heel, Cecil, and people will begin to gather thinking I am a parade!" I complained. My freedom was already restricted, and I hated giving away more.

"You need men to protect you, Majesty, you are the Queen of England and we must preserve your life."

"Fine," I agreed with poor grace. "Now what of de Quadra?"

"This is the second time that the ambassador has been implicated in a plot against you, Majesty," Cecil warned. "We have to believe he is indeed an enemy, rather than a potential friend."

"I have never believed him to be a friend, in any case, Cecil. The man despises me and all for which I stand. I am not in the least surprised he might be involved with a plot on my life. God in Heaven knows, I have often believed the ambassador might be pondering with delight upon my demise when he comes to talk with me at court."

"Take no presents of gloves, foods, perfume or anything else which may contain poison, Majesty," Cecil went on as though I had not spoken.

"I know the rules, Cecil, fear not." I tapped on the table in front of him, making him look up. His face was drawn. "Fear *not*, old friend," I said again, gazing into his eyes. "We are used to this, are we not? Who in Europe, aside from the glorious poet, Erik of Sweden, does *not* want to murder me?"

Cecil's lips bunched together. He did not like my japes on such a grave matter, but what was I supposed to do? Hide under my bed every time there was a threat to my life? "Your Majesty should take this seriously," he admonished.

"My Majesty takes it most seriously."

Cecil grimaced. "Lord Dudley has also been informed and is aware of what precautions to take when you are out riding or hunting," he went on. "Although it would be safer for you to remain inside."

"I *must* be allowed to ride and hunt, Cecil," I protested. "Send all the men you want to follow me, but I will not lose all freedom for fear of death. What is the point of living, if all enjoyment of life is stolen from me?"

"Then I will order many guards to ride with you, Majesty," he said, shaking his head at my resolve. Cecil plunged into detailed descriptions of the security measures he was to impose on my household. I ceased to listen after a while, but I allowed him to go on, listing all his plans. It made him feel better. Cecil liked lists. He had stacks of them everywhere. Since he was involved with all matters of my kingdom, I have no doubt he needed them, but I also saw he used them as a crutch in times of trouble.

I tried to make light of it, but I was unnerved. I jumped at shadows and started at odd noises. My bedroom was searched three times daily, and I was constantly surrounded by armed guards. I became paranoid. Combined with my lack of sleep, I started to believe everyone and everything was out to get me. My ladies were my greatest consolation. They tested my food, at great risk to their own lives, ensured I was always surrounded, and they tried to calm me, when I was made restless with fear. I was grateful to them, especially since Robin was no help at all. He was affronted by my dismissal of him during the summer, and hardly seemed to understand why I had become so worried, and so very tired.

I could not afford another enemy. I had to keep Mary as an ally. Maitland returned for another audience to press me again about altering the Treaty of Edinburgh and I decided to try a new tactic to distract him from talk of the succession, or invasion. "I think your mistress and I should meet in person, my lord ambassador," I announced. "Will you put the idea to her?"

"I am sure nothing would give my Queen more pleasure than to meet with her royal sister," Maitland said, his slack eyes opening a touch wider. "But would you go to Scotland, Majesty, or do you invite my Queen to your court?"

"The details can be worked on in due course." I waved my fingers at him. "I would like first to know my cousin's thoughts on such a meeting. If she is willing, it would please me greatly to see her in the flesh and talk of peace between our nations." I paused and smiled at the ambassador. "It is strange for me to think, at times, that we have *not* met, considering our closeness in age, sex and blood. You must tell me more of her. Does she look like my aunt, Margaret Tudor? Or does she favour her mother?"

Maitland launched into a description of his tall, beautiful and learned mistress as I sat back, happy to see his present distraction. Mary was likely to be interested in meeting me, since then she could put her case for the succession to me in person. If she thought such a meeting might happen, she would be less inclined to consider war against England. Offering her this would divert her, and likely for a long time as all the details were worked out.

"Your mistress sounds like a woman after my own heart," I said as he finished, eventually. "We have such similar tastes. Were I a man, I believe she could win my heart and we two could marry, uniting England and Scotland."

Maitland looked frankly astonished at the idea of me marrying his Queen, but took the opportunity to press for his mistress's rights. When he came to the subject of the use of the arms of England, I interrupted him. "I am willing to discuss the right of your Queen to use the arms of England," I said. "But I would ask that she would not think to do so during my own lifetime. After all, she can hold a *right* to something, and yet choose not to use it, can she not?"

"Indeed, Majesty, although if named heir to the throne, she could use them without offence."

"I will not make the Queen of Scotland my heir through act of Parliament, my lord, not at this time. There may be too many who would seek to use this against me and place her in danger as well. Let us end this meeting now, in high spirits. You will write to your mistress suggesting that we meet. This is a noble task, Maitland. Imagine if you could bring us together? It would be a glorious meeting, and one that would be talked of for all time."

Nils Goransson Gyllenstierna, ambassador to King Erik of Sweden, was lingering at the edges of the Presence Chamber, eager to further his King's suit, so I waved Maitland away. "We will talk more, my lord ambassador," I said as he bowed and left. As Nils approached, I smiled with genuine affection. I always enjoyed talking with him. The man was a born flatterer.

"My lord," I said. "How are you?"

"Not as well as you, obviously, my lady," he gushed. "For you shine at the head of your country. The rest of us are but dull marsh lights to your blazing sun."

I breathed out and leaned back in my chair. No matter if I was never going to accept his master as a husband, I did so enjoy these little visits from Nils.

Chapter Thirty

Whitehall Palace
Autumn 1561

On a bright November morning, I went to watch Robin shoot in a match arranged between him and Pembroke. Both were fine shots with the musket and I had been looking forward to attending as wagers had been laid on the contest throughout court and all were talking of it. The tension, however, between Robin and Pembroke, Arundel, and Norfolk was growing. I did not want to be seen supporting Robin over Pembroke, and cause only more division, so I devised a plan. Disguised as a maid, and following Lady Clinton, my *Fair Geraldine*, I slipped out of Whitehall by a back entrance, and joined Lady Clinton's servants. It was enormously liberating. I hardly remembered a time when I entered a room, or in this case, walked out on a green, and did not have everyone staring at me. Disguised and hidden amongst her servants, I was anonymous. It was a heady sensation, and a startling revelation to understand that there could be such freedom in anonymity. I walked behind Lady Clinton with a cowl over my head to disguise my features. It did not, however, take long for Robin to recognise me.

"I see you have a new maid, Lady Clinton," he said, coming to take a drink from the table set up with refreshments. The match was going in his favour. He and Pembroke had been taking turns to shoot at various articles pinned to the targets. Some were stationary, and others, such as a length of ribbon, moved in the wind, challenging their skill. Pembroke was a fine shot, but Robin was both skilled *and* deeply competitive. Coming in second was not in his nature and he looked set to win.

My *Fair Geraldine* dipped her head. "A cousin of my husband's, my lord," she replied. "Visiting from the country.

But she is shy, so I would beg of you not to importune her. Her father is also very strict and would not approve of her dallying with men of the court."

Robin grinned, casting an amused glance in my direction. "I would never importune a lady who was unwilling."

"Thank you, my lord." Geraldine moved in front of me, thinking my identity was still a secret from my favourite. I knew it was not. Just as I could pick Robin from a score of disguised courtiers in a masque, so he could recognise me where others would fail to.

The match went on, and Robin won, of course. Arundel and Norfolk were not best pleased, but Pembroke lost with grace, shaking Robin's hand, even though there was no love lost between them. As we walked back to the palace, Robin hung back, and fell into step with me. "Are you so displeased with the governance of the realm, then, that you have chosen instead to become a housemaid, my lady?" he whispered.

"I understand you not, my lord," I said, drawing the hood closer and feeling a tingle of elation tickle my spine. "Perhaps you have lingered too long in the sun and have started to imagine things?"

"Perhaps I have… for I see the face of the one I love wherever I turn."

"I pity the lady, then, my lord. Do you think her so commonplace that you see her in every face of every woman? A lady likes to feel special, not ordinary."

"My love is no ordinary woman at all." Robin plucked a wild flower from the hedge, and offered it to me. "But perhaps it is because I long so to see her, that I recognise her spirit in others."

I took the flower. The sun shone down on its pink petals, and a lump grew in my throat. I had been so alone of late, without his friendship. It had been long since I had felt this way… special, free, loved… beautiful. There was a pathetic need in my heart then… I yearned to be loved. "If you long to see your lady, as you protest so passionately, then perhaps you should spend more time with her, my lord," I noted, twirling the flower in my fingertips. "And less with the men of court."

The main party had walked ahead of us as we talked. Robin took my arm, and led me into a bower where we were shaded from view. In the darkness of those shadows, my heart skipped as he drew me near. "Elizabeth," he whispered against my cheek. "How I have longed to have you close."

"I am not Elizabeth," I murmured, lifting my arms about his neck. "As you are not Lord Dudley… For a moment, my love, let me believe I am someone else. Let me be free to do as I will."

His pressed his lips to mine with eagerness. Although the feel of his skin on mine, and his body close to me was exciting, I could not help my old fears returning. I longed for intimacy, and yet I feared it. How I wished I could indeed be another woman: a woman who did not fear closeness; a woman who could give herself up to her passions; a woman who could love, and be loved, as she wanted so desperately to be. But there was always fear for me, in the physical expression of love. It had been that way since the days when Thomas Seymour had hunted me.

A footstep on the path made us draw back. Robin's face was flushed in the shadows of the bower. We listened as the steps moved on. He reached out and put a finger on my lips, resting it there as he gazed into my eyes. "You have been so distant of late," he said quietly. "I thought I had lost you."

"You will never lose me, Robin." I kissed the finger on my lips and he removed it. "I am the Queen, am I not? Queens are hard to lose."

"I thought you were not she, this day?"

I smiled sadly. "That which we wish for seldom comes to pass, Robin."

"It could do," he insisted. "If you had the courage to make it so." I groaned, stepped away from him and walked out of the bower. He chased after me and took hold of my arm, twisting me about to face him. "You do nothing but *avoid* the love between us!" His handsome face was drawn with fury. I pulled my arm from his grasp.

"And you do nothing but seek to pressure me into something for which I am not ready!" I shouted back, not caring that others might hear me. "Each day! Every day! Every moment! In every conversation, and with every word, Robin! There is nothing in your mind but marriage. I have had nothing from you for months but complaints, sulking, and pressure. You accuse me of avoiding my love for you? Perhaps I do, for you are *killing* it, my lord! You strangle it inside me! You allow it not air to breathe, nor room to stretch its limbs. Perhaps I avoid thinking on it for I know I will only have to mourn its demise. You are the one at fault here, Robin! *You!*"

Robin stared at me as though he knew not who I was. "*I?*" he muttered. "I... I kill the love between us?" He scowled. "I am not the one trying to avoid marriage at all costs, Elizabeth."

"And I am not the one working against the wishes of my sovereign, and the woman I claim to love by promising my loyalty to other kings!"

The words just came out, and then I could not stop more tumbling from my lips. All my pent up anger of the last months came rushing to the surface of my skin. "*I* am not the one plotting with the Spanish ambassador, am I, Robin? I am not the one in cahoots with Sidney to make promise that the Catholic faith will be restored to England, am I, Robin? I am not the one taking on the mantle of my Dudley forebears by betraying my Queen and becoming a traitor to her!"

Robin's face was pale with amazement. He blinked and his face turned grey. I curled my lip. How could I have kissed him a moment ago? How could I have forgotten myself... forgotten his deeds? "Oh yes, Robin, I know *all* you have been up to these past months... Do you know that I could have had your head? Do you understand how far you have gone? You accuse *me* of killing the love between us, but *you* are the one who has betrayed me. You have risked all that we had together! And for what? To become King... Do not think I do not know that ambition is stronger within you than your love for me! It is all too clear, my lord!"

"Elizabeth..." He went to move towards me, and that old desperate expression I hated so was back on his face. I stepped away from him.

"You accuse me of much, my lord," I said coldly. "Yet I know you to be guilty of far more evil than I have done. And yet I have not put you in irons, locked you in the Tower, nor taken your head and lands, as my father would have done. I have kept you alive, Robin, and unharmed. I have not punished you, nor revealed your treachery. I have known all you have done and even promoted you further! I did so because I still love you, despite all you have done. Think on *that*, my lord, when you sit alone at night listing my failings and my flaws. Think on the fact that you are only alive because of the love I bear for you. Think on the fact that my love has never been so tested, that I have never been so angered at a person and yet allowed them to keep their liberty and my friendship. Think on all those things, Robin, and consider how fortunate you are to have such a queen!"

I turned from him and almost ran away. Joining the party of Lady Clinton I found none had noted my absence. To them, after all, I was just a maid, and of little consequence. Robin did not join us. He left for his quarters and I did not see him for days. When he returned, nothing was said about our argument. Once more, we hid in silence.

I gave Robin a pension of one thousand pounds a year, as well as more offices which gave him political sway. I was in need of friends, in such dangerous times as these, but in many ways, these gifts were offerings to my guilt. I knew I was at least partly to blame for his actions for I had offered him false hope. He was but acting on that. Robin was pleased with this sign of favour, and became a great deal more attentive and conciliatory than he had been. I hoped that my words had sunk in, and he understood what pain he had caused me. But I also believed this would not last.

There was a creature lurking between us now, and that creature was Robin's ambition.

Chapter Thirty-One

Westminster Palace
Winter 1561

On the 26th of December that year, I finally elevated a Dudley to the House of Lords. It was not Robin, however, who received the honour, but his brother, Ambrose. I liked Ambrose… not as much as I liked Robin, of course, but Ambrose was the elder, and, in fairness, he should have the title of Earl before his brother. I restored the Castle of Warwick to the family, along with lands and other estates, and there was a celebration at court. What came as a surprise to many was how happy Robin was at his brother's elevation.

"It demonstrates the rise of my house, Majesty," he said as we walked in the privy gardens. "And the trust you have in us. Ambrose is delighted. You could not have a more loyal servant in the House of Lords."

"I am pleased you have taken the news so well, Robin," I admitted. "I had thought you might be affronted, and your pride would be bruised."

Robin smiled. "I am not as proud, Majesty, as many believe me to be. And not so foolish that I cannot see what a good event this is for my house."

I put my hand onto his arm, and gazed at him with gentle eyes. I enjoyed it when Robin surprised me, and nothing surprised me more than him being happy to see another elevated rather than him. *Perhaps he has begun to understand*, I thought. *And will now put his days of pride and brashness behind him. Perhaps my words have shown him the error of his ways.*

Later that month, Robin was admitted to membership of the Inner Temple of the Inns of Court. The Inns of Court governed barristers in England and Wales. It was also where most London barristers trained and studied. The benchers, or Masters of the Bench, wanted to honour Robin as he had supported them in a land dispute, and so they held a celebration for their new member, with a feast and plays. We heard of these entertainments at court, and heard that all the plays' themes revolved about marriage, and especially about the duty of a sovereign to marry. Clearly put on to please Robin, they made me wonder if he had not learnt so much after all.

Robin was not the only one enjoying plays that season. Reports came from Randolph, my ambassador in Scotland, that Mary was turning her court into a showcase of talent. My cousin wrote verse and encouraged poets to join her court. She invited philosophers and musicians, and was rumoured to be particularly fond of one new arrival; an Italian named Master David Riccio, or Rizzio, who had become one of her personal musicians. Mary was fond of disguisings and masques, as with her height she could easily pass for a man and fool her court. It was also rumoured she took to disguising herself as a servant and wandering the streets of Edinburgh with her *Maries*. Having recently understood the freedom such a disguise could offer, I understood why she enjoyed this diversion.

Mary put her court in Scotland into mourning that December to mark the anniversary of her husband François's death. Did her thoughts hark back to the time she had been Queen of France *and* Scotland, when the world had been ready to fall at her feet? Had she ever loved that weak and feeble boy whom she had been wed to? What did she think of her fate now? Whatever her thoughts about François, Mary was determined to make the best of what she had been offered now, and that I could applaud.

*

Just before Christmas, my cousin Margaret Douglas, Countess of Lennox offered me an early New Year's present by falling under Cecil's suspicion after sending letters to powerful Catholic houses in Spain and France. The unlucky Countess, who had only recently been released from house arrest, was discovered passing letters to various enemies of England. In actual fact, the letters were rather dull. Written with her heavy Scot's accents braying through the pages, they all noted her link to the royal line, through her mother, Margaret Tudor, and protested she had a valuable, *legitimate* place in the succession. The term legitimate was used *many* times. Whilst they made dreary reading, these letters clearly questioned my right to the throne by insinuating that Margaret was legitimate, where I was not. It was ironic, in some ways, since Margaret's parents had petitioned the Pope to annul their marriage when she was a child, and her status was often called into question because of it. The Pope had proclaimed Margaret legitimate, despite the dissolution of her parent's marriage, but there were many in England and in Scotland, where she had grown up, who saw her as a bastard.

Perhaps it was this shadow, one that had followed her all her life, which made her so aggressive towards me and my status, for I had been declared a bastard too. In me, perhaps, she heard an echo of her own fears. In asserting her legitimacy over and over, she sought to impress on others the difference between us.

In these letters, she sung sweet praises of her boys, particularly the eldest, Henry Darnley, and described herself as *"the second person"* in the realm of England, with a right to be my heir, overlooking the claims of Mary of Scots, or the Greys. I could almost see her heavily-lidded eyes narrowing on the throne she believed should already be hers…

"That woman will never learn," I said to Cecil as we talked about the discovery of Margaret's treachery. "Not even if I take her head, she will never learn. Do you remember when

I was in my sister's custody and Margaret set up a kitchen under my rooms, so she could plague me with banging, crashing, and ill smells of fish frying at all hours of the day and night? I have never lived near a kitchen since, after that experience. She is a petty soul, that one."

"She has, perhaps, moved on in her ambition, Majesty, from merely attempting to annoy you to acting with treasonous intent." Cecil's voice was dry, but serious. "She is a dangerous Catholic intriguer, and must be arrested."

I glanced up at Cecil, my smile wide and wicked. "Nothing would give me greater pleasure, *Spirit*," I announced with glee. "Take her, her husband, both her sons, all her daughters and her servants, will you? It will be delightful to hear her screams of angst mingle with carols throughout the season of Christmas."

My cousin of Lennox should have been used to being on the wrong side of her monarch by now. She had been imprisoned by my father and had come close to losing her head for daring to enter into a privy contract of marriage with Lord Thomas Howard, and had been almost placed under house arrest a few years later when my father uncovered her love affair with another Howard, Lord Charles. It was only because my father had been fond of his niece, *Margett*, as he had called her, that she escaped with her life. My brother had been none too fond of her, since she was a Catholic, but Margaret had been sensible enough to hide her beliefs better than my sister had during Edward's reign. She had lived a life of favour under my sister, and I had been lenient with her, despite knowing that she despised me. But there comes a time when one cannot be lenient any longer, and that time was now. Lennox was held in London, but Margaret tarried in their country estates, claiming illness. Since I had once used such a ruse myself, I knew this was a feint, but I decided to wait for the Countess. Cecil had her house under surveillance in any case.

At times, it seemed those most likely to do me harm were those of my own blood. As I thought on that, I thought of what I had said to Maitland.

Was it not proved true, then, as I had said, that a prince may never look on his heirs with peace in his heart? My sister had not looked happily upon me, and my brother not on her. And I, with cousins aplenty waiting to do me harm, or cause trouble in my realm, perhaps I had it worst of all... Or perhaps not. Having so many possible heirs, even if they were troublesome, meant that armies of disaffected men were not lining up behind one particular candidate.

To name an heir would unite my enemies. I was not one to willingly hand arrows to those poised to shoot me.

*

As snow floated over the gardens of Westminster Palace and settled on rooftops about London, Robin called for his men to put on a play for the court's amusement. We gathered in the great hall, gowns and tunics of red, blue, pink and gold glittering under the orange blaze of the torches. Ladies giggled soft in the darkness as men whispered in their ears, spilling secrets. I settled on my dais with a cushion to support my aching back.... the latest part of my body which had decided to pain me... Holding a cup of small ale in my hands, and tapping my feet, I watched as the players arrived to tell their tale.

The play chosen was *The Tragedy of Gorboduc,* and had been already shown at the Inner Temple. It was about Gorboduc, an ancient King of Britain, whose country descended into chaos when he divided his country amongst his heirs, unable to choose only one to succeed him. His heirs fought each other, leading to civil war and the death of Gorboduc and his Queen. Afterwards, for want of a sole heir, the country fell into disorder and anarchy. The play ended as a foreign prince invaded the fragile state, taking the throne by force. It was a morality play and was, I realised, aimed directly at me, both for not naming an heir, nor providing one from my reluctant womb. It was also the most tedious performance I had ever sat through, which did nothing to improve my mood. The play unfolded, and I heard nothing but the complaints of Robin who wanted to marry me, and the worries of Cecil, who wanted me to get breeding, emerge through the lips of the players. As I sat through this barely concealed, ill-executed farce of a reprimand, anger rose, bitter in my belly.

As I listened to Eubulus, the King's secretary, bemoan the fate of his country, mourning that Parliament should have been called upon to decide on the succession since the King had failed to, I started to tap my fingers on my armrest with irritation. When he continued to ramble on, informing the audience that justice would prevail, no matter the *poor* actions of the King, I grew ever more aggravated. The political uncertainty of my refusal to name an heir was the whole point here. I was apparently condemning my people to the misery of certain war; to the chaos of a realm left without a proper ruler. I was being irresponsible, careless, reckless. Robin was not always a subtle man. This was the least subtle gesture he had made thus far.

He had not listened to me. He had learned nothing. Did he think this was a cunning way to shove me into marriage? What a fool my favourite was.

As the play ended by saying that an English successor should be chosen by the people if there was no named heir, I almost got up and left. They were talking of Katherine Grey and her son, of course. No one wanted the spoilt son of the Lennoxes on the throne, and there were few who would support Mary of Scots, but apparently the child of this insolent, traitorous girl was suitable!

"A dull play for a dull day, my lord," I noted sharply to Robin as he pranced over, his eyes bright with expectation. I was delighted to see the happiness tumble from his face.

"I thought Your Majesty would enjoy this myth of history, being ever an avid reader of historical works," he replied, his eyes suddenly less sure.

"You thought wrong, Robin," I said. "I found the subject matter tiresome, the sentiments ridiculous and the performance dreary. *Do* see that you come up with something entertaining next time, won't you? Or I shall be forced to employ a new Master of Revels. It would seem your imagination has run as dry as a pond in the desert. There are many others, eager for such a prestigious role, waiting for a chance. After today, I have a mind to give it to them."

I walked away from him, stopping to talk with Admiral Clinton and Geraldine, who chuckled at my descriptions of the play as lacklustre and tedious. They laughed heartily as I impersonated one of the more absurd players; a man who believed shouting was the best method of creating dramatic effect. Robin was not pleased with the way I had responded. *Let him sulk*, I thought irritably. I was not about to be altered in my course for my reign or this country by a lifeless play!

*

Later that week, de Quadra came to discuss resuming talks about the suit of Archduke Charles. "I have made up my mind to marry none whom I have not seen or known in person, Your Eminence," I interjected as he extolled the virtues of the Archduke Charles *again*. "And consequently, I may be obliged therefore to marry in England, in which case I can think of no person more fitting than my Lord Robin Dudley."

"In that case, madam, I would delay no further, but satisfy Lord Robin at once," replied de Quadra. "It has been over a year and a half since Lady Amy's death. Would your people not trust in the judgement of their sovereign?"

I had actually only brought up Robin as a suitor to steer de Quadra away from the Hapsburg alliance, for in my present mood I was more likely to break something over Robin's head than offer him my hand. I wondered, however, whether I had uncovered something. Why was de Quadra so supportive of Robin again? Was Robin working again with this man who had been suspected of plotting against me? What had Robin promised to de Quadra this time, to gain Hapsburg support?

"I would like to know if such a match has the support of your master, my lord ambassador," I said carefully, wondering if I could get de Quadra to betray Robin. "Would your master be willing to write to me and show such support as you say he offers freely? If I had such support, it might show my people such a union was endorsed by other princes, and was not done merely to satisfy my own feelings, as many might suspect."

De Quadra laughed, but it was an awkward sound. He knew Phillip would never agree to put such sentiments in writing. "Your Majesty should rest assured, I am the mouthpiece of my lord and emperor," he gushed evasively. "And you, Majesty, should go ahead with what *you* decide is best for the realm, but if your choice did fall on the fortunate head of Lord Dudley, I know my master would be pleased."

De Quadra was well aware that in marrying Robin I would add nothing to my country, nor station and would most likely alienate my people. He believed, eventually, as weak woman, ruled by her emotions, I must give in to the passions of my heart and scupper my own boat. Was this the only reason he supported Robin, though? Or was there something deeper to discover here? I wanted de Quadra to think I might well destroy myself, but I also wanted to know if Robin was conspiring with my enemies again. That winter, I restored lands to Robin which had been lost upon his father's fall and gave him a licence to export wool free of tax.

"My ladies ask me, my lord ambassador, if they should kiss my Lord Robin's hand as well as mine these days," I said to de Quadra, adding a girlish giggle as I implied Robin might soon be of the same status as I. De Quadra smiled at me as though I was a fattened calf ready for slaughter. Rumours murmured from the wood and plaster of my palaces, all saying I was on the verge of announcing my engagement to Robin.

But when Robin pestered, I just said the same thing. "Not this year, Robin. Not this year…"

Chapter Thirty-Two

Westminster Palace
Winter - Spring 1562

Sympathy was strong about England for my cousin, Katherine, and her babe, still prisoners of the Tower. None dared come and say so to my face, knowing the mere mention of Katherine's name was enough to oust a man from favour... but I heard the rumours well and true through Kat and Blanche. I could not understand why Katherine had so many supporters, but then, people are ever wont to support an underdog. I was troubled and had no intention of releasing her when she had so many supporters. Would they revolt, and attempt to place this dim witted girl on the throne in my place? I could never be sure of some of my men.

I was about court a great deal that winter; milling, conversing, showing myself to my people. I wanted to remind my nobles of all I had done for England. The country was growing stable in terms of trade and we had been involved in no conflicts of late, which had been good for England's recovery from the past few turbulent years. I also talked often about the Hapsburg alliance, and about Erik of Sweden. My level of enthusiasm for each match depended on to whom I was speaking. To Protestants I hailed Erik as a fine match, and to Catholics I praised the Archduke Charles. I wanted them all to hope I was about to marry and provide an heir, so they would cease to look to my cousin and her child. At one such gathering in my Presence Chamber, as I flittered like a butterfly from group to group, Cecil wandered to my side. He wanted to point out a promising man who had just been elected to Parliament. His name was Francis Walsingham and Cecil believed he could be useful.

"He is a loyal Protestant, and shows an emerging talent for the type of work Parry was skilled at, Majesty," Cecil said, nodding to the dark-clothed man who bowed in response. At the sound of Parry's name, grief stuck his fingers into my belly and twisted. A little over a year without him, and still the pain was raw when it struck unexpectedly. Cecil, blithely unaware of my feelings, continued. "And he is kin to Mistress Ashley," he went on, "for his mother was of the Denny line and his stepfather was a Carey."

Cecil thought he was being subtle, but I knew what he was up to. I had ever shown preference for promoting kin, and in mentioning Walsingham's connections to my family, and to those I trusted, Cecil hoped to win my favour for this dark-robed man with watchful eyes.

"Well, if you trust him, Cecil, keep an eye for any appointments for which you think he would be suited," I said and then moved on. Walsingham's dark, almost black, eyes followed me as I moved about the chamber.

*

That March, pigeons came in flocks to assault the spring vegetable gardens. My garden maids and servants ran an ongoing battle against these feathered foes, trying to keep them at bay with nets, traps, prowling cats and when those defences failed, they would charge out from the kitchens, waving aprons and swiping at their winged opponents with brooms. Since everyone at court was always looking for something new to wager on, this became a spectacle my courtiers turned out to watch each day. The Battle of the Vegetable Patch, as it became known, was very popular for a while. We ate a good deal of pigeon that spring, their gamey flesh sweet and plump from the tips and buds of the plants they had pilfered.

Other birds were busy too; sparrows took dust baths along the garden paths and jackdaws sought chimneys to make nests in. The air was restless with song and chatter. Nests were being made, and partners being courted. There was a sense of expectation in the air as spring fought to banish the last lingering strands of winter from her domain. As we basked in the hope and joys of spring, however, we received horrifying news from France.

On the 11th of that month, the Duke of Guise was travelling from his palace at Joinville when he heard bells ringing in the streets of a small town. Stopping to ask what was going on, and thinking he might attend Mass in the church, he was informed the town's Huguenots were going to their Sunday service in a barn. Guise was affronted. These lands belonged to his niece, Mary of Scots, as part of her dower lands and therefore he felt he had a responsibility for them. The Duke of Guise despised Protestants at the best of times, but recent talks had agreed that Huguenots were supposed to hold services only outside of towns. Enraged, the Duke went to the barn, apparently to admonish them for flouting the law. When the frightened people inside denied him entrance, Guise's men broke down the doors. They fell upon the crowds in unbounded fury, slaughtering many, and destroying their place of worship with fire.

It was a massacre. The Huguenots bore no weapons, and had hardly expected to be put to the sword as they worshipped. It was no fair fight. Sixty-three people were killed, and hundreds injured. For France, this was a disaster. Existing fear and tension between Huguenots and Catholics reached a fever pitch, even after an investigation was launched by a deeply troubled Catherine de Medici. Leading Huguenots wanted revenge for their slain and leading Catholics wanted the Huguenots crushed for their disobedience. For England, too, there were repercussions. Protestants had been slaughtered by a Catholic power; this led to suspicion and terror creeping through England the like of which had not been seen since my sister's reign. Suddenly, all known Catholics in England were being looked upon as the enemy. Catholics in turn became suspicious of their Protestant neighbours, fearing reprisals. And so the circle of violence began.

It terrified me to see how swiftly my people could be torn apart. And there was another consequence. These lands comprised part of the dowry of my cousin of Scots, and her Guise uncle had acted in her name. This put me in a difficult situation with Mary. What was I to do? Continue talks of meeting her whilst people of my own faith were slaughtered, in her name, and by her own uncle? The news spread like fire through ripe barley. It was all anyone at court could talk of and there were rumours that Protestants in England wanted to avenge the deaths of the slaughtered Huguenots. The massacre troubled me and would not leave my thoughts at rest. Visions of those poor, desperate people trapped in that barn as it was set alight haunted me. I could not believe this was an accident, as the Duke of Guise so casually tried to pass it off as in dispatches. The Guise had long been opponents of the Protestant faith and this slaughter was a symptom of that disease. Besides, how does one *accidentally* massacre a barn full of people? But despite my misgivings about the incident, I was cautious. England was surrounded by Catholic nations. We could not risk open war coming to England's shores.

The massacre at Wassy fired up Cecil and many other members of my Privy Council to lecture me anew on the importance of marrying, bearing an heir, or naming one to follow me. They said my refusal to name an heir left the realm open to the threat Catholics so clearly posed to Protestants. My head aching with their constant protests, I said goodbye to Nils, the Chancellor of Sweden as he left for his homeland. I had tried to delay him for as long as possible, thinking he might head straight to Scotland and offer my cousin the place in Erik of Sweden's bed I had lately said I could not accept at the moment, but Nils was determined to leave.

"I am sad to lose you, ambassador," I said with genuine sorrow. "You have been a balm to my spirits these past months."

"And I am no less grieved to lose your company, my lady," he replied. "But, if I may be so bold, Majesty, I would offer one small token of advice for your future."

"What is that, my lord?" I asked, sure he was about to tell me to marry, or name Katherine Grey my heir, probably as a result of being bribed by Robin, or Cecil.

"That you act ever as I have seen you do, Majesty. Act true to your conscience. No greater master can a person have than an active and loyal conscience, such as you possess. When troubles come *or* when peace prevails, I urge you to listen to the voice within your own soul, and you will be well. I counsel you to be true to yourself. Knowing your good heart and wise soul is leading them, the good men and women of England may rest gentle in their beds."

I gazed at him with startled eyes and then smiled sadly. "Thank you, my lord ambassador... I will ever attempt to do as you have instructed."

At least there is one man who understands me, I thought as I watched him leave. *More the pity, though, he is a foreign lord, and not one of my own men.*

*

There were increasing signs of unrest in France.

The Prince de Conde, claiming he and others were liberating their King from the influence of "evil", meaning the Guise, of course, started to send men to protect Huguenot places of worship, and take control of towns of strategic importance along the Loire Valley. Catholic lords started to make ready, too, and from the deluge of furiously written reports coming from Throckmorton, it seemed civil war was about to break out in France. We watched nervously as events unfolded. Some Huguenots took the opportunity to leave France. They flooded into England, arriving in London, Bristol and other cities.

"We should support the Huguenots and send troops to France," Cecil announced when he arrived to talk with me in private.

"We can do nothing of the sort at this moment, as you are well aware, Cecil," I said with patience. "It is too soon to become involved, *if* England should even become involved in the civil war of another state. The Dowager is arranging talks of peace. Perhaps it will be over soon enough."

"They are determined to exterminate us," Cecil muttered, smoothing his long beard.

"Who, my lord? The Guise? You think they are bound for England, intent on murdering you, do you? Perhaps it would be better if you took some time to think on the poor people in that barn who but went to worship in peace, before deciding all of this was a plot to remove me from the throne, or attack you personally!" I strode out of the room, leaving him gaping. I did not want England to become involved in France's inner turmoil, but others did not think the same. England had intervened before in another country's civil unrest, in Scotland. We had sent troops to support Protestant rebels there against Mary of Guise. This led many to believe I would leap at the opportunity to aid French Protestants. But our intervention then had been about maintaining the security of England, by removing French influence over Scotland, rather than about aiding those of our faith.

I could not risk England in every dispute about faith in Europe. England could not become the shining knight of all Protestant causes in the world. We had enough enemies... *I* had enough enemies. I had worked hard to maintain peace with our Catholic neighbours, many of whom had more resources, more men, and more wealth to use than England if we faced them in war. When I first came to the throne, I had said I meant to live in peace with our Catholic neighbours, as long as they reciprocated. To charge into this looming conflict in France was not only premature, but potentially perilous. It could unite Catholic states against us, causing them to strike at England in retaliation, or simply decide to remove us as a threat before we truly became one. Besides, I did not like war. I wanted France to solve her problems through talk and diplomacy, not through fire and sword. War brought strife and terror and it was always the common man who suffered most. I did not want my people exposed to such horrors. But my Council were keen that England should become involved. They jabbed me with their arguments and I rebuffed them with a shield of words. I was uneasy, often lost in thought, and disturbed by anti-Catholic sentiments I heard about court.

Perhaps it was the wildness of the times, perhaps it was the strangeness of the events, but a thought came and would not leave.

I had been thinking on Mary of Scots, and considering what I would write to her about the Wassy massacre. Such delicate, inflammatory events require some thought before quill is put to paper. We had entered a time of fragile harmony, and I had no wish to see it crumble. I had also been thinking about Mary's suitors. She was eager to marry Don Carlos, and I was just as eager that such an event should never happen. In truth, I little liked the idea of her marrying *any* foreign power. They would arrive with their own ambitions, and should they be Catholic, there was a good chance one of those ambitions would be taking me off England's throne and replacing me with Mary. I hardly wanted my cousin to resume her old stance, and decide she was the true Queen of England. My cousin of Lennox had not given up her old ambition to wed her eldest son to Mary either, and Cecil's men had found many a letter wending its way to Scotland that winter in praise of the match of which I had not approved… Margaret was apparently unaware that she was under surveillance, and that perhaps accounted for her idiotic brashness. Cecil was already asking for more men to investigate the foolish Countess, and I had allowed him free rein to burrow into her affairs. I had Lennox in London, but Margaret still tarried in the country, leading to me order the ports closed in case she and her sons might think of escape. I sent men to bring her to London.

Unfortunately, the elder son, Henry Darnley, got wind of our plans and managed to flee to France before my guards arrived to tear Margaret's house apart. The remaining Lennoxes were arrested and escorted to London as my men ransacked Margaret's house for further evidence. Note, please, that this *angelic* son who rode so high in his mother's estimations did not think to warn the rest of his family they were about to be arrested. Oh no... Henry Darnley was a selfish creature; that was the way he was born, and the way he ever was through life. Some beasts simply never change.

My cousin Mary was unlikely to accept Darnley, knowing how many enemies his father had in Scotland, but what if Mary married an English nobleman of my choosing? One whom I knew would be a friend to England? What if she took a husband who was one of my supporters?

What if, in fact... I offered *Robin* to my cousin?

You perhaps think at this juncture that I had run mad in the spring sunshine, but it was not so. There were advantages to this odd plan. The thought of losing Robin was abhorrent. No matter what he did, my love for him remained... But how strong were his feelings for me? I had suspected his love had waned as his ambition to become King grew. Would this not be a way to discover the truth? If I offered Robin to Mary, he could have all his ambition desired. He could become a king, rule a country, and his children would be heirs not only to the Scottish crown, but potentially to England's as well. Mary was an enticing woman; beautiful, powerful, learned, graceful and charming. Would she not prove tempting to any man? And if he was tempted by her, and her crown, I would finally know that he loved me no more. If he chose to reject the proposal, however, I would know his love was true, for he would be willing to abandon such an alluring prospect for me.

An interesting experiment, indeed.

There were, too, other advantages. I doubted that Mary would accept Robin, but if she did then I would have a friend and ally on the Scottish throne. For all his dealings with Spain, I knew Robin loved England too well to ever actually work against her interests. And even if Mary only considered Robin for a while, it would postpone her securing a match with a foreign power. It might make Robin's enemies less fearful of him if they thought he meant little to me. It might allow my people to finally understand I did not intend to marry him, and therefore remove the lingering suspicion they held about his wife's death. And, for Robin to be considered a worthy husband for a queen, he would have to have greater titles than he presently held. This could allow me to elevate him without everyone thinking I was doing so in order to wed him myself.

There was, of course, one large disadvantage. I did not wish to lose Robin. I had fought hard to keep him and could not imagine being without him. But offering him thus would give me a chance to test his love, and distract Mary.

Yes... A curious thought, an outlandish one, and it was a gamble, but it was worth further consideration. I doubt I would have ever considered it for a moment had I not been so hurt by Robin's power games. He had sprung a few surprises on me of late. It might be quite delightful to see how he would react when I unleashed one of my own. And *what* a surprise I hoped it might be! For him to suddenly discover I was willing to part with him for politics? But first, Robin needed to be lulled, just as he had lulled me, into peaceful, happy slumber before each of his assaults. He needed to think himself secure, just as he had done to me, so I could surprise him properly. Spiteful, yes... but you cannot deny he deserved some payback.

With this in mind, I approved his recent request to alter his crest to include the bear and ragged staff emblems of his family. Since these figures had been present on the arms of his father, the Duke of Northumberland, many took this to mean I intended to elevate Robin, possibly in preparation for marrying him. Robin's new arms were unveiled at a meeting of the Knights of the Garter on St George's Day. I had expected some of my lords, Robin's enemies in particular, to protest, so it came as a vast surprise when it was reported to me that Norfolk stood up and ordered a petition for me to marry Robin!

Norfolk's bizarre outburst did not receive a good reception. Arundel and the Marquis of Northampton disagreed and abruptly departed, but others agreed to sign. When it was delivered to me, I shook my head in wonder. Robin had bribed Norfolk. There was no other explanation. And Robin must have made some hefty promises to overcome Norfolk's loathing for him. What had he offered Norfolk to bring this about? A place on my Privy Council? Cecil's positions? And how much wealth had Robin had to put down as security? Sussex... now Norfolk... No wonder Robin was always in debt, despite his great wealth. These bribes must be decimating his coin chests. And since I had granted him the means to gather such wealth, through lands, estates, positions and liberties with taxes, in essence, I was paying Robin to bribe my men against me!

Oh, Robin, I thought with a wicked smile on my lips. *You will get such a surprise when you see what I have planned for you.*

Publicly, I expressed joy that so many of my men were keen for me to wed Robin, but I said also I needed to give the matter further consideration. Some, however, could not wait for their Queen to gather her thoughts, for later that week Cecil came rushing to my chambers, with fresh rumour to disclose.

Chapter Thirty-Three

Westminster Palace and Nottingham Castle
Spring- Summer 1562

"So… I am *already* married to Lord Robin Dudley?" I asked as Cecil revealed this gossip. "And am I pregnant, my lord, do you know? Or just basking in the bliss of newly married life?"

Cecil blinked, not understanding why I was not taking this seriously. It made me chuckle. "I assure you, Cecil, I am not married, am yet a virgin, and likely to remain so…. Do you not see, *Spirit*? We must laugh at the ridiculous in life for it arms us against the sorrows." I was not overly concerned about the rumour. Such had been said before, and proven false with time. What would prove the gossip wrong this time, would be when I announced Robin as a candidate for Mary's hand. I was warming to the idea by the day.

"I am, of course, delighted to hear your Majesty is so amused," he said, sounding not delighted in the slightest. "But you should also know… the source of this rumour has been traced to de Quadra."

That was more serious. "Is that stinking weasel *ever* doing his actual job, Cecil? Or does he spend his all his days plotting against me?"

"You could say that *is* his job, Majesty. He *is* an ambassador, after all, and a Catholic. We have no reason to trust Catholics at this time."

I shook my head. "Not so fast, Cecil, slow those thoughts down. De Quadra is *one* man. *He* is not *all* Catholics, and neither is his master. Do not throw all Catholics in the same pot and make a pottage of paranoia from their bones. I refuse to believe *all* Catholics in my realm mean me harm. Even less do I believe they are set on slaughtering their countrymen. Tread careful, Cecil. When a bear feels hunted, he turns on those who track him. I will not have my kingdom falling to bits, as France seems poised to, because my men have *created* an enemy by acting as though Catholics *are* the enemy."

"I did not make your cousin of Lennox write to Phillip of Spain, nor the Guise massacre Huguenots in France," Cecil defended himself. "Nor did I make de Quadra plot against you, Majesty. The threat *is* here, and it is not just from one man, but rises from many Catholic quarters."

"I recognise the threat, *Spirit*. I know well enough how many people despise me and would love nothing better than to see me deposed and dead. But even so, these conspirators do not represent *all* Catholics. You will make English Catholics into the very enemy you fear, old friend, by treating them as though they are the enemy before they have done anything... by judging them as a whole, rather than as individuals. Do not drive people from me with suspicion. Do not make them feel unwelcome in their own country, and do not make them feel hunted."

I shivered and stood up, walking to the window. My words felt as though they were coming from another place, another time, as though another Elizabeth looked back on these events and was trying to warn me. "Do not make my people the enemy, Cecil," I murmured as I looked from the window. "I have enough foes."

Later that week, as Cecil's investigation into de Quadra continued, it was found the ambassador had not only been starting rumours, but had taken the time to compose a sonnet about me, and a rather rude one. The sonnet, which I might add was badly written, did not scan with ease, and was packed full of poor insults, *was* offensive, but was also a poor piece of work. I snorted at the verse when a copy was given to me. "The desiccated rodent could at least have made an effort," I said to Kat as I set my copy into the fire's flames. "Why, at one point he tries to rhyme 'heretic' with 'inherited'… a most unwieldy ode."

Kat laughed. "Your Majesty has not found her new court poet, then?"

"My Majesty has not, indeed." I watched the flames consume the parchment, turning de Quadra's words to ash, which was the best use for them. "Does de Quadra think I will be hurt? *Wounded* that he loves me not? I care not for the opinion of those who hate me. It is only the opinion of those I think well of that matters."

Cecil's spy in de Quadra's household, Borghese Venturini, was de Quadra's secretary. He revealed not only this latest plot and the terrible sonnet, but other secrets; the full truth of all that had been offered to Robin, all that Robin had promised in return, and many little incidental and insulting trifles de Quadra had said about me over the years. There was also evidence to suggest that de Quadra had been in talks with Margaret Lennox, via letter, and had offered his support to the notion of Henry Darnley marrying Mary of Scots. It was a damning brief, and not only for de Quadra. Cecil gave his findings to the Council and they were appalled. I was worried for Robin. I had worked hard to foil his plot without bringing public shame upon him, but Cecil had the right to disclose this information to the Council. Although it was supposed to be confidential, the truth, of course, leaked out into court, and from there, to my people. Robin was in disgrace, and many of his previous supporters turned from him, particularly Protestants. He knew this information was not news to me, and I assured him I would protect him as best I could. I could not help but think, though, that this might be good for Robin. Perhaps it could do what I seemed unable to; puncture Robin's pride, and make him aware of the ramifications of his actions.

Lennox was sent to the Tower for his wife's meddling in the succession, and Margaret's second son, Charles, was kept in York as I had his mother and her daughters held at Whitehall and then in the Charterhouse at Sheen for questioning. Rumours of witchcraft and accusations of treason accompanied my cousin, and Cecil was keen to have her attainted for high treason. I attempted to have Margaret proved a bastard, but unfortunately there was not enough evidence to support this. Her letters, however, and the evidence of Venturini, showed that Margaret had declared she was my heir and had asked for the support of Phillip of Spain for her claim. This was more than enough to hold her for suspected treason. Fifteen articles were drawn up against her that spring, all of them damning. Margaret had called me a bastard to her intimates, had conspired with soothsayers and witches to predict my death, and had been attempting to marry her son to Mary of Scots. I did not allow my cousin to be informed of the full extent of the charges against her. It was far more satisfying to know she was sweating away in her comfortable prison, wondering what I might do with her.

It was said about court, with the incarceration of the Lennoxes and Katherine Grey that "the prisons will soon be full of the nearest relations to the crown," and perhaps it was true. But both these cousins *had* committed treason.

As Margaret wrote to me and to Cecil, proclaiming her endless love for me and her innocence of whatever she was accused, Cecil went to de Quadra's house accompanied by the Privy Council. They presented their findings and de Quadra squirmed and slimed, trying to deny involvement. He was not believed. How I would have loved to watch as my Council attacked him! Unfortunately, it was not to be. We had agreed that I, as the Queen, could not be seen to insult Phillip's ambassador and thereby ignite an international incident with Spain. The role of spanking de Quadra was therefore given to my Council, so I could deny knowledge of it should Phillip become enraged. I rolled with laughter when

Cecil told me about the meeting, and made him describe in intimate detail de Quadra's expressions, sweat patterns and excuses. But by the faith! How I would have loved to be there in person to see him wriggle like the worm he was!

I dismissed de Quadra from court, but I was not about to send him home just yet. Everyone knew about Robin's dealings with de Quadra. Robin needed to understand the consequences of his treachery, but I was not willing to desert him. He was facing a great deal of hostility. Sending de Quadra away would mean the only scapegoat left was Robin and I was not going to serve him to his enemies plucked and ready for roasting. It was not a good time to come under such suspicion, with all that was occurring in France. Robin's deep unpopularity made his enemies thirst to destroy him, but my protection ensured his safety. Unable to persuade me to move against Robin, his enemies sought to undermine him in other ways. Tales of his wife's death resurfaced, as did stories of his pride and arrogance, the ills he had done to others, and the nefarious influence he held over me. Had you heard some of the stories circulating about Robin, you might have believed he was a wicked sorcerer, bent on dominating England by possessing its Queen by magical wiles. If Robin were truly capable of witchcraft, however, he and I would have been long married by now.

I kept him close, outwardly showed my support for him, and told all who asked that I believed he had been led astray by de Quadra. Robin and I did not talk about this. There was no need. Robin already knew I had been aware of his plotting with de Quadra, and I had nothing more to say. Robin slipped in and out of court like an eel in the marsh beds of Ely, trying to slither unseen. Fortunately for him, his chambers were close to mine wherever we stayed, and so he could spend most days hidden in my rooms. We played cards and chess, we listened to music together and left the castle quietly to hunt and ride. Robin was grateful; there was a humble air to him at that time. I liked it. It was infinitely preferable to his high-handed arrogance. I hoped he understood what could have happened, had I decided to toss him to the wolves. Robin was wounded, both in his pride, and in his ambition. There were none who would support his suit as my husband. His dreams were thrown to the floor and stamped on. I admit a certain satisfaction in his humiliation; after all, it was deserved, was it not? But I also pitied him. My emotions were rarely straightforward when it came to Robin.

As Robin's popularity plummeted, mine soared. Despite my support for Robin, I was cheered everywhere I went. Such plots, such danger, such insults thrown at their Queen made my people protective. Their love for me swelled just as their hatred for my enemies deepened. They blamed Robin and Spain for conspiring against me. They believed Robin was an ill-influence, but they also celebrated my loyalty to my friends, seeing virtue in me even in the things they saw as flaws. The last time I was this popular was when first I came to the throne. When I travelled, I was greeted by thousands turning out to call my name, to shout "God Save Good Queen Bess!" and to applaud me everywhere I went. When Robin dared to venture out, he was hissed at and booed. I had done well from this incident, and my triumph made me a little more generous towards Robin.

As spring turned to summer, Margaret Lennox and her husband were still being questioned. Margaret wrote to Cecil and to me proclaiming her devotion to me as a kinswoman, and objecting to the incarceration of her family. I did not believe in her innocence. I did not, however, order their executions. Margaret was Catholic, however much she might pretend otherwise, and I had no wish to further rile Catholics in England by ordering her death.

To further demonstrate my wish for peace with those of Catholic faith, I put on a three-day allegorical masque when visiting Nottingham Castle. It was for the benefit of Mary Stewart. Whether we would be able to meet given the Wassy massacre, I knew not, but I was determined to keep peace alive between us. I little needed her to turn to her Guise relatives, and find French troops entering Scotland again. Besides, despite our differences, Mary was fast becoming the cousin I warmed to the most. All the others were either conspiring fantasists, like Margaret, or traitors, like Katherine.

The first night's entertainments started with *Pallas* riding into the hall on a unicorn; a small horse, pure white of coat, with a golden horn attached to his head with gilded ribbons. Flying above *Pallas* was a standard of two female hands clasped together, set on a background of raging crimson. Behind *Pallas* came two women, one riding a red lion, and the other a golden lion. The first woman wore an embroidered shawl with the word *Temperance* upon it, and the other wore one which said *Prudence*. Both women were crowned and dressed in robes of royalty.

The lions, who were actually men of my household in costume, since I had no wish to see my ladies devoured by the beasts of the Tower menagerie, did very well, I thought. They roared into the great hall, making ladies giggle as they swiped them with their tails.

The next day, *Peace* was drawn through the hall on a golden chariot, pulled by an elephant. On the back of the elephant (a creature constructed from yet more obliging servants of my household) sat *Friendship*, waving a white banner of truce. On the last night, a figure called *Malice,* in the form of a silver snake, was trodden underfoot by *Peace, Unity, Prudence* and *Temperance* all working together to stamp him into the ground. Although it was supposed to be a serious allegory, I could not help but chuckle at *Malice* as he cowered on the floor, trying to protect his head from the stomping feet of his assailants.

The object was, of course, to show how Mary and I could overcome our differences and live in peace as neighbours. All of this was reported to my cousin in Scotland and Mary wrote me a rather gushing letter to express her joy. She was keen for us to meet, but with all that was going on in France I wondered if this was going to be possible. I also was a little unsure as meeting with her would only lead to her petitioning me in person to be named heir. I did not want to insult my cousin to her face by having to refuse.

Mary's letters though… They seemed so genuine, so *innocent* in many ways that I pondered seriously about meeting her. I was in need of allies, but perhaps it was more than this… I wanted a friend. Not a friend like Robin, who had damaged my ability to trust him. Not a friend like Cecil, who although I knew to be loyal, would always act as he saw fit. Not even a friend like Kat, who I loved above all others.

Mary was the only person who could understand my position. All others saw my choices, my deliberations, the strains and pressures upon me from a distance. My cousin of Scots was the only one who understood what it was to be a queen; a sole, unwed, and often lonesome, queen. This notion made me write more openly to Mary than ever I had done before. We began to exchange increasingly personal letters. We wrote each other poems. We wrote in Italian to each other and sent gifts. We exchanged experiences and advise. Some of our missives were almost like love letters. Mary sent me her portrait, made into a miniature to be worn about the waist on a golden chain, and with it came a poem expressing love and devotion to me, as her good friend, and her sister.

It was common to overstate devotion and love in diplomatic letters, but all the same, I began to feel as though I had a new suitor, and this time it was not a prince… it was the Queen of Scotland.

Chapter Thirty-Four

Greenwich Palace
Summer 1562

As we heard of growing problems in France, Maitland left on a mission of peace for his Scottish homeland. I instructed him to go to his Queen and tell her of my passionate interest in the meeting.

I was still in two minds about the prospect of meeting my cousin. I was curious about her, and I had never been good at restraining my curiosity. There was a part of me that longed to put a face to all I had heard of her over the years. There was another part of me which was apprehensive. Quite apart from political considerations, I had heard much of her beauty, and I was vain enough to find this threatening. No woman likes to be outdone. I could shine above women with fairer faces than me in England, for the crown made me more beautiful than I was. But Mary had her own crown. She had the potential to outdo my charms.

But there were deeper concerns for me to think on. There always are for a queen. It was not only for my sake I wanted to know my cousin better, but for England as well. I did not like to hear the succession talked of in Council, in Parliament, or at court, but that did not mean I did not think about it. How could I do otherwise? England was my responsibility. This became only more relevant as the investigation into the marriage of Hertford and Katherine Grey reached its conclusion. Their marriage was declared null and void, and any children resulting from it therefore illegitimate. This was good for me as it was the vindication of all I had said and thought on the matter. Katherine's supporters were not pleased, but they could not deny Archbishop Parker's findings. I breathed a sigh of relief, feeling safer than I had done for months.

"The child is illegitimate, Cecil, and the mother proved unsuitable." I could have set my head back and crowed like a triumphant rooster. "Katherine Grey will no longer be considered for the succession."

Cecil moved swiftly on to other business, but I could see that in *his* mind the matter was not finished. After all, *I* had been declared illegitimate, and *I* still sat upon this throne. If anything unexpected were to happen to me, I knew Cecil would work to place Lord Beauchamp on the throne with a regency council to govern until he came of age. Such a result would hold the best of both worlds for my Cecil. He would have a male, Protestant king, and he would be in control of England until the boy came of age. I did not believe Cecil actually *wanted* anything to happen to me. For all the times we disagreed, we were more often united. He had respect for me, even loved me in his own way, I believe. I felt the same for him. We understood each other. We knew the other was capable of duplicity, even evil, but we worked together to maintain goodness. There are princes who will only have men about them who agree with everything they say. Some who take every difference of opinion as an insult, but I was not one of those. I did not tolerate insubordination, or disrespect, but I did not believe in closing my ears. The final decision was always mine, but the manner of reaching that decision should be one that was shared. We were a good team, Cecil and me. Many was the time I was angered by him, but many more were the times I was grateful to have him. But even if he loved me, Cecil wanted a future where *normality* would be restored. He looked to a future where the Protestant line would be assured, and where kings would reign. My growing affection for Mary troubled him. His vision of the future was different to mine.

Tempted though I was to order an Act of Attainder and have Katherine and Hertford branded traitors, I had them instead sentenced to life imprisonment, but they were hardly mistreated. Katherine's chambers in the Tower were hung with rich curtains of velvet and tapestry to keep out the draughts. She had an allowance for coal and wood to keep her chambers warm for her child, a bed with a good mattress, and whatever she wished, within reason, for her table from the private kitchens. Her pet dogs and little apes lived with her, as did a maid, and she was allowed to take exercise in the gardens of the Tower. She had not her freedom, but I made no move to take her life. My forebears would not have been so generous.

Whilst many still hoped there would come a day when I would relent, release Katherine and Hertford, and name her son my heir, I looked in another direction for the future of England... I looked to Scotland, to the young Queen there, who I hoped would not disappoint my growing faith in her abilities.

Chapter Thirty-Five

Greenwich Palace
Summer 1562

France erupted into war.

We had known it was coming, but somehow it still came as a shock. It was civil war of a most unusual kind, made not between royal houses hungry for power, but between Christian faiths, struggling for the very soul of France.

The royal house of Valois, led by Catherine de Medici, was set on reconciliation, or so it appeared. You could never be sure with that slippery eel. Catherine tried to stride through the middle of the troubles, openly supporting neither side. She placated, she pleaded and cajoled, trying to head off war before it roared into full power. I wondered how long this would last, for Catherine and her son could not teeter on a cliff edge between the two sides indefinitely. Eventually they would have to choose, and they were much more likely to choose the Catholic side, than the Protestant.

Reports of the first skirmishes arrived in England. Civil war is dangerous. Weakened by its own people fighting each other, the country is open, too, from attack from other nations, as well as gaining nothing but the destruction of its own people, their lands and livelihoods. I have never understood the use of the word 'civil' when it comes to war. There is nothing civil about war. It is a dirty, foul creature which steals, murders, and rapes its way through a country. It is a beast which stalks the hearts of men, bringing out the worst elements of their characters. We never know what we are capable of until we have feared for our lives. And now, in France, this war set neighbour on neighbour and kin against kin; the dirtiest, vilest kind of conflict.

Throckmorton and Robin added their voices to Cecil's, pleading that England should intervene. Many on the Council were eager for war. They offered many persuasions to entice me to send men to aid the Huguenots, even dangling Calais before me. My sister had lost Calais when she sent men to join her husband's forces against France in war. The loss had been a hideous insult to English pride, and my men knew I wanted it restored. I admit, it was tempting. To restore Calais would bring joy to England, and I knew it would have grieved my father to think it lost forever. There were other considerations too. Cecil pointed out that, should the Huguenots win, and overthrow their Catholic overlords, France might become a Protestant state. The idea of having another Protestant nation near us, and one we had aided, would be advantageous. I could not deny there were reasons to consider aiding the Huguenots. But, of course, if they lost, and the Catholic factions prevailed, we would have a hostile Catholic nation on our doorstep... A much less enticing proposal.

As I pondered, voices rose against my meeting with Mary. Throckmorton wrote, advising that to meet with my cousin at this time would be a poor idea, and impolitic if we *did* wish to support the Huguenots against the Guise, who were, after all, Mary's kin. The fact that this war had sprung from her uncle's attack on Huguenots in Mary's dower lands meant that many viewed her as embroiled, even complicit, in this affair. For me to meet with her might lead people to believe I supported the Catholics, and could alienate Protestant allies, such as Sweden. But, I reasoned, to not meet with Mary may well alienate my nearest neighbour.

To my mind there were as many arguments for getting involved as there were for remaining out of this conflict. My personal inclination was that we should not enter this war. I wanted to meet in peace with Mary, or at least improve relations between us by *acting* as though I was going to meet with her even if it never came to pass. But my men would not let this lie. They wanted to become part of this war, as much for its own sake, I believe, as because of the benefits and morals involved. War is a drug to the hearts of some men. They are raised on stories of it and nurtured by its fantasies. If they believe all they are told, they come to think on war as a glorious event; one in which they are proven men, and made heroes. But that is not the truth. Whilst heroes have been made in battles, and some men have done acts of bravery and compassion in conflict, most of the time war is a filthy thing. To the common people, those ever caught in its crossfire and flame, it is a hideous demon that brings nothing but death, humiliation, and loss. No, I had no wish for war. But my Council did.

"We *should* support the Huguenots," Robin declared with passion to the Council. He had asked permission to come and speak, for he was not a part of my Council, but had said to me that he felt strongly about the issue. "They are men of our faith, my lords, and the Catholic Guise have shown that they have no honour." Robin's cheeks were scarlet. His words were convincing, but I knew what he was up to; trying to resurrect his much-damaged image by reinventing himself as a paragon of Protestantism. I was not about to let him shove me into war as he had tried to force me into marriage.

"Were you not in bed with de Quadra, a Catholic, not so very long ago, my lord?" I asked in a frosty tone. "And yet now, you are here becoming a champion of the Protestant cause? Remind me to take note of your leaps of loyalty, my lord, for there are so many I will lose track." The others chortled at Robin's discomfort. He glowered at the table since he did not dare glare at me. He did not like me bringing up his recent shame, but I was not going to allow him to get away with pretending such zeal when he was in fact only looking after his own interests.

"You cannot meet with Mary of Scots, my lady," Cecil interjected as the laughter died down. "To do so would only strengthen the Guise. England would be seen to be supporting French Catholics, and possibly vindicating the massacre of Wassy. We cannot make enemies with Protestant countries who would look on this meeting with distaste."

"But yet we *can* afford to make enemies of Catholic nations by sending in troops to support the Huguenots?" I asked with incredulity. "I am talking of meeting with my kinswoman, and a fellow head of state, in peace, Cecil, to *talk* of peace. Surely peace is more important than war? Surely peace brings greater benefit?"

"We could regain Calais, Majesty, as you have always longed to," Pembroke noted, looking up from petting his hound. "If we offer support to the Huguenots, they may be willing to barter for its restoration."

"As *many* have said to me over the last few days," I said irritably. "It is as though Calais has transformed by magic into a rump of beef, and you all think me a slathering hound, my lords, willing to do anything for a bite." More chuckling. My men found me amusing, whether they agreed with me or not. "You *will* set the meeting with my royal cousin into motion, my lords. I wish to at least *talk* of meeting with Mary Stewart. If she is anything like as charming in person as she is in her letters I believe we have the potential for friendship, and that is more suited to my heart than war."

I held up a hand as voices broke out in protest. "But I *will* think on the matter of France in all seriousness, I promise you. Do not believe my heart is cold when I hear about those of our faith being so abused. Do not believe I feel no temptation to aid them. Do not think I hear not the cries of mothers, whose sons have died, or feel not the grief of God for seeing His children butchered. I still believe it is not our place to enter this conflict, and yet I will consider your opinions, my lords. But I have to think of what this will bring to my own people. England must always be my first, and most important, concern."

Two weeks later, Maitland returned to court. I discussed plans with him about the proposed summit. We discussed York as a possible meeting place, and plans were set in motion for tournaments, entertainments and public meetings between Mary and me. Much to my satisfaction, peace was brokered in France between the warring sides. It was an uneasy truce, to be sure, but at least it was peace. My Council, many of them clearly disappointed, decided the need for England to become engaged in war was required no longer.

I sat back, breathed a sigh of relief for having managed to avoid becoming entangled in war, and started to instead contemplate how to outshine a woman who was younger and prettier than me. I admit it was a high concern for me, not only as a woman, but as a queen. But my curiosity about Mary was starting to outweigh my reservations.

As I read Mary's letters, all containing great joy about my continued resolve for us to meet, I began to think I might actually enjoy meeting her... If, that was, I could contain the envy I might encounter upon seeing her, or jealousy, if my people decided she was more beautiful than I was.

*

Cecil had become obsessed with the weather.

As talks went on about the English-Scottish summit meeting, Cecil came up with a seemingly never-ending list of problems which, in his mind, should delay the meeting. Each day he arrived with more: the autumn rains would make travel impossible, he said; the wheels of carriages and wagons would be clogged with mud, he said; there were shortages of fowl and wine in the north of England, he muttered; the planned entertainments would be ruined by hail, rain, wind, snow, storms, tempests and mudslides... Cecil did not want the meeting to go ahead, that I knew, but the barrage of excuses he presented was getting faintly ridiculous.

"You seem to have become *most* interested in practical matters, *Spirit*," I noted calmly as he finished another list showing why it was *clearly* impossible for me to meet my cousin that autumn. "I have ever known you fond of maps, but did not know that travel and travelling, weather and wagons, were such passions of yours."

"The meeting is impractical, and cannot go ahead," he said stiffly.

"The meeting is un-retractable, and therefore *will* go ahead. Do not test my patience, Cecil. You know I have little as it is."

Cecil went off muttering into his beard. Unable to reason with me, Cecil decided to take matters into his own hands. He went to Maitland, informing the Scots' ambassador the meeting was not to be. When I heard this I was furious. Another one seeking to overstep his authority!

"The meeting will *assuredly* go ahead, ambassador," I said to a heated Maitland, who came to protest this abrupt cancellation. The Presence Chamber was packed that morning with petitioners. "I know not to whom you have been speaking, but they do not speak for me. I am quite capable of doing that for myself, my lord. My wishes are unchanged. I want to meet my good sister of Scotland and know her better. Ignore these triflers who play with you, they speak not for me."

I glared openly at Cecil. Chatter broke out, and even some muffled laughter. Cecil was a powerful man, and power attracts enemies like flies to rotting flesh. There were many happy to see he had slipped in my estimations. Cecil was aghast, not only that I still wanted to meet Mary, but that I had shamed him in public. I suffered no remorse. How many times was I going to have to slap my men about their well-fed buttocks before they understood who was master here?

"My royal cousin will have one thousand attendants, as will I," I went on briskly, enjoying the pallor on Cecil's face. "We will meet in September, in the north of England, at York. And whilst in England, my cousin will be granted dispensation to worship in the Catholic faith as though she were at home."

There was a lot of muttering at that. Cecil went white as the moon. Maitland was taken aback, and hardly knew what to say. "That is… most generous, Majesty," he said eventually. "My Queen will be overjoyed at such a munificent offer from her beloved sister. She did not expect you to be so magnanimous in terms of religion."

"Whilst England will always be a Protestant nation, my lord ambassador, I believe there is small difference between the Christian faiths. We all worship the same God. I am happy to make concessions for your Queen, and I am sure she will respond in kind with the same open friendship. We may be of different faiths in practice, but I believe we are of one belief at heart."

There! I thought happily. *Let Cecil understand the more he opposes me, the more I will work to make peace with my cousin of Scots.*

Cecil was not the only one unhappy with my proposals. There were plenty at court who were vastly displeased with me, but the more they fought me the more resolved I became to actually go ahead with this meeting. Maitland made for Scotland a day later, and Mary was overcome by my generosity. I sent Maitland with letters for Mary, and finally sent a portrait to my cousin. She had sent me several, but I had waited until I had one which satisfied my desire to outmatch my cousin. I was not as pretty as her, but the portrait I sent was impressive. My red hair flamed against my pale skin. My black eyes were bright and bold. I was dressed in red, golden and ermine trimmed robes, and looked every inch a Tudor. I was pleased with the effect, and it seemed

Mary was as interested in me as I was about her, for she quizzed Randolph when the portrait arrived. He sent me a full report of their meeting.

"How like is it, unto the Queen, your Mistress's lively face?" Mary asked, gazing at the portrait.

"Your Majesty will shortly be the judge of the likeness when you meet my mistress... but when you meet with her, I assure you, you will find more perfection than could be set forth by the arts of man," answered Randolph.

What a lovely man Randolph was. I did so like to hear such things.

"To meet with my cousin is the thing I have most desired ever since it was suggested," Mary went on, walking about the portrait and leaning in to examine it closely. "Let God be my witness, I honour her in my heart and love her as my dear and natural sister."

Randolph wrote further to say he believed Mary's expressions were honest. It was rather sweet, in a strange way, that Mary should be so affected by the idea of us meeting. I wondered if she felt that sense of loneliness that our positions could bring. A queen is surrounded by people, and yet is alone in her station. *Could we ever be close enough to become friends*, I wondered, *or are we too close to one another, too close in position and rank to ever be true friends?* In the end, I did not have to wonder on the subject. Fate stepped in to thwart our plans.

Disturbing reports arrived from Randolph that my cousin was actively giving support to her Guise relations by urging them to overthrow the still–rebellious Huguenots. Her Council would not approve sending troops, but Mary's support for her Catholic uncles set us on opposite sides. Increasing pressures were already upon me not to meet with Mary, and now the silly chit had thrown her lot in with the Guise! I knew they were her kin, and there is loyalty demanded to family, but she must have understood the position she was putting me in. And could she not see her support for the Guise would be dangerous to her own position in Scotland? Her men, her lords, her clergy, they were all Protestants. Mary was wagering much on a risky hand.

Word arrived that talks of peace had failed, and war was upon France once again. We were petitioned for help from Huguenot leaders, and my men assaulted me over and over in Council on the matter. Reluctantly, believing the Huguenots may be crushed by the Catholic Guise, and thinking if the Guise prevailed then England would have sure enemies as neighbours, I gave the order for troops to be mustered to support the Prince de Conde and Admiral de Coligny. I hoped our intervention would maintain a Protestant presence in France. Certainly, if the Guise won, they would work to stamp out Protestantism in France, and might turn their ambitions on England as well.

I sent Henry Sidney to Scotland to inform Mary that under the present circumstances we could not meet. I proposed we delay for a year, when all of these troubles might have passed. At the same time, I urged her not to support her Guise relations, for that would put her in direct opposition, not only to me, but to her Protestant subjects as well. *"You must see the danger with which you dance, sister,"* I wrote. *"To support those whom your own people and lords view as their enemies will only bring grief to you, no matter what loyalties of blood and birth you owe to them."*

There was a marked period of silence after that letter. I do not think my cousin of Scots was overly pleased I had highlighted the fragility of her position.

Sidney wrote from Scotland, informing me that when he told Mary the meeting was postponed, she had left him and made for her bedchamber where she fell *"to furious weeping."* He managed to rally my cousin by telling her I was just as disappointed as she. Although I was pleased Mary genuinely wished for this meeting, it was outlandish to me that she should dissolve into tears every time something happened that was not to her liking. Her emotions burst from her like a rotting quince upon the ground in November. I was unsure what to make of this behaviour.

Since I had delayed my meeting with Mary, many thought now was a good moment to resurrect the idea of Katherine Grey becoming my heir. Was the girl to haunt me forever? Hertford and Katherine were appealing the verdict that their marriage was unlawful. They had the right to appeal, but I resented it. How often were they to defy me? Had I not been generous? As they put their case forward, some nobles sought to thrust Katherine Grey forward as my successor. I just as keenly thrust their ideas back.

As I fenced and parried with my cousins, fresh rumours of a match between Robin and me resurfaced. I was not sure where this gossip sprang from this time. I did wonder if Robin himself had spread the rumour; testing the water, perhaps, in light of his outspoken defence of the Huguenots. But he had been quite well-behaved of late and I did not want to think we were entering another period of plotting. There was much opposition to the idea this time, even more so than before, mainly due to his uncovered dealings with de Quadra. Clearly his efforts to be seen as a defender of Protestantism had not worked in all quarters. Muttering grew about court, and none would believe me, of course, when I said loud and clear I was not about to marry Robin.

I did not need rumour of marriage with Robin to add to my problems. He was unpopular in England, and although rumours of our marriage had aided me before to side-step other proposals, I did not want to be so closely associated with him now. I decided to take steps. I wanted my people to think I was bent on marrying another. This would halt all those thrusting Katherine Grey under my nose, and would remove the stain of Robert's present reputation from me. I needed to resurrect a suitor, and I needed help. In secret, I met with Kat and one of my maids, Dorothy Bradbelt. It was not challenging to meet in secret with my ladies. My Bedchamber was their domain, and they ruled over its privacy as lionesses, for within those chambers I was theirs, as they were mine.

"I need you to help me to resurrect the alliance with Sweden," I said to them as they sat with dice ready to play and coin ready to wager. I spoke in a low tone. I did not want everyone to hear.

"You would accept Erik of Sweden, Majesty?" Dorothy asked, surprised, and I smiled at her innocence. I liked Dorothy and trusted her. She had previously served me as a chamberer when I was under house arrest in various palaces during my sister's reign. Recently I had rewarded her long service by making her one of my Ladies of the Presence Chamber. Since she was not of noble birth, it would not have been fitting to immediately elevate her to the Bedchamber, where the most important positions were, but she was young and had time to rise further. Dorothy was responsible for caring for the various beasts that inhabited my chambers, my lapdogs, my parrot and Gardiner, the little ape. She had an affinity with animals, able with a calm or sharp word to call them to order.

"Actually, I intend nothing of the sort, Dorothy," I said, still smiling as I glanced at Kat's soft-smirking face. "But I want you two to make it appear as though I do, if you understand me?"

Dorothy's brow furrowed. "I am afraid I do not understand, Majesty."

I beckoned them closer. "Then lean in, Dorothy, and I shall tell you all that I want you and Kat to do to help me."

"Majesty…" Dorothy hesitated, but there was an edge of excitement in her hushed voice. "Did you not say when we were initiated into your household that we were forbidden to play with politics?"

I grinned. "I did, Dorothy… But you are *also* sworn to do all that I ask of you, are you not?" She nodded and I continued. "Then allow me to temporarily relieve you of one oath, in preference of another. For when your Queen orders you to serve as her soldier in the secret wars of court, Mistress Bradbelt, then serve you shall."

As before, when I had used Mary Sidney to encourage de Quadra to believe I longed for marriage with the Archduke Charles, so now I formed a plan with my ladies to breathe new life into the idea of a union with Erik of Sweden. If there was a chance that I would marry and breed, then my men would cease to talk of Katherine Grey. If I was thought to be in love with Erik, then Robin's unpopularity could affect me no more. I just needed my spies to trip forth from my chambers, and sow discord and confusion with their merry and talented tongues.

Chapter Thirty-Six

Greenwich Palace
Summer 1562

"We have written to the Swedish ambassador, Nils," Kat whispered into my ear as she hung a necklace of coral beads and diamonds about my neck. "And have informed him that your Majesty is *most* keen for the match with Erik to go ahead, but draws back from opening discussion due to your delicate feminine modesty."

I snorted indelicately, giving lie to that famous delicacy of mine I so often heard about. "People will believe anything of a woman, will they not, Kat?" I murmured, barely moving my lips. "It seems to me that as long as whatever is said makes no sense, men will believe it of a woman."

"More to our advantage than disadvantage here, my lady," Kat observed, pretending to play with the clasp to keep her lips close to my ear. "And you yourself have often used such ploys, playing on your sex to your advantage."

"That does not mean I have to like it, Kat," I sniffed. "A soldier may lift a rock to break the skull of his foe, but he would rather bear a sword. We must use what we can to survive, that is the only honest truth."

"Then I would urge your Majesty to be most girlish and whim-some in response when Nils writes to you," Kat said dryly. "And there is another element we have added, Majesty. John and I have a friend named John Dymock, a London jewel merchant."

"I know the man," I said, turning this way and that to admire the necklace in the mirror. "He came last year with jewels to tempt me."

"He is at court again, and bound for Sweden after this visit," Kat said. "I have advised him to show you jewels intended for the King of Sweden, Majesty, to allow you to publicly demonstrate you may be interested in Erik as a husband."

"In what way?"

Kat walked around to my front, apparently intent on examining the set of the necklace against my white skin. "Oh... I am *sure* Your Majesty will find a way," she said, putting a hand to the necklace and adjusting it.

"Your faith in me is gratifying."

Kat grinned. "My faith in your abilities is endless, Elizabeth."

Later that week Dymock came to court. In his vast selection of fabulous jewels there was a large, rather splendid ruby. I took it in my hands, keeping an eye on the full Presence Chamber as they watched me admire its quality by holding it up to the light. "A beautiful gem," I noted and then sighed, handing it back. "But I cannot possibly afford such baubles, however much I might desire them."

Primed by Kat, Dymock smiled and bowed. "I am bound for the Court of Sweden, Your Majesty," he said, his bright eyes narrowing. "Perhaps I might suggest to King Erik that he purchase the jewel for you, as a token of love and friendship."

"If it should chance that the King and I were to be married," I said loudly, chuckling. "Then it would be said that a liberal and generous King were joined with a niggardly princess! You do not think King Erik would think ill of me, do you, sir?"

"The King, as all know, has long been enamoured of Your Majesty. I am sure it would be a great pleasure for him to purchase this jewel as a gift for you."

"It takes a good man to act for his lady's interests," I said. "And I have only ever heard fine reports of the King. I hope you will send my warm regards to him. I was quite taken with his latest poem. It caused a fluttering in my heart so loud that for a while I believed I was taken ill… and perhaps I was. Perhaps I was heart-sick, for him."

I talked excitedly to Dymock about Erik, and gave him a pair of fine velvet gloves, one of my best mastiffs, and a French translation of Castiglione's *The Book of the Courtier*, to take with him as presents for Erik. It was enough to ignite furious conversation in the Presence Chamber that day, and later, the only gossip at court was about my fresh interest in Erik. Within a day, the city of London was on fire with speculation. Protestant members of my Council were pleased. Catholics were worried.

Dymock sent back letters from Erik when he reached Sweden, all filled with declarations of love and joy to hear I was considering him anew. Two jewels, one of them the fabulous ruby, and a portrait of the young man arrived after. Holding the ruby in my hands, I was pleased that even if these talks were going nowhere, I had at least profited from them. I wore the ruby about court, took hold of it and sighed. Everyone believed I was overcome with love.

Kat and Dorothy were hard at work in those late summer months, spreading rumours that I had spoken of the Swedish King's appearance with warm approval, and was indeed considering giving up my virgin state. Pleased to imagine I had finally seen sense, my men stopped pestering me about Katherine Grey, and the rumours about Robin and me died away. Encouraged by the apparent about-turn of their mistress, the court lapsed into a period where all that was talked of was love. Love poems were traded, passed about, and made into songs. Masques became flush with tales of romance and devotion. Robin went about with a face like a spoilt lapdog left out in the rain.

As more serious talks of marriage got underway, and my Council proposed inviting Erik to England, I decided enough was enough. I had no wish for Erik to actually visit England. I had to end this deception, and end it carefully. I instructed Kat to send letters to Nils, letters I knew would be intercepted by Cecil. The letters urged Erik to visit England so that he and I could meet but were clearly sent from Kat and Dorothy, not from me. "You will have to take the blame, as we discussed when first this was put into motion," I said to Kat and Dorothy. "But have no fear. When the storm has passed, you will be rewarded."

Cecil came to my chambers that same night to inform me he had unearthed a *scandalous* plot within my own household, and my own ladies were involved. How I wanted to laugh! "Whatever their intentions, Majesty..." he said, after revealing what Kat and Dorothy had been up to. "... And I do believe they intended good rather than ill, they have overstepped the mark. They have played with politics. These matters are for you and the Council to act upon, not mere ladies of court!" Cecil was regarding me with eyes heavy with suspicion, but I played my part well.

"This is *unbelievable*!" I shouted, rising with flushed cheeks and heated eyes. "That my own ladies would go against all I have impressed upon them!"

"They can be dismissed for this, Majesty." Those eyes were close on me as I raged about my chamber. My wily Cecil clearly believed I might be involved in this plot.

"You will write *this night* to Chancellor Nils Gyllenstierna and tell him his informants are idle cheats who spin falsehoods!" I cried, rounding on Cecil as though I were furious. "Confine Mistress Bradbelt to her quarters and send Mistress Ashley to me! I will have none of this!"

Cecil left to carry out my orders, his brow still dark with suspicion. When Kat arrived, I sent all others from the chamber, closed the door and shouted loud and long at my Chief Lady of the Bedchamber. I complained, I screamed, I upbraided her, I called her names and insulted her... even as Kat knelt, doubled up with laughter, crying weakly and pushing her handkerchief into her mouth to conceal the sound of her mirth. I censured her so all outside could hear me and all the time I scolded Kat, I had a huge grin upon my face.

How I kept from spoiling the whole performance and bursting into gales of laughter, I will never know. Outside of the chamber, all those listening at the door were convinced I was livid with Kat. There were rumours she and Dorothy would be sent away for good, and wagers started on who would replace them. For the sake of appearances, both were banished from court, but it was the shortest punishment ever I doled out. Within two weeks, Kat and Dorothy were back in my service, and no more was said. I told Cecil this was due to my high regard for both women. I told him they had shown due penance and sorrow for acting without my permission. I doubt he believed me.

Marriage talks with Sweden still went on, although with less vigour than before. The plan had worked and I made many secret, generous gifts to my loyal women for helping me to confuse and bamboozle my court once again.

Chapter Thirty-Seven

Hampton Court
Autumn 1562

We came to Hampton Court and I was in high spirits. The brightness in my soul reflected keenly against the darkness in Robin's, for since talks about marriage with Sweden had resumed, he had become morose. But I could not worry on that now. Robin had proved more a liability than a love in these past months.

Hampton was glorious that autumn. The trees in the park glowed with red fire and golden warmth. The gardens my father had transformed in the year of my birth were infused with the last glory of the end of summer. I ordered my horses brought out often, so I could ride and hunt in the parks.

In my Presence Chamber at Hampton the court would gather; thronging and milling amidst tapestry, pearl-covered tablecloths and milling before my throne of rich brown velvet, embroidered with golden thread and encrusted with diamonds. Over my head hung a canopy of estate, bearing the royal arms of England and studded with huge pearls and diamonds. It had been made for my father. I liked to use items my father had used in his lifetime. They gave me a link to him which was important, not only for my own standing, but also just because they reminded me of him. Next door to the Presence Chamber was the library, where many glorious books were stored. Maids removed dust and dirt from them each day with brushes made of horse hair. In here there were also curiosities, some that my father had collected, and some that had come to me as gifts. There was a chess set of alabaster, a jewelled water clock, a walking stick made from the horn of a unicorn, and a magical cup which would break if poison was poured into it.

The palace had many conveniences, such as lead piping which brought fresh spring water to the kitchens, brewhouses and to my rooms. My bathroom was covered with glazed and decorated tiles from roof to ceiling, and had a little stove in it, which, when fed with coal and water, allowed the room to fill with steam. On cold days I would sit in here with my ladies, in naught but our undergarments, breathing in the good, thick steam and relishing the sensation of all our bodily ills being drawn out by the hot vapours.

The weather was clement and I took to the park with my ladies. Robin and Thomas Heneage joined us, and we made merry in the falling light of the season. But as we gloried in the beauty of the autumn, all talk in Council was of war. I had agreed to send troops to support the Huguenots but it did not sit easily with me. "*Support* is all it will be, my lords," I said grimly, tapping my fingers on the piled parchments my men had gathered. "Support to give the Huguenots a chance against the Guise. This is not our war, and I think it important to remember that."

"The Mother of the King has ceased to talk to her Huguenot subjects, Majesty," Cecil said. "Which does not allow talks of peace to resume. There is no chance to reconcile the two sides now. War has come and must be fought."

"I don't believe for a moment Catherine de Medici is any fonder of the Guise and their Catholic supporters than I, Cecil, even if she shares a faith with them... and will you stop calling her that? *The Mother of the King...* what a ridiculous title! The only reason that Medici woman uses it is because it takes longer to say and so she thinks it gives her more authority! Call her what you need to on diplomatic papers, *Spirit*, but in here she is either Catherine de Medici or the Dowager. Those titles will do her well enough!"

Pembroke and many of the others chuckled, but Robin had been rather quiet. "You say little today, my lord," I noted, turning to him. "Do you have no opinion? You asked again to attend Council… was it for no reason, then?"

"I am delighted we are *at last* to send support to our Protestant brothers and sisters, Majesty, and that you have put your trust in my good brother, Ambrose, to lead your troops," Robin replied, making me groan inwardly.

This play-acting of Robin's, trying to reform himself into a guardian angel of Protestants, was wearisome. He thought he could restore his reputation by doing so, and perhaps he was right, but I would have welcomed a real opinion, not one fabricated to win supporters. In truth, Robin wore his faith light about his shoulders. Mistake me not, Robin loved God and honoured Him, but he would have been happy enough to worship as a Catholic or Protestant. But since the affair with de Quadra had come out, Robin had made a public change from a measured way of seeing religion, and was edging towards becoming a zealot. I despised fanatics and hardly wanted one at my side every day.

"Well the six thousand troops we are sending with your brother in command, along with hundred and forty thousand crowns should support them well." My mouth twisted as I considered the sum. That money would have had more use for my own people.

"The Huguenot leaders have sent word that they will grant you La Havre as a pledge, Majesty, until they can return Calais." Cecil looked up from his notes. "But they promise they *will* return Calais, as soon as they have taken it from the Catholics."

"Then there will be something to cheer my heart, *Spirit*," I said unhappily. "Let us hope that with our intervention the Crown will open talks again, and promote peace."

"The King and… his *mother*…" Cecil grinned as I flashed him a look, reminding him not to use the title Catherine de Medici had made up. "… Seem resolute to remain impartial in the war, Majesty, a most unusual situation when the Crown will not support either side in a civil war."

"You mean the Medici snake is waiting to see which side looks set to win before she picks a bed to slither into," I interjected, making Pembroke guffaw. "I don't believe she is impartial for a moment, Cecil. She pauses to gain advantage, and I don't believe Conde, Coligny or the Guise believe her either. They know well of what she is made."

"Of course, Majesty… I but pass on what is in the papers from France."

"Is Throckmorton home yet?" We had called him back. With England planning to intervene in France, and even with the royal family adopting a position of neutrality in the war, it would be inadvisable to have him at the French Court much longer.

"He will come soon, Majesty," Pembroke said. "He wrote and said he had a few loose ends to secure before making for England."

"Good enough," I said, putting my hands to the table and rising. "Muster the troops and make ready to sail. I will give the final order for our forces to leave England when we are ready."

"Your Majesty is also aware of the outbreak of smallpox at court?" Cecil asked as the others rose. "I have commanded that none who have been near the sickness will be allowed to attend upon you, and none who have suffered and recovered are to come to court for at least a month. Some are not pleased with my sanctions, but…"

"They are important sanctions, Cecil, and will be upheld. We can have no one spreading the sickness."

My men left, carrying various orders with them. I heaved a sigh, once more thinking I did not want to be involved in this war. But still, the amounts of men and coin, although large, were hardly enough to win a war. They would give the Huguenots a chance against the vastly better armed and prepared Catholics. And who knew? If they won, France might become a Protestant ally. I was still thinking uncomfortable thoughts later that week, however. The men were gathered, the arms prepared, the ships were ready... all was prepared for the English to cross the Channel and enter France. And then, I almost destroyed the hopes and dreams of my men. I almost denied the Huguenots their support. I almost brought chaos upon my country.

Death was at my door. Not knowing He was there, I opened it and let Him in.

Chapter Thirty-Eight

Hampton Court
Autumn 1562

It started with a pain in my head and another in my belly. At first, I thought little of these pains. Recently, I had found I was subject to many aches. I put these new ones down as another sign of my youth deserting me.

We do not believe, when we are young, there will come a day when our bodies will turn against us. We believe every day will follow much as the day before; that we will awake with full and bright health, zest and vim always in our bones and blood. But recently, I had become aware this was a fiction born of inexperience. As I grew older, parts of my body I had little thought on before wanted to make me suffer. Restless nights brought on headaches and lack of appetite sapped my energy. My teeth pained me often and my back and shoulders were at times determined to rebel against me.

I was hardly old, being twenty-nine, but I was coming to understand there was more to growing older than simply gaining wisdom or grey hairs. I seemed to gain aches at the same rate as experience. And it was not the case anymore that there needed to be a *reason* for a pain to develop. When I was young, there was always a reason for pain… Now, I could simply wake up to find a part of my body wished to hurt me. I could do something as slight as bending to tie a shoe ribbon, and find I had pulled my back, or wrenched my shoulder. No one tells you this as you grow older. It had come as an unpleasant surprise, although when I complained to Kat, I had received an annoying, knowing grin in response.

So when a pain in my head arrived and would not leave, and an accompanying ache began in my belly, I did not send for my doctors right away. I sipped plain broth, and watered ale. I tried to rest, thinking this would ease the pain in my head, but after several days, and as the pains increased, I gave in and sent for my physicians. At first, they did not think much of it either. They bled me, gave me pills and bitter herbs and I wrote a letter to my cousin in Scotland, but had to cut it short as I started to feel increasingly unwell. I took a bath, and followed it with a bracing walk through Hampton's park, thinking I had lingered too long in the dull confines of the palace and this was affecting my heath. When I returned, Kat stared in horror at my bright, flushed cheeks and glassy eyes, and sent me straight to bed.

"There is nothing wrong with me, Kat," I protested as she all but tore my clothes from me and ushered me into the glorious bed, calling for warming pans and for the fire to be stoked. But as I got under the sheets, a violent chill shuddered through me, and I was suddenly glad of the warm covers. "Well, perhaps just for today," I said, shivering under my blankets as I pulled them up to my neck.

But the next day I did not rise at all.

The chill settled into my bones. I ran hot and then cold, sweating profusely, then shivering so hard my teeth rattled in my head. Grievous pains of the belly assailed me so I could not rest. I lay doubled up in misery and pain. My hands shook when I tried to lift a cup to my mouth. My fingers were numb, but my face was flushed scarlet with prickly, uncomfortable heat. I could not sleep, and yet could not stay awake. I drifted in a state between sleep and waking, muttering as I saw shadows race before me. When I awoke properly, hours later, Kat and Blanche were at my bedside, their faces wan.

My doctors were at a loss. They believed they saw symptoms of the dreaded smallpox, and yet there were no physical signs; no blemishes or spots. A German physician, much respected at court, was sent for, and he too said it was the pox.

"But I have no spots!" I cried out, and then fell to coughing which hurt my head. "See?" I held out my white, unmarked arms to Doctor Burcot who looked at me with steady eyes.

"Sometimes the affliction does not *immediately* present on the skin, Majesty," he said in a patronising manner that made me angry.

"Then why call it the *pox*?" I shouted. "Remove this knave from my chambers! Clearly he knows nothing! Bring me proper doctors!" Burcot was removed. Muttering darkly about the rudeness of the Queen of England, he left the chambers in high dudgeon. My remaining doctors started treating me for a simple fever, perhaps caught when I walked in the park after taking a bath, they said.

"The warm bath opened the pores of your skin, Majesty," one explained. "And then your walk in the cold air allowed a wandering fever to enter your body. You should not take such dire risks. Bathing during the autumn or winter can be perilous."

"I have bathed, winter or summer, all my life," I rasped. My throat was on fire.

"But you are older now, Majesty. The years take their toll."

That was not likely to please me. No matter if I admitted the years creeping up on me to myself, I did not want others observing this. I think he realised by my livid expression it might be ill-advised to continue to talk of my age in relation to my illness. Although my face was pallid and drawn, it did not damage the impact of the dark anger in my black eyes as I glowered at him.

After another day, I was glowering no longer. I had not the energy to speak or open my eyes. My ladies could not rouse me fully. I could hear them, but I could not respond. My skin was alive with prickles and itching, as though it were infested with thousands of tiny, crawling, scratching spiders. My flesh roasted upon my bones. I called out in pain and cried out as shadows crept upon me, hunting me in my half-dreams. My tongue was dry and my head a hideous riot of noise and screaming.

When I was able to open my eyes, I stared out at the world with glassy, unclear vision. I saw shapes around me, but knew not who they were. I recoiled from hands that tried to touch me, shrinking from them. I could hear muttering, and yet knew not from where it came. I slipped from consciousness, and fell into a world of nightmares. My fevered dreams brought forth monsters to hunt me through the dark tunnels of my imagination. Scaly hands touched me. They sought to lift my nightshift, to abuse me, to rape me. I screamed, flailing about, my covers wrapped around me in knots like a thousand hands trying to hold me down. I know not how long I battled through that horrible world of demons. After a while, I lost the ability to fight them. I lost my courage and what strength I had left and collapsed into a sleep so deep, that when I awoke, gazing blearily about me, my ladies almost fell at my side, relieved I had not died.

"What is going on?" I croaked as Kat pressed a cup of boiled herb-water to my cracked lips. I sipped and then coughed the mixture up again, soiling the bedcovers. I felt faint. Even lying in bed, prostrate, I was dizzy. The world would not fall into focus. I knew then I was truly sick unto death.

"You are sick, my sweet," Kat murmured, her voice thick with tears. "But we are going to make you well again."

At the edge of my vision, I could just about see Cecil's pallid face. Everything that was not right before my eyes was shadow and shade. I seemed to see people moving in the darkness… People who were not, could not, be there. I could catch the black snap of my mother's eyes floating behind Cecil. I saw a glimpse of my father's red hair. I saw Parry, standing with that steady expression he always wore on his face. Little Jane Seymour laughed at his side… There was Amy Dudley, stood with her hands about her throat, staring at me with goggled eyes bulging from her head. The ghosts of my past had come to flock about me. For a while I blinked and stared at them, not knowing whether to be afraid of them or not. As I gaped, my sister stepped forward, her arm entwined with my brother's. Mary lifted her hand, and beckoned to me. I screamed, looking over Cecil's shoulder and pointing at the beckoning form of my ghostly sister. Cecil and my women ran to me, blocking out the sight of those phantoms, but even so, it was a while before I was calm enough to lie flat and still.

"*Spirit*," I wheezed as hands forced me back on the bed. "Do not let these ghosts take me. They want me, Cecil… They want me to go to them." I do not think he knew what I was speaking of, for only I could see these shades of my past.

"Your Majesty has been very ill," Cecil said. I blinked at him, seeing his face flicker and distort. "We must make preparation, Majesty… in case you do not recover."

"Am I dying, Cecil?" My voice was faint. I did not sound like me.

Cecil nodded, and I was amazed to see his eyes overflow with tears. "Majesty… we must make preparation for England, for the succession."

"I am dying." I lay back on my covers and Kat flapped forwards.

"You are *not* dying, Elizabeth!" she exclaimed, throwing a blazing look at Cecil. "I will not *let* you die!"

"Peace, Kat... peace," I pleaded. Her cries hammered in my aching head. "I must think of England... of my people." Members of my Privy Council appeared from nowhere, and gathered beside Cecil. They were dressed in black, as though I were already dead.

"I do not want to die." The words came from me as though a child spoke. The voice was tiny, helpless. Several of my men broke down, turning their faces from me as grief and fear overcame them. I felt tears on my own cheeks, but I could not feel them falling from my eyes. I stared up at them, my unfocused eyes begging them to help me. My men looked at each other, and then began to talk over each other.

"None of the doctors even know what this illness is!" Pembroke exploded in frustration.

"None will commit to any remedies!" called another.

"We must bring them *all* here and have them all work on the Queen until they find what this is! By God's Holy Spirit! It must be *something*!" Robin's voice; breaking with sorrow, harsh with impotent rage. I held out a hand.

"Robin?" I asked, my eyes closed. Their shouting was hurting my head. If I opened my eyes, I believed they would bleed. His warm hand clasped about my own, and his weight came down upon the bed beside me. Soft lips kissed my hand.

"Do not..." I whispered. "Do not... You will put yourself in danger, Robin... I could never live knowing I had done you harm." There was a noise from my side, a choking sound, as Robin sank into helpless tears. I managed to open my heavy eyes, and saw him bent over, holding my hand. Cecil had his hand on Robin's back, trying to comfort him. "Robin..." I croaked. "You must marry... with another... you must go on to have children. When I am gone...."

I did not get to finish my speech of noble sentiment.

"Do not speak so, Elizabeth!" Robin roared, rising from the bed, his eyes flashing about, filled with wildness and desperation. "Do none of the doctors here know what is wrong with the Queen? Do none have any skill?"

"Doctor Burcot said he believed the illness to be smallpox," Mary Sidney answered. "But there are no spots or pustules..."

"Get him back here now!" Robin demanded, turning on Lord Hunsdon who stood nearby. "Bring him here!"

"He will not come," said Kat. "Her Majesty sent him away, and called him a knave. He said he would never return after being so insulted."

Robin faced Hunsdon. "*Drag* the man here if you must!" he ordered. With a grim face, Hunsdon left the chamber, shouting for his men to follow him.

"You *will* recover, my love," Robin whispered, sitting on the bed and taking my hand. "You will."

Doctor Burcot arrived perhaps an hour later, looking utterly terrified. I heard later he had refused to come, and Hunsdon had drawn a dagger on him, threatening the doctor with a painful, lingering and bloody death if he did not attend upon me. Burcot set to work. Laying a blissfully cool hand to my face, he ordered everyone out but Kat and Mary Sidney, who refused to leave. Burcot had taken Hunsdon's threats to heart, for the pace he set was confounding to watch. I admit, I was hardly in a lucid state, but all the same, the doctor seemed to move as though the Devil Himself were at his elbow. Burcot wrapped me in red flannel, lifted me from the bed as I weakly protested, and set me before a roaring fire in the chambers. The hot fire burned against my fevered skin. I feebly tried to remove myself from its heat, but Burnet held me firm in the chair.

"Drink!" he ordered in his guttural English, thrusting a potion into my hands. I could not take the cup; it slid from my feeble grasp. Kat caught it and fed it to me, little by little. Within an hour, the awful wheals and pimples of smallpox rose upon my white skin. I recoiled from them in horror. To my fevered mind, I had become one of the scaly devils of my nightmares. Mary Sidney, too, gazed at me in dismay. Even if one recovered from smallpox, its spots often left disfiguring marks on the skin, marring beauty and making even the most striking of people into fearsome demons. Mary Sidney put a cloth to my head as I sweated before the fire, weeping half for fear of dying, and half for the loss of any beauty I may once have had. "I am a monster," I mourned, my mouth slack, dribble melding with the tears running down my face. "I am a monster."

"The sickness *must* be drawn out of the body," Burnet said, regarding my distress with calm control. "Inside the body, it is more dangerous. Now we can see it, Majesty, we can fight it."

But even if the sickness had shown itself, I was still dangerously ill. I hovered between life and death for several days, and eventually, fearing that I was to die, my men came again, gathering about the bed to hear my commands for my realm after my death.

"Lord Robert Dudley will be appointed Lord Protector of England until such a time as a new monarch is chosen by God," I muttered. I was only half conscious, but in the darkness of my dreams, there had been only one man I believed I could trust to act as I would have done for England. Cecil would make my country into a state only for Protestants. He would put Katherine Grey or her son on my throne. The others were not qualified to lead as I knew Robin could, if he were given the chance. Even in my delirium, I knew none but Norfolk would accept Mary of Scots.

"Lord Robin Dudley will govern this realm when I am dead. And I would have all know that whilst I love and admire Lord Robin as I do no other, nothing unseemly has ever passed between us. He will act as I would for the good of England. He will cherish and nurture my people, with you, my lords, at his side to advise him." My lips burbled. I hardly heard what I was saying.

There was shocked silence. Cecil was lost for words. They agreed to honour my wishes, perhaps because no one wanted to distress me further in my perilous state. When my men left and Burcot returned, he found me trying to focus my hazy eyes on my skin. When I let out another sob, he grew angry. "God's pestilence!" the man exploded. "Which is better? To have a pox on the hands or in the face, or in the *heart* where it will fester and kill the whole body? Think not on vanity, Majesty, but of the wellness of your body!"

Sensible advice. But I was not really listening. I stared blankly at him and then sank into the bedcovers to sleep. When I awoke, Burcot was shouting at Cecil instead of me. "The spots are a *good* sign!" Burcot ran his hands through his hair. "They show the worst is over. The pustules will dry and fall off, and with them this fever will fall from the Queen's blood."

"You mean… the Queen will recover?" Cecil's voice was desperate. He did not want to hand England over to Robin.

"If there are no complications and *if* the patient will listen to her doctor!"

But no matter his exasperation with me, Burcot's methods worked. The next day my head felt clearer. I took some broth and drank a great deal of watered ale. The day after that I could sit up in bed, inspecting the spots which covered my skin with anxious horror. Within a week, my fever had broken. The hideous dreams ceased to plague me. When I slept, it was dreamless and peaceful. My headache drifted away as did the pain in my belly. Within a week, I was almost myself again.

And the spots did as Burcot said they would; dried, scabbed and fell away. He bound cloth about my hands to keep me from scratching at the itchy sores, and doused me all over with a thick camomile balm. As they healed, I noted with great relief that few had left scars. There were some marks, here and there on my body, but those would be covered by my clothing. There were some light scars on my neck, and a few on my face, but Burcot assured me I was lucky, and he would give me an ointment to apply to my skin which would cause the marks to fade if I used it each night.

"You are fortunate to be alive," he muttered after telling my ladies all they could do to help my skin heal. "Your Majesty should be grateful for that!"

"I am grateful for *you*, good doctor," I said. "Without you I would have died. You were generous enough to return even after I insulted you. I am sorry for what I said. I should not have treated you so rudely. Anything you wish of me, you shall have."

The good doctor looked pacified, and even chuckled. "Never have I had a more difficult patient," he admitted. "And never have I been brought to the bed of a patient by the sharp point of a dagger! But at least it shows, Majesty, how deeply your men love you. Lord Hunsdon was ready to kill me if I refused."

"Then I will reward him even as I reward you." I smiled weakly. "And you will become a court physician, doctor, with a pension, if you will accept it. I owe you my life."

"Well," he said, a becoming cherry blush spreading over his wide cheekbones. "It is pleasing to know I did some good, Majesty."

I only allowed Robin and Cecil to visit me as I recovered from the pox as I did not want rumours to grow that I was unsightly, and I knew I could trust these two to guard the reputation of my appearance.

"Am I repulsive, Robin?" I asked as I glanced at the healing scabs on my face using a hand glass.

"You are beautiful, my love," he said, coming to sit on the bed.

"And you are a liar," I laughed. "Look at this face, Robin! I am covered in horrible, scabby sores! You cannot look on me now and say I am a beauty."

He kissed my hand, his expression warm and loving. "I look on you with the eyes of love, Elizabeth, and I am glad that you are here, alive, and with me still. I care not for some flaking skin and itching flesh. I care only for you and your happiness."

"At least you admit to the existence of these unsightly sores, Robin, or else I might have thought those eyes of love had rendered you blind!" I sighed, putting the glass to one side and resisting the impulse to scratch. "The Council were surprised when I made you Lord Protector?"

Robin chuckled. "I think *surprised* is too weak a word, Majesty," he grinned ruefully. "Cecil told everyone that you were in a fever and you had clearly lost your mind."

"I was in a fever," I agreed. "But my mind was clear. Whatever has passed between us, Robin, I know you love England as I do. I know that had you been offered the position, you would have made a good Protector."

"Then I am as flattered by your fevered assessment of me as by your calm one," he replied. "But I would not want that position, Majesty, for it would mean I had lost you. Coming so close to losing you, Elizabeth… It put so many of our late troubles into clear relief. I have been a fool. I treated you badly. Mistress Ashley was quick to point out that I should have been consoling you rather than opposed to you after you lost Parry. She pointed out a *great* deal, in her anguish. Much I did not want to hear, but that I needed to. I have been a fool, Elizabeth… I wonder that you have had the patience you have shown when dealing with me."

"You are *my* fool, Robert Dudley." I smiled, leaning forward to put my cloth-bound hands against his face. I felt my love for him might suffocate me. If I had to go through another illness, another brush with Death, I would have done so happily to bring my Robin back to me.

"Do not seek to make me Lord Protector again." He kissed my palm, sending shivers down my spine. "I would be lost and alone in the darkness, without you."

We sat and played at cards and chess on my bed as I recovered. Robin told me tales of what went on at court, and danced with my ladies to entertain me. I was a few weeks in my bed, and my Privy Council had to be brought to me. My ladies were diligent, and in my weakened state I had no chance to escape Kat and Blanche as they constantly, relentlessly, pushed food down my throat. I gave in. It was, in truth, pleasing to have them all show how much they loved me. I ate better in the weeks after I escaped Death than I had done for over a year.

But even as we rejoiced that I was well, Mary Sidney, Robin's sister, fell ill with smallpox. She had caught it from me after refusing to leave my side during my illness. She suffered now for her loyalty to me. When I was well enough to walk, I went to her. My men were not at all happy, thinking

I might catch the illness again, but Burcot assured me that now I had had the sickness, I would not suffer from it again.

Mary's chambers were in almost complete darkness as I entered. I sat at the side of her bed and as she looked up, I had trouble controlling my face. I stared at the vision before me in dumb horror. Mary's fever had broken, she was out of danger, but her beautiful face had been ravaged. By the light of one candle I saw the edge of one of her upper eye lids was folded down and pinned to her cheek. Her once-clear skin was torn by silver-red scars. Her face was a mottled crater where red blood mingled with glaring white chalk. She smiled sadly. "Worry not, Majesty," she whispered. "I have seen what it has done to me."

"Oh, Mary…" I dissolved into tears. To see her made so frightful, when once she had been so very beautiful was horrific, and she had caught this in caring for me, in serving me! "I am so sorry, Mary."

"When Phillip returns from his mission abroad," she whispered, "I will not let him see me without a veil. I would have him remember me as I was, not as I am now."

"You are still beautiful." I pressed my hands about hers and kissed her warm skin. "For the light which shines from your soul has no comparison."

We sat together for some time. She wanted to leave court, but I persuaded her to remain, for I did not want to lose her. She gave in to my demands somewhat, but spent a lot of time away from court in the years that followed. She could not bear the staring eyes of those who tried to glimpse the monster hidden under her veil. For the rest of her days, Mary Sidney wore a deep, dark veil over her maimed face, but she continued to serve me loyally and faithfully. I made a promise to myself that I would never forget her sacrifice. Unfortunately, and to my deep shame, over the years that followed I would not always treat this dear woman as she deserved.

When I recovered, I gave Robin a permanent place on my Privy Council. He had sent Hudson to Burcot, and that had saved my life. No one put up too much of a protest. They were evidently so relieved I was alive that I could have ordered anything at that time and got away with it.

The pox marks on my face faded, but scars remained. From then on I had to wear a thicker layer of the cosmetics I used on my skin; powder of alabaster, puffed over a paste of almond milk, egg and white lead, hid most of my scars. I hardly wanted anyone to look on the marks of smallpox and believe I was instead marred by sores of syphilis. I had enough ambassadors and princes willing to make trouble for me without adding a question over my reputation. With my face covered in paint, my thinning hair concealed by wigs, my lithe body presented in marvellous gowns, and my lips painted red with crushed rose petals, I could appear as though I were still a girl of eighteen, rather than a woman nearing thirty years of age.

It was trickery, of course it was, but a queen must be magnificent before her people. I needed no further rumour of my death to surface. My people were wild with joy to hear that I had triumphed over Death. They had feared what would come if I died, and my salvation from Death was heralded as a direct intervention from God. It was good that I had their love and devotion, for I had enough problems, and they were not over yet.

My cousin Katherine had prepared a surprise for me. It was not a welcome one.

Chapter Thirty-Nine

Whitehall Palace
Autumn - Winter 1562

Whilst I lay sick unto death, three men were discovered plotting against me. Discovered in their treachery, they tried to make for France, but were captured and put in the Tower. Planning to depose me, and place Mary of Scots on my throne, Arthur and Edmund Pole, and their brother-in-law, Anthony Fortescue, were charged with treason. When questioned, they revealed that the Catholic Guise, Ambassador de Quadra and Phillip of Spain were all involved. When I recovered, and Cecil informed me of this, I wrote to Phillip, telling him that should his ambassador interfere with English affairs again, I would send him back to Spain in disgrace.

Whilst they had been laying their plans for some time, these plotters had been spurred to action by my illness. Thinking I was about to die, they had revealed themselves and Cecil moved on them. Under interrogation they swore they only intended to bring an army into England when I died. They had been taking the advice of a Catholic necromancer and alchemist who told them I would be long dead before their plans came to fruition.

"They will face trial, Cecil," I said. "And I will consider what is to be done with them when the verdict comes back."

"They should be executed, Majesty," said Cecil. "They were set to bring a foreign army into England and put your cousin on the throne."

"I know what they did, Cecil," I said, waving him away.

Whatever else I experienced from this ill news, it made me less regretful about intervening in France. If I could give the Duke of Guise any trouble, then I was glad of it.

A few days later, all gladness was ripped from my soul.

*

"What do you mean, the Lady Katherine Grey is with child again?" I screamed at Cecil. "How has this happened when she is locked in the Tower and away from her husband? Tell me, Cecil, is this a miracle birth? Has an angel visited her?"

Cecil blanched at my blasphemy, but he did not confront me about it. He could see this was a dangerous moment. I could not believe what I was hearing. My cousin Katherine Grey was once more with child! How had this happened? She was a prisoner in the Tower still, as was her Ned… Had she played the jade with her jailers, then?

"It would seem, Majesty, her gaolers took pity on the couple and allowed them to meet on some evenings… and without a guard." Cecil took a step backwards as he watched my face turn purple.

"It is *Hertford's* child?"

"Apparently so, Your Majesty."

I had to try hard… very hard… not to fly at Cecil and unleash my anger on him. "What am I to say to that?" I asked him. "Who allowed this to happen?"

"Sir Edward Warner, Lieutenant of the Tower," Cecil answered. "I assure Your Majesty he is being dealt with most seriously."

"He will be dismissed of his post, immediately," I commanded. "And Hertford will stand trial before the Court of the Star Chamber. Their marriage was found to be null and void. He has therefore not only deflowered a virgin of the royal blood once, but now twice! You will set up new officers in the Tower, Cecil. I will not have those two meeting again, ever. And someone tell that girl I am seriously considering changing the laws surrounding the execution of pregnant women!"

"Majesty," Cecil agreed, removing himself from my presence as swiftly as he could.

For days I was almost insensible with rage. I paced about my chambers and on my early morning walks in the gardens, my face and form filled with wrath. Not only could I not believe that my own guards, my own Lieutenant of the Tower, had disobeyed my orders with such *breathtaking* arrogance, but I could not believe Katherine had succeeded in flouting me again! Pregnant! Again! Another bastard to add to her growing collection! Another child to throw in my face and taunt me with!

I ordered that Hertford and Katherine were never to see one another again, and this time I was going to be sure this was done. I would not have two prisoners defy me so openly. It made a mockery of my authority. And yet, I could not throw the girl into a cell as I wanted. I could not order her death, even though I could have arranged something once her child was born. Katherine would remain a prisoner for the rest of her life, and her children would suffer with her. No more would I allow visitations. Hertford would not see this child he and Katherine had made. Let that be his punishment for disobeying me! Let the couple ever be apart now they had defied me once more!

That November, I released the Lennoxes from prison and returned them to liberty and favour. Tensions were high, and Catholics were much suspected. Although they attended the Protestant Mass for the sake of appearances, Margaret and her sons were known Catholics. I believed setting them free might help to reassure Catholics hidden in my realm I was not after them *all*. This was my first reason. The second was that I could not stand to receive another letter of complaint from that damned, screeching harpy! I had given Margaret permission to write to me, for when I was in a similar situation and that right had been denied to me I had keenly resented it. I had not foreseen, however, that in giving this right to my cousin I would be bombarded by missives every dawn, noon, dusk and every hour in between. Margaret must have sent *hundreds* of letters. I could have used them to light every fire in every palace in England for a hundred years and still have enough to stuff a mattress. I could stand no more.

I had one final reason for releasing Margaret. With Katherine Grey pregnant once more, I wanted another English heir at liberty so that those who might think to support Katherine would have another to focus upon. It was true that Catholics tended to favour Margaret, and Protestants Katherine, but the claims of English blood held much sway, and I knew that in releasing Margaret I would add confusion to the succession discussion, and thereby, hopefully, split some of Katherine's supporters.

At first I had Margaret and Lennox kept under house arrest, but I soon allowed them permission to visit court. Margaret and Lennox swore a solemn oath never to attempt to marry their son to Mary of Scots, and although this was not nearly enough for Cecil, I decided it would do well enough for me... for now. Given the seriousness of the *many* charges against them, their release was remarkably tolerant, but the accusations of witchcraft had not been proved, nor had Margaret's dealings with de Quadra. And technically, since Darnley was my cousin, there was no crime in his mother attempting to marry him to Mary of Scots. The charges of imagining my death and calling me a bastard I chose to overlook, much to Margaret's relief.

The Lennoxes were eventually allowed back to their own estates, and given permission to visit court. Margaret continued to protest her innocence, and was not in the least humbled by her experience. I think she believed I could not, or would not dare, do anything against her, but she was wrong. I had no compunction about executing Margaret if I had to, if she posed a genuine threat to England or to me, and in many ways it would have removed a most irksome boil from my royal bottom to do so... But I was not about to do it without good reason. The executions of close family, friends and loved ones had eroded my father's soul, and haunted my sister's spirits. Besides, there were other ways to ensure Margaret's loyalty. I had her sons, Henry and Charles, brought to court permanently. They would be politely held hostages to secure their mother's good behaviour. Cecil also put her household under further observation. Forgive, I could. Forget, I would not.

As I struggled with one of my possible heirs, my cousin in Scotland was encountering fresh conflict all her own. Randolph wrote to inform me that Mary had foiled a plot to kidnap her. She had been having troubles with the Earl of Huntley. Huntley was a leading Catholic noble of the Gordon clan, an influential family who had managed the estates of Mar and Moray on behalf of the Crown for many years. Mary had grown annoyed with the Earl when he spoke out in opposition to our summit meeting, and her anger had only grown as Mary found more to dislike about Huntley.

Huntley felt cheated. He believed the estates his family had managed should have been granted to him, but upon her arrival back in Scotland, Mary had given them instead to her bastard half-brother, Lord James. Whilst on progress, Mary arrived at Aberdeen only to find Huntley had brought fifteen hundred retainers when all lords present were supposed to only bring one hundred. When she went on to Inverness, she found the captain, one of Huntley's men, had been instructed to bar her from the city.

You would have thought that a leading Catholic, who had been a great supporter of Mary of Guise, would have instinctively supported her daughter, but Huntley was a brash fool. Resentful that his Queen would not alter the religion of her country, troubled by her overtures of friendship to me and enraged she would not elevate him, Huntley decided to rebel. Mary responded with defiance. She elevated her bastard brother, now her best advisor, to the title of Earl of Moray that Huntley had coveted, rode to Inverness with a huge force of men, and took the city. She hung Huntley's captain from the city walls, but graciously spared those under his command. Mary set her eyes then on Huntley; she would find him and make him pay for his treachery.

As Mary rode back to Aberdeen, her party came under attack from Huntley's men. One of his young sons, Sir James Gordon, led the attack at the River Spey, thinking to overcome the young Queen's small forces, and take her prisoner so his father could command her actions and choices. But they were deceived. I laughed aloud when I read Randolph's report. Mary had realised Huntley was up to something, and whilst she rode with only two hundred men at her side, she had *three thousand* hidden in the forest. Gordon attacked with one thousand men, but as they charged the river, Mary's secret forces surged forth from their hiding places. Gordon's men faltered, turned, and then ran for their lives. The plot was foiled, my cousin was jubilant, and Huntley and his men went into hiding.

"That is how a *true* Queen acts, Cecil!" I crowed as I thrust the report under his nose. "Tell me now that Katherine Grey, that traitorous jade, is more suited to becoming my heir than my cousin of Scots! Read the missive, *Spirit*! My good sister of Scotland is proved a wily vixen amongst her Scottish foxes!" Even Cecil had to admit, grudgingly, that Mary had done well.

"Better than *well*, Cecil." I cackled like a merry witch. "To think, she had all those men hidden, and led her enemies into a trap!" I shook my head, marvelling at my cousin's adventure. How satisfying it must have been to see the expression of horror on her foes' faces!

Randolph had been with Mary when the attack came, and even though he was supposed to be a neutral party, being an ambassador, he had been so caught up in the excitement that he had taken to arms and rushed in with the rest to defend Mary. Cecil was not pleased to hear this, and although it was worrying, indicating that yet *another* ambassador had fallen for my cousin's charms, I was not displeased. Were I there, I believe I would have done the same. Mary had acted with wisdom, courage and fire. I had sometimes dismissed her in the past as hesitant and immature, but with this clever ruse Mary had shown herself to be a worthy queen.

My Council did not agree. They believed that her actions, and her victory, were due, in large part, to the intervention and advice of her brother, the new Earl of Moray. But men are often wont to *allow* a woman to be lucky if she succeeds, and ever cast about for the man who *must* have been responsible if she was clever. I did not think the same way.

Huntley retaliated by trying to attack Aberdeen. He wanted to murder Randolph and Maitland, who, as ambassadors, he saw as directly responsible for trying to bring Mary and me together as friends. He failed in both ambitions. With Mary's forces on their way to engage him, Huntley went on the run. My cousin hunted him through Scotland until his forces met hers at Corrichie. Outgunned and outnumbered, Huntley tried to flee, but he and two of his sons were captured. Sir James Gordon was executed with his brother at Aberdeen but Huntley decided to spare Mary the trouble of executing him herself, and suffered a fit upon his horse, losing the power of speech and dying a day later. His corpse was embalmed, and put on trial. With the coffin stood upright in court, he was tried and found guilty of treason. The corpse was condemned and his family estates were declared forfeit to the Crown.

Letters I had sent to Mary just before I fell ill arrived in Scotland as she celebrated her victory. Explaining my intervention in the war in France, I had laid out my position for my cousin, and also asked her to excuse the shortness of the letter as I was by that time already burning with fever. When Mary heard this, having suffered from the same illness when she was a child, she became distressed. She assured Randolph that after careful consideration, she had decided to be neutral in the affairs of France, and would no more offer her support to the Guise. She also said I had intervened for a 'godly cause', adding that the King of France would surely one day thank me for my actions on behalf of the Huguenots. Mary sent a letter, commiserating on my illness and enclosed, too, a bottle of a potion she had found beneficial. *"This potion helps to reduce the scarring of the smallpox,"* she wrote. *"I hope that my good sister will have the same success I did, and her beautiful face will remain un-marred by the echoes of this terrible sickness."*

Cecil would not let me have the bottle until it had been examined for poison. "Why would it aid her to kill me now, Cecil?" I asked as I furiously demanded the present. "And in such an obvious way? Do you really think the Queen of Scots would be so foolish as to *openly* send a bottle of poisoned potion to me?"

"Even if she would not, *others* may seek to use her gift against both you and her, Majesty," Cecil protested, refusing to give up the bottle. "It could have been intercepted. It could have been tampered with. You must be more careful, Majesty. We have already nearly lost you once!"

Cecil was furious at me for my lack of care, as he saw it, and perhaps he was right, but I was touched by Mary's gesture. It took a woman to truly understand what such a gift could mean. It took a woman to understand how valuable our looks can be in this hard world, where we are so often judged by what lies on our faces, rather than by our courage, strength, or spirit.

Unfortunately, after this happy gesture, Mary was taken to bed with a cold. She was ill, and it had not helped that her spirits had been brought low by learning that, when I was ill, only a single voice of my Privy Council had supported her as my successor. All others had refused to consider her. It seemed, no matter her virtues and obvious courage, my men did not warm to the Queen of Scots. There had been support for Katherine Grey and her son, which not only irked me, but disappointed me too. They would rather pick an infant, just because he was a male, than view Mary as my successor.

Chapter Forty

Richmond Palace
February 1603

Hope, trust, belief… We find them in unlikely places, we hold on to them in times of trial.

As I recovered from the smallpox, I found my position on the throne had altered. Brushing so close to Death, coming so close to losing my life, I wanted to set aside thoughts of my demise and concentrate on the future, but my Council, my nobles, my men… they all thought otherwise. They saw my death as something which was ever present; a shadow hanging over them. They feared what would come for England, should I die suddenly, unexpectedly, as so many did. They looked back to my father, to the man whose marital history had changed England, and they forgot the upheavals he had caused. They remembered only his dedication to producing an heir.

It had been the desire which had defined him. My father had searched in love, in hate, in lust and in diplomacy to find a mate who would give him what he needed; an heir, and a spare… He got the heir. He never found the spare. My father never intended for my sister or me to reign. He believed only a man could unite the country, could bring the warring factions of court in line… He did not see that a woman could do such a thing.

He had been wrong.

And yet, my men gazed back through time, and sighed for a monarch who would give such dedication to the quest for an heir. They were baffled by my desire to never marry. They were worried by my refusal to name a successor. They wanted to know that England would be safe, when I was gone. But I was a creature of the present. That is how survivors are. We learn to live in the present, for we know not how long we have to enjoy it. I did not want to think of my own death, who does? Who would want to be presented every day with lists of those who will take your throne, shoulder the care of your people, take up the work you have started... once you are dead and cold in the grave?

They thrust my own demise under my nose. They stalked me with images of my death. They ran after me, showing me what would come when I was gone. How could anyone live, when they exist under their own death shroud?

I loved my people, I loved England. I would rule for as long as God permitted, and then allow Him to choose who was to succeed me. In my mind, then, was my cousin, Mary. She had the blood, the spirit and the courage to do what was best, for both our nations. I put my trust in her. I placed my hope in her. I was not ready to die just yet... and even now, as Death watches on as I tell my tale, I tarry still. But when I did die, I believed Mary was the one destined to replace me.

Still, I did not love to hear of my own death. I did not revel in this discussion. But I was about to find that even if I did not wish to hear, there were many others willing to speak...

And Death... Did He feel cheated to have failed to take my life? Perhaps so, for He came back... And in the place of one life He failed to take, He would steal many, so many more.

Chapter Forty-One

Windsor Castle
Winter 1563

That January, plague crept into England.

And this was not the sweat, nor smallpox. This was the plague that once, a few hundred years ago, had wiped out one third of Europe. They called it the Black Death and never was a name more feared.

The plague began with a fever, headache, chills, swelling, and lumps which formed under the arms, at the neck and at the groin. As the sickness ate into the body, the lumps turned black, and extremities would rot and fall away. There was no treatment. People were ordered to stay inside, rest and pray they would be one of the few and fortunate to survive. All we could do when the plague came was to lock those affected inside their houses, and hope to contain the number who died. People carried garlands of flowers, wrapped their faces in cloths soaked in wormwood and vinegar, and petitioned God and Saint Roch to spare them. The holy cross was carved on the doors of those who fell to the illness, in the hope that God would see them, and cure them... It was done, too, to make others aware the plague was within that house, so they would not to go near.

Within weeks thousands had died.

The city stunk as Death walked free and easy in her streets. Churches, markets, shops and parks were closed. Mass graves were made outside of London, and those who had survived the plague drove carts about the city in the gloom of night, removing corpses from infected houses and throwing them into pits. Priests stood, mumbling nervous, harried prayers over the ravaged bodies of the dead. Everyone carried talismans, relics and prayer books, trying to keep themselves safe. Each night the creaking wheels of the wagons sounded through London. Each day, more died.

Death was busy, that winter.

Did He feel cheated, in failing to take my life? Did He come to exact His revenge on my people? Spiteful Death. He struck out like a child. He came for petty vengeance.

The risks presented by the plague were enormous, and therefore the precautions against it had to respond in kind. No one was allowed to transport goods in or out of London by boat or road and anyone who broke this sanction would be turned from their house. Any found concealing the pestilence inside their house was fined. Anyone found trying to escape London and therefore possibly spread the plague to other towns, villages or cities, was hanged.

The court was rushed to Windsor, for as much as that castle was a palace, it was also a fortress that could be secured. Provisions were hoarded, so we did not have to risk the plague entering upon wagons of wheat, or in stocks of meat, grain, vegetables or cloth. No one was allowed to enter Windsor if they had visited London in the past month. Foreign ambassadors, newly arriving in England, were sent to safe houses outside of the city, and were told they would not be received at court until they had spent forty days in England without coming near the sickness, or presenting any symptoms. Ambassadors and dignitaries already at court were hustled to Windsor with us.

I was moved into the closest thing to seclusion I would ever experience as Queen. I was served only by my ladies, and only by those ladies who had been with me before the outbreak, had showed no signs of sickness, and had not been into London itself before the court moved. My servants were reduced in number, and kept apart from the servants of other lords. My kitchens were guarded, the servants there also reduced, and no produce was allowed to be used for my meals unless it had been inspected and passed Cecil's rigorous tests. I was permitted my apothecary, and my doctors, but they were not allowed to treat others. I was not allowed outside. Every day, all my servants were checked over for signs of the plague, as was I. In light of my recent brush with death, and the mounting piles of dead in London, Cecil and my Privy Council were taking no chances. Fortunately, it was winter. The plague was always more virulent if it came when the summer's heat allowed it to fester and spread. We hoped winter's cold would force it to retreat.

*

By January, the numbers of dead and newly infected were falling rapidly. The plague had taken a horrific toll, but it had begun to dissipate. Feeling safe enough, I called Parliament to reconvene. I regretted it almost immediately. At the opening ceremony I was upbraided by Alexander Nowell, Dean of St Paul's, for failing to marry. With Death still cackling merrily in some parts of London, and considering my close brush with death by smallpox, Parliament had become obsessed with my demise. I sat listening to Nowell, as he criticized me. I did not listen with good grace.

"Just as Queen Mary's marriage was a terrible plague to all England," the man began, setting my spine into brisk bristles. "So now the want of Queen Elizabeth's marriage and issue is like to prove as great a plague! If your parents, madam, had been of such a mind, where would you be now? Alack! What is to become of us?"

I felt the use of 'Alack' was rather over the top... Did Nowell believe he was in a play? I spent the rest of his address fuming in silence as men all around me thumped their fists against wood in agreement with the Dean and added their complaints to his. Both Houses agreed they would issue petitions for me to marry; an event they believed would "strike terror" into my enemies and replenish my subjects "with immortal joy!"

My subjects may well have had *immortal* joy at the prospect of my marriage, but *I* did not. What business was it of theirs whom and when I might marry? I understood my sister's feelings perfectly whenever I was admonished to marry. Mary had once said she must marry according to her own private inclination, as was the right of all men and women. At the time, I had censured her for this. Now, I believed there was something in what she had said. My inclination was never to marry. Why could my people not look on me now, in the present day, for once, rather than harping constantly on the time I would die? I was insulted. Was there was nothing I could do, myself, for the good of England, then? Was there nothing more worthy I could ever achieve than marrying a man, and birthing a babe? Was that really all they thought me good for? Had I not proved my intelligence, my wit, and my political skills? Was it only my womb they wanted me for, rather than my mind?

And yes, in saying all this, of course I understood that they wanted to secure their future. But there were *always* other options for the throne; my people just had to be willing to *see* them. I did not believe that if I died childless the realm would fall into chaos.

When the petitions arrived for me to look over, I found them replete with warnings under their civility: reminders of the horrors of civil war; the meddling of foreign lords into an unstable England; the destruction of noble houses and the slaughter of my people... All of which would apparently *absolutely* occur unless I gave in. What did these people believe marriage was? A magic talisman against evil? It was ludicrous. But there was a later passage which made me more nervous.

"We fear a faction of heretics in your realm, contentious and malicious Papists. From the Conquest to the present day,

the realm was never left as it is now without a certain heir. If Your Highness could conceive or imagine the comfort, surety and delight that should happen to yourself by beholding a child of your own, it would sufficiently satisfy all manner of impediments and scruples."

I did not like the constant emphasis on the supposed evil of Catholics. More than that, I did not like the idea my men believed I had only to hold a child in my arms and *I* would be made whole. Was *I* not a *whole* person without a babe dribbling upon my arm? Was the worth of a woman not measured on any scale other than how many brats she could squeeze from her quinny? Was I never to be recognised as worth something *on my own*, without a child?

And quite aside from my natural impulses and fears of marriage… What if I could not breed as other women could? I did not want a child. I did not yearn for one. But even if I did, was I capable? My mother had suffered failed pregnancies, and my sister had grown only ghosts in her belly. My father had had six wives and many mistresses, and yet his offspring had hardly been numerous. What if there was a fault in the fertility of my line? If I subjected myself to marriage, what if then I could *not* bear children? I would be humiliated. And since it was commonly held that women were always the ones at fault in matters of fertility, my people would blame me if I failed, just as they had blamed my mother, and my sister.

No, it was better to remain true to the natural impulses of my own heart and soul. I would rule as a woman, alone. I would show my Council and my people that a woman needs neither man nor child to make her whole. She is a person in her own right. She is a woman without the presence of a husband or child. She is whole, by her own self. *She* is a person.

But I could hardly be honest about these thoughts. I would have to find ways to pacify, distract and confuse them…

Business as usual, then, for this last Queen of the Tudor line.

I was also far from pleased when Katherine Knollys informed me that the speech given by the Dean at the opening or Parliament had been encouraged, and part written, by none other than *Robin*. So much for his protestations after I recovered from illness that all he wanted was my happiness! And after I had protected him as best I could from the de Quadra scandal, too... Ungrateful, scheming wretch! Revenge on Robin would, unfortunately, have to wait. I had to deal with my Parliament first. Both Houses wanted me to marry, and in the meantime, to name a successor. I would do neither, but with the war in France, and our troops supporting the French Huguenots, I needed money. The fastest way for a prince to get money is through Parliament, so I could not dismiss them, nor openly refuse their petitions.

At the end of January, with the Speaker of the Commons on his knees to present the House's petition, I assured my men that the matter of the succession had also been on my mind. "When Death possessed every joint of me," I said loudly. "I know now, as well as I did before, that I am mortal. I know also that I must one day seek to discharge myself of the great burden that God has laid upon me. But this matter is no light subject, good Masters. I must be given the time to think on it with all seriousness, both for the good of my realm and the good of my people."

That bought me space to breathe, but it was not enough to silence them. A few days later, the petition of the Lords arrived and it was much the same as that of the Commons. They would not let the matter lie. Since I had already said to my Parliament I would give serious thought to the matter, I was angered when they continued to harass me.

"Think you these marks upon my face are *wrinkles* of old age, my lords?" I snarled at the Lords. "They are none such! I am marked by the illness which I lately recovered from, and not by the stains of age. And although I may be older than I was when first I came to this glorious throne, I am not so old that I may not bear fruit yet of my womb. God could still send to me an heir, my lords, just as He did with Saint Elizabeth!"

They were none too pleased at my statement, and rankled at my obvious anger, but they waited for me to agree to marry, and to agree upon an heir.

The succession was not the only business of my Parliament that year. They discussed further measures to ensure my safety from Catholic plots and talked over our intervention in France. They discussed furthering the religious settlement I had made when first I came to the throne, as well as new ways to enforce it. The Oath of Supremacy was to be widened to include any who held public office. I agreed to this bill, but made sure my Archbishop of Canterbury knew not to tender the act a second time, as I had no intention of making nobles swear the oath and force Catholics amongst them to choose allegiance between me and the Pope. There were other matters too; the plot which had been uncovered as I lay ill was brought to the attention of Parliament. A new act against sorcery and witchcraft, when used for harmful purposes, was passed, which also included a ban on the use of prophesy to foretell my death. Anyone indulging in the magical arts for malicious purposes would be fined and imprisoned. A second offence would mean life imprisonment, or execution, and the forfeiture of their goods.

My attempts to avoid naming an heir were compounded when the odious Katherine Grey gave birth to a second male child in February. My twenty-two-year-old traitorous, brainless cousin now had *two* male heirs. This hardly helped me as I tried to dodge and duck Parliament. That girl was set on making trouble for me, I could feel it. I just had to hold out until Parliament had voted through the funds I needed, and I turned to my greatest weapon, to words, to stall them.

"If any here doubt that I am bent never to trade that way of life, and by that I mean to remain an unwed woman, let them put that kind of heresy from their thoughts. Your belief, if it tends that way, is awry. For although I think the unwed state is best for a private woman, yet I do strive to believe it is not best for a prince. And if I can bend my liking to your need, I will not resist such a thought. I hope I shall die in quiet, with *Nunc Dimittis*, the Song of Simon, in my ears. But think not that I do not understand your need to know whom you will follow after my graved bones are laid to rest. I hear you, my lords, and I will attempt to bend my will to that of yours."

That was all I said. Parliament, happy to hear I was disposed to bend my will to theirs, even though I had not said *when* or *how much*, granted me the funds I required. I dissolved Parliament amidst some general sense of confusion in the Commons and the Lords, who had expected a further, clearer answer from me on both the matter of my marriage and the succession.

They should have learned by now not to grant me what I wanted before receiving the answers they desired.

I was never one to give a clear answer when it was much more to my advantage to offer a confusing one.

Chapter Forty-Two

Windsor Castle
Spring 1563

I was not best pleased with Robin.

Having discovered his involvement with my rebellious Parliament, I found myself often sharp, hard and vexed with him. When we rode into Windsor Park, when it was allowed, due to the still lingering plague, I said few words to him. When I was in my chambers I did not call for him, and when he was present, I brushed past him as though he were nothing more than a candlestick upon my fireplace. Robin did not react well to being treated thus, and acted confused, hurt and petulant. He did not know I had uncovered this most recent betrayal. He did not understand why I had grown cold.

Robin was playing the part of the cold wind in the fables of Aesop. If you do not know the tale, I shall tell it to you. One day, having little else to do, the wind turned to the sun and laid down a challenge. They will see who can make a lonely walker travelling over the hills remove his heavy cloak. The bold wind decides to try first. He blows and blows into the man's face, whips his body, and batters him with his cold breath trying to force him to remove the coat. Chilled by the wind, the man pulls his heavy cloak only tighter about him and struggles on. The sun smiles. She flies into the heavens and burns brilliant and bright in the sky above. She rains down gentle warmth. The man basks in the lovely sunshine, and suddenly finds his cloak is too hot. He takes it off and hangs it over his arm, continuing on his journey with the warmth of the soothing sun upon his shoulders.

Robin was making me pull my cloak tight about me. There was no gentle sun in my life.

And it was not only I who was having trouble with certain men who believed their desires were more important than another's choices. A young man, named Pierre de Boscosel, the Seigneur de Chastelard, was found hiding in my cousin of Scots' bedchamber. Apparently infatuated with Mary, the young man had hidden himself under her bed. He thought to wait for her servants to depart, and to make love to the Queen when she got into her bed. Many dullards found this tale highly romantic. The fact that Chastelard was *armed* with a dagger and a sword hardly made the story sound like a romance to me... What was he planning to do? Take my cousin by force if she would not submit? The thought must have occurred to him, otherwise why bring weapons? I am sure if you ask any woman, the idea of a stranger leaping out from under one's bed, heavily armed and with rape in mind, is not something to light sparks of love in one's heart...

Luckily for my poor cousin, Chastelard was discovered during the nightly search of her rooms, and despite his ludicrous claim that he was only there because he had had *nowhere else to sleep*, he was not believed. Nowhere else to sleep! What a feeble-minded excuse for attempting to rape my cousin! Mary was so scared by the incident that she never slept alone again. When later questioned, Chastelard revealed that the plot went even deeper. Sent, apparently, by Huguenots in France, who had been angered by Mary's support for the Guise, Chastelard had been ordered to infiltrate Mary's chambers and find a method to defame the Queen. He was to sully her honour in the eyes of her people, playing upon the idea, of course, that should a man rape a woman, *she* is to blame, and not *him*.

What a convenient myth that was for men who wanted to assault women! To my mind, it was as insulting to men as it was to women. It was a slight to every man who would never dream of doing such a hideous act just as it was an insult that women were often accused of having *encouraged* men to rape them; by smiling at them, by wearing a certain dress, by talking to them, or even by showing no interest at all. I did not believe the myth. It was created and used to excuse rapists. It was maintained by those who sought to place the blame onto the shoulders of women. That was what was behind this event. It would not be the morals of Chastelard that were called into question had he achieved his revolting aim; it would be those of Mary.

I wonder if this will ever change? That one day, people will hear of a woman assaulted, and blame her attacker rather than first looking to see what she must have done to *deserve* her attack? When we hear of people who have been stolen from, we do not say they should not have had anything worth stealing. When we hear of a murder, we do not say the victim must have beckoned Death. Why then do we maintain that a woman must be guilty when she is raped? Why do we maintain this lie, allowing it to survive, generation after generation? All those who maintain this myth maintain evil. They allow rapists to continue to spread fear, misery... to steal a part of a woman's life, by excusing her attacker.

Chastelard was beheaded. Knox took the opportunity to blame Mary for the incident, saying that she had led Chastelard on by choosing to dance with him at court. Another perpetrator of evil.

I made it clear to my court that I wanted no slander on the character or virtue of my cousin to be spoken in my hearing. I could not stop the rumours altogether, especially from those who would use this incident against my Catholic cousin, but I wanted it made clear that I saw she was not to blame. It was the man himself who should be seen as culpable, not her.

*

In February, the conspirators Arthur Pole and his brother Edmund were tried for high treason. Under the new laws against sorcery and witchcraft brought forth by Parliament, they were sentenced to death, but I commuted their sentences to life imprisonment, showing mercy they little deserved.

The involvement of the Guise and Phillip of Spain in this plot was disconcerting. They had been prepared to send men into England to capture my throne once I was dead, and replace me with my Scottish cousin. Randolph said that as far as he was aware, Mary had known nothing of this plot. I wanted to believe him. Many times when I was a princess I had been used by intriguers without my knowledge. I hoped this was the case now, with my cousin. Under interrogation, de Quadra's name had been mentioned, *yet again*. Were that man a subject of mine, his head would have spun from his neck long before now. I wrote to Phillip, asking him to cease to meddle in England's affairs, and to make it clear that should de Quadra be found to be involved in one more plot he would be sent home in disgrace, or worse. In the meantime, the Spanish ambassador was put under house arrest. It was vastly unhelpful for international relations to do so, but what choice had the man left me? De Quadra was a liability, and it was clear I could not leave him at liberty in England. Cecil and many others wanted me to execute the conspirators, but I would not make sacred martyrs from foolish mortals. In the same way, I would not move further against de Quadra. It occurred to me de Quadra might even *want* me to move against him, in order to start a war he knew I could not win. I was not going to give him that satisfaction.

A welcome distraction came in the shape of letters from Doctor John Dee. Now studying at Antwerp, he had begun work on the mystery of ciphers, was still adding to his growing library of learned books, and was also studying the mystical arts of the Cabala. The Cabala was a combination of language, mathematics and mystery, based on ancient Hebrew texts. Interest in Hebrew had grown apace over the years, as it was believed that its study could release certain secrets and knowledge hidden in ancient texts and Biblical works. Scholars were searching for numerical patterns in texts using *Gematria*; where numbers are substituted for letters of the Hebrew alphabet. They were trying to demonstrate a mathematical relationship was underlying the language, and reveal hidden secrets. Cabalism also had a magical and practical side; incantations could be used to summon spirits, angels and even to influence events. Dee assured me he was not studying the Cabala for this purpose, for it could be viewed as a use of the dark arts, and if used for ill-purpose, would be illegal in England, but he spoke warmly on the mathematical pleasures he found in his studies, and on the delights of Antwerp.

"Antwerp is a lively and marvellous city, Your Majesty," he wrote to me. *"Filled with the rattle and clank of printing presses, where thousands of pamphlets and books are made on the study of humanism and Christian faith. Where the streets are filled with scholars, and the inns are made lively with talk of mathematics, cosmology and science. Knowing that you, my Queen, are so avid and devoted a pupil to all new learning which comes your way, I can only mourn that your duties bind you to England. But I promise that I will return with many wonders to delight and tickle your imagination and your mind."*

Dee sent maps for Cecil and books for me, delighting us both. It was good to have a distraction, especially since I swiftly had to deal with another act of treachery from de Quadra. Cecil had long had the Spanish embassy at Durham House in London under his watchful eye, so when it was reported that a disturbance had broken out inside, Cecil's men investigated. It turned out that two Italians had broken into an argument, but as this brawl was investigated, more secrets came to light. De Quadra was allowed to hear the Catholic Mass in his house. It was his right as a foreign ambassador, but my men found he was advertising this to my subjects, inviting them to come to Mass, and breaking my laws by doing so. Even under house arrest, the Spanish ambassador was apparently unable to do anything unless it was to my detriment.

"Who do you have inside the house, Cecil?"

"Several members of de Quadra's household are my secret servants," was his quick answer. Cecil had many eyes and ears about England.

"He will abuse his diplomatic privilege no longer," I sniffed. "Have the locks changed on his house and give the keys to a new custodian in your pay. We shall let the ambassador know that he cannot flout my laws." I stretched my shoulders back and cracked my fingers. "If only he were an Englishman, Cecil... How I would like to see his irksome head tumble from his neck."

De Quadra protested at this rude handling. Saying his diplomatic rights were being interfered with, he complained to my Council, who were entirely unmoved. We all knew what de Quadra was up to. He was encouraging dissent, inciting law breaking, and acting against me. And don't believe for one moment that he was doing this for devotion to his faith. He wanted to cause trouble for *me*. That was his sole aim. But he was going to find it a great deal more difficult to act against me now that we had his household in a tight grip. When the time was right, or when I lost all patience, I would send him from England in disgrace.

As it transpired, I had no need to move on de Quadra. There was someone else with an eye on him.

Chapter Forty-Three

Greenwich Palace
Spring - Summer 1563

English forces had landed in France just after I recovered from smallpox, but it quickly became apparent this war was not going to go in our favour. In January, Huguenot forces had been defeated at Dreux and one of their leaders, Conde, was captured. Then in February the Duke of Guise had been shot by an assassin and died six days later. Some said he would have recovered from his wound, had his own doctors not bled him to death. The two sides made peace, and then, to my horror, they both turned on our English troops! I could understand the Catholic factions attacking us, but why our allies, the Huguenots, would choose to do so was a mystery. Cecil believed they must have come to an agreement in their peace talks. Since the Catholic side were still stronger, despite the loss of their leader the Duke, perhaps they had demanded the Huguenots expel their allies from the conflict.

Surrounded at La Havre, Ambrose Dudley had small choice but to secure the city and defend it. He tried inviting Huguenot leaders to talks, all of which were refused. As summer began, in the cramped, dirty conditions inside the city an epidemic of plague broke out. It tore through our English troops and decimated them. Ambrose was sure he could eventually come to an understanding and bargain for Calais, but as the months went on our intervention was becoming not only more costly, but increasingly pointless. I was stricken with remorse for getting England involved at all.

When I heard of the death of her uncle, I wrote Mary a letter of condolence. In truth, I did not sorrow for his death. The Duke of Guise had been a liability when he lived, both for France and for me, and was now, in death, being turned into a Catholic saint. A less likely saint I could hardly imagine...

would one of his holy miracles be the slaughter of innocent people in a barn? But still, it was politic to write to my cousin and commiserate. The mention of Mary's name in the plot of Edmund and Arthur Pole had made my Council suspicious of her, but I hoped she had been unaware of it, as was protested. Maitland was due to return to England soon and whilst I was happy to keep lines of communication and affection open with Mary, I did not relish another round of fencing with her ambassador over the succession.

"I am in such a labyrinth with the succession, Cecil," I said to him one evening as we sat at my fire. "I believe my cousin Mary to be the best candidate, and yet I know many will never accept her. I cannot condone the elevation of the Greys, and never would I support a Lennox for the throne."

My cousin of Lennox had been trying very hard that summer to wend her way back into my favour. Wanting to show her favour over Katherine Grey, I had agreed to write to Mary Stewart about Lennox reclaiming his Scottish titles. Lennox's titles and blood were Scottish. He hailed from one of the greatest noble Scottish houses, and was descended from James II in the female line. Brought up in France, since Scotland was considered too dangerous after the assassination of his father by the Hamilton clan, Lennox had returned to Scotland as a young man, determined to be named Mary Stewart's heir in defiance of the Regent, Arran, who was head of the clan who had murdered his father. Lennox claimed that James V, Mary's father, had named him her heir, although others contested this. Whilst in Scotland Lennox had tried to woo Mary's mother, Marie of Guise, in an attempt to make her his wife, but the canny Regent had played him, keeping him close and yet holding him away. Lennox had previously sworn fealty to the French King, François I, but upon realising he would get nowhere with Marie, he switched his allegiance to England, and to my father, which had made him no friends amongst the Scots or the French. Working on behalf of my father to marry Mary Stewart to my brother Edward, Lennox had effectively committed treason in Scotland. He had led my father's troops during the *Rough Wooing*, as it had been called, where my father attempted to take Scotland by force and secure Mary of Scots for his son. When the *Rough Wooing* failed, Lennox had been attained for high treason by Marie of Guise, lost his estates to the Scot's Crown, and had fled to England. An exile in England, Lennox had retained his titles, although they were not recognised in Scotland, and had remained in England ever since.

Lennox and his wife were keen to regain their lands and titles in Scotland, and in agreeing to this project I was demonstrating my favour for them over Katherine Grey as an heir. I had also hinted I might consider the match between Darnley and my cousin of Scots. Margaret had come to court, and I made sure I was seen often with her. Although I despised her company, my Lennox cousin was of use to me in rupturing support for Katherine Grey.

"To marry and bear a child of your own would solve all problems, Majesty," Cecil reminded me; it was his constant refrain, his answer to all questions.

"You speak so because you have become a father again," I noted. Cecil's second wife, Mildred, had given birth that June to a son, named Robert in honour of my favourite.

"I admit that the birth of another son brings me much comfort, even if his health gives us cause for concern," Cecil said. "And I wish, madam, that you could feel the same pleasing warmth that children may bring to the life of a parent." Seeing my disgruntled face, my Secretary hurried on. "But I agree you cannot exclude the Queen of Scotland entirely, for to do such would only bring trouble, even war upon England, I believe."

"If she pursues a match with Don Carlos, my people will certainly never accept her," I said. "They have no wish to have Spain as a master over them again. If Mary marries into Spain, she will bring that threat to our shores. If only Mary could be prevailed upon to marry one we approved of, that would solve many problems."

I did not say I was considering offering Robin to Mary, but it was in my thoughts, especially given his late involvement with my Parliament. I began to draft an agreement for Mary; if I was allowed to dictate whom she married, she would have her claim to the throne recognised. I did not show it yet to Cecil, for I knew he would protest. As for my plan to test my favourite... Robin was not, as yet, high enough in title or wealth to be an inviting prospect for my cousin, so I made moves to make him so. I would have to tread carefully, but I was determined not only to test Robin, but to have my revenge on him as well. Oh, I was a wicked woman then! And why should I not have been? Robin deserved a shock.

I gave Robin Kenilworth Castle in Warwickshire. It was a fine prize and Robin was pleased, but also clearly baffled. I had been cool with him of late... and now I granted him such a gift... What was going on? The flickering emotions of doubt and joy on his face were pleasing. He would understand... soon enough.

He was pleased to have the castle, despite his doubts about my motives. It stood but a few miles from his brother's seat at Warwick, making them close neighbours. Ambrose was still in France, battling both the united French forces and plague, but in July I sent word that he was to surrender to the French and return home. It was obvious we were going to gain nothing by remaining in France. When Ambrose returned from this disastrous campaign, we found he had been injured. He walked with the use of a stick for the rest of his life. I did not blame Ambrose for the failure of the mission. He could hardly have foreseen our own allies would turn on us, but I was angered at our losses. All we had done *was* lost. Calais was not returned, our former allies had betrayed us, and we had lost men and money on the campaign. What I had said before was true; no good came of war.

The return of the soldiers also unleashed a fresh outbreak of plague. We had just managed to get it under control in London when they came home. I believed God was sending England a message not to become involved in conflicts again. And what a message! Three thousand in London died each week, and as it started to spread to other areas of England, sanctions had to be firmly set in place again. I had to order Katherine Grey, Hertford and their sons moved from the Tower and placed under house arrest in the country, for it was too dangerous to leave them in London. I would not have anyone accuse me of bringing about her death through lack of care. Katherine was sent to her uncle, John Grey, along with her baby, and the elder son, Lord Beauchamp, was sent to his grandmother, the Duchess of Somerset, along with his father. I was not about to put Katherine and Hertford in the same house, but I thought it fair to share their children between them. Katherine was not given leave to write to Hertford, to anyone in his household, to her sister or anyone at court. I sent her with Thomas's nurse, three ladies in waiting and two manservants. Katherine sent a letter to Cecil, thanking him for saving her family from the plague and asked him to seek forgiveness for her from me.

"I have shown her enough generosity already, *Spirit*," I said. "She has proved she cannot be trusted, twice. And she should thank *me*, not you, for having her moved to safety. I could have refused, just as I could have taken her husband's head, and hers, for their betrayal."

Katherine's chambers in the Tower, when inspected, horrified me. Her fine hangings and furniture had been all but destroyed by her dogs and her pet apes, and they stunk of shit and piss. Clearly the maids I had sent had failed in their duties, so perhaps it was just as well Katherine was now housed with family instead. But still, Katherine's fate could have been much worse, had I made it so. Soon after her arrival at his house, John Grey wrote to Cecil, alarmed for his niece. He believed she was pining away for Katherine had stopped eating and said she would welcome death if not for her children and husband. She missed her eldest son horribly, and was especially depressed when she missed his second birthday.

"And would Hertford not be depressed in spirit to see neither of his children?" I asked Cecil. "Should I give both to Katherine, and leave the father never seeing either child until they were grown men?" I shook my head. "She had two years with the elder, and now Hertford will take his turn. I cannot put the two back together, but I will not ignore Hertford's right to his children. Katherine has her babe. Let her concentrate on him."

As the court removed to Windsor again, marriage talks reopened with the Hapsburgs. With de Quadra locked in his house in London, and muttering against Catholics growing in England, talks about a match between the Archduke Charles and me resumed at perhaps the worst time possible. It was only at Cecil's urging I allowed it. Our intervention in France had not been appreciated by the ruling Valois and due to de Quadra's meddling, relations between Spain and England were strained. Cecil wanted England to have at least one friend and so I grudgingly allowed him to open negotiations. As I considered the idea, I found I did not mind so much. Spain and the Hapsburgs were all vastly unpopular with my subjects. I could refuse the suit at any point, and say I did so for love of my people, which would be at least partly true. Randolph wrote from Scotland that Maitland had said "there are three factions in England; the Catholics, the Protestants, and Queen Elizabeth." I found this highly amusing, but it was true enough. I had to keep a balance.

As part of these negotiations, Emperor Ferdinand wrote asking me to allow English Catholics to have the use of one chapel in each city where they might practise the old faith in peace and without hindrance. I found this rather hypocritical, seeing as Protestants were not given those rights in *his* country…

My religious settlement was generous, and I did not persecute Catholics, all I asked for was public obedience. If Catholics wished to be Catholics, they could remain so in their own hearts. But in my realm I would have order, and I would have unity.

"This request," I wrote in response to the Emperor, *"is of such a kind and beset with so many difficulties that we cannot allow it without hurt to our country and to our own honour… To found churches expressly for divine rites, besides being repugnant to the enactments of our Supreme Parliament, would be but to graft religion upon religion, to the distraction of good men's minds, the fostering of zeal of the factious, the sorry blending of the functions of church and state, and the utter confounding of all things human and divine in this, our now peaceful state. This would be a thing evil in itself, and of the worst example pernicious to our people, and to those themselves, in whose interest it is craved, neither advantageous nor indeed without peril."*

Phillip of Spain was not keen on the idea either. He believed it would allow me to single out Catholics, and move against them. Why he believed me to be made of the same spirit as he, I know not, for in so many ways I had proven myself lenient and patient in terms of religion.

"He should look at the practices of his dead wife, my sister, or at his own horrific Inquisition, if he wants to see what persecuting people for their faith truly is!" I huffed to Kat as she undressed me.

"Indeed, Majesty," Kat agreed. "Phillip is hardly innocent of acting against those of our faith."

I was not the only one struggling with religion. Reports that Mary was considering a Catholic match had leaked out, and

Knox was after my cousin. He preached against her proposed marriage to Don Carlos, and my cousin called him to her. Making it clear that she had endured a great deal of insult from him and yet still left him at liberty, Randolph reported that she became tearful. "I shall be revenged," she said, her eyes swimming. "What have you to do with my marriage?"

"Your nobles are flatterers and neither God nor the Commonwealth are represented well at court," Knox replied.

"What are you to do with this Commonwealth?" Mary demanded.

"I am a subject born within this realm, Majesty," Knox stiffly replied. "And albeit I neither be earl, lord or baron, yet God has made me a profitable member of this kingdom. If you marry a Catholic, you betray Scotland and all the promises you made when first you came here. Marry a Catholic and you will end your days in anguish and sorrow."

Knox was dallying with danger. He spoke to Mary as though she were his equal. Mary, unused to anyone daring to address her in such a way, burst into tears. If I were her, I would have screamed at him, even though I can't deny his stance against a Catholic match was in England's favour. Knox watched her cry. "I have never been moved by a woman's weeping," he said. "I can scarce abide the tears of my own sons when I beat them. I have spoken nothing other than the truth, Majesty, and you have no cause to be therefore offended. I will not betray my Commonwealth by remaining silent."

Mary stood up and shouted he was to leave the chamber. Knox departed, but Mary knew she would face further battles. And in his mind, she could never win. Knox despised female rulers, believing they ruled from the heart, and possessed no reason. Knox also believed Catholics and Catholic women in particular, were savage with lust. Knox had recently written to Cecil, praising me over his Queen, for I was Protestant, and had therefore chosen reason over emotion, and was a queen *"by the miraculous dispensation of God."* So he now approved of me, even though being a woman and in power I was apparently deviating from the natural order.

Despite my cousin's habit of breaking into tears, were we so very different? Mary had shown she could rule wisely, justly and fairly in her realm. She had conquered rebellion and had not imposed her faith upon her people. If I did not burst into tears before my men, I often enough lost control of my temper. Knox ignored all slander which had been made against my name over the years, because it suited his theory to believe me rational and strong, and Mary irrational and weak. It was true my cousin could be naïve and impulsive, but she had not learnt her craft as long as I had, and it was not as though I was a creature without fault or flaw.

The only difference was our faiths. Knox was willing to stuff Mary with every sin for her faith, and lay every virtue over my shoulders for mine.

Chapter Forty-Four

Windsor Castle and Oatlands Park
Summer 1563

In August, de Quadra died of the plague.

It was the only thing he ever did that pleased me.

I did not sorrow. I did not shed a tear. Had it not been a public insult to Spain, I would have ordered the court into a round of furious celebration upon the death of my enemy. For once, I thanked Death.

I am sure Phillip of Spain believed I had poisoned de Quadra, or had left him under house arrest in London hoping he would catch the plague; neither was true, although I will admit the ambassador was not one of my first concerns. Perhaps I was guilty of neglect, but I had no reason to sorrow that the grating, infuriating weasel was gone. I sent word of our sorrow for the loss of the *"good ambassador de Quadra"* to Phillip, and asked for a replacement.

Phillip was cool towards England after de Quadra's death, and this carried the added benefit that he was not keen to pursue the match between me and his cousin. De Quadra, clearly, was of more use to me dead than alive. With Hapsburg negotiations frosty, and relations with France strained, I decided to work on Scotland. I formally asked my cousin to give me the authority to select her husband. If Mary would content me in this request, I wrote, I would proceed with her right to be named my heir. Cecil stepped in to amend my letter, saying that her right to the throne would be *investigated*, rather than immediately approved, which I allowed. I asked Mary to marry an English nobleman; one who was committed to friendship between our countries. I said that she might marry a foreigner, but only if he was committed to peace, and asked her not to marry with France, Spain or Austria. Cecil wanted Mary to submit evidence for her claim and if it was upheld by Parliament, I would accept Mary as my natural sister or daughter. I believed it was a generous offer, but my cousin thought otherwise. She could not understand why I would seek to barter, or why she should have to prove her claim.

"Who else in England, or any court of the world, would my good sister regard as having more right to be her heir than me?" Mary asked Randolph. "Do I not hold the royal blood of Scotland, France and England within me?"

Randolph acquitted himself well, but my cousin was clearly lost as to why I should not name her my heir and was not eager to hand me the right to choose her husband. I could understand this, but still I wanted her to agree. I would work to give her what she wanted, if she would satisfy me. It was a compromise; I would secure her future, if she would secure England's present. Mary said she would think about it, but it was clear she was not enthusiastic about my proposition.

*

Phillip of Spain was quick to send a replacement for de Quadra. I was not looking forward to meeting him, seeing as my relationship with his predecessor had been less than perfect, but from the moment he arrived at court, I knew Don Diego Guzman de Silva was different. De Silva was about the same height as me, with dark, short hair which was curly and often plump when the weather was humid or wet. He had a short, clipped moustache, and a ready, merry sense of humour. It was also clear that rather than being intent on spreading discord, de Silva's desire was to make friends and allies. Upon his arrival I had Darnley go out to meet him as another sign of favour to the Lennoxes, and de Silva was brought to me later that week.

"You are most welcome, my lord," I said as we were introduced. I watched the way his curly hair sprang as he rose from his bow. There was something endearing about it. "I hope, my lord, that you and I will come to understand each other well."

"My master has often spoken with great warmth about you, Majesty," de Silva replied smoothly. "For myself, I hope to discover *all* there is to know about you, Majesty, and your beautiful country. Never have I seen a land more green! Although I would not speak ill of those who have passed from life, I believe Bishop de Quadra perhaps had other notions in mind when he came to serve. You will find that although I hold the same post, my intentions are only to make you and my master the very best of friends, and allies."

"Then you are even more welcome," I said dryly, not entirely ready to believe him. "For all I have ever wanted was a good relationship with my brother of Spain. I believe his last ambassador hindered that, rather than helped it."

"Sometimes, Majesty, a man cannot see past his own beliefs to make friends with those who are otherwise inclined." De Silva's smile shifted into a tight grin. "But *I* find that the more variety there is in life, the more interesting it becomes. As one sits down to a feast, one does not expect only to be served old, well-known dishes. Such a fate would be tedious indeed!"

"Then I hope you will feast well on the offerings of the Court of England," I agreed. De Silva had an open air about him, most unusual in an ambassador. It would not do to trust him without question, but still, I liked him.

"I am sure England has much to offer both Spain and me," he replied. "And I can only hope that I can return such a gift in kind."

"You have not asked me yet on the subject of Archduke Charles," I noted, playing with a ribbon on my dress. "De

Quadra was wont to thrust at least one sentence on marriage into every conversation we held."

"How very dull, Majesty!" He grimaced, almost making me giggle. "I wonder that you were able to bear meeting with the man at all, if that was all he spoke of! A lady should not be *hounded* into marriage; to do so removes all possibility of romance, does it not? And for all they put up with in life, women should all have a chance at romance. I shall wait for you to tell me of your inclination. If your choice falls upon a Hapsburg, I shall be the happiest of men, but I will never chase you, Your Majesty. Please do not judge my character, and certainly not those of all Spaniards on the merits, or failings, of but one man."

"I will certainly try, my lord ambassador, to please you," I said warmly. If there was but one person who did not press me constantly on the subject of marriage, he would come as a most refreshing change. "If you promise to do the same with the English."

"Done, Majesty." De Silva beamed, his moustache ruffling against his cheeks.

De Silva was true to his word. Believing there was much damage to repair, de Silva adopted an entirely different attitude to de Quadra. He told me should I wish to talk about the Archduke, he was at my disposal, and would always consider the matter open as long as neither of us married, but he did not wish to enter into talks unless I was serious. He worked to become my friend, and I was hungry for friendship then. He liked to tell me tales of mishaps which befell nobles for he found I was easily amused by such stories. He gossiped like a kitchen maid and discovered all that was going on at court within a breathtakingly short period of time. It was not only me he charmed. Within a week, he had made many friends at court, including Cecil.

"What do you think of him, *Spirit*?" I asked as we wandered the grounds of Oatlands Park one bright morning. Clouds rested in the blues skies and birds sung in the tall trees. The air was warm and there was a balmy, sweet breeze. It was a good day to be outside.

"I find him so different to de Quadra that I half expect all this to be a ruse, Majesty." Cecil ran an appreciative hand over a bush of thyme. The oily, rich scent of the tiny dark leaves washed up into my nose.

"He does seem to have different objectives to de Quadra," I agreed. "Oddly, his remit seems to be to make friends. What a strange idea, *Spirit*... That an ambassador should be occupied with making friends between countries, as he is supposed to, rather than plotting to undermine and divide them!"

"Indeed, Majesty, and that is what makes me a touch suspicious, although I cannot deny he appears genuine enough."

"Wouldn't it be nice to believe, Cecil, just for once, that someone *was* what they appeared to be?"

Cecil grinned. "I quite agree, Your Majesty."

*

Later that week I came down with a light fever. It was nothing serious, but given my late brush with Death it was enough to send all at court flapping like ducks caught in a storm. Doctors flocked about me, and I was prodded and poked so much that I started to lose my temper. "All I require is rest and some sleep," I bleated. "*Please*, gentlemen... peace!"

They left me after taking samples of my urine and stool to test and taste. Eventually I was left with Kat, who believed every problem could be solved by the constant imbibing of broth and bread, and Bess St Loe, who was visiting court. Bess did not hold a position in my chambers anymore, but I welcomed her company when she visited court. At least she, unlike Kat, was of a mind to let me do as I wished.

"I am sorry that you became so involved in the troubles with my cousin, Katherine Grey," I said to Bess as Kat moved off to order pottage of cock brains and rice from my kitchens. "You were placed in an unfortunate position."

"I am just relieved, Majesty, that you understood I knew nothing of the scandal until Lady Grey spoke to me," Bess said, moving to plump the cushions at my back. "I have known her all my life, Majesty, and to own the truth, she more often acts when she should deliberate, and rarely heeds the warnings of others."

"Her father's true daughter, then," I said, making Bess smile sadly. "Henry Grey never seemed to consider *anything* before rushing headlong into peril, and not only his peril."

"It is true, her father was a foolish man." Bess sighed, and sat down on the bed. "I often wonder if his daughter Jane would still be alive, if it were not for him, madam."

"I don't believe my sister ever wished to harm Jane Grey," I agreed. "Mary only had Jane executed because Henry Grey made repeated trouble. I believe, had he not risen in rebellion time and time again, my sister would have let Jane go free, eventually. She grieved to kill our cousin for she knew Jane was used by Northumberland and Grey. In truth, it was Henry Grey who signed his daughter's death warrant, not my sister. What other choice was my sister left with? Henry Grey ensured Jane was too dangerous to be left alive."

I leaned back on the cushions. "And now his second daughter is acting as her father did; without consideration that her actions may put her and her children in danger."

"You have been generous with them, Majesty, none can doubt that."

"And if she continues to make trouble for me? What then, Bess? Shall I have to ever watch my cousin over one shoulder, as men scheme to use her and her bastards against me? Will I be put in the same position as my sister; forced to execute a woman of my own house and blood?"

"None can know the future, Majesty, but I hope that will not be the case."

"Why do you have no children with St Loe, Bess?" I asked suddenly. "It seems that the two of you were fertile enough in your previous marriages?"

Bess coloured prettily. "My husband and I have more than enough children from previous marriages between us, my lady," she replied. "We decided… Well, William more so than me… decided he did not wish to risk my health. He said he would rather have me than risk my life to gain children and so I took advice from a cunning woman, and now eat a dish of wild leaves each day which brings on my monthly courses. I agreed because it made William happy, although I am not sure more children would put me in peril of my life. I am a sturdy woman."

"You have great strength, Bess," I said. She was a stout woman, but her generous curves only gave her more beauty in my eyes. And she was not only physically strong, but hale in spirit.

"Have you had any more trouble with your husband's brother?" I asked.

Her mouth twisted. "There is no firm evidence he was involved in the plot to poison me, Majesty, but I cannot look on him with a contented eye. I feel there is trouble yet to come, but what can I do? One cannot act unless he first commits a crime. I am careful, I am watchful. This is all I can do. " Bess's face looked uncertain for a moment. "Majesty, there *is* a matter I was hoping to ask you about, if you would not mind?"

"Ask all you wish."

"My late husband, Lord Cavendish, left me with many debts when he died, Majesty, and I have struggled to pay them off for some time. I fear the remaining debt may take my beloved Chatsworth from me, and I would be desolate to lose my house."

I narrowed my eyes, but I did not feel ungenerous. Her husband was important to me, and Bess had put up with a great deal when accused of involvement with my scandalous cousin. I was intending to restore Bess's position in my chambers one day, for I was fond of her. "You wish me to release you of your debt?" Bess's cheeks ignited, but she nodded.

I tilted my head back. "I will consider your request carefully, Bess," I said. "But do not think I am unsympathetic. I know you suffered from this affair with my cousin, and that you were innocent of what you stood accused. Having once been in such a position myself, I understand what it cost you."

"Your Majesty was generous enough to release me when I was found innocent," Bess said. "And I would not ask for help now, if I were not in dire need."

"I know that, Bess," I agreed. It was true. She was not one to ask a favour on a whim, nor did she pepper me with requests from others. When I rose from my sickbed, I pardoned Bess and St Loe of Cavendish's debt on condition they paid one thousand pounds to the exchequer over a period of several years. That way I was not left out of pocket, but Bess was relieved of the pressure put upon her by her second husband's debts.

*

As the last days of summer shone over England, the plague continued to rage in London. Death was everywhere. When I was well again, we moved the court. As soon as we reached Windsor, however, panic broke out as many courtiers fell ill. Fortunately, it was not the plague. Windsor was a draughty palace, and often cold, and this gave life to a new illness. Cecil came down with it one day, and the next I was in bed, too. My doctors named the sickness as *pooss*. It brought fever to the blood and swelling in the ears, eyes and throat. Poor Cecil could hardly see for days, his eyes were so sore and swollen. I suffered pains in my head, nose and eyes. Many more people caught the pooss, and some died of it, but in a week or so I was out of bed, swearing never to return.

"I am sick of being sick!" I cried at Kat who was attempting to keep me in my bed. "If I do not get out into the park and on a horse soon, I shall run mad!"

"You need to take care, Elizabeth." She *tsked*. "We only have one of you."

"I am so tired of hearing that, Kat," I sighed. "If everyone could stop talking of my demise I would be a happier and healthier woman, I am sure of it!"

We recovered, but from the window, Death surrounded us. The scent of decay rose from the city. The sight of men toiling to dig pits to throw the dead into were haunting. And from the crossroads, the creaking sound of the gallows, with bodies swaying gently in the late summer breeze, invaded our thoughts. Men swung there who had been executed for trying to escape plague-ridden areas. They had attempted to flee Death, only to find He had followed them. Death does not like to lose His prey. He always finds a way.

Chapter Forty-Five

Windsor Castle
Autumn 1563

"My master wishes to meet Lord Robert Dudley, Your Majesty," said the French ambassador, Paul de Foix.

"Why should your King wish to know *one* of my lords over another, my lord ambassador?" I asked. De Foix had sought audience that morning, obviously with something in mind. His rapid request about Robin made me suspicious,

"My master believes you intend to marry Lord Robert," said de Foix. "And so wishes to meet your future consort. Lord Robert will then, after all, be as a brother to my King."

Ah... there it was. Was Robin working with a new ambassador? Wanting to discover more, I giggled, as though I were happy to hear Robin suggested as my husband. "It would scarcely be honourable to send a *groom* to see so great a King," I said, watching Robin's cheeks turn pink as I spoke of him with so little regard. "And besides, I cannot do without my Lord Robert. He is like my little *dog*, my lord ambassador; for he is always at my heel. Whenever he comes into a room everyone at once assumes that I myself am near." The court chortled as Robin went crimson with shame.

"I am sure Your Majesty thinks more highly of Lord Robert than you admit," the ambassador said politely. "Long have many of us known that you esteem him."

"Esteem I hold for many men, my lord," I replied. "But think you that a woman should marry every man she admires? I must act as is best for my country, not for my own impulses." I smiled, seeing de Silva at the edge of the crowds. "And for that purpose, one of your fellow ambassadors is here, you see? To discuss the issue of my marriage."

Negotiations were continuing with the Hapsburgs, but Charles's father, Emperor Ferdinand, was deeply suspicious of my motives. As well he should be, for all I wanted was something to placate my lords and Parliament. "How is my good brother's son, Don Carlos?" I asked de Silva. "We hear the Prince was taken ill, and we are concerned for him."

"My master will be deeply moved to hear of your concern, Majesty." De Silva bobbed his curly head down in a graceful bow and rose to gaze warmly at me.

"Having so lately known illness myself, my lord, I can only commiserate on the state of the Prince's health, and understand the deep fear of his father, my beloved brother. A parent experiences their children's pain as deep as if it were their own. I have felt such for my own people, as the pestilence continues."

"It is true, Majesty, my master is distressed, but the Prince has a fine constitution, and an able mind. These strengths will aid in his recovery."

What a fine liar de Silva was! Don Carlos was presently as frail in body as he was in mind. Had de Quadra said this I would have looked down on him, but since the liar was de Silva, and I was growing increasingly fond of him, I celebrated his cleverness. Friendship is the best sauce; it disguises ugliness and smoothes all bitterness. "Have you written to Emperor Ferdinand about opening talks of marriage with his son anew?" I asked.

De Silva dipped his head. "I have, Majesty. I have also taken the liberty to counsel the Emperor that he must proceed slowly and with gentle care. I have told him acting in haste will only alarm you for I know your Majesty is naturally inclined to a maiden's life. Rest assured, Majesty, my master will take the time that must be allowed for you to prevail over your instincts. You will find him a gracious and tender negotiator."

Oh! I could have bounded to de Silva and kissed the man! What a marvellous ruse! He had ensured all talks of marriage would go ahead with all the speed of an ancient slug meandering over a tasty lettuce! With de Silva as my ally I could pull back from the talks, or put them on hold with ease.

"This would be pleasing, lord ambassador," I said. "For too often have men not understood my heart." I glanced at Robin, his face still afire from my previous insults. I kept my eyes on him. "Too often have suitors tried to push me into doing their will; that is the way of *some* men when they deal with women… They try to force themselves upon us making us feel only disdain for them. With your care for my comfort and sensibilities, ambassador, I believe these negotiations may run smooth."

"I admit myself horrified to hear you have been so rudely handed, Your Majesty," de Silva said, looking genuinely upset. "You will find that neither I, nor my master is made of such mettle. Rest assured, Majesty, we will move at the pace which suits you. Women are to be flattered, after all, rather than *forced* into the state of matrimony."

"I wish more men thought as you do, my dear ambassador," I said, gazing at Robin. If his cheeks grew any redder, I could have set him on a pole in my gardens to illuminate the dark pathways at night.

Good, I thought, let Robin understand all he has done. *Let him understand that he has tried to force me just as that knave who hid in my cousin's bedchamber attempted to force her!* One act of force was physical, and one mental. But were they not all part of the same evil?

Storms of autumn arrived. Gusting gales of chilled wind from the north blew over England, throwing golden leaves and brown stalks whirling through the air and pelting the heads of field workers with hard and bitter rains. In the forests and woodlands mice and voles scampered between heavy droplets, stoically gathering nuts and berries. And, as the countryside fell from autumn and into winter, Cecil descended into incessant nagging about my cousin, Mary of Scots.

We had agreed we would ask for evidence about Mary's dynastic rights and would ascertain her claim to the throne. Cecil now demanded this investigation. It would take into account all other heirs, and my father's will, which had expressly eliminated the heirs of Margaret Tudor in favour of the Greys, as Cecil knew. He wanted to prove Mary had no right to the English throne, but since I was sure his investigation would show the opposite, I allowed it. Mary was displeased to hear of this, so I attempted to soften the insult by sending her a gift. It was a ring; a great diamond, set in gold, and of most pleasing clarity. My cousin received it with great affection, wore it every day, and made a point of kissing it before her court. Some began to jest it was an engagement ring.

If she was pleased with her new ring, however, Mary was apparently much less enamoured about me choosing her husband. She was, for once, clever about hiding her feelings, but Randolph was sure she was never going to acquiesce to my demand. Whenever he tried to broach the subject, she distracted him. I could admire this feint, but it still irritated me. One day, she held out her hands to Randolph displaying the ring I had given her and another which had been a present from François, saying, "two jewels I have now that must die with me and shall never be willingly let out of my sight." Then, as Randolph tried to press her, she shouted to her court, "Randolph would have me marry into England, my lords!"

The Duke of Argyll called back, "why? Has the Queen of England become a man?" Her courtiers laughed heartily and Mary went on to sport with Randolph. I had not disclosed any potential suitors to Mary as I was not quite ready to reveal Robin as my choice yet. Mary believed Randolph knew who I wanted her to marry, so she tried to tease it from him, and then dodged his constant petition that she accept me as her matchmaker. My ambassador was reduced to great embarrassment as Mary toyed with him. My cousin and her court found it amusing, I less so. My offer had been serious.

Although only twenty-one, my cousin seemed to be in regular ill-health. Randolph wrote that she was given to even more frequent outbursts of weeping, and had a pain in her side. Which side it was that Mary felt pain in, Randolph could not decide, for sometimes he wrote it was her left and at others her right.

"As long as she does not become a pain in *my* side," I muttered to myself as I read Randolph's reports. "For she is clearly not taking the notion I decide on her husband as serious."

*

Another cousin was bent on vexing me that autumn. And it was not only Katherine Grey I grew angry at, but Robin and Cecil as well.

Robin brought a petition from Katherine. It was accompanied by letters from John Grey and Cecil and was stuffed full of pretty phrases, all begging for mercy. At the same time, I learned of a book written in support of both Katherine's marriage and her right to be named heir. Written by a man named Hales, the text said that since Katherine and Hertford had been married with joint consent, and had consummated the match, their marriage was legal. It also cited the stipulation of common law in England, which said that only

Englishmen could inherit property or title in England, and not foreigners. Although this stipulation did not, in fact, apply directly to the crown, there were many who took it to mean such. It was a direct strike against Mary of Scots ever being named my heir, and that made it potentially dangerous for our delicate friendship.

The book further called upon scholars in Europe to decide on the legality of Katherine's marriage. I was enraged that anyone would seek to undermine my authority and that of the English Church who had conducted the investigation. I had John Grey and others questioned about the book, and many fingers pointed at Cecil as the true author.

I took the petition silently from Robin when he arrived with it, and sent him away. When I had read it, I called for Cecil. "This petition is your work, is it not?" I asked, waving the parchment at him. "Yours and Robin's. Katherine Grey has never written like this before, Cecil. I hear your words through her mouth."

Cecil was not fool enough to deny this. "Your Majesty, Lord Grey contacted me in despair for Lady Katherine's health. Have they not been punished enough?"

I drew myself up and glared at him. "Have I not been generous, Cecil? Have I taken their lives, or removed their sons to the houses of strangers? Have I thrown them into prisons without comfort, or denied them servants to tend to their needs? There is much more I could have done with Hertford and Katherine. There is much more my father would have done." I threw the paper on the table. "Tempt me not, Cecil, to become as my father was to his enemies."

"They do not have to be enemies, Majesty."

"Those who act against my laws and against my will are my enemies. Those who defy me are my foes. Those who do not show outward obedience to me will be punished." I looked long and hard into his eyes. "Do not become my enemy, Cecil."

"Your Majesty... I work ever for your wishes and for England..."

"And the book, Cecil? The book apparently by Hales, but which many say was penned by you? Is that your work also?" Cecil went to protest, but I stopped him.

"My wishes are England's wishes," I said, my tone baleful. "My will is England's will. *I am England*, Cecil. If you betray me, you betray your country." I shook my head. "If you choose to work for my cousin, then you are working against me. Think carefully, old friend. Choose your side well. I shall not offer you another chance."

I knew the petition was Cecil's work, but I did not believe the book was. I did not believe Cecil would do something as idiotic as that, but I was angry at both Cecil and Robin for working behind my back. I sent word that I would not forgive Katherine or her family. Katherine was plunged into misery, and refused to leave her bed. When the Seymour and Grey families found out about the failed petition, they all blamed each other. The Seymours blamed John Grey for getting involved, and he protested he maintained Katherine, and bought everything for her, so was he not in the position of a father, or husband and therefore honour-bound to protect her? He said he had been given little from the Crown for her upkeep, which was true enough. I had been forced to pay for my imprisonment when my sister held me captive and I had not even been found guilty of treason. I saw no reason to take on the cost of Katherine's upkeep, when her family could provide for her. Both families viewed my actions as cruel, but why should I pay for a twice-proved traitor to live in comfort?

I had Katherine and her youngest son moved from John Grey's house, for I believed he was an ill influence. An investigation went on into the book, but so many names emerged who were involved that I knew I could do nothing about it. Cecil, Robin, and Cecil's brother-in-law, Nicholas Bacon, were all implicated. The author of the book, Hales, was arrested and put in the Tower, Bacon was banished from court and John Grey lived in terror he would be arrested too. I was troubled by how many high-ranking supporters Katherine had. It made me all the more determined to court my cousin of Scots, especially since so many of her supporters had read Hale's book with horror and were writing responses to it. Katherine's supporters, too, wrote responses to those responses, and so the circle continued on. I felt as though I would never be rid of this abhorrent girl and all the strife she had caused me.

I removed Hertford from his mother's house, so he could influence his son no more. Katherine I left at Ingatestone with her baby. I would find other ways to punish Cecil and Robin. It was time to offer Robin to Mary, and to show my displeasure to Cecil, I would promote Mary of Scots as my heir.

Chapter Forty-Six

Windsor Castle
Autumn - Winter 1563

As the plague started to dissipate in London, I took the opportunity to ride out and hunt each day in Windsor's great park. Arriving back one afternoon, news came of a ship arriving at Dover. The previous year, a captain named John Hawkins had departed for Sierra Leone. He arrived back in London that autumn with a great profit in his pocket. Part of Hawkins's newfound wealth had come from the sale of slaves from Africa; a trade which was illegal in England, and one I was not enamoured of at all. When Hawkins arrived in English waters, however, his reports explained that the slaves he had taken and sold had defected from their Spanish and Portuguese masters, and gone to Hawkins, asking to be sold on to better owners. Hawkins said they had suffered from poor treatment, and had been grateful for his help. Spain and Portugal held many slave plantations in Africa, and had reduced much of the native population to slavery to support their ambitions. Slaves could not be brought into England, since there were laws in place which prohibited slavery, and the colour of a man's skin, or the country he originated from did not excuse infraction of the law. The other problem with Hawkins bringing such people to England was that their legal status was in doubt, for although they could not be kept as slaves, they were not Crown subjects either. He had therefore traded them outside of England, apparently according to their wishes, and had returned home a rich man.

"And you maintain they came to you *willingly*, Captain Hawkins?" I asked. I had read his statement in detail, and found no fault in law with what he had done. If the slaves he had traded had indeed asked to be taken to kinder masters then he had done right by them. But the idea of a man owning the freedom of another was repugnant to me. Should it not be to all people?

"They suffered under abusive masters, Your Majesty," Hawkins replied, his weather-beaten face ruddy under the candlelight. "And I left them with better ones. I had no legal power to alter their status, and it was not within my authority to bring them into England, but I assure you, they came to me and asked for my aid. This worked to our advantage, as you have no doubt read in my dispatches."

I tapped my finger on my chair as I pondered on his words. There were plenty of Moors and Africans in England, but they were free men and women. Some ran shops, worked in trades of pin-making or silk-spinning, and others were servants. The English did not keep slaves... Not since the days when William the Conqueror invaded England and dissolved the practice. All Moors, African and Saracens living in England were free, had been baptised and christened, and were accepted into society. There was a commonly held theory that they were, in essence, a more ancient, purer race and often they would find they could gain greater wages than others, for lords and ladies liked to employ them. There were even some depictions I had heard of where the Virgin Mary was represented as a black maiden. Whilst it was true that some regarded those of black complexions as frightening, and even ungodly, to my mind, the varied skills Moors brought to England were valuable to trade and commerce and they played a worthwhile part in England's society and Church. I had several Moors in my household, all of whom were loyal and useful servants.

So, therefore the thought of trading in people was unsettling. but I had to admit that Hawkins seemed to not only have made a good profit, but had done well, if he had indeed acted in these slaves' interests. He was right when he said he had no power to change their legal status, and he had sold them where they had asked to be sold... It was a complicated idea, and I must admit I was not wholly comfortable with it, but a queen also has obligations to her treasury, and mine was always running low.

"And if I gave you money to further this trade, would I have your assurance that the people you trade would go willingly with you, be removed from bad owners, and sold on only when they wished to be?" I asked, still struggling with the idea. Partly, you see, I liked the idea of disrupting Spanish interests in Africa, as long as my men were not caught. But I wanted to make sure that none of these slaves were traded in England, and that we *were* acting to free slaves of bad masters. I had no authority to alter the status of a slave who was not one of my own people, but that did not mean I could not be involved with stealing slaves from the Spanish and taking them elsewhere.

Hawkins assured me he had not thought to trade slaves at first, and had in fact been seeking gold and jewels. He told me stories of how the people had come to him, and where he had sold them. I felt assured he had acted in good faith and gave him leave to continue, as long as he did not bring slaves to England, unless they *wished* to come and work here as free servants or tradesmen. I also invested money, so he could continue to steal disgruntled slaves from their present masters and sell them on to better ones.

I will admit to you that I remained uneasy, for in allowing Hawkins to act in this way, I was aware that I was giving unofficial leave to others in England to do the same.

No matter what, I understood this could be a practice open to much abuse.

*

An important book was published that year. Called *Actes and Monuments*, its author was Master John Foxe and his work became widely known as the *Book of English Martyrs*. The work celebrated those who died for the Protestant faith, and called them the true heirs of the Apostles for their sacrifice. Priests were encouraged to leave the text next to the Bible in churches, and copies were held by almost everyone at court.

"Mary," I called to Mary Grey as I entered my chambers. The girl came running. Since her sister's disgrace, Mary had experienced a hard time in my chambers. It had ever been my habit to express my dissatisfaction at one member of a family by treating others badly. I was no saint. But I had been feeling bad that Mary suffered for her sister's sins, and when this opportunity came to make some amends, I wanted to take it.

"I have a gift for you, Mary," I said, holding out a new copy of Foxe's book. "I am sure that you will have heard of it. There are many fine passages on your sister, Jane. I thought you might like to read them."

The girl blushed and ducked into an awkward curtsey. She was not a graceful woman. Her height and roundness made it hard for her to be so. "Majesty," she breathed, taking the book. "I am more grateful than I can say."

"It is a good copy," I added. "And I hope it brings you some comfort." I glanced off to one side where my detestable cousin Margaret Lennox was conversing with her son. Darnley was often in my chambers, called to sing for me, and his mother was delighted to see him treated as a prince. I stared at Margaret for a moment, watching her heavily-lidded eyes rest with naked adulation on her son. Was this what motherhood did to a woman? Removed all sense and reason? She could not see his flaws, nor did she note his arrogance.

"I have longed to read what was written of my sister. Thank you, Majesty." Mary said, pulling my wandering eyes back to her. I was surprised to see that the girl looked a little overwhelmed.

"I hope you find all you are seeking in the text," I said.

At least one Grey understands she should be grateful to me, I thought as Mary left, hugging the book to her chest.

*

That Christmas, as the English court settled into a riotous round of celebration and enjoyment, my cousin of Scots was holding a rather different kind of audience. Mary was resolved to take care of John Knox.

Mary had experienced repeated difficulties with Knox. Quite aside from his attacks on her faith, morals and marriage plans, in the summer, two Calvinist priests had threatened one of her priests and had been arrested. Knox had put together what he called *'a convocation of the brethren'* to free them. Speeches he gave demonstrated he was quite happy with acts of violence done against Catholics, and Mary's Privy Council believed him guilty of treason. Mary decided enough was enough. She put Knox on trial for treason and sedition.

Upon entering court, Mary was amused when Knox took his cap off, showing respect, something he had little thought to do before. "This is a good beginning," she chuckled loudly. "The man made me weep and shed never a tear himself. I will see today if I can make him weep instead." Many of her advisors were shocked, and counselled her to take care for Knox could still stir trouble. Charged with 'raising a tumult' against his Queen, and encouraging others to rebel, Knox conducted his own defence.

Unfortunately Knox was an able debater. The vote was taken whilst Mary was absent from court, and Knox was acquitted. When Mary returned she refused to accept the verdict, and it was taken again, only for the same result to occur. Mary's half-brother, Lord James, Earl of Moray was the cause. Irritated to see others promoted above him at court, and nervous about Mary moving against Scotland's premier Protestant, he had secretly worked to ensure Knox would be acquitted. It was the first in a long line of betrayals of his half-sister and Queen. Mary was humiliated. Knox had prevailed and it was clear that dangerous factions were growing at court against her. Although she deported herself well, and sought to make peace with her brother, I believe she was lonely. The reason I had cause to believe this was because she started to write more letters to me.

We had a bond. It was a strange bond, for often we were hardly friends. In many ways we were rivals... but the connection was there. Call us friendly foes, or fractured allies if you will, but there was an understanding between us at that time in our reigns. Mary even wrote that I might suggest some lords I believed suitable to be her husband and she would consider them. My cousin was seeking a friend and ally.

I wish we could have stayed that way; close and yet apart, together and estranged, friend and yet stranger... At that time, we were the closest we had ever been to truly being sisters, as we so often called each other.

Chapter Forty-Seven

Windsor Castle
Winter 1564

Amidst the snows of winter, the Duke of Wurttemberg, envoy of Emperor Ferdinand, arrived to test how serious I was about marrying Archduke Charles. Ferdinand did not trust me. I heard in private he referred to me as "that bastard English fox" which tickled me. But, with the help of de Silva, who was ensuring all parties knew about my *fragile sensibilities* I was unafraid of these negotiations. I met the servant of the Duke, and told him I believed it had been the Emperor's fault talks had stalled last time, since he had not allowed his son to visit me. I veered between simpering enthusiasm and blushing modesty. The envoy went away in a state of abject bafflement, although Cecil later assured him I was in earnest about marriage.

"Was I lying, Majesty?" he asked, taking a seat in my chambers.

"Not if you believed what you said, Cecil." I smiled. "That is the nature of truth is it not? All men see their own."

"You know what I mean, Majesty," he said, taking a goblet of wine from Anne Parry. "Are you serious about wanting to wed Archduke Charles?"

"As serious as ever I was, Cecil," I flippantly admitted, receiving a great sigh in return. "You know my mind, Cecil. I am not made for matrimony. But, old friend, I promise not to die until I am in my grey hairs. You will have me for as long as I can cling to life, and I have always had a talent for survival."

"Then you must name an heir for the security of the kingdom."

"I must *not* name an heir, for the security of the kingdom. Naming an heir will bring division and rebellion."

"Not naming one may do the same," he disagreed.

"Not so, *Spirit*. I know the temper of the English. This is the right way to play this game, I know it."

*

As wild storms battled the English coastline, political tempests rose in Flanders and the Low Countries. Phillip's bastard half-sister, Margaret of Parma, ruled there as regent, and since she had come to that position many Protestants in her realm had left, fleeing persecution. Where their father, Charles, had been surprisingly lenient with Protestants, Margaret and Phillip were not. Ever since the reign of my grandfather, England had held a valuable trade agreement with Flanders and the Low Countries. The cloth trade was important to England and, more particularly, to me. It allowed me means to raise income without always needing to turn to Parliament. Since Parliament always wanted concessions before agreeing funds, the wool trade was vital to my personal freedom. I did not wish to lose it.

Reports reached us of increased searches and arrests being carried out, all in the name of stamping out 'heresy'. The Inquisition, that horrific order Phillip of Spain was so enamoured with, was strong in the Low Countries, and their increasing power was regarded with great fear by those of our faith. Protestants, led by the Prince of Orange, petitioned for leniency, but were often ignored. English privateers and merchants were subject to interrogation if suspected of crimes when on Margaret's lands, and we heard of arrests of our people occurring with increasing regularity. Determined to retaliate for this persecution, English captains began to attack Iberian ships. Perhaps four hundred English ships were involved, although they did not band together to attack, since that would have looked like a declaration of war. Phillip ordered that these 'pirates', as he called them, were to be arrested, their ships seized and their contents confiscated. Margaret sent her ambassador, Christophe d'Assonleville, to me with a long list of grievance against English captains wreaking havoc in Hapsburg waters.

We had to keep the peace, but I was secretly proud of these wily captains. Given Phillip's involvement in plots against me, I could not think ill of my captains causing him trouble for a change. I also benefited secretly from their efforts, since these captains paid me a portion of their plundered profits for looking the other way, and so had no intention of punishing them. But a queen has to make it appear she is concerned for the dignity of other rulers, even when she is not. Unfortunately, my efforts to persuade the ambassador I would do all I could to stop these men did not convince him. Margaret closed her ports to English vessels and we were in danger of losing the trade. It did the cloth trade in Flanders no good either. English wool was the best there was, and without our raw materials coming to market in Flanders, the cloth trade there collapsed. Many people were made destitute for want of work and income. Angered, disaffected masses opened their hearts to the words of Calvinist preachers, who spoke out against the hard, grasping rule of Catholic overlords. Muttering of rebellion began. Margaret became nervous, keeping to her palaces, rather than travelling through the streets. I told her ambassador I was more than willing to open the trade up again, as soon as his mistress was ready, but there are some people who would rather cut their own arm off than admit defeat, and the Regent Margaret was one of them.

Phillip of Spain took the whole event as a personal insult. In his eyes he had been *lenient* with me. I was the bastard, heretic Queen. He had more right to the throne than I did, so he thought. Having once been England's King-consort, had he wished to, he believed, he could have deposed me and taken my kingdom. What a fantasist! The slack-brained, puffed-up, bobolyne believed my reaction smacked of *ingratitude*. As though I had anything to be thankful for from Phillip of Spain! And besides, Phillip could hardly have known I was not in earnest about stopping my captains from ship raiding. I had made all diplomatic pleasantries required…

As the disaffected numbers grew, and more turned to Protestant preachers, Phillip viewed me as directly responsible for encouraging rebellion and heresy in his lands. We entered a secret war. It was one not fought with ship or sword, musket or cannon, but with spies and secrets. As Protestant rebels grew in the Netherlands, Phillip and his sister came to regard me not simply with suspicion anymore, but with outright hostility. We had to keep the peace on the surface, but under this cloak of pleasantries, spies moved.

As I struggled with Phillip and Margaret, a new maid entered my household. Her name was Mary Radcliffe. She was that same daughter of Sir Humphrey Radcliffe who had been offered as a New Year's gift to me some years before. Finally of an age to take a place in my household, the girl arrived at court. She was young, being only thirteen when she entered my service, and an innocent in the ways of the court. Raised on her father's estates in the country, she arrived with wide eyes and a humble, gentle nature to which I warmed. But there was strength, courage, and conviction under her humility; qualities I admired.

"You will be expected to be humble, gentle, and deport yourself with grace and virtue," I said, ending my induction speech. "When you marry, you will be expected to keep your children at the estates of your future husband. Child-bearing will not be allowed to interfere with your duties at court. I have few places in my household, and since they are precious, you must make serving me your first priority. "

"I have no intention of ever taking a husband, Your Majesty," the girl announced, causing many of my ladies to blink with surprise. "I will follow the example of my Queen and give myself entirely to the office God has chosen me to perform. I believe that, were I to marry, it would distract me from my duties, Majesty. I have no wish for anything come between me and the service I will give to you."

I was astounded. It might have seemed she was too young to make such a choice, yet in her eyes I could see determination. I sensed we were of the same spirit. I could understand well, where others could not, the freedom that came in remaining unwed. I found her resolve so pleasing that I paid her a wage, something I did not do for every maid in my service. Eventually, she would become one of the women who served me the longest, and also a close and good friend.

Like calls to like, after all...

Chapter Forty-Eight

Greenwich Palace
Winter - Spring 1564

"One hundred and fifty-seven are *actively* hostile to the policies of your Majesty's government," Cecil said, reading from one of his habitual piles of parchment.

"Out of eight hundred and fifty-two, Cecil, I do not consider those bad odds," I noted, looking out of the window, its panes made dark by the falling rain.

"There are more who are marked as indifferent or unfavourable."

"Still, Cecil, I am not discouraged."

The reports we were going over were from my bishops. They had been tasked to conduct a survey of the Justices of the Peace, classifying them according to religion and discovering their sentiments about my religious settlement. Opposition was strongest in the east and north of England, with blotches of resistance in Staffordshire and Buckinghamshire. Without the aid of local law enforcers we could not maintain control, and if too many were allowing transgressors to flout the law, my middle way would never succeed.

All knew there were priests hidden in many houses in England. They knew if you came to a certain door at a certain time and made a certain knock, you could be admitted to hear a Catholic Mass. This, I saw little harm in, as long as it was kept secret. What concerned me was what those priests were up to when not holding Mass. There had been occasions where the Catholic faith had led to problems for my security and for my wellbeing. Secret Masses I cared not for, even if my men did… Plotting and planning against my life, I certainly did care about. I was not willing to believe that all Catholics desired my death but was prepared to admit there were zealots willing to take up arms against me. I could also see, however, the same was true of fanatical Protestants who thought my religious settlement did not go far enough. I was trying, trying very hard to maintain peace in my realm and prevent my Council from implementing extreme measures. Whenever a plot was uncovered, the fire was rekindled in my men. The desire to stamp out Catholics was increasing.

"What will be done about this?" Cecil asked, glancing up with a smudge of ink on his cheek.

"Nothing," I said softly and turned around. "I am happy with the way the religious settlement advances, Cecil. This is not a war. Justices of the Peace do not spring from the earth, Cecil. We cannot replace all the men who cause you disquiet; we have not the resources. Let them be. They know we have an eye on them."

"You give them too much leniency," Cecil said. "You will regret this, one day, Majesty. I feel it in my bones."

"Let me tell you what I think, old friend. I believe if you constantly act against a sect of people, if you treat them as outcasts, act as though they are the enemy, then you make them into the very enemy you fear. I have said before, *Spirit*, not to turn my people against me. I will not have this realm becoming a mirror image of the horrors my sister inflicted on those of our faith."

"I wish I had your faith, Majesty," Cecil said, his face grim. "But I do not believe Catholics will be so generous."

"Then we will show more generosity, *Spirit*, and more, until they understand."

"Catholics are not loyal to you first, Majesty, but to the Pope. Their hearts will always be papal purple, rather than Tudor green." I gazed out of the window, attempting to ignore Cecil as he continued his lecture. "Catholics *are* a threat to you, Majesty, it is only fitting that we keep a close eye upon them."

"*Spirit*," I said wearily, twisting my neck to look at him. "I have tried very hard to ensure my realm does not become a divided nation. Persecuting Catholics will only ensure more rise to take their place. Children will see their parents hurt and humiliated, and they will turn on us. You will breed a new generation opposed to me, and to my government, from birth." Cecil was shaking his head. He did not think I was correct. "Think of it as a plant gone to seed, old friend," I said. "Shake the plant, and the seeds fall further; they spread, and more plants grow. Leave the stem untroubled, and perhaps it will simply rot away. That is what I want... a slow and gentle passing of Catholicism. And in its place, the English Church will grow. In one more generation the people of England will be united under one faith."

"What we wish for, we cannot always have, Majesty," Cecil warned.

"*What* a surprise, Cecil," I said waspishly. "I had never considered such might be the case." I cracked my knuckles, making Cecil flinch. "I will not sanction persecution of Catholics as my sister did to Protestants. I will not do it, Cecil. If you must keep an eye on certain people determined to make trouble, then do so, but have a *reason* to do so... and not just a prejudice against them."

"I am not prejudiced against them," sniffed Cecil.

"Yes you are, my old friend, and well do I know it." I sighed heavily. "I believe it is possible for those who still worship in the Catholic faith to be loyal to me. I will not push them to choose between me and Rome. And besides, I have no wish to make further enemies in Europe by hunting down Catholics and putting them to the sword. Leave them be, Cecil. If they have done no harm, then no harm shall we bring to them."

"Majesty," Cecil bowed and left, a deep crease furrowed into his brow. I returned to stare at the window. Outside, rain was falling fast and the skies were dark. In the window pane I could see my own ghostly image staring back. I stared into my reflected eyes; black and bold, they twinkled back at me. My mother's eyes... Sometimes I saw people start when I looked at them for the first time. Robin said staring into my eyes made him feel like I could read his thoughts. Unusual eyes... yes... but I believed they saw much others could not... I shook my head, thinking on all I had struggled with to get my religious settlement passed. It would be easier to believe it was never going to work fully, to give up, but I would not. War is easy to make, evil is effortless to fall into. Sin appeals to the laziness within us. Evil is so quick, so swift.

Peace and unity do not happen overnight. Most things in life, most *good* things, take a great deal of hard work to achieve. Goodness takes work and diligence. Perhaps that is God's greatest lesson. If something seems too easy, then that is where evil may be found, waiting for us to give up, give in. I had faith then that I could prevail. I just had to keep toiling.

*

At Shrovetide, my cousin of Scots put on an entertainment. It was not a normal festival of court, it was a sign she wanted to increase the friendship between us, and bring us closer together.

At a grand feast, Mary put on a show for my ambassadors. A boy dressed as *Cupid*, representing love, led a procession into her hall. He was accompanied by Mary's choir singing Italian madrigals. After a course of food was served and the diners had washed their hands and faces in silver bowls, a girl representing *Chastity* entered the hall followed by another procession of singers. As Mary's servants served the last course, Latin verses were spoken, proclaiming the virtues of a pure mind and radiant beauty. The last figure entered as the feast ended; a boy symbolising *Time*. Mary's choir sang of how friendship between England and Scotland would be praised in the future.

Randolph was excited by this, as it presented an opportunity for him to open fresh talks with my cousin about her marriage. But her men intervened. Maitland, Moray and Argyll all argued that the postponed meeting between Mary and me should go ahead before any agreement was reached. Randolph wrote that they were particularly concerned with Mary and me meeting without intervention from any of my subjects, meaning Cecil, of course.

Mary called Randolph to her. "Princes at all times do not have their wills, but my heart being my own, is immutable," she said. Mary wanted me to reveal my choice for her husband. Randolph wrote that Mary spoke of her love for me, and longed for friendship, but could not continue with this uncertainty. If I wanted to choose her husband, she wanted to know his name. Only then, she would decide. *"The word of a prince,"* Randolph wrote, *"is of far greater worth than the mutable mind of inconsistent people."*

The time had come. When Maitland returned to court that spring, I ensured the Presence Chamber was stuffed with courtiers, Robin amongst them. "I would be prepared to offer your Queen a husband from amongst my own men, one whom all know to be dear to my heart. I am sure, if your mistress considered him as a husband, she would prefer him to all the princes in the world."

I extended my hand, and pointed to Robin.

There was silence. The horrified look on Robin's face was truly delightful. *Taken by surprise, dear Robin?* I thought.

Amazed I would be willing to part with you? I could not think ill of my actions. Robin had interfered in politics too many times. I needed to know where his loyalties truly were.

"This is proof of how much I love your Queen, my cousin," I went on. "That I am willing to give up a creature I so dearly prize, and give him instead to your mistress."

"My Queen will need time to consider your offer, Majesty," Maitland said, glancing at Robin who had gone white as the Virgin's undergarments. "Of course there is the issue that Lord Robert Dudley is not high enough in title to match my Queen..."

"Such matters can be altered, ambassador," I purred. "It is a shame, however that the Earl of Warwick, Ambrose Dudley, is not *quite* as handsome as Lord Robin, his brother, otherwise I would have offered the elder brother over the younger. And it is true also that this is a great sacrifice for me..." I gazed lovingly at Robin who was staring at me in disbelief, his mouth opening and closing like a freshly caught fish. "... For Lord Robin is, as all know, well-beloved of my heart."

Got you, Robin, I thought, enjoying his horror.

If Robin was dismayed, Cecil was keen. He was the only one besides me to think well of the idea. Even Norfolk was opposed to it, and he had more reason to wish Robin gone from court than anyone. But Norfolk despised the idea of Robin becoming a king, for then, Robin would outrank Norfolk. What an idea! Cecil's enthusiasm had less to do with recognising Robin's possible virtues as a king, and more to do with wanting to pluck Robin out of the English Court for good, but all the same, I valued Cecil's help, especially when he decided to seek Maitland out and praised Robin. It only added to the notion that I fully supported this plan, and that was what I wanted Robin to believe.

Robin arrived at my door the next day, in an unusually humble frame of mind. He stood restlessly, waiting for my ladies to move to another part of the chamber. When he looked at me, his eyes were haunted with sorrow and incredulity. "You would rid yourself of me?" he asked. I could hear sadness in his voice, and anger too. I took great satisfaction in his fear and worry. Let him, for once, understand the pain he had caused me.

"Is there a reason I should have you stay, Robin?" I asked, my tone careless. "Have you not given every reason for me to distrust you? Have you not worked with my enemies? Have you not worked against me, with my own lords and Parliament, trying to force me to wed? Have you not conspired to make that loathsome Grey girl my heir?" My tone was flippant, light as the summer breeze. My feelings were anything but.

"Have you given up on the idea of us marrying at all?"

"At this present time, Robin… yes," I said. My tone altered as my hurt and anger, stored up for so long, broke over my control. "You have done nothing to make me believe it is *me* you love, and not the throne. Nothing to make me think *I* am your true desire, rather than power. At every step you have tried to flout me, to dupe me and to play me as a fool. You should know by now, my lord, this is no way to win a woman's heart."

"But I only did thus to get you to see reason!" he exclaimed, running his hands through his hair and gazing at me with feral eyes.

"It is *my* reason which will prevail in *my* realm, Lord Dudley, and no other. Keep that in mind. Do not toy with my patience. Take not the path forged by your father and grandsire, the path of treason and betrayal. It leads only to death, and believe me, I have considered offering you that fate many times."

He had no answer. To deny my accusations would be a lie, and to admit to them would be dangerous. Robin often acted recklessly, but he was no dullard. He was not about to put himself in clear danger.

I sniffed loudly, resuming my facetious tone. "I do not see *why* you are so aghast, my lord. You wish to be a king, do you not? I offer you a queen. You can become a king, Robin. You can rule at Mary's side, and your sons would be heirs not only to Scotland, but mayhap to England as well some day. Think you not that your Queen has offered you a fine gift? If ambition and power are all that matter to you, you can have all you want of them. I am handing you your desires. I might expect you to be grateful."

"I do not want to marry another," he almost whispered. His eyes fell. I almost felt sorry for him, but I steeled my heart. "I love *you*, Elizabeth," he murmured. "I want to marry *you*."

"Perhaps that is the problem, my lord," I said. "You already think of me *as* a wife, do you not? And to you, as to so many others, a wife is a possession to be controlled and managed by her husband, by her *master*. When I revealed my love, you believed I had already given you such power over me. You would be my master, Robin. You seek to command me, to control me."

His eyes darted to my face. About to deny my words, he opened his mouth to speak, but I held up an imperious hand and he closed his mouth. "You do not see that I am not as other women, my lord," I continued. "I will not suffer a master. Even if you were chosen to be my husband, Robin, you would not be the chosen of God as I am. *I* was set on this throne to rule England by God. You were not. And despite this, you think yourself above me, and that is why you treat my position, my wishes, and my affection with such disdain. How can you be surprised, then, that I turn my face from you and offer you to another? This plan will give you a wife, a pretty wife, and it will make you a king. You will have your ambition to keep you warm at night, my lord, along with my beautiful cousin."

"You are more important to me than any ambition," he said. His voice was harsh. It scraped from his throat as though he had swallowed gravel.

"I do not believe you, Robin," I said coldly. "And should you ever wish me to believe in you again, I would urge you to act for my welfare, for my interests, and be my friend, rather than working with my enemies, and against me time and time again."

I made for the gardens. I did not want my fine speech ruined by Robin seeing the tears in my eyes.

Chapter Forty-Nine

Greenwich Palace
Winter - Spring 1564

I sent Randolph a letter in which I formally offered Robin to Mary. My cousin was startled and suspicious. Seeing that Robin was not a prince, or even an earl or duke, Mary was affronted. Although Randolph did much to convince her that Robin was important to me, and therefore what I was offering was a true sacrifice, she was still unsure whether to view the offer of his hand as a slight. But Mary could not reject my offer immediately. She needed me. I was not only the one who could grant her the throne she wanted, but my support was important against men such as Knox and other Protestants who would flaunt her will. Mary was confused. She suspected I was playing games with her, which I was in part, but my true opponent was Robin.

Robin was doing all he could to make sure the match never went ahead. Working with all those who supported him, and anyone he could bribe, my favourite was a busy man as the winds of winter softened and took on the shallow warmth of spring. He went to Cecil, to convince him he was an unsuitable husband for Mary. He went to Norfolk, who was already opposed to the idea, and won his support. Robin positively *flew* about court trying to keep his nest in England. I heard of his scheming through Kat, who I had instructed to watch him. From all outward signs, Robin was desperate. He told anyone who would listen that he loved me and did not wish to leave England. I had run my bird into a trap, and now he struggled to be released.

I was pleased by Robin's misery, comforted by it even. The pallor of his face, the frantic efforts he went to, the people he would align himself to as an ally... Yes, all this was sweet to my fractured love and weary soul. Perhaps he did love me. I would certainly have loved to believe it. But there was not enough evidence yet for this belief to thrive in my heart. Robin was so busy racing about trying to stop the match he did not think to work on his relationship with me. That displeased me.

The news soon spread to the courts of Europe and was greeted with derision. Phillip of Spain thought I was attempting to slight Mary by handing her my cast-off. No one believed I was serious but I insisted that Robin cooperate with the marriage negotiations to make it appear as though I was. Maitland was at a loss to know how to react, much like his mistress. A further proposition I added, that Mary and Robin could live at the English Court with me so I would not be separated from Robin entirely, did not go over well either. I was only half-serious on this in any case. It was security in case Mary should actually agree to my plan.

"I think we should talk again about a meeting between my cousin and me," I said to Maitland. "The circumstances which prevented it before no longer restrict us. I am sure if my good sister and I could meet, we would come to an easy and quick settlement on this and other issues. She could meet Lord Dudley at the same time, and assess his worthiness."

"I will certainly put the idea to my Queen, Majesty," he agreed.

When word came from Scotland it was not positive. English spies in Mary's court told us my cousin was quietly still seeking a match with Spain, and was playing us for time. Mary declined to meet that summer, saying there was not time to adequately prepare. I knew she was stalling and that roused my temper. Her refusal to meet me led to a time of coolness between us. Mary was not willing for me to act as a father to her, and I was not willing to name her my heir without that relationship. We were at an impasse, and each of us was too stubborn and proud to allow the other to take the lead.

When ill weather drove us inside the warm confines of the palace, I spent time with my ladies. Where once Robin would have been a perpetual presence there, he was now far too busy attempting to thwart my plans to spend time with me. Robin had missed the point; it was my affection and love which would prove key to his staying in England.

Too many tricks... Too many games... Robin had become lost in them. Sometimes I wondered if I had, too.

In the absence of Robin, I had another man in constant attendance in my chambers. Ordinarily I would have had as little to do with him as possible, but he had a sweet voice, and I was vulnerable to the appeal of music. Lord Darnley was a regular visitor. Accompanied by musicians on the virginals or lute, he would entertain me. I had no love for Darnley; he was arrogant, foolish and selfish, but he had the voice of an angel. It was just a shame that this one virtue did not extend to aid the rest of him. The voice of an angel he had, yes... but he had the soul of a demon.

Some of my ladies, especially the younger, more impressionable maids of honour, were impressed by Darnley. He was handsome and had good legs, which he was inordinately fond of displaying in tight, white hose. He was rich, and noble, to be sure... All things which may recommend a man to a woman's affections, but to me, his handsome face was vaguely unsettling. He looked almost like a woman, so delicate was his beauty, and yet, in the cruel curl of his lips, and in the glance of his eyes, there was such lasciviousness that I found him uncomfortable to be around. He possessed an air of wanton, lewd experience, which made me shudder. He reminded me too much of Thomas Seymour. He did not look like Seymour, but there was something similar about their characters which made me uncomfortable. Something predatory. He was also conceited, callous, stupid and vain. He had little conversation, and what little there was, was about himself. Darnley was a strutting coxcomb, a narcissistic, brash borachio. Hearing him sing though... Ah, then you might have believed there was indeed an angelic spirit hidden deep in the folds of sexuality and licentious hunger. When he lifted his head and sang, it was easier to see what women saw in him. When I heard of his exploits in Southwark, however, I was further repulsed.

"The boy will be riddled with pox, if he continues this way," I said to Cecil. Cecil's face was dark with disapproval. He liked the boy no better than I.

"From what I hear, Majesty, he already is." Cecil shook his head. "It is in the nature of young men, with money enough in their purse, to be wild in youth... but Darnley takes such ambition to new heights."

"Or lows, Cecil, as may be." I had no illusions that many men at court had mistresses, and visited the stews at Southwark, but most were discreet. Darnley hid little of his reckless adventures with staggering numbers of prostitutes of both sexes. It amazed me that women could hear of this, and still want to bed him, since they must have known there was a risk of pox. But I had to admit he did radiate a kind of brazen invitation in his manner of talking, walking and conversing. Some people find such blatant sexuality appealing, and even more fall into the trap of projecting the fantasy of a fallen man, who can be saved *only* by the one he loves. Darnley's admirers may have thought they could redeem him, make him a good man. How many times have people of either sex fallen for such a myth? More times than can be counted.

Sometimes when Darnley turned up in my chambers it was clear he was still drunk from the previous night; the scent of sour wine on his breath and leeching from his skin not quite covered by the rose perfume he liberally doused himself with. There was no law against men being drunk at court, but

I hardly expected my servants to arrive to entertain me with bleary eyes or unsteady stomachs. At such times, I kept his visits short, and sent him away so he could stick his head in the privy and void his festering belly. Ordinarily I would have detained him as punishment, but I could not stand his stench.

You might think this would be enough for me to banish him from court, and believe me, I considered it. But having him here, under my careful eye, meant I had my cousin Margaret's precious son just where he was most of use to me. I could strike fear into her whenever I wished, since I had her son under my power. It was enough, I hoped, to stop her conspiring against me. Darnley was my prisoner to ensure his mother's good behaviour. Soon enough, however, Cecil thought of another use for this repellent boy.

Chapter Fifty

Greenwich Palace
Spring - Summer 1564

English engagement in the wars in France was brought to an official end that spring with the Treaty of Troyes. We did not do well from the treaty, but there was little we could do about it. We had lost men, money and status in this failed venture and Calais was not included as part of England's settlement. With that treaty I lost the final scrap of belief that England would ever regain Calais along with any enthusiasm to join a foreign war again. In the days following the treaty talks I was downcast, thinking how disappointed my father would have been in me. I had longed to recover Calais ever since coming to the throne. Now it looked as though that would never be. The wound we took when Calais was stolen from us would remain, open, bleeding, festering in English pride for generations to come.

That same month, my dear Bess Parr, Marchioness of Northampton, requested to leave and travel to Antwerp with Doctor John Dee. The lump in her breast was growing and she was often in pain. Her appetite was feeble, and her husband told me he often found her vomiting, although she took pains to hide much of her suffering from him, knowing how he worried for her. Parr suspected that Bess was sicker than she allowed anyone to see, and he was frightened. The physicians of Antwerp were world-renowned and they were her last hope. My doctors could do nothing more for her.

"Be sure that you take good care of my friend," I said to the handsome, grave-faced man as they came to take their leave of me. Dee had only just returned to England on a short visit home, but was eager to return to Antwerp. "I shall expect her brought home in bonny health."

"I have assured the Marchioness that the physicians of Antwerp are the very best she will find, Majesty," Dee said. "And with their help and the grace of God, we will find a cure for her malady."

"Bess," I put my hands into hers, squeezing her fingers. "You are *commanded* to return home a well woman. I will hold your posts in my household until you come once more to claim them."

"Thank you, Your Majesty," she said. "I hope I will return soon."

As Bess and Dee walked from the chamber, so Cecil entered. "Your royal cousin of Scots has agreed to allow the Earl of Lennox to return to his estates in Scotland, Majesty."

"Good," I said. "Perhaps it will get the troublesome man and his odious wife out of my hair."

I had written to Mary some time ago about allowing Lennox to return. He was a handsome, well-proportioned man; tall, fair of skin, and with a rather long nose. His years in France as a youth had left him with a heavily accented voice, and he carried his pride with him like the scent of overpowering perfume; cloying and nauseous. My father had no doubt granted Margaret to him as a wife as he saw Lennox's potential for the Scot's throne, but none in Scotland wanted a traitor who so easily switched sides as their King. Lennox was officially a Protestant, but his faith was as easily changed as his loyalty. He had converted to Catholicism under my father, changed again under my brother and then again under my sister. Margaret's *Mathieu*, as she called him, was a man who would do anything for advancement, and who would give up anything for power. He wanted his Scottish titles and estates back. Granting him this excursion to Scotland was a mark of favour, but it had occurred to me this would be a way to rid myself of Margaret Lennox for good. A pleasing notion, although not one likely to happen for some time since we had had reports of late that Margaret had been conspiring *once again* to offer Darnley as a husband for Mary. Releasing Margaret into Scotland would only bring trouble. I may have hinted to my Lennox cousin about the idea of allowing the match, but had no intention of actually allowing it to happen.

"Lennox has leave to go whenever he is ready," I said. "But his children and wife will remain here."

"Perhaps, Majesty, it might be an advantage to consider releasing Darnley to accompany his father," Cecil said, causing me to lift my eyebrows almost into my hairline with surprise. Cecil smiled. "Unless Your Majesty cannot do without his stimulating company?"

"Have you run mad, Cecil? You want me to send a single and unmarried man with royal English blood in his veins into Scotland to meet with my cousin?" My cousin was searching for a husband... Did Cecil mean to send Darnley to Mary as a potential mate? Had Robin got to Cecil and persuaded him to endorse a different match for my cousin?

When Cecil did not immediately answer, I continued. "Or have you changed your mind and decided to support my cousin's claim to the throne? You must know that such a match would only increase her eligibility?"

"I doubt if she would marry beneath her, Majesty, especially given her reaction to Lord Robin... But Darnley is a handsome young gallant. Perhaps his presence would distract your cousin? Prevent her from setting her sights and ambitions on Spain, if only for a time?"

"And if she married him?" I asked.

"Darnley is an English subject, and would require your permission to wed, Majesty."

"A fact that has not prevented other cousins from acting as they want rather than observing the wishes of their sovereign," I reminded him. "This plan is dangerous, Cecil. If Mary married the boy she would increase her claim, and that of any heirs the two might produce… She might even decide not to wait for me to die, and move to take my throne by force." I stared at Cecil. "I ask again, Cecil, have you changed your mind about the succession? Or has Robin asked you to make this suggestion?"

Cecil smiled. "Your favourite has presented *many* ideas to me, Majesty, to prevent his being sent to Scotland, but this is not one of them. I do not believe the Queen would wed Darnley. I simply think he would serve as a good distraction. He is handsome enough to turn a woman's head, and she would toy with the idea since he is of royal blood, but eventually she would surely see he is not powerful enough to bring her what she needs… I believe he might buy us some time, and with time, Don Carlos may marry another. Also, Darnley is officially Protestant. I believe your cousin cherishes hope of a Catholic marriage, does she not?"

"Lord Darnley changes his religion as often as he changes beds," I said. "His mother is Catholic, as you well know. The Lennoxes attend the Protestant ceremony to avoid suspicion, but all know where Margaret's heart lies… and, besides, what man would not agree to alter his religion for a crown?" I stared at Cecil, pondering the matter. "Is there *another* reason you want to thrust him in her face, Cecil? Are you hoping Mary will marry the whoring yaldson and be saddled with a ridiculous husband?"

Cecil's continued reluctance to admit to this only confirmed my suspicions. Darnley's drinking, whoring and other unsavoury adventures were common knowledge at court. In place of a mind, he had pride, and in place of emotions he had lust. If I was right, then my Secretary was willing to trade all dangers of Mary marrying a member of the blood royal in return for handing her a husband who would bring her peril. I could see advantages as well as disadvantages to this notion. Whatever Cecil's motivations were, if Mary were to marry Darnley, her claim to the throne of England would be bolstered. Since I preferred her as a successor over any of my other cousins, despite her faults, then if she married Darnley this would help. All well and good, but on the other hand it meant the possibility of Darnley one day becoming King of England. Inflicting him on my court was one thing, inflicting him on my people, quite another... It would also impose Darnley on Mary, and I was not quite angry enough at her to think well of this. *And* it would mean my odious cousin Margaret would triumph by making her son a king; a vastly displeasing notion. It also presented the added danger that Mary might indeed forgo friendship between us and invade England, bolstered by the English husband at her side. But still... it bore consideration. Darnley was less dangerous than Don Carlos as a husband for my cousin.

"I will think on it, Cecil."

"There is one more thing, Majesty," Cecil went on. "In the letter I received from Randolph, Mary of Scots says she wishes representatives from your court and hers to meet at Berwick-on-Tweed to discuss terms for the union with Lord Robin. She has decided to consider the match."

My heart dropped. Mary was willing to consider Robin? I had never thought she would actually go ahead with it. I had wanted Robin to turn to me again, to show that he loved me, to mend the hurt between us. I had wanted to buy time before proposing another English suitor. I could not lose Robin. The thought of him with another woman was too hard to bear. Sharp slivers of jealousy cut through my blood and bone. But then, when I had a moment to consider, I wondered if Mary was playing with me, as I had done with her. Was she, in fact, only going ahead to barter for time to pursue Don Carlos? Was she trying to trick me? For a moment I thought well of sending Darnley to Scotland, just to spite her.

"Tell my cousin I will be *delighted* to send an envoy to meet hers," I said in a level tone. "And will start to make preparations to ensure Lord Dudley is ready to meet his bride." I looked at Cecil closely as another concern sprung to my mind. "How is your son, *Spirit*?" I asked. His new son, Robert, had never been a hale babe and I had been told of late that he had developed a curved spine, which was further impeding his health.

Cecil sighed. "Mildred and I are often most concerned for him," he said. "But my wife, much like my Queen, is a determined woman. She tends to Robert's care with great diligence, and has made up her mind already that he will be tutored at home, when he is old enough to hold a quill."

"If you need any advice from my physicians, *Spirit*, then you have only to say."

My Secretary smiled. "I will take you up on the offer, madam, if needs be."

As Cecil departed, I send Kat to bring Robin to me at once. Leaving my chambers for the Privy Gardens, I waited for him. It was time to find out the truth of his feelings.

*

"You sent for me, Majesty?" Robin's voice came from behind me as I stood admiring the gardens at Greenwich. I had been lost in thought. Cecil's plan to send Darnley to Scotland had consumed me.

I turned. "I did, Lord Dudley," I said formally. "I wanted to inform you that Queen Mary of Scotland wishes to send an envoy to talk about your suit."

"It is not *my* suit," Robin protested, his tone plaintive. "It is your wish that I be sent from you, from England, and from all that I love."

"Do not sulk like a little boy, Robin," I said. "As I have told you before, I am acting as any good master would who cares for her servant. I am giving you all you want."

"There is but one thing I want, and that is you." He gazed at me so sadly I thought my heart might break.

"I cannot believe in something there is no evidence for," I said. "You have shown me that all you care for is the throne. And now, I offer you one."

"I care nothing for the throne, neither the one you offer me nor the one you deny me. What I care for, is you. I want to be with you, Elizabeth, why can you not see that?"

"Because you court me no longer, Robin; you court power." I glanced away, tracing the flight of a bird in the skies. Shadowed dark against white clouds, it swooped and danced in the air, riding the breeze. "You said once that I was in your heart, but I believe this lie no more."

His hand came down on my shoulder. He spun me about to face him, his expression furious. "How can you believe such of me?" he shouted. "When all I have done, I have done for us!"

"All you have done you have done for *you*!" I shouted back. "You have done nothing *for* me, Robin, only *against* me!"

"All I have done, I have done to bring us together."

"And all you have achieved is to drive us apart." I tossed my head. "You do not see, even now, what you have done? How you have tried to squash my power with your intrigues and double-dealing? You are a fool indeed, Robin, if see this you cannot."

"And you are a fool, my Queen, to remain blind to the horrors you inflict upon me!" he shouted. "You would send me away? From you? From court? From my family, my friends and the land I hold dear? You would offer me to another woman? You would betray me and my love for you, for spite?"

I shook his hand off. "Why should I not be spiteful, my lord? When a heart is abused it becomes dark and rotten. That is what you have done with my love! I am what you have made me!"

"And I am what *you* have made me," he replied. "*You* have made me into this creature... this desperate, grabbing, grasping beast. You play with my feelings, madam! You say that you love me. You say you will marry me, you raise my hopes and then you dash them to the ground! I am your plaything. I am the doll you bring out, taunt your friends with, and then throw on the floor and forget about." His lip curled with disgust. "You beckon me on, and then you refuse me. You toy with my love, Elizabeth, you abuse my feelings, and you demean both me and yourself in doing so."

I stared at him. His words struck me deep. Although I had not intended to treat him in such a way, I could not deny that from Robin's point of view, this was the truth. And yet... he did not admit to all *he* had done. Much blame was mine indeed, but I was not the only one guilty here.

"And you work with my enemies, plot with my advisors, and bribe my lords to bend me to your will," I said coldly. "You are a traitor, Robin. To me, and to our love."

Robin glanced at his fine shoes. For a moment there was silence. "Do you want to be rid of me?" he asked softly.

"I do not."

Robin glanced up, that desperate hope in his eyes again. "Then do not pursue these negotiations to marry me to your cousin," he pleaded. "Finish this darkness and malice between us, Elizabeth. Marry me."

"That, I will not do either," I said. "I have lost faith in your love, Robin, and such cannot be mended with words." I held up a hand as he went to protest. "But I will not be parted from you, either."

I sighed and waved at him to follow me as I walked. "I cannot live without you, Robin," I said, refusing to look at him. "But I cannot give you to another. It would break my heart... And yet, I cannot marry you, not with all that has happened. I am torn and my heart is wounded."

"I never intended to hurt you."

"And yet you have... and I have hurt you." I paused, stopping by a fountain where blue waters shone, dappled silver under the sun. "It will take time to mend the ills we have caused each other. But I am willing to try, if you are, Robin."

"I want nothing more than to have your love."

"It will take time for me to believe that again," I said. "But I will make you an offer, Robin; a token of friendship. I will give you something you have long wanted in return for your promise that you will attempt to make amends for your part in the strife between us."

"You will marry me?"

A breath hissed from my lips and I stared at him with a strained expression. "Do not ruin all my good intentions, my lord, by making me decide to ship you to Scotland after all," I warned. "Should my cousin see you, I am sure there would be no force in Heaven or on earth to persuade her to give you up."

Robin breathed out heavily. "Then what do you offer me that I want more than anything?"

I smiled, turning my gaze back to the horizon. "In order to be considered noble enough to be a true suitor for my cousin, you would need a grander title than the one you have." My tone was offhand, careless, but I saw interest flicker in his eyes. "You would need to be an earl, really..." I looked at him and my grin broadened. "How like you the title of Earl of Leicester, my lord?"

Robin was suspicious. "Not at all, if it allowed me to be considered for your cousin."

I chuckled. "My cousin is not serious about wanting to marry you, Robin," I said. "But as these talks go on, we must make sure that we play the game as well as she. Mary will pretend to consider you as a suitor, even as she works secretly to snare Don Carlos. And if my offer is to be seen as serious, then I must elevate you. That is the next move, Robin, and playing with Mary will allow me to elevate you without much trouble at court... Norfolk will protest of course, but then he always does, but Cecil will support your elevation if he thinks he has a chance to get you gone."

"What are you saying, then?" Robin asked, confused.

"I say, Robin Dudley, that I will not be parted from you, even though I do not entirely trust you anymore. I say that I will use you to play this game with my cousin in Scotland... and I say that I am sorry for the pain I have caused you. I offer you an earldom as a peace offering."

"And if I accept... you will not send me to Scotland?"

"No, my lord. You will stay with me, and I with you. This is merely an opportunity to elevate you, without scandal attaching itself to my name, and with the support of many lords at court who would dearly love to see you gone from England."

He stared at me as though he had not considered this, and then a great smirk broke over his lips. I chuckled. "Pick your seat in the House of Lords, Robin," I said, taking his arm. "You are about to become an earl."

Chapter Fifty-One

Greenwich Palace and Cambridge
Summer 1564

As I left for progress that year, so my cousin in Scotland did too. After declaring she was willing to discuss terms of marriage to Robin, Mary effectively disappeared, and the stream of dispatches from Scotland tumbled into a mere trickle of information. Her rapid disappearance confirmed my suspicions that Mary had no serious intention of accepting Robin. This knowledge put my mind at rest. It did mean, however, that my cousin was clearly capable of duplicitous guile, and I would have to take that into account in the future. Announcing that whenever the Queen of Scotland re-emerged from progress, I would send men to her immediately to continue talks, I went on with plans to ennoble Robin.

My Robin! The knowledge that I was not serious about parting with him had brought a skip to his step. I have no doubt the prospect of becoming an earl added to his new lightness of spirit. He was a regular visitor to my chambers, and whilst he attempted to put on a good show of malcontent for the court, in my rooms he was happy and sweet.

"You will have to continue with all the plotting you were up to before I informed you of this," I told him. "My nobles must believe you still think I will send you away. If they catch scent of the truth, they might oppose your elevation."

Robin chuckled. "I will be utterly downcast and miserable when I come to perform for them, Majesty," he said, pulling his lips down and bowing his head like a beaten hound. "How is this?" he asked.

"Entirely unconvincing," I replied and chuckled. "You are a poor liar, Robin."

He pulled his lips down further, making himself so ugly I laughed even harder. He bowed his head, wrung his hands and dropped to his knees. "How about this, my Queen?"

"Worse." I indicated for him to rise, marvelling at the warmth in his dark eyes. "You must spend time with your company of players and learn their tricks," I scolded. "You will give everything away if I send you out to weave our blanket of lies now."

"I will call to mind the harshness of our late sorrows," he said. "And therein, I will find all the grief I need." He lifted my hands and kissed my fingers. Sparkling shudders of pleasure flashed though my blood. My cheeks warmed as I stroked his face.

"I am more pleased than I can say, my *Eyes*, that we are friends again."

"No joy, even yours, can match my own."

"Get you gone," I teased him. I needed to curtail my emotions before they got the better of me. It had not taken much for me to start to forget all of Robin's misdemeanours. I had said it would take time to mend the hurt between us and I meant it. It would not do to falter in this resolution by immediately giving in to all his protests of devotion and love. "Get to your packing, my lord," I said. "We leave for Cambridge with the dawn's first light. Make sure my horse is ready."

"My lady's stables are never unprepared," Robin protested, but agreed to leave. I found it hard to believe I had ever been angry with him... How quickly we forget ill deeds and times, when we reconcile with the one we love.

Before the sun rose, the court left for Cambridge. We stayed there for five days and it was a goodly time, only made more pleasurable by my reconciliation with Robin. Wearing a gown of black velvet, slashed with a delicate underlay of rose-coloured silk, and with a jewelled cap upon my head, I entered the city to grand acclaim.

As we entered the city, cannons fired from the walls, trumpets blew and crowds cheered. The streets were packed. Young maids carrying hot baked pies and ale drifted through the crowds selling their wares. Merchants brayed at passing folk trying to entice them to stalls laden with silk, ribbons and spices. The scent of the hot summer and my people's sweat was cloying, but I minded not. To see so many turned out to welcome me was joyous. People jostled in the streets and hung from windows and balconies above. The sound of a thousand voices surrounded us, along with the glorious sight of their waving hands and beaming faces. Cecil greeted us at the University, for one of his many titles was Chancellor of Cambridge University, and, surrounded by dark-robed scholars, crying *"Vivat Regina!"* we were ushered into its beautiful halls.

Robin arranged all the entertainments, and there were many. Not just feasting and dancing as was normal on such visits, but many scholarly diversions, too. I visited all the colleges, many of them founded by my forbears, attended lectures, watched plays in Latin, and gave speeches in that same language. Gifts of books, gloves, sweetmeats and flowers were piled on me and each day my ladies and menservants staggered back to my chambers with stacks of lovely presents.

"Have a special care with the books, Kat," I reminded her as she gazed about the spectacular chaos of my ante-chamber and attempted to bring order. I had been given so many presents that Kat believed we might need to hire three extra wagons to carry them all back to London. "I shall want my books preserved against the weather and the dust of the journey."

"Have I ever allowed one of your books to come to harm, Majesty?" she asked in an acidic tone. I said nothing and eventually she turned to look at me, letting out a sigh when she saw my raised eyebrows. "I am sorry, Majesty," she apologised. "I have had a pain in my head these last few days and it robs me of my patience."

"If you need to rest, old friend, then do so," I said, touching her shoulder with concern. "There are other servants who could organise my packing."

"And have everything arrive in London in a great mess?" she exclaimed, aghast at the notion. "The flowers put in with the books and the gloves with the comfits?" Kat shook her head. "The only other person who could be trusted with this is Blanche, Majesty. The others would not know where to start."

I smiled at her proud manner, but it was true Kat had a particular talent for packing and organising. She was always in charge, and since that had *always* been her role she was unwilling to give it up. "Well, you continue to organise this mess, then," I agreed. "But have my doctors give you something for that head, Kat."

"I am getting old, Majesty, that is all," Kat said. I frowned at her. Kat never seemed old to me, but she was over sixty now. "And with age, so come more ailments." She put her hands on her hips and scowled at the mess as though she meant to frighten it into submission. "I will be fine, Majesty."

*

The end of our stay in Cambridge came with more speeches, and one by the Public Orator surprised me. Taking an entirely different point of view from every other man in my realm, he openly praised my virginity and status as an unmarried Queen. "There are some who mourn our Queen's unmarried state," he said. "But I say to them, do not mourn; celebrate such a happy event! Our Queen, unlike all others in this world, hath given herself completely to the service of her people. She has chosen *us* over the claims of blood, children and family. We are fortunate, good people, to have such a Queen. We are her children and England is her husband. With her ruling over us, we have our eternal mother; a maiden as devoted to her duty as the Holy Virgin herself was."

His words caught me off-guard. In a moment of uncharacteristic embarrassment, I flushed red as tears sprang into my eyes. Biting my lips and playing with my fingers, I spoke. "God's blessing on your heart," I said softly, deeply touched by his words.

The Orator went on, extolling my virtues and reducing me to such a state that I thought I might weep in public like my cousin of Scots. It was so surprising to hear a public exultation of my unwed state. So many thought it unnatural, bizarre, and bad for England, so to hear someone talk on the virtues, rather than the sins, of my status was almost unprecedented. I was grateful to know that at least *some* of my subjects understood me.

We left Cambridge, making for London, only to find fresh rumour of my marriage to Archduke Charles had broken out. I had no idea where this new rumour came from... We had re-started talks, yes, but that was no new event. Perhaps it was a quiet season in London, and people were desperate for gossip. Before it could reach a fever-pitch however, Ferdinand of Austria died, bringing talks of marriage to his son to an end for a while. I breathed a sigh of relief, thanking Death for his visit to the Emperor.

Soon enough, I was to thank Death no more.

*

As we returned to London, Dee and Bess returned from Antwerp. Sadly, the physicians there had found there was nothing they could do for her condition, but Bess was not willing to admit defeat. "I will be consulting with your doctors, as you have so kindly offered, Majesty," she said. She was pale and gaunt. My spirits trembled to see her this way. "And there is a cunning woman in one of the villages on our estates who I have turned to before for advice. I mean to speak with her and her son, who is training as her apprentice, when William and I return to our lands."

"Often there is more wisdom in the minds of such women than in the words of trained doctors," I agreed. I rose and walked to her, putting my hands on her shoulders. "Rest often, though, Bess. Tiredness can be dangerous to any condition. Do not wear yourself out."

"I do hope my good wife listens to *you*, Majesty," William Parr interjected before Bess could answer. "For she listens not to me."

Bess smiled and leaned in to whisper to my ear. "My husband would wrap me in fleece, Your Majesty, and lock me in a cupboard along with his stores of sugar to keep me safe."

I gazed with affection at my good uncle. "He loves you, Bess," I replied. "And if you will not listen to him, I shall make my request into a royal command. If I hear from my uncle you are exhausting yourself, I shall put you in the Tower, where I may keep an eye on you."

Bess and Parr laughed. They left for their country seat later that day, and I made Bess promise to write to me often, especially with regards to her health.

With Bess, Dee returned, his bags and trunks stuffed with books and his mind afire with new thoughts. He showed me his newest work, called the *Monas*, a most interesting study filled with magical ideas and notions many considered pagan, and therefore heretical, on numerology, cosmology and mathematics. It was also clearly influenced by his study of the Cabala. Since it was a potentially inflammatory work, Dee chose not to dedicate it to me, but to the newly crowned Holy Roman Emperor, Maximilian II. His caution was understandable and I praised him for his forethought. I had no wish to be accused of heresy by either Catholics or Protestants, who were both likely to object to this work. There were enough people in the world who believed me to be a heretic queen as it was.

"I admit myself somewhat baffled by much in this text," I confessed to Dee when I had read it. "Much of this theory is beyond my scope of knowledge."

"Only because you have no grounding in it, Your Majesty," he flattered. "Remember, I have worked for many years on these studies. It is easy for anyone to believe they have no understanding of a subject, when they first start to study it. That is where many people give up. The trick is to plough on, and engage the mind."

"I believe your idea is that you believe astrological symbols to be part of a lost language, Doctor Dee," I went on. "And wish to test this hypothesis?"

"You have the main thrust entirely, Majesty," he said, looking impressed.

"Would you come to court, and instruct me so I might better understand your theories?" I asked. "It has been some time since I was a pupil. I would love to learn at your side, Doctor, if you were willing to tutor me."

"I would be honoured, Majesty," Dee said, with an expression of clear astonishment and interest on his face. "And it would aid me also."

"In what manner would my becoming your pupil help you?"

Dee smiled. "When a scholar becomes a teacher, Majesty, he understands his subject all the clearer for having to explain it to another person."

Dee was a good, wise man. There were many who suspected him and his work, thinking he was exploring pagan, ungodly studies. But I saw him for what he was; a seeker of truth. He was a talented scholar, often apt to become so lost in his work he forgot to eat or sleep. Dee took a house in London, and I promised him I would become a patron of his work, if he would share all he found with me. There were many who would have liked to see me arrest him, and search his house, fearing he might be practising dark arts. But there are always those who fear others with more knowledge than they. This is the way of the world. Often, those who seek truth and knowledge become suspected by those who dwell in ignorance and fear. But the way of truth is the way of light, just as the path of ignorance is bound in shadow.

Chapter Fifty-Two

Windsor Castle
Autumn 1564

In September as farmers in the fields were busy gathering in the last of the crops, as England was filled with the steady refrain of singing workers harvesting barley, hay, hops and wheat, the Count of Lennox rode for Scotland. He left alone, despite Cecil's notion to send Darnley. I was still wavering on the idea, but if a time came when a match with Spain or France was on the horizon, I would consider sending Darnley.

As Lennox rode for Scotland, Ambassador Melville arrived in England. Having heard little from my cousin that summer, I was determined to catch up on news from our neighbour. I greeted him, and later called him to my apartments to view my collection of miniature portraits. When he arrived, I was gazing on one of Robin, thinking of the days when I had promised him my heart... how happy I had been then in my innocence.

"You are most fond of Lord Dudley, Majesty," Melville noted, regarding the inscription on the bottom of the portrait. It read *"My Lord's picture"*; a rather personal inscription.

I brushed a finger over the soft paper which held the portrait safe and smiled. "No other man has my regard as he does," I confessed. "And I can think of no other man I would be willing to offer as a consort to my good sister in Scotland."

"I wonder that you would wish to be parted from him, Majesty," Melville said, narrowing his eyes. "For surely, his loss would cause you pain?"

"As it would bring pleasure and comfort to my sister," I said, setting the portrait down. "And for such grace, I would be willing to give up a great deal." I gestured to a picture of Mary on the table. "I gaze often on the face of my cousin, wondering on her," I told him. "Is it a good likeness?"

Melville stood over it and considered the portrait. "It is a fair likeness, Majesty, although I would say it does not do due justice to my Queen's beauty."

I nodded. "Then I have to meet with her, do you see, my lord? For how can we ever truly see or know each other without meeting?"

Melville glanced back to the portrait of Robin. "Would your Majesty allow me to take this portrait of Lord Dudley back to Scotland?" he asked. "I believe my Queen would be interested to see the face of the man you wish her to marry."

"I have but one miniature of my lord," I protested, holding Robin's portrait to me as though Maitland were about to snatch it away. "I cannot part with it."

"But your Majesty has the original in her keeping," Melville said with a short smile.

"For now, my lord... but all the same, I would not wish to lose this picture."

"Then will your Majesty send another token to my Queen?" he went on. "Perhaps the ruby you showed to me earlier?"

The gem he spoke of was in my private collection. It was a large jewel, big as a tennis ball... I had no wish to give it to my cousin. "I will send my cousin a diamond," I said, noting his disappointment. "For the diamond signifies purity and wisdom, and those are qualities I believe both I and my dear cousin possess." Asking Kat to clear the portraits away, I took the ambassador's arm. "Will you tell me about my good sister?" I asked.

"What would you know, Majesty?"

"Everything!" I cried, leading him into the gardens. "Everything there is to know. Tell me of her face and her character. Tell me of her wishes and aspirations. I would become close to my good sister in Scotland, and you, my lord, are my means of so doing."

The gardens were glorious. The last of the summer warmth held on tight as autumn strove to usurp her throne. Aromatic herbs puffed forth delicate scents on the warm breeze, and flowers planted in rows and geometric patterns made the grounds bright and gay. Marble statues were dotted through the gardens, rising up from grassy avenues and fountains whose waters sang like delicate music. We walked to the centre of the gardens where a sundial counted the hours, and a fountain shot water up, sparkling in the sunshine, as it fell into a pond. "Talk to me of my cousin," I insisted.

Melville did as I asked. As he rambled on and on about Mary, I allowed my thoughts to roam, thinking on other matters as he was distracted by speaking of her. "I am tired now, ambassador," I said as he ended his praises. "We will talk again later in the week."

I held Melville at bay, for I knew he wanted to press me about the succession. Every time he came to me I asked him about my cousin. He found he had to embark on answering many pointless questions, rather than getting to the one point he wanted to speak on. I diverted him with my apparent obsession with my cousin's looks. "Which of us is the fairer?" I asked of him, smoothing the front of my gown of gold and crimson velvet, allowing him to see the whiteness of my own hands.

"Each of you is the fairest within your own kingdoms, Majesty," Melville replied with great tact. "Although I will allow that your Majesty has the whiter complexion... But my Queen is equal to you in loveliness just as she is equal in blood."

He was trying to steer me towards the succession again, but he would be thwarted! "Which of us is the taller, then?" I asked.

"My Queen is taller, Majesty," he said. "She is five feet and eleven inches, and stands taller than many men of the court."

"Then she is too tall," I said, pretending to pout. "For men say that I am neither too high nor too low, and that is the perfect height, is it not, my lord?" Before Melville could answer, I continued. "Does my cousin like to hunt... or perhaps she favours reading as a pastime?"

"My mistress enjoys the hunt, and loves to ride, as I believe Your Majesty does," the poor fellow went on, seemingly baffled as to why I would have more interest in Mary as a person than as a successor.

"And does she like music?" I asked.

"My Queen is... reasonably accomplished as a musician, Majesty," said the man. "But she has a fine, sweet voice."

That evening Kat took Melville to a gallery which overlooked one of Windsor's chambers, and I told her to have him stand there so I could impress him with my skill on the virginals. I loved music. I practised my skills daily, and I knew that in this I could outshine my younger, more beautiful cousin. After listening to me play, Melville was forced to admit I was indeed the better musician.

Some of this show was of course vanity. I *was* vain. I have no call to deny it. Knowing myself to be not as beautiful or as young as many other women, I had to find ways to satisfy my thirst for admiration. Perhaps it was due to the fact that I had known myself unwanted as a child. My father had wanted a boy, my mother had scarce had time to show affection for me before her head was sliced off, and I had lived a rather neglected youth. My father had thrust all his adoration and ambition into my brother, and even though I knew he had loved me, I had still felt unwanted, unimportant at times. As I had grown, I had known what it was to be outshone by other women. Striking, I was, but beauty is not the same beast. So, yes... I craved admiration. We all want what we do not have. To be admired for grace and skill was *almost* as good as being admired for beauty. I took admiration where I could and was not averse to demonstrating my skills to earn more esteem.

But all this performance was not all about vanity. I wanted to show my cousin that if she could toy with my interests, then I would retaliate. Had Mary not done the same with Randolph? Distracting him with talk of other matters so she would not have to converse on the subject of marriage?

At the end of Melville's stay, I ordered him to stay for another two days, so I might further impress him with my dancing. Whilst I wanted him to admire my talent and my strength, I had another reason for detaining him. Henry Darnley was attending this event, and I was keen to know what my cousin might think of him. Melville's opinion was important, for if he believed Mary might find Darnley attractive that was good, but if he believed she might actually consider marrying the young fool that was another matter. Taking to the floor with Robin, I danced eight galliards without tiring. Afterwards, and much to my satisfaction, the ambassador confessed that his Queen had nothing like my strength and grace in the dance.

"What do you think your Queen would think of our shared cousin of Lennox?" I asked Melville as we stood drinking ale.

"Some have remarked that he, as my cousin's kinsman, would make a good choice of husband for her."

Melville glanced over. Darnley was lounging, surrounded by his usual gang of young pretty lads at the edge of the hall. His rosebud lip curled as he made a no doubt scathing remark about one of the dancers, and his band laughed with sycophantic appreciation. Melville shook his head. "No woman of spirit would choose such a man that is more like a woman than a man, Majesty," he said in a scathing tone. "I regard Lord Darnley as a rather lusty, beardless lad, with a face more at home on a lady than a man."

I snorted with amusement, and Melville grinned. "I heard the Cardinal of Lorraine once referred to him as a polished trifler," I whispered to the ambassador. "A rather polite way of describing him, do you not think, my lord?"

"It is a shame he is heir to so much and yet has so little to recommend him," Melville agreed. "And no, Majesty, I do not believe my mistress would find him suitable as a husband. He has too many faults, despite his titles and blood."

Good, I thought. If I did send Darnley to Scotland then he would prove a momentary distraction for Mary and nothing more. That would be helpful. As I was talking to Maitland, Robin joined us. Bringing a fresh cup of wine for me, he stood waiting to join the conversation, but without seeking to interrupt. I smiled affectionately at him. Robin had been so pleasing of late. I really believed we had left our times of trial behind us.

"Will you be staying for the ceremony for my Lord Robin, ambassador?" I asked, putting my hand on Robin's sleeve. "In a few days we will make him an earl. I hope that this elevation will make him more suited to your Queen, in terms of title at least." I gazed lovingly at Robin. "For I already know he is suited to her in spirit and in character."

"I shall stay, of course, if you wish me to attend, Majesty," Melville replied.

"I should like your Queen to know I do all I can to advance Lord Dudley's suit in her estimations," I said. "I know that, should she choose him as her husband, she would become the happiest of women."

Robin chuckled. "My Queen is ever kind to me, lord ambassador," he said. "But I am eager to meet the Queen of Scotland and put my suit to her in person."

"I am sure my Queen is no less interested in meeting you, my lord." Melville bowed. "To meet the man who has so captivated the heart of her good sister, and to discover if he has the power to bewitch her heart as well."

I patted Robin's arm. I was pleased with his dissembling. Had I been Melville, I am sure I would have believed Robin was in earnest. Robin was becoming quite talented at pretence. The thought pleased me then, but later I came to be disturbed by it. If he was so talented, was there a chance he was play-acting when it came to our relationship? I cast the thought from my mind. I was sure Robin was in earnest. The truth of his love was there, returned in every word and gesture... Or at least, I hoped it was.

Chapter Fifty-Three

St James's Palace
Autumn - Winter 1564

Robin finally achieved *one* of his ambitions that September. In a glorious ceremony in the Presence Chamber at St James's Palace, I made him an earl and a baron. Robin Dudley took the titles of Earl of Leicester and Baron of Denbigh. The title of Earl of Leicester was important as four previous earls of that name had been sons of English kings. At the same time, I made Robin order a new book of his lineage, which showed his descent, in the female line, from King Edmund Ironside.

At last raised to the peerage, ostensibly in the name of making him more acceptable to Mary, Robin entered arrayed in a glorious tunic of russet silk and cloth of silver, with robes of estate draped over his broad shoulders and a great sword in his strong hands. I stood with my cousin, Lady Strange, holding my train, as I marvelled at Robin's fine form and grace. He was so solemn and proud during the ceremony, I could not resist reaching down and tickling him playfully under the chin as I invested him with the collar of his earldom and his ermine-lined robes. Norfolk let out a barely concealed snort of disgust as he saw me tickle Robin, and my actions were censured for being too familiar, but I cared not. I was happy, restored to full friendship with Robin. There seemed to be nothing which could incite me to displeasure.

"How like you my new creation?" I asked Melville as we stood chatting after the ceremony. I gazed at Robin, knowing I could never be parted from him. Even if he could not be mine, I would not allow him to belong to any other either. I could not. For all that had come between us, all of the hurt, misery and pain, I loved him. I always would.

"The Earl of Leicester is a fortunate man to have such a loving Queen," Melville said. I noted he avoided commenting on Robin's suitability as a husband for my cousin. I was not surprised. From Cecil's spies and from de Silva himself, I had heard Melville had used his time at the English Court to visit the Spanish ambassador, attempting to resurrect negotiations of marriage to Don Carlos. Mary was not serious about marrying my Robin; that was clear now.

More fool you, sweet coz! I thought. Any woman would be lucky to have Robin as a husband. Of course, none of them were going to... He was mine.

I excused myself from Melville and went to Robin. "My dear Earl," I said happily. "How do you like your new collar? It suits you, Robin. You were born to be a peer."

"Thank you, Your Majesty." He kissed my hand, his bright eyes gleaming over the top of my pale skin. "I find it most comfortable, although I still am nervous that your cousin may take up your offer of my hand."

"Worry not, Robin." I took his arm. "My cousin has been sending her ambassador to talk in secret with de Silva. She wants mad Don Carlos, and so I am sorry to tell you, my lord Earl, you will have no cause to leave England. You must stay here..." I smiled wickedly. "But if you lose a crown in Scotland, you get to keep your English earldom, so whichever way, you have won, have you not?"

"I would rather remain a merry Englishman, Majesty, than become a poor-tempered Scot."

I laughed, feeling joyous. All that remained was to stop my cousin marrying into Spain to make me satisfied on all counts. "Cecil wants to send Darnley to Scotland," I said. "He thinks the lad will distract Mary from her plans to wed elsewhere. What do you think?"

"Surely handing her a potential husband of royal blood would be dangerous, Majesty?"

"It would," I agreed. "But even more dangerous would be a match with Spain. Tensions in the Low Countries continue, and Phillip blames me for the uprisings. If Mary marries Don Carlos, we could find a fleet at our door in a short space of time. They might gain papal approval, and invade." I stared over at Darnley. "My cousin will not listen to me about taking a *good* Englishman for her husband, but I wonder… would she take a *bad* one instead? If she married Darnley it would cause some problems for us, but would they be less than if she married with Spain? Darnley has no fleet, no army. He may yet prove to be the lesser evil."

"If he is the lesser evil for England, Majesty, then I say send him." Robin took a goblet of ale from a passing servant and drank deep. "At the least his handsome face will distract the Queen, and at the most she will take a fool for a husband."

"There is something in me that wants Mary to refuse him," I said. "There is something in me that wants her to be clever, Robin… to see through him, even though I know that her marrying with Spain instead would be disastrous." I sighed. "Sometimes the wishes of my heart and the best outcome for my country are not in agreement with each other."

To my surprise, Robin did not seek to bring up another event where my heart's desires and the best interests for England were not aligned. "You like her, don't you?" he asked.

"I do," I admitted. "She has wit and guile, Robin. She has the instincts of a survivor. I believe, given the chance, she could be a worthy heir… but I know many would not accept her. *I* change my mind about her often enough."

"There were some who did not want you on the throne, Majesty," Robin said. "You did not let that stand in your way. Perhaps your cousin will prove the same."

"A part of me hopes that very much Robin," I confessed, taking a sip of my wine. "Just as another part, the part which must think for England, hopes that she will fail."

*

The creaking carts moved slowly against the dense, thick mud and tumbling water on the roads. We were travelling only a mile from St James's Palace to Whitehall, and yet the distance might as well have been twenty for the struggle of the wagons carrying my goods.

"We will ride on ahead," I called to my servants. I nodded to my ladies, who wore miserable expressions as they sat upon their horses. Sleet fell from the skies and water dribbled from their hoods. From the river we could hear shouting. The River Thames had frozen solid, and a market had been constructed on its icy surface. Beside the market, people played football, bowls and skittles. The game of football was a rather unruly sport. Two teams, usually numbering men of fifty or more on each side, would gather and try to get a ball made of hog-skin into their opponent's goal. It often became rowdy, and sometimes ended in fights. My father had disapproved of the sport, and had banned it in favour of archery practice, but I allowed it as long as it did not get out of hand.

Riding on ahead of the struggling carts, we reached Whitehall in good time, but I was chilled to the bone. Forced that night to sit before the fire and warm my blood with spiced wine and good flames, I did not attend the dances at court. A few days later, I was taken with a sudden, violent pain in my gut. I almost did not make it to the privy. An explosion of such horrific violence came from my bowels that I thought I might pass all my inner organs out through my rear. Can you imagine how hard it was for me to get upon the privy in time when struck with a flux of the belly? The gowns I wore were so heavy, bejewelled and intricate and were usually pinned on me. It took several of my women to aid me in the privy on a normal day, but as this hideous sickness took hold of me I had to be stripped to my undergarments, so that I was capable of voiding all within me quickly and without damage to my fine clothes.

Shivering and shaking from loss of fluids, I was put to bed by Kat. I spent that night either in bed or dashing from it. God's blood! What a horrible time that was! A day later, Kat and Blanche were confined to separate beds with the same sickness. Another day and poor Mary Sidney was struck down with it, too. From under her dark veil she apologised for having to retire from my service for a few days, and then raced out. I had no illusions where the poor woman was going...

As always, when I was ill, there was an immediate fluster that I was to die and leave England with no heir. Although I felt truly rotten, I knew my life was not in danger. Mary Radcliffe took over, and organised care of the other stricken ladies, too. Pouring ale and water down my throat in vast quantities to make up for all I lost, and rallying my remaining ladies into caring for the sick, Mary proved herself an able commander of the Bedchamber. I lost weight, but I was never in peril for my life. Trying to convince my men I was safe was, however, a hard task. You never would have seen a group of men so afraid. They were like squawking hens flapping about a barn upon the intrusion of a hungry vixen.

Although my bowels eventually decided to stop punishing me, my illness continued on through the festivities. I was weak, and continued to experience pains in the belly, which did not inspire me to eat a great deal. I could not feast and dance as I would have liked to, particularly this year since we had much to celebrate with Robin's ennoblement.

My cousin in Scotland sent a letter mourning my sickness, but this time her sentiments hardly rang true. I'm afraid my thoughts on my cousin had turned less generous after Melville's visit. When he had returned, Randolph had discovered that Melville had told Mary I was a dissembler and could not be trusted. Mary's letters became less frequent, less affectionate and more insistent about the succession. Robin had ceased to pester me, and so Mary had stepped in to take his place. I knew she was thinking if I should die, as was widely rumoured, then she could come to claim my throne.

De Silva was a regular visitor to my sick room. I was glad to see him for he often was able to brighten my spirits. "I have such pains in my belly," I told him on the first day he came. I had been out of bed for a few days, and no longer required to be dressed only in nightclothes, but I was still unwell. "I hope you will dispel my pains by talking with me."

"Shall I tell you a tale I heard lately, Majesty?" he asked.

"Only if it is amusing, my lord," I said, shifting uncomfortably.

"It is a tale of the Bishop of Leon and how he took a fall in front of the whole Spanish Court, Majesty," said de Silva, grinning wide. His voice fell to a conspiratorial whisper. "But... if I dare tell you, you must promise to tell no other, for the bishop displayed much he did not intend to as he tumbled before my King!"

I laughed. De Silva knew I had a passion for the ridiculous, and delighted in finding stories which would amuse me. With him at my side I was cheered. My doctors, however, could always ruin any happiness. Blaming this illness on my virgin state, they nagged me. "Remaining a virgin, Majesty, is hazardous for a woman," said one of them in a grave tone. He looked so young he could have been my son. "For the passions and urges within a woman for sex are stronger than those within a man. Keeping them pent up allows illness to enter the body as it is weakened from this excess of passion."

Excess of passion! What a belief! That I was dwelling in a state of ever un-sated lust and made ill because of it! The only man I had ever desired truly was Robin and although I loved him I was *not* pining away for want of his body next to mine! Eventually the only man I would allow entrance to my chambers was my apothecary, John Hemingway, who decided I had eaten or drunk something which was infested with sickness. At least he did not attempt to blame all ills on a maiden's thwarted desires!

"After all, Majesty," he said as he prepared a potion. "If this was caused by your virginity, then why would married ladies in your service suffer from the same illness?"

It was a good point, and one my other doctors seemed incapable of recognising. I wondered sometimes if Cecil or Robin had told them to put all my illnesses down to my virginity, in an effort to scare me into marriage. I recovered, but I emerged wasted and thin. Long hours spent in my stuffy bedchamber made me yearn for the outdoors, but Kat, who was better by that time, turned wild at the thought of me riding into the countryside. To appease her temper, and save myself a round of lectures, I remained indoors. But I was not happy about it.

"I am not a child, Mistress Ashley!" I cried at her as she pestered me to eat and then turn in early for bed.

"You are to me, *Majesty*," she huffed. "You are like my own daughter, and at times such as these, will obey me as such!"

Blanche stepped in to take Kat away. "She only acts this way for love of you," Blanche said when she returned.

"She should have a mind who is Queen!" I retorted, vastly annoyed with my oldest friend.

"So she should, Majesty... Now, how about a nice bowl of pottage before bed?"

I glowered at Blanche. "You are as bad as she is."

"If you mean I love you as well as Mistress Ashley, madam, then you are quite correct," Blanche said, coming to the bed with a bowl of broth and holding out a full spoon to me. "Now, open wide, Your Majesty."

I chuckled at her, and obediently opened my mouth.

Chapter Fifty-Four

Whitehall Palace
Winter 1565

"The man claims he can make base metal into pure gold, if given the correct financial support to set up the enterprise," I said, reading from the parchment in my hands even as I spoke to Robin. Lounging on cushions before the crackling fire, Robin looked quite at home. The dance of the flames played on his skin, and revealed lighter hints of colour in his beard. His eyes mirrored the fire as he gazed on it. I could see bright embers and flickering flame against the dark night of his eyes. He was so handsome, he almost stole my breath. Robin's recent ennoblement and return to my favour suited him. He looked happier than he had done for months. The pleasure of knowing he was to remain an Englishman and had my favour once more made him as cheery and bright as the fire.

"Dee has said the same to me, Majesty," he noted from his comfortable seat. "Although *he* seems to think there is more to this art than any have managed to discover thus far."

"Lannoy also believes he can make an elixir of eternal life," I mentioned. "He says as much in this letter." I put the parchment to one side. Could it be true? If so, it was worth a little financial risk to put into practice. The letter was from Cornelius de Lannoy, an alchemist from the Low Countries. Keen to escape the troubles presently besetting his homeland, and even more eager to work on his theories, he had written asking that I take him in and give him funds to practise his craft. Alchemy was technically illegal in England, but if I chose to I could allow Lannoy to practise by issuing a dispensation. Lannoy believed he could conjure the Philosopher's Stone; a fabled gem that could turn base metal to gold and create a potion of perpetual life and health.

If true, it would certainly solve all my problems, both financial and in the case of the succession. If I were to live forever, there would be no need for an heir. What a way to prevent my Council and Parliament ever bringing up the subject again!

"What do you think of the idea, Robin... to live forever?"

"All men desire immortality," he said, playing with the tassels on one of the cushions. "But I have ever believed only God was capable of such a feat."

"It sounds lonely to me," I said, crossing to the fire and sitting next to him on the floor cushions. "To live forever, as those you love wither and die? To have those you love pass into Heaven, leaving you to face aeons of existence alone, until the end of days?"

"I suppose you could feed this fabled potion to those you love, Majesty, and maintain the court in all its splendour until the final day of reckoning." Robin smiled at me and took my hands in his. They were warm. I could feel the calluses on them against my soft skin. "Eternity would not be lonely, if you were at my side. In this life, I need no other but you."

My heart sang. The pestering stranger who had worn Robin's face had gone. Now, the man I loved had returned. I stroked my fingers against his and kissed their tips. Then I breathed in and smiled, pulling my hands away. "Shall I give Lannoy dispensation to practise his art in England, then?" I asked, drawing us back to business. "He offers the princely sum of thirty-three thousand in gold and precious stones per annum if it works."

"What a very *specific* amount," Rob marvelled with mocking eyes. Robin did not believe this art could bear fruit, at least not in the hands of Lannoy. "The alchemist must have worked his sums to the last shilling! I must tell Dee of this.

He will be fascinated to hear how the man could be so exact!"

I laughed. "I will send word to Lannoy to come to England, and I will offer him a pension," I said. "The distilling rooms in Somerset House should suit him, and if he succeeds, who knows what may come, Robin? England may well have a queen to rule over its people forever, *and* become a rich nation in the process."

"It sounds like an ideal future to me, Elizabeth." I did not remark on his familiarity, I liked it. Not since the days when Amy Dudley was still alive, and I had offered my heart to him, had I been so happy. There was much to content me. Talks had resumed on my proposed marriage to Archduke Charles but were moving at a satisfyingly slow turn of speed thanks to the good offices of my friend de Silva. Mary was sending delegates to meet mine in the north of England, but these negotiations, too, were not serious in the slightest. I had recovered of my late illness and Robin was back at my side. Life was sweet in those hard days of winter.

*

Another, rather more surprising marriage proposal arrived, too, that winter, in the shape of the fourteen-year-old King of France. Catherine de Medici had evidently decided the best way to stop me interfering in France was to saddle me with her son.

"People will say that I am marrying my grandson," I had remarked dryly when the idea was presented. I have to admit, my feelings were bruised when many in the Presence Chamber laughed heartily at my jest.

It was true enough, however. I was thirty-one to this King's fourteen years. Although I had to show due respect for the offer in public, I was not enthused. There were rumours that the young King was about as hale as his late brother had been, and, according to the newly returned Throckmorton,

Charles was under his mother's complete control. My new ambassador, Sir Thomas Smith, wrote that the King was tall, but had knobbly-knees, thick ankles and ill-proportioned legs. When I put this image of a weak, gangly, mother-led lad next to my bold, hale, handsome Robin, I could only find the idea repellent.

I had to maintain talks for the good of England, however. The French ambassador, de Foix, appeared to lose heart after my jest, so I pretended to be affronted, telling him I had only wished to point out the difficulties of the match, and I was still open to talk about it. It was a way of keeping negotiations open with France, and showing the Hapsburgs I had other options as well. As soon as they heard France's offer, the Hapsburgs were *most* eager to talk about trade and negotiate for the release of their ban on English ships. Seeing Hapsburg interest renewed, the French were under pressure to court my desires too. Having them both at my mercy was vastly satisfying. But I ran into troubles with my Council, who, as ever, took any proposal of marriage as serious, and never saw the potential benefits of stringing suitors along. To me, this was an opportunity to make trade deals, and barter with my fellow monarchs. My Council, however, were generally opposed to a match with France. I turned to Robin as I needed at least one on the Council to show interest. Everyone knew my regard for him, so if he spoke in favour of the match, it would buy me time for other negotiations.

"I need someone to act as though they think the French marriage a good idea, Robin," I said. "Otherwise the Council will make me abandon it, and in doing so I will be under more pressure to accept Archduke Charles. I want time to bargain with both sides. Besides, if there are two suitors, then no two men will ever agree. If there is one, they might unite."

"I am at your service, Majesty," he said with a devilish grin. "Anything to prevent you marrying another man. I will gladly help. France is *obviously* my first choice. "

De Foix was encouraged by Robin's enthusiasm. King Charles declared himself in love with me, no doubt at the urging of his overbearing mother, and started to pen the most appalling poetry in an effort to win my heart. I had thought the worst poet in Europe was Erik of Sweden. I was mistaken.

There was another string to this lute played by the French, for in addition to offering Charles as a suitor to me, Catherine de Medici offered her second son, Henry, Duke of Anjou, to Mary. I am sure it would have suited that devious Medici snake well to tie her house to both England and Scotland in marriage. It certainly made Phillip of Spain nervous. Although Spain and France were generally united in religion, they had never been easy neighbours. I think they had spent more time at war with each other than ever at peace. The idea that France, Scotland, and England could become united made Phillip twitch on his throne as though his clothes were infested with hungry fleas. It was therefore as much for my own amusement as for political gain that I decided to stretch negotiations out. Mary, however, was repulsed by the notion of marrying her former brother-in-law. Having known Anjou since he was a child, Mary was in a position to know his character and looks in ways I could only guess on with Charles. Mary refused to consider the proposal, but she seemed to have turned cool on the idea of marrying Don Carlos too. The reason being, that another suitor was being offered.

Lennox had been greeted at Mary's court and had managed to become a firm favourite with her in a short space of time. Mary had agreed to reverse the attainder against him for his past treachery, and had welcomed him with open arms to rounds of feasting, dancing and hunting. Installed in glorious apartments in Holyrood Palace, Lennox wasted no time in not only restoring his own titles, but seeking to add to those of his son as well.

Lennox was pouring sweet promises into Mary's ear. Randolph informed me that Lennox had presented my cousin with a miniature of Darnley, and spent his days telling Mary *what* a man his son was; handsome, learned, wise, chivalrous... Lennox must either have had more imagination than I would have credited him for, or he was blind to his son's flaws. Lennox was keen to sell his son. He told Mary not only of Darnley's many apparent virtues, but also that marriage to his son would aid her in her quest for the English throne. I was obviously supposed to know nothing of this. Lennox knew I would disapprove, and he also knew it was in my power to decide whom Darnley would marry. But ambassadors have long, keen ears. Randolph concealed his findings in cipher, and Cecil and I devoured the papers he sent from Scotland.

Darnley was still at my court, but there would soon come a time when I knew I would have to choose whether to allow him to join his father in Scotland or not. If I did, and Mary liked him, would she be so foolish as to marry him? Perhaps this would be a good test of whether she was indeed suited to be my heir. A true Queen must choose her head over her heart, as I had done. I had tested Robin's loyalties, and he had prevailed. Perhaps this was a way to test my cousin... But still, I wavered.

If I was unsure, the Lennoxes were not. Cecil's spies watching Margaret Lennox had found out that when Melville returned to Scotland she had given him something for Mary. Although we were unsure what this gift was, to my mind there was only one thing it could be; the Lennox Jewel. It was a fabulous trinket, designed as a pendant to wear about the neck or on the girdle. It was a golden heart, with a crown at the top, surrounded by fleurs-de-lis, on a background of dazzling azure enamel. Under the crown, which was mounted with rubies and emeralds, was a winged heart with a huge sapphire set into its centre. Crafted in gold were the figures of *Faith, Hope, Truth* and *Victory* and about the border, the motto "*Who hopes still constantly with patience shall obtain victory in their pretence.*" Not the snappiest of mottos, I grant you, but the jewel was famous. It had been commissioned the previous year to celebrate the marriage of Lennox and Margaret, and demonstrated their obvious links to the crowns of both Scotland and England. Lennox wanted Mary for his son and thought to buy Mary's affection with this shiny trinket and with all his pretty, pretty lies.

As a sudden thaw came in January, causing flooding and distress in many parts of my realm, much of my time was taken up with organising repair crews, charity and aid to those affected. Whilst I was busy acting for my people, my cousin was busy reconsidering her choice of husband. Cecil informed me that Melville had met with Margaret Lennox often whilst he had visited court, and my wily *Spirit* had no doubt that my duplicitous cousin was working hard to ensure her son became a king. In doing so, Margaret was going directly against the oath she had sworn to me. I doubted this troubled Margaret a great deal. Any promise to me she would have seen as easily forgotten.

My cousin of Scots was as keen to marry as I was to remain single. I came to think that perhaps my cousin and I were not as alike as I would have once liked to believe.

Chapter Fifty-Five

Greenwich Palace
Winter 1565

Robin had made me most content since his return to favour. We were free and easy in each other's company. Winter passed in perfect happiness and I had just started to sink into this blissful bath of contentment when Robin evidently decided enough was enough. Perhaps believing my memory was lapsing, Robin held an entertainment in my honour. During the day we attended a joust where Robin rode, wearing my favours. To see him, riding out into the lists, his armour shining in the watery sunshine... Ah, it was like watching a god of old come back to grace us mere mortals with his sacred presence. He rode against Norfolk, Pembroke, Heneage and Sussex, and won against them all.

After the joust there was a wrestling competition, which was exciting to watch, and even more thrilling to wager upon. I won myself a fine pile of coins from betting against my ladies. When dusk began to fall, we raced inside to don gown or tunic and emerge for an evening supper party. A select group of courtiers and my ladies were chosen to attend. It was a pleasant, intimate, evening. Then came the entertainment Robin had selected. It was a play, a comedy, as he came to tell me, so no immediate lights of alarm blazed in my mind as the players strolled out onto their makeshift stage.

When the drama unfolded however, my contentment and happiness seeped from me. Sadness invaded my bones and blood. This comedy, if that was what it was, was *all* about marriage. It was a play about the gods of ancient Rome. *Juno* advocated matrimony to *Diana,* who was opposed, and both gave their cases to *Jupiter* to decide. *Strangely* enough, don't you think, *Jupiter* supported marriage over chastity; a depressingly tedious, predictable verdict. Admittedly, some of the players gave foolish, and therefore amusing, reasons for either marrying or remaining single, but since the whole tenor of the play revolved around advocating marriage, I was not pleased. I sat there listening to the players, glancing at Robin's shining face. Why could he never leave well alone? Did he think his recent good behaviour would have altered my opinion? Or... a different and much more unpleasant thought reared up in my mind... had all his recent good behaviour been just another deception? Had all of his efforts at friendship been a feint, to once more lull me into a state of happiness, so he could pounce on me, and take me off-guard? I pursed my lips, feeling foolish for having believed in my favourite, as *Jupiter* spoke final, glowing words about the *glorious* state of matrimony. I turned to de Silva who was at my elbow. "This is all about me!" I muttered out of the side of my mouth. His lips broke into a sympathetic smile.

"It may be that is the case, Majesty," he murmured, glancing at Robin. "Your people wish to see you married, madam, none can ever doubt that... and none more so, I believe, than your good friend, the Earl of Leicester."

I twisted my face into a look of annoyance. "*Good* friend!" I muttered irritably. *Was* Robin a good friend? I did not know. I felt cheated, tricked, deceived... It was a dirty feeling. I found myself mistrusting every sweet moment between Robin and me of late.

Lifting my voice, so that many could hear me, I spoke loudly. "Marriage is a state for which I never had any inclination, my lord ambassador. My subjects, however, press me so that I cannot act according to my private inclination, but must marry or take the other course, which is a very difficult one. There is a strong idea in the world that a woman cannot *live* unless she is married, or at all events, that if she refrains from marriage, then she does so for some bad reason. They said of me, in the past, that I did not marry because of my fondness for the Earl of Leicester, and the sole reason I would not marry him then was because he had a wife already. And yet, you see... Although he hath no wife alive now, I still do not marry him. I cannot cover everyone's mouth; people will hold their own opinions... I must content myself with doing my duty and trusting in God, for in doing that, the truth will at last be made manifest. God alone knows my heart. And what lies within it is very different from what people believe, as you will see some day."

"I do not think your heart is so very different to those of other women, Majesty," Silva said, adjusting a stray ribbon on his tunic. "You are merely different in the manner in which you choose to live your life, Majesty. I do wonder if, watching your example, many women would choose to marry not, if they were allowed to do so."

I smiled. "Most women *should* marry, my lord ambassador. What would men do without us?"

He smiled and glanced at me with sparkling eyes. "Without women, my lady, men would be a poor lot, indeed. How *would* we men know what to do with ourselves, if we did not have our wives, sisters, mothers, daughters, aunts *and* nieces all at hand to instruct us?"

"'Tis true," I agreed, chuckling.

"We would be lost." De Silva's voice was mocking. He put a hand to his chest and sighed dramatically and then smiled. "But in all seriousness, madam, if I had not women in my life, I should be a pauper, and not only in terms of the money in my purse." He turned to me, his face affectionate. "Women have different ways to men, and men to women, but when set in the right alignment, they meld together so well that then, then I appreciate why God made us as He did."

I snorted. "You know that oftentimes, de Silva, my reluctance for the state of marriage has led some to believe that I *am* a man in disguise." I shook my head. "I wonder why they think this? Why, if I were a man, would I pretend to be a woman? Had I been born a man, as my parents so desired, it would have alleviated many of the problems I have encountered."

"And replaced them only with different ones," he noted. He looked me up and down. I almost blushed as his gaze lingered on my white bosom, and drifted over the curve of my delicate jaw. De Silva lifted his shoulders. "To claim such a fantasy, such people must not have seen you, Majesty. It is plain you are a woman indeed, and a beauteous one."

"People are apt to comment well and heartily on all they have never seen, my lord ambassador, do you notice that? Any man may be thought a scholar of a subject if he speaks with confidence. And often, the more outlandish the claim, the more it is believed. Speak bold, speak loud and you can win people over to the most ridiculous of notions."

De Silva leaned down to my ear. "As we have ample and daily proof, Majesty, in Lord Darnley," he whispered. I giggled.

"True... that is how the boy gains his followers. See them now?" I pointed to Darnley's gang hanging on his every word. "He speaks with brash boldness, and they feed on his confidence. Just as well, for there is no other sustenance in his company." As I looked their way, I caught Robin's eye. He started to wend his way through the chattering crowds, his eyes alight with expectation.

Ah, there he is again, I thought, feeling the good humour de Silva had restored to me being torn away. *That stranger who steals my friend's face...*

"What thought you of the play, Majesty?" Robin asked as he joined us.

"What I always seem to think of *your* plays, my lord Earl," I said, rising and taking de Silva's arm. I gazed coldly at Robin and he started at my expression. I had become winter. "I think the comedy, if that is what it was supposed to be, was not amusing enough to bear such a name. I think the play was ill-chosen, and ruined this day which had been so delightful for me." I sniffed, holding de Silva tight to me. "I think, as ever, that you ought to ponder more on the contentment of your Queen, if pleasing her is what you aim to do. And if you do not aim to do this, I shall have you replaced."

Robin stared at me, his face growing red. I put my hand on his arm. "I warned you once before, my lord Earl, about your plays. I will not sit through another like this, I assure you. Present one more entertainment that fails to amuse me, and I shall employ another to take your place," I nodded at Thomas Heneage who was laughing with a group of ladies not far away. "Heneage has a lively spirit," I said airily. "Perhaps he can find ways to please his Queen, rather than seeking many and various ways to ruin her happiness."

Not waiting for an answer, I led de Silva off. We joined Heneage and his admirers. It did not take long for us to be enveloped in the conversation, roaring with laughter as my good Spaniard traded quips with Heneage.

I glanced only once more at Robin for the rest of the night, and when I did, I saw a sour expression on his face. Once again, his play had not worked the magic he hoped it would on me. Once again, I had lost my friend.

Chapter Fifty-Six

Greenwich Palace
Winter 1565

"The Council are here to talk about the suit of the Archduke, Majesty," said Kat, walking into the Bedchamber the next day. "They are gathering in the Privy Chamber."

"*Ugh*." The noise I made was more expressive than a grunt, less so than a word. "I have no wish to talk about marriage at all, after being bombarded by Robin's players on the subject last night."

Kat smiled. "It was a poor concealment of his intentions," she agreed. "The Earl has many good qualities. Subtlety is not one of them."

"Nor the presence of mind to think before he acts," I muttered and huffed out a breath. "We had just got to a stage where I believed he was my friend again, Kat... Why could he not leave well alone? I told him that the restoration of our friendship would take time... Does he think a few weeks makes up for these past years of treasonous behaviour?"

"I have often thought, Majesty, that Lord Robert's impression of time is not like that of other people," she said. "After his wife died, he believed a few weeks would be enough to erase the memory of that ill event. When you told him to wait, he seemed to think you meant a few hours."

"Remind me to get him a clock for New Year's," I said. "Methinks the Earl of Leicester needs to learn to tell the time again."

Kat giggled. "The Council are waiting for you, Majesty," she reminded me. I frowned, and entered the chamber.

If Robin's play had worked no magic on me, it was apparent it had fired everyone else into thinking of nothing else. *Curse you, Robin!* I thought, seeing him on his chair, *Even if you failed to entice me into matrimony, you have kindled the thought anew in my Privy Council.* Had that been another of his aims? He was not above using my men against me.

Cecil, along with Sussex and Norfolk were all keen on the match with Archduke Charles. Robin, looking a touch sheepish, advocated for France. As he spoke in favour of France, I noticed he did not dare to look at me, obviously sensing the wrath radiating from my skin. He was still going ahead with our plan, perhaps by way of an apology, or perhaps just to prevent me marrying anyone else.

"France is dejected, brought low and has far less resources than Spain!" Norfolk cried eventually, banging his fist on the table. Cecil, who had clearly been thinking of other matters as the stale old arguments went on, jumped in his seat. "And there is still the matter of the religious divide and all the dangers it presents," Norfolk went on. "The Hapsburgs can be the only choice!"

"*My* choice is the only choice, Your Grace," I reminded Norfolk. He sat down abruptly, seeing my face of stone. Norfolk was not a member of the Council, but had asked to present his opinion. I was starting to regret I had allowed him to attend.

"Of course, Majesty... I meant... it is the *better* choice."

"In your opinion, Your Grace, and yet members of my Council are opposed. I shall consider all options, and hear all voices." I glanced at Robin. "Could you ask Ambassador de Foix to attend on me in the Presence Chamber after this meeting, my lord Earl? You have made some good points about France and her King. I would like to discuss them with our ambassador." I put a finger to my lips and tapped it upon them. "I wonder if I have not given due consideration to King Charles as a suitor," I said. "It is true there is a disparity in our ages, but then the same is true in many marriages, is it not? And the King has shown himself to be wise beyond his years... patient enough to woo a woman. Perhaps the French-style manner of courting would suit me better; for every woman wishes to be wooed, rather than *battered* into the wedded state." Without looking at Robin, I dismissed the Council and made for the Presence Chamber.

"A French Charles, a Hapsburg Charles..." I muttered to Kat as I sat listening to de Foix ramble on. "... Is there anyone in this world they wish to marry, aside from a *Charles*? Are there no other men left?"

"What about a Robin, my lady?" Kat murmured.

"A Robin..." I shook my head. "Do you ever note that they are possessive, territorial birds, Kat? I have had enough of robins and their warbling."

"*Poor* chick," Kat murmured without a shred of compassion in her voice.

"We are delighted by the wondrous virtues of your master, lord ambassador," I said, turning my attention back to de Foix. "But, to my endless sorrow, I have other matters to attend to. Will you ask your master to send a portrait of himself to me? So I might look upon the face belonging to the hand which writes such beautiful poetry?"

"I will send the request this very day, Majesty," said de Foix, looking pleased. The poor man! He believed I was seriously considering his gangly-legged, ill-proportioned, spotty youth of a King. Anxious to relay my request to his master, de Foix left.

"Lord Darnley?" I called, seeing him waiting. "You have come to take your leave?" Darnley was to go to Scotland. I had finally made up my mind to send him and see what happened. Mary was becoming interested in Don Carlos again and it was too troubling to ignore. I had given permission for Darnley to visit his father in Scotland for three months; long enough to distract Mary, and short enough so that she could form no serious ideas about making him her husband. Reports from Scotland suggested that Mary's Protestant lords would not look favourably on a match with a secret, albeit known, Catholic, and Cecil had further reassured me that Darnley would not risk his English inheritance by marrying Mary without permission. I had hopes that Mary would pass my test, and see his true nature.

I watched Darnley approach and bow with fluid grace. Some of my maids of honour stared at him with eyes of desire. I could not understand the attraction. Darnley made me feel as though I needed to wash whenever I was near him. "You are to join your father in Scotland, my lord?" I said.

"Indeed, Your Majesty, I ride on the morn." Even his voice was displeasing when he was not singing: high, fragile, whiney, and grating. There was the tone of his mother in there, that shrieking harpy who even in her letters wailed like a banshee.

"I give you leave to go, Lord Darnley, and ask that you offer my best wishes to my royal cousin, along with my hopes for us to meet soon in the future. You carry with you the pride of England, cousin. Do not forget that as you visit the Court of Scotland."

I dismissed the other petitioners. I had had quite enough of petitions after watching the performance of last night. I was left worrying about Mary and Darnley. Speaking that evening with Cecil, I made him swear that if anything happened to me he would see to it Darnley was rendered powerless. "I fear such a man to come to my throne upon my death," I mourned, even though the lad had not even left England yet.

"I would never allow that to happen, Majesty," Cecil promised. "And you know there *are* other options to your cousin of Scots as heir… Katherine Grey is not suitable, I agree, but her sons are young. If they were raised by trusted lords they could be brought up to be suitable successors."

"I *will not* hear you, Cecil." I wanted to grind my teeth until they shattered. "I will not release her from house arrest, and I have no wish to consider those boys to be anything other than products of a treasonous affair between two intriguers. Speak not of them; they are not, and never will be, my heirs."

"If your Majesty never produces children of her own then she must acquiesce to choosing a successor!" Cecil's normally composed manner fell away. "And the people of England will never accept your cousin of Scots, Majesty."

"You mean *you* will not, Cecil," I snapped. "And who knows, Cecil? Should Lannoy's plans to make an elixir of life come to pass, you may have a Queen forever on the throne of England… *me*. Then you will be forced to deal with me, old friend, until the end of your days. Wouldn't that be a relief?"

We glowered at each other for a moment and then Cecil bowed shortly and strode off, not wishing to say more that would only incur my wrath, or further reveal his. I sat by the window that evening, listening to Lady Cobham play on the virginals with Lady Strange accompanying her with a song, but barely hearing the music as I thought. I was disappointed; in Robin, in Cecil… and wondered if I was about to be disappointed in Mary, too. Lost in my thoughts, staring with unseeing eyes at my hands, it took a moment for me to realise there was a figure standing behind me. I looked up and saw a white, gaunt face behind me in the dark window. The sight froze my heart. For a moment, I thought there was a ghost looming behind me. I made a strangled noise of alarm and my heart leapt with fright, but then I realised it was not a ghost, but Kat. I started to chuckle, pressing a hand to my swift-beating heart, but the mirth froze in my throat as I saw her expression. She held piece of parchment in her hands; her face a mask of sorrow and dumb disbelief.

I twisted about sharply to face her. "What is wrong, Kat?"

She held out the missive and I read much I wished I had not. The letter was from Bess St Loe. Her husband, William, my good and able captain of the Yeomen Guard was sick unto death at his house in London. He had taken a leave of absence recently, one of very few he had ever asked for, to see his family. Bess's servants had written that she was to come with all haste from Chatsworth, for he was perilously ill. I could see Bess's terror plain in her scribbled words. And there was more. Her husband had fallen gravely ill *just* at the time when his brother, Edward, was paying a visit. Knowing her suspicions about Edward St Loe, I had no illusions that Bess believed her brother-in-law had made an attempt on her husband's life. She was asking for my help.

"I read here that my good William St Loe is dangerously sick," I said. "Mistress Radcliffe!" I called. "Go to my physicians and send them to St Loe." I thought for a moment and then added, "and have some of my Yeomen guards go with them. Take this note and they will understand why." I hastily scrawled some words onto a piece of parchment, and thrust it into Mary's hands. Seeing the urgency in my face, she ran for my doctors' apartments. I knew from the letter that Bess was already riding hard for London. My doctors would get there before her, and I hoped they could aid William. I hoped also that my guards would separate Edward St Loe from his brother, if he was indeed up to something wicked. I wanted to go, but Cecil would not permit it.

"If he is suffering from anything contagious, madam, then you could catch it too!" he said when he arrived, looking rather dishevelled. I suspected he had already been abed with his Mildred.

"Then I hope Bess gets there in my place," I said.

But Bess did not reach her husband in time. She was too late.

William St Loe died even as Bess galloped into London. It transpired that Edward St Loe had been at his brother's side all through this short and *most* unexpected illness. As Bess arrived, wanting to throw Edward St Loe from the house, her smirking brother-in-law produced an indenture, apparently signed by William before his death, claiming legal right to Sutton Court, one of their properties. Edward had claimed he had a right to Sutton Court before and William had fought this with great passion, so to find that this document existed was a nasty surprise for Bess. She immediately suspected foul play. The matter was investigated, but no trace of poison was found. The indenture went later to the legal courts, but the signature was thought to be genuine. How Edward St Loe got his brother to sign, if indeed he *did* sign, I knew not. Had Edward poisoned his brother and then, in William's weakened state, thrust the parchment under his nose claiming it was something else entirely?

There was nothing anyone could do. Sutton Court was lost to Bess, but her own properties of Chatsworth and Hardwick Hall, inherited from her previous husbands, remained hers. Edward St Loe could not touch them, but he was not done with Bess and the St Loe wealth as yet. William had left only small, personal bequests to his children. The bulk of his wealth was left to Bess and Edward St Loe and one of Bess's stepdaughters contested William's will. When Bess briefly visited court after William's funeral, she came with a dark cloud of gossip about her. People believed it was unnatural for a father to leave no provision for his children and some accused her of having stolen the inheritance of the St Loe children. It was a cloud that was to follow Bess for the rest of her life, giving her an unfair reputation for being grasping and self-serving. None of this was true. I was sure William had left Bess his wealth for he knew his children were well cared for, and comfortable in their situations. When Bess's previous husband, Lord Cavendish, had died, he had left her a great deal of debt. William, ever a vigilant guard, would never have wanted to place his beloved Bess in the same situation.

The affair and all the legalities of it went on for years and I helped Bess as much as I could. My finest moment came, I believe, in securing a distant post for the repulsive Edward St Loe in Ireland, which brought a smile to Bess's face. Eventually there was a settlement, and Bess kept much of what William left to her, but the courts ordered her to make payments to compensate the losses of St Loe's children and Edward St Loe. I told her I would have her back in my household. I knew it would not compensate for her loss, but it was all I could do. Then, I went about the sad task of replacing William St Loe.

There were many times, in the years that passed, especially when I walked through my gardens in the morning, when I would think on the quiet, loyal, good-natured man who had watched over me for so many years. There was never another who guarded me who had the quietness of St Loe. Never another who had the ability to make me feel as though I was alone, as I needed to be, whilst being yet protected. There was never another who could take his place... that watchful, gentle presence. That good, sweet heart.

Another of my friends was gone. Another life ended too soon.

Chapter Fifty-Seven

Whitehall Palace
Winter-Spring 1565

"There are rumours that the Queen of Scots is in *love* with Lord Darnley," Cecil exalted. "She seems taken with the lad, Majesty."

"You will write to Lord Darnley and his father immediately and remind them Henry Darnley is unable to marry anyone without my permission!" I said, then let out a sigh and sat down. "Not that it will do any good... Is she really in love with him, Cecil? I find the notion so repellent. He is such an oily little tick."

"Many women find a girlish look on a man attractive, Majesty," Cecil said. "Although I must admit I fail to see the attraction... Perhaps he simply appears less fearsome than her brash Highland lords."

I felt so let down. I could hardly express my disenchantment in Mary. It was as though my own child had done something vile. She had failed me. Darnley! What a husband to choose! "She will regret it if she puts a crown on that dullard's head," I said. "He will try to rule her... He is too proud and stupid to take the place of a humble consort. He will bring misery to her and trouble to her country."

"Internal disorder in Scotland can only be an advantage to England, Majesty, since then no one there will be thinking about England," Cecil went on with distasteful relish. "And you must admit this is a better outcome than your cousin uniting Scotland with Spain."

"Better for us, Cecil, disastrous for her... I feel it in my bones, *Spirit*, that man will do her no good."

I had no idea how quickly I would be proved right.

My letter, demanding that Lennox and his son should return to England, was sent in early March but was delayed by a late fall of snow over England. It reached Mary by the 14th. It contained threats. I was appalled she would consider Darnley. I regretted listening to Cecil and sending the boy. He was supposed to be a distraction, not a viable candidate for the throne! Amongst my demands that Lennox and Darnley return to England, I added, as another warning, that nothing would now be decided about the succession until I was married. I also reminded Mary that Darnley required my approval to wed, and I would not give it. It was not one of my most diplomatic missives. Mary received it and was angered.

My cousin called for Randolph and accused me of playing games with her, saying I "answered her with nothing," in terms of the succession. She would have been "bound to my sister, your mistress," she said. "But to rely or trust much from her for that matter, I will not." As the conversation continued, and Randolph tried to calm her, she only became more furious. Mary flounced out and went out hunting, leaving Randolph to wonder what was to be done to mend this situation.

Whilst the court watched Darnley and his friends ride at the rings the next day, Mary approached Randolph, apparently with her humour restored. Mary told him that she loved "her good sister, his Queen," and owed me her obedience as "if to her own mother," but these sentiments were just empty words. Mary's true purpose that day was to get me to approve safe conduct of passage for Maitland through England and into France. The rumour was that Mary was contacting her family in France about Darnley. Unsurprisingly, I did not give permission.

Darnley and Mary were reported as being almost inseparable, but I do not believe she made up her mind until an accident of fate occurred. Darnley fell sick with a cold which developed into a fever accompanied by a rash, and sharp pangs in his head and belly. Many of us in England suspected syphilis, knowing well Darnley's predilection for cavorting with Southwark jades. But even these unpleasant rumours did not deter Mary. In fact, his illness broke into the core of her heart, turning gentle affection into love. Cecil found this baffling, but I understood her warped reasoning. Wasn't it only to be expected? Her first husband, whom many swore she had loved deeply, had been a sickly youth, and then a sickly king. Perhaps, seeing Darnley brought low reminded her of François and made Mary only more determined to cling to him. I believe my cousin had a passion for men who looked like boys. François had been a boy. She had never seen him grow to be a man. Was it therefore so unreasonable that Mary would fall for a man who looked like a boy, a boy who was sick and vulnerable, as her beloved had been too? Was it so unlikely she would cherish Darnley all the more when Death seemed bent on stealing him away?

The past has a strange way of creeping back into our lives and deciding our fates, if we let it. I am sure my cousin did not recognise this was the reason she fell for Darnley. I am sure she did not realise, as she gazed on the handsome face of this sick young man, that she was transferring the genuine love she had felt for François, into Darnley. He became to her, I believe, a handsome shell into which she put all the hopes, dreams and aspirations she had shared with François. Mary could not see Darnley for what he was. The glimmer of her fantasies was glowing too bright over his true face. And there was the added benefit he would help her in her pursuit of the English throne. Whatever the reason for her alteration from affectionate monarch to loving woman, it happened. By the end of the spring, Cecil's spies in Mary's court told us that they were sure to wed, and she would brook no refusal.

Cecil was privately delighted, although he could hardly reveal his happiness in public. Most other members of the Council were horrified. They, like me, had no wish to see Darnley on any throne, English or Scottish. My Privy Council met to see what was to be done to stop the marriage, and we were not alone. There were many in Scotland, Mary's bastard brother Moray included, who were violently opposed. Her detractors believed Darnley would be an enemy to the Protestant faith since his family were known Catholic sympathisers. They also did not see the mark of a strong or wise King in this simpering eighteen-year-old lad.

Ordered to leave court in disgrace after opposing the match, Moray left in high anger, furious at his sister. It was the start of a serious rift but Mary did not seem to care. There were others who pledged their support; both for political reasons and personal ones. Maitland, who wished to marry one of Mary's *Maries*, supported his Queen, hoping she would allow his marriage. Some of her Council saw that marrying Darnley would put her in a good position for the English throne. A benefit, they saw, that was perhaps worth putting up with a dullard as their Queen's consort. Mary believed she had enough support to go ahead. She would lose my friendship, but in marrying Darnley, she believed she could only strengthen her position, and besides, she had a great fancy for him, as all who saw them together noted.

Margaret Lennox, who had been in high favour until this point, suddenly found herself surrounded by my wrath. I had never enjoyed pretending to be friends with her, and so it was almost with relief that I snubbed her openly at court. Maitland arrived in London to ask permission for Darnley to wed Mary, and for me to name Mary my heir, both of which were refused. A little later that month I sent word to Margaret that she was to keep to her own chambers at Whitehall. She was not officially under arrest, but the conditions were much the same.

Cursing myself for ever having listened to Cecil, who was almost skipping about the palace for having engineered this ill fate for Scotland and eliminating the threat of Spain entering Mary's bed, I tried to prevent the marriage. I sent Throckmorton to Scotland. Having been once close to Mary he was, I hoped, the best person to reason with her. I also said I had heard rumours that Mary and Darnley were already lovers, and was concerned for my cousin's honour, but when Throckmorton arrived at Stirling, he found the gates of the castle closed to him. When finally he did manage to gain an interview, he gave Mary the document asking her to put Darnley aside and wed either Robin or another lord of my choosing. My cousin refused.

Pointing out that I had petitioned her to marry an Englishman, Mary protested she had done only as I had asked. "The Queen of England cannot expect to control *all* aspects of my heart and my life, lord ambassador," she said coolly. "And since I have chosen a man who is my good sister's kinsman, I could only believe your mistress would be *delighted* with the proposal."

Leaving Throckmorton at a loss for words, Mary went off and straight away made her new love a knight, then a baron, and ended the day by granting him the title of Earl of Ross. What a busy lady my cousin was! Whilst she also planned to make Darnley the Duke of Albany, a title which only royal Scots had previously held, Mary paused to see what my reaction would be. In the interim, apparently enraged by the delay, Darnley drew his dagger on Lord Ruthven, who had but come to deliver the message that Darnley's further ennoblement was postponed. Randolph reported that Darnley had shouted at Ruthven, and others in the room, saying they were attempting to thwart his natural rights as the future King of Scotland. Quite an overreaction, I am sure you will agree, and one that was talked about with amazement at Mary's court, and mine.

If my cousin was at all perturbed by these emerging character defects, she did not remark on it. Mary appeared utterly infatuated with the strutting halfwit, and went out of her way to placate and please him. If she thought gentle treatment would inspire good behaviour, she was much mistaken. Darnley was a spoilt little boy, used to getting his own way without question. He was often drunk at court, even when attending serious meetings. He lurched about entertainments in the evening; bragging, boasting and making swift enemies with her lords with his lewd and outlandish behaviour. There were rumours he had taken up with a parade of whores in Edinburgh, yet still, my cousin did not seem to see any fault in him. I knew not from one day to the next whether Mary was blinded by love, or by ambition.

Darnley developed an intimate friendship with Mary's musician and personal favourite, David Rizzio, leading to gossip that they were lovers. It was well-known that Darnley had taken up with as many lads as lasses whilst in England, and many of the whorehouses he frequented were known to provide boys for men who wanted them. Although this was shocking to some, I found it less so. I found men attractive, why should other men not look with the same eyes upon their sex? It was against Church law, of course, but there were many who indulged in adultery and other sins, and were not judged as harshly as those who had a predilection for their own sex. And it was hardly as though Darnley was the first young man to experiment with his sexuality. There were plenty of men at court who had done so before marriage and some I knew of who kept secret male lovers in their households. But what *was* shocking to me was that Darnley was shedding the fine veneer of his charm with astounding speed. He was revealing his true, most unpleasant, colours, and yet Mary still wanted him.

Love is strange, is it not? Even when it is a false love, as I believed this was. This was an infatuation based on what Mary *wanted* Darnley to be, not on what he actually was. It could be nothing else, in truth, for what he was, was repellent and odious. Desperate for love, for one to call her own, for a man to support her and share her burden, and for a greater claim to my throne, Mary plastered Darnley with her fantasies.

When the plaster dried, when her illusions crumbled, she was going to find out just what kind of a man she had invited to her bed.

Chapter Fifty-Eight

Whitehall Palace
Late Spring - Summer 1565

In May, as my cousin fluttered like a delicate butterfly about her new love, a game of tennis was arranged at court to distract me from my woes. Robin was playing Norfolk, and at a break in the match he came over to talk to me. The sight of Robin sweating and flushed was quite distracting, and therefore I barely noticed when he slipped my handkerchief from my sleeve and dabbed his forehead with it.

"You play well, my lord," I noted as he wiped his face. I was about to continue, enjoying Robin's impish eyes and the scent of his body, when Norfolk erupted into furious anger. Storming towards Robin, snatching the cloth from his hands, Norfolk went an unearthly shade of purple as he bellowed at Robin.

"You go too far, sir!" he screamed, his eyes bulging and nostrils flaring so wide I believed they would part company with his face. "You are too *saucy* with the Queen, my lord! You take liberties! I swear upon God's blood, I will take my racket and break it over your head for your lack of respect!"

I doubt that Norfolk really cared about anyone showing me a lack of respect. He showed precious little himself. Rising from my chair, I rounded on him. "Hush your mouth, Your Grace, or I will shut it for you!" I cried, blazing at him. "How dare you tell me to whom I may or may not offer a handkerchief? Is it not *my* cloth? Am I not your Queen and master? Remove yourself! The records shall show that the game was won by the Earl of Leicester, for the ill manners of the Duke of Norfolk have disqualified him!"

Gaping at me in horror and surprise, Norfolk could barely bow due to the rigid anger in his bones. He stalked off like an outraged heron. Robin handed my cloth back to me, smirking.

"And don't think you are without blame, *again*, Robin!" I whispered harshly, snatching the cloth from his hands. "You know such familiarities incense Norfolk. You did this on purpose, to rattle him!" Robin said naught, but bowed and left to play another opponent.

"The Earl plays well," de Silva interjected smoothly as the match resumed, even though he had heard all I had said to both men.

"He does," I grimly agreed. "If only his games about court were as subtle as his playing on *this* court."

"Some are more talented at certain games than others," de Silva agreed. "But I do not think you are as enraged with the Earl as you say, Majesty."

"Am I not?" I asked coldly.

"How can a heart, so open, be easily closed against the one that brings it such pleasure?" de Silva asked. "For all his faults and imperfections, Majesty, you love the Earl, I am sure of it."

I allowed a small huff of breath to leave my nose. "Truly, ambassador, is it not the faults of a person which make them real, rather than imaginary? There is no such thing as a perfect person. When one loves another, it is as much for their imperfections as for their perfections. My cousin of Scots will come to understand this when she sees past the handsome fantasy she has thrown over Darnley. In him, there is too great an imbalance of imperfection. She has deluded herself into false love by believing him to be perfect.

If she sees not his flaws, then she knows him not enough to love him truly. "

"Let us hope she sees his flaws soon, Majesty," de Silva sighed. "And yet you see the Earl's faults, and love him still. It is a fortunate man who knows himself loved despite his failings. Perhaps Lord Darnley will come to know the same grace, if the Queen of Scotland continues to adore him."

"Lord Darnley will *never* know himself fortunate, my lord," I said, frowning as I watched the match. "He will never be satisfied with what he has... He yearns only for more; more titles, more wealth, and more prestige." I nodded at Robin, who was bounding about the court like a stag. "And my lord Earl is the same, in some ways. He does not think himself fortunate to merely be loved. All he sees is what he does not have, rather than what he does."

"Then I pity him," de Silva said. "For to know oneself to be loved... Is it not what we all wish for, no matter in what circumstances?"

"It would be enough for me, ambassador, but it is not enough for the Earl." My lips curled. "Nor will it be for Darnley, as I am sure we will see if my cousin has not the sense to put him aside."

After the incident between Robin and Norfolk, their supporters and servants suddenly took to being well-armed about court, and especially when they came near each other. It disturbed me, but men were permitted to carry swords and daggers, so I could not stop them. But if any used them on each other I swore I would make sure they regretted it.

*

At the pressing of my Privy Council, I sent another order recalling Lennox and Darnley, but I knew it was to no avail even as I penned it. My cousin was lost in her love for this

Darnley dullard and enthused with the idea he could win her the English throne. She would not listen. Had I not been so horrified by the idea of Darnley becoming a king, I might have realised that by demanding she return Darnley to England, it would only make her more resolved to keep him. There is nothing like adversity to encourage love, after all. Since Cecil read all my letters before they were sent, he could have warned me off, but he had no reason to do so. Cecil wanted Mary to marry Darnley. He did not try to warn me. He wanted me to react thus, and my enraged response only drove Mary closer to her obnoxious fiancé.

Mary defied me. Commanding Darnley and Lennox to remain in Scotland, she started to make preparations to wed. "Let her not be offended with my marriage, as I will not be with hers," she said to Randolph when he protested. "You can never persuade me that I have failed your mistress, but she has failed *me*." With that, she left my ambassador with tears in her eyes.

As we struggled on with Scotland, Death took His opportunity. Bess Parr died at her country estates. Her end was not easy. It was painful, confusing and messy. Bess lost control of her bowels, her breathing and at the end, her mind. She struggled towards Death, falling into His embrace a wraith of her former self. We all long for an easy death; a smooth transition from this life to the next. Only the fortunate are blessed with such a happy, sweet end. So often death is ugly, bruising and humiliating, not only for the person who dies, but for those who have to face their demise with them. It was so for my Bess; an ungainly, horrific end to a gracious, adventurous life. And my poor uncle, who sat with her until the end, had to watch the woman he loved suffer and die in agony and ignominy.

"My dearest uncle." I clasped my hands about those of William Parr when he arrived to give me the news. My eyes were bleary with tears. My heart throbbed with grief. "I don't know what I can say. I loved Bess as though she was my own sister, and to have to do without her now…" I trailed off, losing my ability to speak.

Parr squeezed my hands and bowed his head over them. His shoulders trembled. He had loved Bess. Parr could not speak. His face was gaunt and hollowed by his loss, mirroring the emptiness of his poor heart. I could barely believe that Bess was gone. She had been so vital, so strong.

"We will see she is given to God with all the grace she deserves, uncle. She was a good woman, and a good wife. We will never forget her." Parr staggered from the audience, his legs only barely holding him upright.

"Will they all leave me, Kat?" I asked her as we settled into bed that night. "We have lost so many friends… so many of the old flock of Hatfield. Parry, St Loe and now Bess. She was one of the first to spy for me, did you know? I sent her on many a mission when I was a princess in danger. And now she is taken from me, as others have been too." I sighed. "My life has become about loss, Kat. Those I love rush to leave me and the spaces they leave are never truly filled."

"Death is a cruel companion," Kat agreed, putting her arms about me. "He steals where He knows it will cause the most pain, and tricks us into thinking He is gone when in fact He is ever hiding in the shadows behind us."

"What can be done against such a foe?" I asked, putting my head to her breast as though I were a child again. The scent of her warm skin washed over me. The smell of lavender, from her perfume, calmed my frayed emotions.

"*Live*, Elizabeth. That is all that can be done against Death. Live each day and know the beauty of life. Laugh with friends, and know that even when Death separates us, we are never lost to one another. Love those who deserve your love, and be grateful to be loved in return." Kat wrapped her arms tight about me. "Speak the names of those who have died, so that they are not lost from memory. Step out into the sunshine and the rain with equal joy, and cherish the feel of the wind upon your skin. Know that to live is a gift, and even when it is taken from us, understand we have been fortunate to possess such grace."

She pulled me closer. "That is all that can be done, Elizabeth, to thwart Death. None of us can escape Him for all time, nor should we mourn such a fact. When He is done with His work, He takes us to join those we have loved and lost in Heaven. But enjoy life for as long as it is yours. In that way do we defy Death. In that way do we learn to live without fear of Him."

"If only I could not feel the sting of the sorrow He brings," I murmured against her breast. "Then I could do as you say."

She stroked my hair. "Such sorrow will pass, with time," she said. "All things, good and bad, pass with time."

Chapter Fifty-Nine

Whitehall Palace
Summer 1565

Now my cousin of Scots had made up her mind to marry, everyone in England thought I should follow her *good* example. Despite various efforts on my part to converse on another subject, my Privy Council were determined to talk of nothing but marriage. *Curse you, cousin!* I thought grimly as I listened to my men raise the subject for the forth day in a row. *Why could you not remain single and unwed, as I am resolved to?*

My nerves were strained. Bess Parr's death hung heavy on me, adding to the weight of losing St Loe. I had been downcast for a while, but as I listened to my men bleat on like lost lambs, anger surged within my blood. Eventually, I exploded. "You would seek to ruin me!" I screamed, standing and slamming my hands down on the table with a great bang. Robin, Cecil and Pembroke all bounced half a foot in the air, all at the same time. I had little time to think on this magic my men had performed, as I raged on.

"You see the Queen of Scots pursue a halfwit *bedswerver* and you pressure me to follow her lead?" I shrieked, my voice reaching octaves which no doubt caused mice in the palace walls to cringe. "You think I should follow her example, my lords? Take a dunce as my mate? Inflict an unwelcome whoreson on England as well as myself?"

"Majesty…" Cecil said, staring at me in astonishment. "No one suggests you take a husband like Darnley…"

"But I should take one such as the Archduke who I have never met?" I fumed. "Or accept the boy-King of France and spend my life buttoning up his tunic and wiping his nose? Or perhaps you think I should marry the Earl of Leicester, finally, eh, Cecil? And inflict upon England a proud, disdainful and arrogant consort?"

"Majesty!" Robin objected, but I was too angry to hear him.

"All know that Your Majesty is so enamoured of the Earl of Leicester she can think on no other man as a mate," Norfolk interjected grimly, earning him a glare from Robin and from me.

"Get out!" I shouted. "Get out, all of you! Knaves and dissemblers! You would have me marry as swift as possible to *any* man who saunters along. You do not care who or *what* I will be saddled with, do you? You have no care for my country, for my people, or for me. My cousin even now forgets the duties she owes to her people, to her country by taking that wretch as a husband, and you think I should follow her example? Should I have moved faster, my lords, and taken Darnley as *my* husband? Would that have pleased you, gentlemen... to have a king such as Darnley rule over you? Perhaps, my lords, I would do you a favour, and die as soon as I wedded him, then you could have what you always wanted; a dullard on the throne under your control!" I glowered at them. They sat, frozen with horror. "Get out!" I screamed again. They were swift to exit. I sat down heavily on a chair.

"Was that *wonderful* performance truly in earnest, Majesty?" Kat asked, appearing from the shadows with a tight smirk on her face.

I glared at her, but then my face broke into a grin. "In part," I admitted. I had wanted to send them off knowing not to raise the subject of marriage with me again for a while. I believe my *performance*, as Kat called it, had accomplished that aim. But my annoyance was real enough, even if I would not naturally have lost my temper quite *so* well.

"They fled quickly enough," Kat said, putting her hand to her head and applying pressure to her temples. The headaches she had begun to suffer last year had become more frequent. She said they were nothing, but they worried me.

"What man would not flee from a woman who seems to have lost her senses?" I asked, rising and putting my cool hand against her brow. She closed her eyes and sighed with contentment at my touch. "You should use more of the poppy potion my doctors gave you," I said disapprovingly. "And take more rest."

"Who is the lady and who her governess?" Kat opened her eyes and gave me a look reminiscent of times past when she had scolded me. I had to smile.

"Who is the Queen and who her servant?" I retorted.

"It appears we are at an impasse." She slipped her hand into mine. "I will take more care, my lady, but *you* must promise the same. Playing your men like this... It can only last so long. Perhaps it is time to actually consider the idea of marriage and family. Not all fates turn out the same. You will not necessarily have a union like those of your father, or your sister. You do not have to live alone, Elizabeth. This single life, this lonely existence, it is not the only way to be."

"I am not alone," I said. "I have you."

"Ambassador de Silva is here to see you, Majesty," Mary Grey said, approaching and hovering behind us.

"Bring him in." I kissed Kat's hand and released it so she could stand at my side. "It is good to see you, ambassador," I greeted him as he entered. "To what do I owe this pleasure?"

"The Earl of Leicester sent me, Majesty," de Silva confessed with open honesty. "He believed I might cheer you up, for he said you were low in spirits."

"*High in anger*, I believe he meant," I said, making de Silva chuckle. "And he sends you to face my wrath, ambassador? Perhaps you should check if you are really good friends, if my lord Earl is so ready to throw you to the lions."

"He trusts in my ability to make you laugh, Majesty, and so it is proved, for I note the smile emerging on those pretty lips."

I laughed. "You do have a talent, de Silva, I admit, for bringing me happiness."

"Then my life's ambition is complete," he said as he performed a ridiculously overdone bow. "But if you will tell me your troubles, Majesty, then I will prove myself a useful friend. Allow me to listen to your woes, and I will do my best to offer advice. Then, when we are done, I will tell you more tales I heard of the French Court this week. I have a good one about a lord who tumbled from his horse into a pile of manure!"

I smiled. I had never met another who was de Silva's match when it came to the performance of comic humour. The man should have been on the stage.

I rolled my eyes. "They press me to marry, and they are not busy with that, they charge me with a great many things," I complained bitterly. "Amongst others, that I show more favour to Robert than is fitting. Even when I insult him, they say I adore him! And their belief that they know *all* within my heart and head leads them to think ill of me. They speak of me as they might of an immodest woman. But God knows how great a slander it is and a time will come when the world will know it, too. My life is in the open. I have so many witnesses that I cannot understand how so bad a judgement can have been formed of me."

"It is a hard task, to be a Queen, ruling alone, my lady," de Silva said. "For men will judge the woman first and not her titles. Ever have I seen it, and ever I suspect it will be. But there are times when one needs to listen to those about us, and learn from their point of view as well as consulting our own."

"And so you think I should marry with the first lord I meet and have done with it?" I asked. "Are *you* married, my lord? I would relish a husband with your sense of humour."

"Sadly, madam, I am," he smiled. "Otherwise I would be at your immediate disposal."

"That is a shame, my lord ambassador, for I begin to find I value silver over gold, the more I am in your company."

De Silva bowed. "As I find the comfort of your company, madam, to be more precious than any jewel."

I chuckled and rose, taking his arm. "Let us to the gardens go," I said. "And you will distract me by telling me tales of men falling down and ladies showing their undergarments. I have had enough of talk of marriage and the future. Allow me to lose myself in your stories."

My men duly avoided the subject of marriage for some time, thankfully.

*

That summer, my cousin Katherine Knollys fell gravely ill. Fearing I would lose her, I sent my physician, Doctor Robert Huick, to look after her. Katherine was at her country estates and I ordered that messengers would travel between her house and the court daily, to bring me news. Her eldest son, Henry, was to marry soon, and I was not about to allow Death to come for Katherine at a time when only joy should be present in our lives. She improved rapidly, and I breathed a sigh of relief. There had been too much death over these past years. It was as though, with the demise of Amy Dudley, Death had taken up residence at my court. But Katherine was set on defying Death, and I was glad of it. As Katherine recovered, so I tried to mend the frictions between Norfolk and Robin. Their men were still marching about the court as though they were on their way to battle, and I liked it not. Sussex had joined in to support Norfolk, and both of them seemed set on removing Robin from life, as well as from my favour. My efforts managed a temporary reprieve of tension between them, but neither was willing to make efforts to be friends.

Katherine was not the only one who fell ill. In June, the headaches which had beset Kat for most of the year sent her to her bed. She suffered such pains that she vomited often and I was terrified she might not leave her bed, but with a few days of rest, and me flapping at her side, she recovered.

"Finally I understand," she said weakly.

"Understand what, Kat?"

"How very irritating it was when I lectured you on your health, Majesty," she said. I beamed at her.

"And you have only yourself to blame, Kat," I told her. "For how do we learn to behave but from those who raised us?"

That made her laugh. But even when she was recovered, the headaches continued. I was sure she was taking too much upon herself, and issued many of her duties to Blanche and Mary Radcliffe. Kat objected, of course, but I insisted that she take more time to rest.

Later that month, I had a headache of my own in the shape of my cousin of Scots. She had the banns of her marriage read in public. Mary was ready to wed the drunken weasel, and it seemed no power on earth could stop her. Although still wary of my wrath, my Council resumed talks on the succession and marriage. To put them off, I made much of Robin, calling him to talk with me everywhere I went.

Robin visited my bedchamber each morning as I was being dressed, and one morning I made a show of kissing his cheek as he passed me my shift, which got the court talking. The shift is the most basic of undergarments, which led many to believe, when they heard the tale, that I had been *naked* in front of Robin! I had in fact been fully clothed, and he was handing me the shift to give to one of my ladies to take for washing, but I have to admit the story helped me spread the idea I was on the verge of marrying Robin.

If my Council believed I was set on marrying Robin, I reasoned they might leave me alone. After all, they did not seem to care whom I married, as long as I married. Cecil was worried. He believed Robin would bring no benefit to England, which was true enough, but also that should he become King, he would control me utterly. Norfolk was, of course, horrified by the idea and made no attempt to hide it. My late efforts to reconcile them were undone, but I could do little about that. Norfolk joined with Sussex, and also the lords Hudson and Howard of Effingham. My court was full of strutting peacocks, stretching their talons and hissing at each other.

And yes, I was using Robin again. I felt guilty, but had he not soured our friendship again with his loathsome play? And yet, eager guilt gnawed at my gut. My angst at Mary, sorrow for Bess Parr and St Loe, and the knowledge that I was using Robin pained me. I became ill. My doctors were convinced I had a stone forming in my kidneys, and this would lead to consumption and death. Death! Had there ever been a time anyone thought of anything else? Death plagued me, followed me, haunted me. His silhouette was cast over everything I did or said. At least being ill made it impossible for my men to badger me.

If I was low that summer, I was not the only one. We had reports from Scotland that Darnley was misbehaving. Randolph was filled with great sympathy for Mary. *"This Queen is so far past in this matter with Lord Darnley, that I fear it is irrevocable,"* he wrote. *"I voiced my concerns to Her Majesty, that she was rushing into marriage too fast, but I believe her bewitched by Lord Darnley. She is so altered in her affection towards him that she hath brought her honour into question, her estate into hazard, her country to be torn in pieces. I see also the amity between countries like to be dissolved, and great mischiefs to ensue."* Randolf clearly thought this marriage would bring no good to Mary, or her country. He wrote that Darnley continued to be drunk and unruly about court; that his boasting was winning him few friends, and many were dismayed by his behaviour. He reported even Mary had become downcast. *"Her Majesty is laid aside,"* he wrote. *"Her wits are not what they were, her beauty is other than it was, her cheer and countenance changed into I know not what."*

If Randolph was at a loss to know why Mary was suddenly downcast, I was not. I could see it all as clear as if I stood there. Mary's fantasy was fading. The paint she had used to cover Darnley's faults was flaking. But now, she was stuck, was she not? She no doubt believed to go back on her resolve to wed Darnley would make her appear weak, especially after all the bold defiance she had thrown at me. Mary wanted to appear independent, strong, and courageous. She did not see that sometimes the bravest thing we can do is admit we have made a mistake, and retract it. Until she married him, she had the option to escape. Mary did not take it.

Cecil took this opportunity to convene the Council and discuss Mary's right to the succession. Since I was absent, he knew he could get away with much. Mary's life story was told to the Council, and not a single detail was omitted that might cause her to be found wanting. By the end of that long day, Mary was found to be not only unsuited to the English throne, but dangerous to England as well. Now that she was poised to take a husband, Cecil argued, she had become a threat. It was likely that her heirs would rule England rather than mine. This would cause my people to turn to her, Cecil said, and be drawn away from their allegiance to me, causing possible rebellion. He also argued if Mary married Darnley without my consent this was a hostile act in itself. She was flouting my authority over my own subjects, he declared, and it was only a small step from that act, to inciting revolt.

I could not deny Cecil had a point. But I did not agree that my people would turn so easily from me. I also did not favour the notion that England should rise to meet this threat, as some suggested. It was discussed that Darnley, as an Englishman, might be able to gather an army against me in England, and so, some men asked, should we not gather our forces now, and pre-empt such an attack? In the end, it was thankfully decided that war should not be the first action England took in response to Mary's marriage. Cecil came to me later with a report of the meeting, and a petition that I look more favourably on Katherine Grey. They did not ask me to name her my heir, for they knew how I would react, but that was what they wanted.

I ignored the petition but I took many of their arguments seriously. "I do not believe my people would rise up against me in favour of Mary and Darnley, Cecil," I protested. "Mary has never been popular, and Darnley, although English, is hardly an inspiring leader."

"But secret Catholics hidden in your realm would rise, if they believed it would bring them a Catholic queen," Cecil said, sitting on a chair beside me. "And although you do not wish to believe this, Majesty, there *are* those willing to support Mary, over you."

I frowned. I did not want to believe it, and yet I could not deny it was possible. "We will take precautions," I said.

"Order the Earl of Bedford to keep a close eye on my cousin." Bedford was the highest ranking man posted to the English borders. "And tell him to aid Randolph. I want more ears and eyes in Mary's court. Issue them with further funds, Cecil. If we have to buy loyalties, we will."

"It will be done, my lady," Cecil said. "I also thought we should put the Countess of Lennox in the Tower. Her husband and son have defied your command to return, therefore they are traitors. You have just cause to formally imprison her on that count, and it would remove one who could be used by Mary or Darnley as a spy in your court."

I grinned. "Nothing would give me more pleasure, Cecil," I purred. "Have the Countess taken to the Tower, and have her son, Charles, removed from her and taken for questioning." I stretched my arms up, thinking that there was at least one event to bring me happiness in all this mess. Charles was only eight, so I doubted there was much he could tell my men, but separating him from Margaret would impress the gravity of her situation upon her. "How many times will that be that Margaret has been an inmate of the Tower, Cecil? My father imprisoned her when she dared to think of marrying men he did not approve of, and I have sent her there a few times myself. She should take up residence there and have done with it."

"I will reissue demands for Darnley and Lennox to return," said Cecil. "And inform them that the Countess is to be arrested for their defiance."

"It will not stop them, Cecil," I said. "Darnley cares for no one but himself, Lennox is blinded by the prospect of the crown and Mary is too far into this now. She thinks that by defying me she is being strong and bold. She will learn, eventually, that this union will only make her weaker."

"If she becomes pregnant, Majesty, she will be in a stronger position than you," Cecil pointed out.

"But she will *always* have that dunce beside her, Cecil. He will counter any advantage she wins."

Margaret was taken to the Tower of London that June and put into the Lieutenant's Lodgings with a small body of servants. Facing Tower Green, the apartments I chose for Margaret were intended to make her well aware of how close she was brushing to Death. On the green before her chambers many other royal women had met their end; my mother included.

Although she was a prisoner, Margaret's apartments were well-furnished and stuffed full of glorious cloth and tapestry. She had access to a small garden for exercise and her table was stocked well with fine foods. Mary sent me messages, asking that I release Margaret. I sent Mary letters commanding her to return Darnley and Lennox to England. We, each of us, ignored the demands of the other. Maitland, aware that he was not about to get my permission for the marriage left for Scotland.

At the end of July, Mary made Darnley the Duke of Albany. One week later she married him. I could hardly believe how swift she was moving. Heralds arrived in Edinburgh to announce that Darnley was to be named King of Scotland, something he had apparently insisted on, despite such an event normally requiring the support of Parliament. Mary's Council were divided and Darnley was hardly helping his supporters, for lately he had been heard to say he cared more for English Catholics than for Scots Protestants, which lost him much goodwill. But Mary was resolute that he should have the title. Perhaps suffering under the old, tired strain of marriage; that a wife, no matter her title, must be subject to her husband, my cousin pushed for Darnley to be made King.

Mary and her new husband celebrated, but there was, even then, a hollow, ominous feel to the festivities. Few were willing to wait upon Darnley, and some of Mary's lords refused to attend the wedding or celebrations which followed.

Already there were lords in Scotland preparing to rebel against my cousin. Although we knew it not at the time, Mary was in a great deal more peril from this marriage than we in England were.

Chapter Sixty

Durham House
London
Summer 1565

"Cousin," I said warmly as I approached Katherine Knollys. "My heart is made whole again to see you." Katherine curtseyed and then rose to take my outstretched hands.

"I am so grateful that you sent Doctor Huick, Majesty," she said. "He was marvellous. It is because of him that I am here to see the wedding of my son."

"The occasion could not be whole without you, Katherine," I said. I looked on her pink cheeks and merry face with satisfaction. I had stolen her from the greedy hands of Death. Henry Knollys, Katherine's eldest son, was to be wed this day to Margaret Cave, one of my maids of honour. We were at Durham House, on the Strand in London and almost the whole court had managed to get themselves invited. The groom was wandering with his men in the gardens, laughing and jesting, and Margaret was having the final touches made to her best gown of red silk. There was talk and song on the air; merriment flowing through every passageway and corridor. It was a good day.

I smiled at my Knollys cousin. I had always had more affection for Katherine than any of my other cousins, with the possible exception of Lady Strange. Perhaps it was because Katherine was related to me through my mother's blood and therefore presented no threat to my throne. There was, of course, a possibility that she held more royal blood than was publicly admitted, for her mother, Mary Carey *nee* Boleyn, and my father had once been lovers. Although my father had never acknowledged either of Mary Carey's children, there was a possibility that both Katherine and her brother Henry were his. This would make them my cousins *and* my half-brother and sister. Henry Carey certainly resembled my father. But even if this were true, it did not matter for the succession. Unlike her sister, Mary Carey had never been married to my father; illegitimate blood could not rise to the throne.

"Tell me your plans for the day," I said, leading her into the house. "Will the couple be put to bed here?"

Katherine nodded. "They will spend the wedding night and a few days here, together," she said and then smiled with an indulgent look on her face. "My son is eager to finally become a husband. He and Margaret love each other dearly."

"Margaret has been almost unable to contain her excitement," I said. "She has skipped about her duties in my chamber of late."

"I thought the girl might fly from one of the windows yesterday," said Kat from behind us. "She was so excited I believe I saw wings sprouting from her shoulder blades."

I chuckled. "Love gives us wings to fly to happiness."

I glanced at Robin as I said this. Standing some way off, talking to the groom, he cut a fine figure in blue silk and silver trimmings. His tunic was tight across his chest. His hose were dark black silk, hugging his fine legs. My heart called out; it tried to make me remember that yearning, wanting, nagging need to make him mine. I turned my gaze away. I no longer listened to my heart when it spoke of Robin. At least... I tried not to.

The wedding was a brief ceremony in the chapel at Durham. The bride was in her best red dress, and the groom matched her in a russet doublet. They were a handsome young couple. Standing before the light of God, she promised to obey him, to be bonny and buxom in bed, and to protect and care for him. As was ever the way, he promised the same, but did not have to swear to be ever-ready to receive her in bed, nor to obey her. I wondered, at times, about the service of marriage; that women should have to swear to give up their independence and freedom of choice where men do not. Had God really intended this? Or were these words made only by men, by the Church, to fashion the world as they wanted it? If I ever married, I would have to swear to obey another. How could I keep such a promise? How could I ever promise to obey a man, when the care of this country was granted to me and to me alone, by God? I liked not the notion of such obedience. It was not in my nature. I also did not welcome the idea that ever after the ceremony of marriage I should be expected to give my body to my husband whenever he desired. Surely, God gave us free will, and granted it to both men and women? The ceremony of marriage, to my mind, removed a woman's right to free will. But if I minded this, all others about me did not. Perhaps to them, the words of the service were but words. I knew plenty of women who did not keep to their oath to obey, just as I knew plenty of men who did not keep to their vows to be faithful... Words... They seem so powerful, yet they only have power if we believe they do.

That night we danced in the great hall, and feasted. The young couple sat happy, and flushed as they stared into each other's eyes. Henry fed Margaret with titbits from his plate and she filled his cup with wine. I noted, however, that she had her servants mix plenty of boiled water into his goblet. *Clever girl,* I thought admiringly, *she does not want a wine-soaked husband in her virgin's bed.*

We feasted on delicate courses of egg and saffron broth, buttered nettles and beer and cheese soup. Fresh, green sallats of spinach with currents and pottage of lamb with dried plums tempted the taste-buds. Then came roasted conies, peahens, capon and lamb so tender it dissolved upon the tongue. There was baked venison with frumenty, roasted hog and gammon with egg, and capon layered with blackened-roasted lemon slices. Thick lamb stew glittering with fresh Alexander leaves bubbled on the tables. Lobster tart, lamb pie, pig trotters in jelly and baked flounder with white wine sauce were dished out from shared platters. Pike in rosemary, roasted conger eel, fresh salmon and fried whiting disappeared into eager mouths. Golden baked pies of mutton, beef, cheese and egg oozed out sweet fillings of dates, raisins, pepper and salt when sliced open. Roasted hare, mutton steaks, ale stew, and lampreys in broth puffed savoury scents into the warm air. Beef olive pie, stuffed with finely diced leaves of violets, strawberries, spinach, and sorrel was cut open to reveal tumbling, steaming hot prunes and dates. Chicken pie with ginger, grapes, and berries was handed out in hearty slices as egg and kidney pancakes with sweet-sour fruits were served. Meatballs in white sauce glistened in silver bowls as roasted crane, quail, heron and woodcock enticed already full bellies to further gluttony. Artichokes boiled in sweet broth sat beside rice of Genoa, rich with almond milk. Spears of bright green asparagus and cold spiced vegetables slathered in honey sauce just about managed to slide in between the many other dishes.

We held a private banquet of sweets later, in another chamber, as the rest of the court tried to resume dancing. Many were far too full to attempt such a feat. In the side chamber, I laughed with the young couple as we supped on walnut comfits, sugar paste shaped into love hearts and marchpane knots. There was almond gingerbread, rosewater marzipan, delicate apple pies and almond butter laced with bright pink pomegranate seeds. Pies and pastries stuffed with summer fruits, or imported bitter-sweet oranges and lemons tingled on the tongue. We nibbled on eggs poached in rosewater and sugar, mottled so their skins looked like the moon, then devoured little biscuits flavoured with caraway seed, dipped in spiced honey custard.

That night I led the party of ladies who were to put Margaret to bed. I instructed Robin, who was leading the men, to ensure the groom was not far behind. Margaret had controlled her new husband's consumption of wine, and he was not too intoxicated. I understood she was hoping for a caring lover to take her maidenhead, rather than a drunken ass cavorting in her bed. I hardly wanted all her good work ruined if the groom was enticed into carousing with his men.

"I will deliver him as soon as possible, Majesty," Robin said with a naughty grin. "Henry Knollys is more eager for his wife than for wine, in any case."

"Remind him that *I* will be in the room when he arrives," I said, eyeballing Robin with a steely gaze. "*That* should keep him sober."

Robin laughed and went on his way to locate the groom as I took Margaret and my ladies upstairs. In the upstairs chamber, experienced matrons explained Margaret's duties to her. They made the whole experience sound so painful and distressing that I pitied the girl, although they did add that there was great pleasure to be found, if the husband had the patience to take his time.

Happy to see Henry Knollys arrive at least mostly sober on the shoulders of his men, we ladies kissed Margaret and vacated the chamber. We made our way back to the great hall, to continue to dance and drink as the young couple made their marriage legal. I danced with Thomas Heneage and then with Robin when he came down. Pink cheeked and happy, I took a break to drink some ale and refresh my senses.

"I wish I could see such a day come for you, my lady," said a voice at my side. Half-expecting it to be Robin, and yet knowing it could not be since the voice was female, I turned and shook my head at Kat.

"Today was a fine day, and a good night," I agreed. "But I would rather be a watcher, than a participant." I laced my arm through hers. "And after all the ghastly detail I heard in that bedchamber, I am surprised any maid has the courage to go ahead with the deed!"

Kat chuckled. "It is true the first time is not the greatest experience for a woman," she said and pulled a rueful face. "Although John did not seem to notice anything amiss when we were put to bed together..."

I laughed. "Was your John a beast, then? Should I have him put in the Tower for hurting my Kat?"

"He was... eager, Majesty. But I assure you he has made up for it a thousand times and more in all the years we have been together." My already pink cheeks flushed scarlet and Kat laughed at me. "You are far too mature, Majesty, to have colour flood into those cheeks upon mention of what goes on in a bed of marriage."

"One is easily embarrassed by events one knows nothing of," I said. "Come, we will move on to other topics. For if you speak anymore of your John in such a way I shall never be able to talk to him again."

Kat giggled like a girl, and we made our way through the crowds. Arm in arm, surrounded by happy faces, we stopped to talk and chat. The hall was filled with the scent of sweat, wine, spice and sugar. Ale flowed long and deep into the night. I danced galliards and voltas and pranced about the chamber with a light step. I was bright, happy and free and went to my bed that night with a mind seeped in joy.

Chapter Sixty-One

Richmond Palace
Summer 1565

After the fuss of the wedding had ended, Kat fell ill again.

The headaches were growing worse and no infusions or potion of poppy juice or willow bark could abate them. She grew tired and clumsy. I sent her to her bed often, but she always returned within a day, refusing to give up her duties.

One day, when she was dressing me, Kat was holding out a ribbon ready to tie it to my gown. Blanche later told me that Kat had seemed confused; she could not get the ribbon to go where she wanted. I did not see Kat as she fumbled. I just seemed to sense something. It was as though, for a moment, I could feel the hand of Fate reaching out to Kat. It was as if a strand of the future looped back and touched the present, warning me of what was about to happen. Feeling this eerie sense, I shivered and turned around. Kat's eyes were unfocused. Her hand trembled as she tried to fasten the ribbon to my sleeve. Her mouth dropped open slowly, as though an invisible person whispered shocking gossip in her ear. Her warm brown eyes fluttered, cresting backwards so I could see only the whites of her eyes. She tried to say something, but the word caught in her throat. The ribbon slipped from her fingers and fluttered slowly to the floor. Kat's knees buckled. She moaned, as though in terrible pain.

"Kat!" I cried, scrambling to catch her.

I failed. I caught the sleeve of her gown. The fabric ripped, and I was left holding her sleeve as Kat's legs gave way. She fell. Blanche caught Kat's head but a moment before it slammed against the wooden, rush-covered floor. I dived to Kat's side. Her body started twitching and convulsing. Her eyes rolled back in her head. Blanche held her, trying not to hold too firm lest she hurt her friend. Kat's limbs moved as though lightning bolts were pulsing through her. Her hands and feet thumped and flopped against the carpet, echoing the thunderous beat of my heart. I stared at her in horror. I could not move.

Kat jerked as though demons were pulling and poking her. Spittle fell from her open mouth. Her tongue lolled from between her lips. Sounds came from her throat as if she was being throttled by unseen hands. Blanche's eyes, which stared up at me in dreadful fear, chilled my blood.

"Send for my doctors!" I screamed at Lady Cobham, who, pale-faced and terrified, raced off to find them. She pushed past maids of honour and ladies who stood gathered helplessly about us, staring down on the Chief Lady of the Bedchamber in disbelief and horror. I sat at Kat's side, trying to hold her hand as she flinched and shuddered and moaned. I gazed at Blanche over Kat's body. We did not need to say anything; we both knew how afraid the other was.

The fit ended before the doctors got to us. They arrived, flush-faced and gasping from running clear across court, and ushered the other woman back and away. Kat was still, her face pale and drawn. She was unconscious, but she was breathing. The doctors helped us to move her to my bed where she slept as they fussed about her, touching her head and hands, exchanging useless stories with one another on similar cases. I stood next to the bed, unable to think, unable to do anything to help. My hands fluttered at my sides. I began to pace, restlessly, uselessly.

The doctors were troubled by the thinness of her body as we undressed her. I had not noticed Kat had lost weight. She had hidden it from me. Kat had plumped her gowns out with thick petticoats and pieces of cloth, just as my sister had done to conceal her fragile health. Kat had obviously been unwell for some time, and had masked the truth from those about her.

"I did not know either," muttered Blanche, her eyes swum with tears as she stared at the thick petticoats and undergarments in her hands. "She never said a word."

"She has not had a good appetite for some time," her husband John admitted when he arrived and I asked him about it. "But she said it was nothing to worry about..." With desperate eyes he stared at Kat, white and wan in the bed. "I should have known!" he shouted. "I should have said something!"

"If you think your wife would have listened, John, you are more fool than ever I took you for." I put my hand on his shoulder. I tried to smile, but it came out as more of a grimace. "It matters not now. She has been a naughty sprite, and we will scold her when she is well, John. What matters now is that she gets well."

The doctors worked on her; taking blood from her veins to balance her humours, applying poultices to her neck and chest. Kat slept on as they toiled about her, as I stood there, watching with eyes of helpless dread.

When she opened her eyes late that night, I was at her side. "Kat..." I whispered, holding her hand so tight that I must have hurt her, although she said nothing.

"What happened?" she asked. Her eyes were unfocussed and unsettling to look upon. She looked as though she were drunk, even though I knew Kat rarely imbibed much alcohol, taking her example from me.

"You fainted," I said, my voice wobbling. "You have taken too much upon yourself, Kat, as always. I will see to it that you get well, and when you do I will give your duties to others. I will not have you suffer for serving me."

"I have never felt my duties to you to be onerous, Elizabeth," she whispered. "To be with my girl, to stand with her through all the challenges of life… That has never been a trial. It has been an honour to be your servant, and your friend, my lady."

"You *will* listen to me, Kat, *and* obey me," I commanded, my voice catching. "I will not lose you. You will get well. You will be at my side for a long time yet."

I did not know I was lying when I spoke these words.

Over the days that passed, Kat would seem to rally and then another fit would assault her. Each time the convulsions came, she weakened. She looked so small in that great bed. So unlike the great force I had ever known at my side. John sat with her whenever I went to try to sleep, but sleep did not come to visit me. John's haunted face spoke of the terrible fear in his heart. We did not say what we feared. We spoke words of comfort to each other. We told each other she would be well, and when she was we would make her rest more often. We swore we would take greater care of this woman we loved so dear.

We knew we were lying, but we continued to tell our tales. We made up fairy stories to comfort one another. The truth was too hard to face. We were losing her. The doctors could do nothing.

One night, when I was alone, sitting up reading to her, she opened her eyes and gazed at me. Not noting that she was staring at me for a while, I finally looked up from the book. She was gazing at me with such warmth, such tenderness. It was a beautiful expression; peaceful, calm, as though her spirit had found its home. "What is it?" I asked, smiling at the affection in her gaze.

"I was dreaming of the old days, my lady," she said. Her voice was faint and weak, but her smile shone in her eyes. She looked proud. Proud of me.

"I was dreaming about the day they came to tell you that you were Queen. You were stood under that great oak tree at Hatfield. The light of the setting sun was shining over you. You looked like an angel, Elizabeth. Your red hair lit up like fire against the red-gold of the trees…"

Her smile grew, flooding her face with beauty. "Do you remember the early days, Elizabeth? The day we met? I loved you from the first moment I saw you; so bold and so proud… yet so sad. You stood there in your fine gown, wearing such a grave expression. You looked as though all the cares of the world were upon your small shoulders, even then. I had never met a child more serious. You hardly laughed until I found ways to tease mirth from you. So serious, so grave… a poor, motherless little girl. It seemed as though so many others had forgotten you, that since your brother's birth you had been pushed to one side. You felt it. I know you did. But I saw what others did not. I saw your courage. I saw your strength. I knew that you would become great, and you will be greater still." She paused and sighed. "I just wish I could be there to watch over you, always."

"Kat… don't speak that way. You *will* be here." Sudden fear flashed through my blood and into my bones. I felt weak. The dread of her admission flooded through me; Kat knew she was dying. "You swore you would never leave me, Kat. You must keep your promise."

"I fear, my lady, I will not be able to keep to my oath… not in life."

"You must." I put aside the book. As I tried to place it on the bed, it fell to the floor with a bang. Its pages opened, moving, flicking in the breeze which crept from behind the tapestry. Pages of words and thought turned as though a phantom hand leafed through the book, seeking wisdom. I slipped my hands into hers. "You must keep your promise, Kat. I cannot do without you."

"You have grown into a fine woman; into a great prince," she said faintly. "I could not be prouder of you, Elizabeth. I never had a daughter, but even if I had, there would never have been even a child of my blood who I would love as I love you. You are my daughter, as much as you ever belonged to your mother and father, you are mine, too. And as you grew, I had the privilege to know you as a friend. Nothing could have made me happier than to see you as you are now. You are the Queen England was supposed to have. You are the master of all you meet; a ruler who governs with wisdom, power and grace. I am so proud of you, my little girl."

"Kat..." My voice broke. I struggled to speak. What can one person say to another at such a time? How could I ever tell her what she meant to me... all that she was to me? Words are feeble when they try to express the love and devotion of hearts joined by bonds unbreakable. "Please," I whispered, feeling my heart tear within me. "*Please*, Kat, do not talk so. You will be well again, I will make it so."

"Not even you, my little love, have such power over Death," she murmured. Her eyes fluttered and she made to close them. A shiver ran through my bones. In the shadows behind the bed I seemed to see a figure. Cloaked and hooded, He stood too near. I knew why He was here.

"Kat... no..." I called out, my voice hard, desperate. "You may not leave me. You shall not leave me! I command you to stay! I order you to live!"

"Such things as these even you cannot command." Her voice was faint. She was falling from me. "I have lived well and full," she murmured. "I have known love and been loved in return. Such grace must be enough for anyone."

"*Please*, Kat..." I fell to my knees at her side, clutching her hand and feeling the life seep from her flesh. "*Please*... Please, Kat. Do not leave me here. Do not leave me here alone. I love you. I cannot do without you."

"I will always be with you." Her voice was barely audible. My heart was breaking. I could feel it; rending and snapping and tearing and ripping. "I will always watch over you... My girl... My little girl... You are mine, Elizabeth. My child. My daughter. I will always be with you... My love will never leave you."

"Kat, I love you too!" I exclaimed, breaking into tears. "*Please*, Kat. Do not go."

She spoke no more. I ran for the doctors who were sleeping in the next set of rooms. There was nothing they could do. I stared at them as though I knew not what they were saying as they explained to me that the end had come. They called for John, and they called for a priest. The last rites were given to Kat even though she could only breathe as a response. Four hours later, as John and I stood lost in a mist of grief, a doctor put his hands to her neck and chest. He lifted his head and shook it just once.

"She is with God, now," he said.

I could not move. I could not speak. As others broke into weeping around me I only seemed to hear a soft sound near to the bed, as though two people had joined hands. I thought I could hear footsteps moving away. Death had taken her from me. Kat was gone.

I stood there gazing on her still body. She looked so small. So very small. Her eyes were closed, her face was at peace. She could have been sleeping, had it not been for the pallor of her skin. Hands tried to coax me to move, but I would not leave her. I could not leave her. She was my Kat, my friend. The only mother I had ever known.

I stood there, frozen like a statue. I could not make sense of what had happened. I could not make sense of my loss. I could not find words to honour her. I could do nothing but stare.

And then, without making a sound, I fell. I heard people scream and rush to aid me. It sounded as though they were far, far away.

Darkness swallowed me.

Chapter Sixty-Two

Richmond Palace
Summer 1565

Blankness.

That is what I felt when I awoke. That is what I felt when I remembered Kat was dead. My heart had been taken from me. I was empty. I did not rise. I lay in my bed that day allowing no one into my chamber but Blanche. I could not bear to see another face but hers.

Kat was gone. She was *gone*.

It was not like any other time I had experienced the harshness of death. There were no thoughts in my head. No memories replayed. I thought not of the past, nor of her poor body lying in the next room. There was nothing in me anymore. There was only the awful blankness. This terrible, aching emptiness. The vacuum of loss. The long dark.

Grief was not beside me. Grief was within me. There was a part of me which never left the room where Kat had died; a part of me that would forever stand, silent, motionless, staring at her face. For the rest of my life I would carry grief inside me. He had entered my heart. He was within my mind… inside my soul. I stared at the window, but I saw nothing. I stared at the coverings of my bed and saw nothing there either. Blanche brought me broth on silent feet and I left it to congeal on the table. I did not drink. I did not eat. I stared and I was empty. Grief had made me hollow. Grief had made me lost.

Others did not mourn for Kat as I did. Phillip of Spain rejoiced, saying that she had been "such a heretic" he was glad for her death. The French Court felt the same. But they had known nothing of the woman I had lost. They knew nothing of her heart; her good heart. They had not known her as a friend. They had not been with her since they were children. Those who rejoiced in her demise had not known her pride, her wit, her spirit, her courage. They had not slept beside her every night since they were small. They had not held her hand or laughed at her jests. They had not had such a friend as I once did and so they understood not that a great soul had been taken.

I could not remember a time when Kat had not been with me. I did not want to think of a time when I would have to face this world without her.

I wanted to die, I think, in those first, awful, hollow days. I wanted to be with Kat. I did not want to live without her. I did not want to rise knowing I would never laugh with her again. That I would never go to her with talk or plans or gossip. That I would never again feel the warmth of her arms wrapped about me in the darkness of night. I did not want to participate in life, without her. Kat had been my gentle comfort, my summer warmth, my winter spark. She had been my mirth, my pleasure, and my scolding conscience. She had occupied my heart in a way no other ever would again. Without her, I did not know who I was.

If you have lost someone, then you understand all I went through. If you have not, then prepare yourself, for we are all fated to lose those we love. It is the price of living. It is the tax of life. And, in truth, we can none of us ever be prepared for loss. The dead leave a space, a gap, which is never filled. All joy had gone from the world. I was lost, naked and alone, in the wilderness. Afraid, raw, broken... bereft of hope and joy.

I rose from my bed after two days. I went about my duties with a mechanical air. I had become one of my father's clocks, ticking and clicking through the hours of the day, but without heart or soul within me. Every day, for the rest of my life, I had to wake knowing she was no longer with me.

Meetings were kept short. My audiences in the Presence Chamber were cancelled. All I wanted was to curl up and disappear inside the aching hole within me. In the day, my bruised eyes shied from the light of the sun, as though looking upon it would cause me to see, only more clearly, Kat's shadow missing beside mine. Everything was too bright, too loud. I wanted to hide in darkness, crawl into my bed and never emerge.

At night, Blanche took Kat's place in my bed. In those long nights, when the dark emptiness threatened to engulf me, Blanche took me in her arms and sang soft Welsh lullabies, trying to lull me into sleep. But sleep did not come, even though I was exhausted by sorrow. As Blanche slept, I would lie with eyes staring and glassy, remembering every day, every event, and every moment I had spent with Kat. Memories flickered, competing with one another. There was the sight of her laughing; the expression on her face as she scolded me; the swish of her silk dress as she marched through my chambers; the warmth of her brown eyes; the memory of her soft hands folding gowns; the scent of her warm skin.

At times, when I caught the scent of lavender, I believed I would drown in sorrow.

I went about court dressed in deepest black; my face plastered with thick powder to hide the ravages of my grief. I saved my tears for the nights, heaving silent sobs against Blanche's soft embrace. I rose each day feeling lifeless. My skin grew grey under my powder. My gowns hung from my skeletal frame.

Blanche became Chief Lady of the Bedchamber, and in those days when I lost Kat, she was my closest friend, my constant companion. She hardly spoke, understanding there are some feelings which cannot be expressed in words. But every night when I returned to my chambers she was there ready to take me in her arms. Blanche, in those days, was my strength, my courage. She was the only reason I did not fall into the arms of Death to join my beloved Kat.

"*Benthyg dros amser byr yw popeth a geir yn y byd hwn,*" she whispered to me one night. "Everything you have in this world is but borrowed for a short time." She stroked my arm as we wept together, and then started to sing to me. She sung a tale of chivalry and sorrow. I fell into dreams of knights, justice and mercy.

Slowly, slowly, the court returned to normal. People who had not known Kat forgot her. But as I sat on my throne, meeting with ambassadors and dignitaries, as my Privy Council argued on what was to be done with Scotland, France or Spain, I heard but little. Others could forget. I could not.

Every time I looked to my side, I saw the gap Kat had left there. Sometimes, I thought I caught a glimpse of her shadow from the corner of my eye. In those moments, my heart leapt with desperate hope. Hope that all of this horror had been but a dream, a nightmare. If I turned my head, she would be there. The nightmare would be ended. The spell would be broken.

But when I snapped my head about to try to see her face, the shadow faded away, just as Kat had. My heart died all over again. The rawness of my grief consumed me. I knew I was alone. Alone in this world without my friend.

Chapter Sixty-Three

Windsor Castle
Summer 1565

"Do not use lavender in the trunks, Blanche," I murmured. "I would that you would cease to use that scent at all, now."

We were packing to leave. Blanche knew why I asked this. The scent reminded me too painfully of Kat. My days were hard enough as it was. Memories of Kat were everywhere; in my palaces, in my chambers, in my bed, in my gardens. Kat stole upon me as I tried, tried so hard to get on with my days, with my work. But that scent... when I smelt it, it was enough to bring me crashing to my knees. I lost all courage. I lost all faith. I could not summon the energy to carry on.

Blanche ordered rose petals from Richmond Palace gardens to perfume the trunks with as we packed and made for Windsor.

Smell is such a powerful sense; capable of bringing memory to the mind more powerfully than sight or sound. There is nothing that can bring memory swimming into our heads like scent. I could not bear to smell the scent which had lived on Kat's warm skin. Every time I caught a trace of it about me, I lost her again.

As we came to Windsor, I was taken low with a fever. Kat's death lay upon me like a shroud and I was drained by emptiness. I had had little will to undertake my duties and little strength to resist this illness when it fell upon me. I was taken to my bed with a cold, fever and a pain in my shoulder. I let the doctors fuss about me, giving in, where in all past times I would have objected. I had no spirit to fight them. I did not want to be before the court in any case. I did not want to have to work and face each day as though nothing had happened.

Blanche read to me each night; poetry we had shared when Kat was alive. Her voice took me into sleep where nothing else would. When I recovered from my fever, I went riding with Blanche and Robin. Often we would not say a word to each other for the whole day as we rode out through the countryside. They understood I wished to lose myself in the silence and peace of my England. But if they understood my need for peace, others did not. An anonymous petition, calling upon me to marry, circulated at court and was brought to me by Cecil. *"We must despair of your marriage,"* it said, *"as we may despair of your issue."*

I stared at the parchment as Cecil wordlessly handed it to me. Words jumped out from the creamy parchment. Accusations and recriminations assaulted me. How could they bring this to me *now*? Could I not be given a moment, just a moment, to try to come to terms with my grief? I was enraged by the petition. Anger was the first new emotion I had experienced since Kat died. Whilst any feeling other than aching blankness or gaping, raw sorrow should have been welcome, anger is not the most helpful of emotions. I threw the parchment into the fire and ran from Cecil. I raged that night, screaming about the uncharitable, unfeeling nature of my subjects. Shouting that they were false, that they cared not, that they loved me not. Blanche brought Robin in to calm me. It did no good.

"Mistress Ashley would not have wanted you to grieve like this," he said.

"Kat is no longer here, Robin, to tell me how she would have me behave," I said stiffly. "And so I will have to behave as *I* have a mind to." I turned away. "Leave me, and do not return until you are sent for, my lord."

I was treating Robin badly, but I could not see it then. Blinded by grief, maimed by sorrow, I hobbled on like a wounded stag seeking a place to hide, a place to die. I turned my anger on Robin and used him ill. Robin became my whipping boy, and even if he understood my reasons, he did not welcome such treatment.

Later that week, I formally rejected the suit of Charles of France. I said that he was too young for me, which he was, but in truth I could not bear the French ambassador speaking to me on the subject any longer.

"A husband can only be of true use to my country if he is old enough to give me sons," I said to de Foix, my tone flat, invested with no emotion. "That would be his chief function, to be of any use to England. His Majesty, the King of France, is too young for me, and I too old for him. It is with regret that I say this, but I believe a match is not to be between us."

My rejection of Charles led Cecil, Sussex and Norfolk to think it was time to throw the Archduke Charles of Austria at me anew. I pretended interest, and asked Robin to do the same. The only reason I wanted Robin to support the match was because Norfolk did, and I wanted those two to mend their relationship. They would never be friends, but if Norfolk could see Robin for one moment not as an enemy, then peace might be easier at court. And I needed peace. I could not bear to hear raised voices, or feel tension about me. I had not the strength to endure it.

Robin obeyed, being wary of my temper which was apt to explode without warning. I hovered between dull flatness and sudden outbursts of rage. I had no control. Seeking to appease me, Robin even went so far as to have a public talk with de Silva, saying he was sure I would never marry him. "The Queen has decided to marry a great prince, or to all events, never to marry with a subject of her own," Robin said, within clear hearing distance of Norfolk. It earned a time of truce between them, but only for a while.

"This feeling will pass with time," Robin said as he sat holding my hand one night.

With time… How many times had I heard that? When I had refused his hand when his wife had died, it seemed that was all anyone could say. What fools they were to believe that Time could counter grief! Time only gave one the chance to get used to heaving grief about; it did not lessen it.

"I will be well, soon," I said, lying, my voice as dull as my heart.

When meeting with Adam Zwetkovich, ambassador of Austria, I told him at one time I was interested in the Archduke, and at another I was unsure. I went through the motions of the old games I played with ambassadors and my men. I did the same as ever I had done, but the enjoyment had gone. I went through the motions of life, and found no joy in it.

"The House of Hapsburg is determined to suspect me of ill-doings," I said to him, speaking of rumours of Robin and me which were abroad. "But they will only find I have ever behaved with due decorum."

"Of course, Majesty, my masters do not listen to idle rumour and gossip," the ambassador assured me, lying through his beard. "And if you cannot marry without seeing a suitor, and my master cannot come here for fear of loss of dignity, would you perhaps send an envoy to my master, to view him for you… to be your *eyes*, if you will?"

"A state of affairs open to much abuse, my lord ambassador, as any who survived my father's reign could inform you," I replied, thinking of the disastrous affair of my father's marriage to Anne of Cleves, and the heads that had rolled when the lady turned out to be far from my father's fantasies. "I can trust no other to be my eyes." I agreed to the

Archduke coming to England, and then talks broke down as everyone disagreed over who would pay for his lodgings whilst he was here. Refusing to pay for his keep bought me time. Negotiations continued.

"I thought *I* was your eyes," Robin said to me later.

"You are." I put my head against his shoulder and felt his arms fold around me. "But if you are my eyes, Robin, I believe Kat was my heart. For as she is gone, so all love within me has drained away."

"Including your love for me?" His arms stiffened.

I pulled away and stared at him with eyes full of disdain. "Even now... You think only and ever of yourself," I said. Cold anger poisoned my blood. "Never once do you think of others. Even when that other is me... the one you swore to love more than you loved your own soul."

I left his embrace and I left the room. Even now, when all I needed was a friend to comfort me, Robin could not set aside the one thought which was always with him. This was no time for games and tricks. I needed my friend. When he returned to attend on me, I was cold and abrasive. I took my anger at Kat's death out on him. I could not help myself.

Margaret Lennox was still under arrest in the Tower for the continued disobedience of her husband and son. I also had her property seized. Since prisoners had to pay for their own incarceration, this meant that Margaret was swiftly running up debts. Even this brought me no pleasure where once I may have skipped with glee to humiliate my cousin as once she had done to me. It caused me more pain than pleasure, in fact, for Margaret started to write to me. Letters arrived thrice daily, all containing the same words and protestations. I read some, I did not read them all. Margaret protested she was innocent and that her son had only done as was his birthright and freedom to do. He could not help who he fell in love with, she argued. He could not help who had fallen in love with him. De Silva took it upon himself to petition for clemency for Margaret, and received a baleful glare from me in response. Being a wise man, de Silva left his requests there for the moment, but in truth, I no longer cared. I acted as though I did. I pretended as though I did, but I cared not. Let my cousin take the fool as a husband! I only wanted to be left alone.

But solitude is a luxury not granted to queens. I had no choice but to carry on, as every day memories of my most beloved friend haunted my steps.

*

There was news from Scotland. Darnley wanted to be crowned King Consort, but this was blocked by ruling members of Mary's Council. He was styled 'King Henry' about her court but it was an empty title. At Cecil's urging, I sent a small sum of money to Mary's brother, Moray, to support him. Mary wrote angrily, telling me to meddle no more in Scottish affairs, and then promptly had Throckmorton arrested. The grounds were that safe conduct had not been allowed for her new husband to visit his mother, and I was enraged. Not only was the arrest of Throckmorton, my ambassador, an insult, but I was within my legal rights to offer or refuse conduct through my kingdom! I grew furious at Mary although I doubt my rage would have been so strong had I not been affected by Kat's loss. My previous affection and hope in my royal cousin drained away. Everyone was failing me. Mary had disappointed me, Kat had dared to leave me, Robin was small comfort and all my Council and people wanted was to talk of marriage. I was alone. My anger was the only thing that gave me energy and so I gave in to it. I let it rage, greeting it, as though it might do me good. It did not. Whenever it left me, I felt only tired, old and lonely.

In previous times I had thought Mary proven wise and courageous, but with her imprudent marriage to Darnley and subsequent actions, a veil had been lifted from my eyes. What a fool this woman was! I began to think then that Cecil and all the others who had railed against Mary from the start were right; she was no proper successor. Cecil and my Privy Council wanted me to announce Katherine Grey as my heir as my cousin of Scots celebrated her wedding, just to teach Mary a lesson, but even in my confused temper of rage and sorrow, I did not want to do anything so rash.

De Silva came to me again. He said that Margaret Lennox was in dire need of items of dress and furniture in the Tower.

"Lady Lennox deceived me," I replied as he finished. "She and her son. And this is not the first time I have had lies from them. Why should I deal fairly with those who will not do so with me?"

"Your Majesty has always shown great clemency," de Silva agreed. "You have always shown a valiant spirit and only the timid are cruel. Your cousin may have betrayed you, but to leave her now without succour would not be in keeping with the greatness of your own spirit."

I admit I felt a touch abashed by de Silva. I agreed to send various items of dress and furniture to Margaret from my own Royal Wardrobe. I did, however, insist that Margaret paid for all that was granted to her. I saw no reason why I should reward her for her son's treachery. Since Margaret was already in financial difficulties, and now had no property to provide her with an income, she was wallowing in debt. As my cousin of Lennox turned fifty, the world must have seemed a rather dull and bleak place to be. She could comfort herself that her son was a king, but she was a prisoner, and I had not quite made up my mind on what was to be done with her.

*

Trouble began to break out in Scotland. Moray was proclaimed a rebel for his outspoken hatred of Mary's marriage. I sent John Thomworth, a man of my Privy Chamber, to reason with Mary about the imprisonment of Throckmorton, but was sent nothing encouraging in response. *"Her Majesty lectured me as though I were her pupil!"* Thomworth wrote. *"She said that a Queen had every right to marry without rendering account to other princes. It had not been her practice, she went on, to enquire what kind of order her good sister observed within her realm, nor did she believe it was the usual custom of princes to interfere so in the internal affairs of neighbouring states. Princes were subject to God alone, she said, which was a sentiment she felt sure Your Majesty would agree with. She ended her speech to me by saying that her heart was her own, and she alone would be master of it."*

I could do nothing. What was I to do? Invade Scotland? There were some at court who wanted me to do just that. They wanted me to raise an army, to cut off the threat Mary and Darnley posed before it had a chance to grow. I admit, in my anger, there were times I thought most warmly about such a notion. But thankfully, I still had enough intelligence left to curtail the idea.

Mary had the upper hand, there was no denying that. She was younger than me, more beautiful than me, a queen like me... And now she was married and I was not. People gazed on me with scathing eyes, asking silently why I could not be like Mary and marry. Mary rose in people's estimations just as I fell. Eyes were on my back and whispers dogged my heels. I hated all who would censure me. I raged in the seclusion of my chambers; against Mary, against Robin, against all who would judge me against my cousin. But in truth, I was raging only for one thing. For Kat.

And as all about me thought on marriage, as my defiant cousin struggled to control the behaviour of her new husband, a fresh secret emerged.

Marriage must have been in the air that summer, for another rebellious bride lurking in my midst was about to reveal herself.

Chapter Sixty-Four

Windsor Castle
Summer's End 1565

"I am married, Majesty." The small voice echoed about the Bedchamber.

I stared at the bowed head of Mary Grey, dizzy with anger, frustration and disbelief. "What do you *mean*, you are married?" My voice emerged with more collected calm than was in my soul. I was ready to kill the girl; strangle her with my own hands. Was every Grey a traitor?

"I have been joined in marriage, with witnesses and in a *Protestant* ceremony to Master Thomas Keyes of Lewisham, Majesty," Mary Grey went on, daring, finally to lift her fearful eyes to mine. "We are husband and wife."

"Get out." My tone was clipped and I saw terror stealing over her face. My anger was rising, boiling and bubbling. I could barely hold myself back from striking the girl. "*Get out!*" I shouted, rising from the chair as she dithered. I stalked towards her. "You prepared your evidence well, did you not, you bold chit? You think yourself safe, do you, Mary? Making sure there were witnesses and a Protestant priest, unlike the wedding of your *whore* of a sister?"

Mary rose, stumbling backwards on her awkward legs as I advanced on her. "You are a ward of the Crown!" I screamed. Blanche and Katherine Knollys came running, seeking to hold me back as I towered over the slight girl. "You *cannot* marry without the permission of your Queen! You think yourself safe because of your priest and witnesses, Mary? Think again!" I spun about. "Arrest her!" I bellowed at my guards. "She will be taken into custody. And then get after this Thomas Keyes and take him to the Fleet

Prison! Both of them will remain under guard until I decide what to do with them!"

"You can keep us apart, but he will be in my heart for all my life, Majesty," the girl said boldly, and foolishly. "He is my husband, as I am his wife. Only God can separate us."

I lost any control I had. I tore my arm from Blanche's grip. My hand lashed out and cracked against Mary's cheek, sending her sprawling to the floor. "Do not think to speak to me as though you were my *equal*, girl!" I screamed. "Think you that you will be kept near to your husband so he can lay a seed in your belly as your sister's lover did? It will never be so!" The guards helped Mary up and took her from the room.

"You will never see your lover again!" I screamed at Mary as she was half-carried down the hall. "Never again! My promise to God!"

As I turned back, I saw my ladies staring at me open-mouthed. I was often loose with my hands, slapping or pinching them if they cut my skin or were too rough combing my hair. But this total loss of control was something they had never witnessed before. I glowered at them and, suddenly, they all found urgent tasks to attend to. "Another Grey set to disobey me and turn traitor at the first chance!" I fumed, to no one in particular. "They all seek to defy me!" I looked at Blanche, since she was the only one who dared meet my eyes. I was shaking. "And who is this Keyes? Who is this man who dares deflower a ward of the Crown?"

"He is the Sergeant Porter, Majesty." Blanche tried to calm me, tried to get me to sit down, but I pulled my arms from her grip. "You know him, Majesty... The tall one?"

I tried to think. It was not easy. I did know him, I realised... to say "good morrow" to at least. Keyes was the tallest man at court; one of my guards and a man of no title or consequence. Mary's marriage, then, could do me no harm.

But that did not mean I was about to forgive her after she had gone behind my back! Was the girl possessed of no wits? She had seen what had happened to her sister, and yet taken the same path!

"Bring me Cecil!" I stormed back into the Privy Chamber. "Mary goes into custody here, at Windsor, where I can keep an eye on her and Keyes to the Fleet!" I commanded when he arrived and I told him Mary's news. "And never shall they meet again. Mary knew all too well what would happen if she married without permission. She is even more guilty than Katherine! If I hear that girl is with child, Cecil, after all I have endured with her sister, I *swear* I shall have Keyes's head for it! I want to know who those witnesses she spoke of are, and what they thought they were doing attending such a ceremony. And when you find them, they will go to the Tower. They find out what happens when they flaunt the will of their Queen!"

*

As troubles dogged me, so, too, they came for my cousin Mary. Over the border, my cousin was struggling to contain rebellion. Incensed by the marriage between her and Darnley, many nobles had taken up with Moray. Afraid that her marriage to this English Catholic, no matter his blood, would mean a shift in religion, they meant to make war on their Queen. Mary took to her troubles with grace, however, and no matter how annoyed I was with her, I will admit my cousin conducted herself as a true and politic Queen. Mary attended a Protestant baptism, ate meat in Lent, and went to the Catholic Mass less frequently... all signs to her people that she had no intention of altering their religion. All well and good, but in secret she was gathering an army as well. But ten days after her ill-thought-out-match with Darnley, Mary had seven thousand troops at her command and was ready to face Moray. At this time also, Mary recalled the Earl of Bothwell to Scotland.

Bothwell was a formidable adversary for Moray, and Mary knew it. Bothwell was a man of action and of war. A stocky man, of medium height, he had been long in France. Throckmorton, who had by now been released, described him as rash and vainglorious. He was known for fighting duels, and saw himself as a man of honour, although later events would strain that assertion. Resolutely opposed to England, he was the man Mary needed now to stand against her enemies in Scotland and give her hope for the future in any entanglements with England. He had also long been an enemy to Moray, and was more than happy to undertake a mission to destroy this rebel lord. Bothwell had a certain lawlessness to his character, which my cousin believed would work to her advantage, but many of her nobles were not happy Bothwell was coming back. As Mary prepared for war, all in England watched and waited to see what would come of this.

Cecil was pleased. He believed that his plan to destabilise Scotland was going well. Not even ten days wed and already Mary's lords were rising against her! There were few things that pleased *Spirit* more than seeing disruption in other countries that were a potential threat to England. And seeing as he had no wish to see Mary ever named my heir, Cecil had high hopes that these events would ruin her reputation for good in the eyes of my people.

*

Zwetkowich came to take formal leave of me at Windsor in August, accompanied by my dear de Silva who was to stay on. We had settled on conditions in order for negotiations of marriage to the Archduke to continue, so Zwetkowich was to return and relay them to his master. There was a mix-up with their chambers when they arrived, and the two men were given but one room to share. When I learned this I was appalled. Handing them the keys to my own rooms, I told them this slight was not intended. "You shall occupy my own chamber, my lords," I said.

"Majesty," de Silva said, smiling affectionately. "It was a mistake. There is no insult. We have no wish to deprive you of your own bed!"

"Indeed, Your Majesty is most generous," Zwetkowich went on. "But we will be fine as we are. I will be sure to tell all who ask, though, that once the Queen of England offered me her bed when I was without one."

"Be sure to tell them that *I* was not offered along with the bed, ambassador," I said dryly, making de Silva chortle. "For I know well enough the way naughty minds will turn such a story against me."

The next morning Robin took Zwetkowich and de Silva for a stroll through the gardens. Making their way back along the riverside, they passed under the building where my Privy Gardens lay. Robin's fool was gambolling and making them laugh by doing impressions. He did a particularly fine Norfolk... As they approached, I heard laughing and shouting, and came to my window, wondering what was going on. It was early and I was not fully dressed. All three men happened to looked up at the exact moment I appeared at the window in my nightshift. Robin's fool pointed upwards. "A merry sight to see the Queen, my lords, and to see *so* much of her!" he cried out. Mortified, my cheeks on fire, I stepped back, leaving the men gaping to see me so immodestly presented. Fully-dressed, and with all my cosmetics applied, I joined them perhaps an hour later.

"Majesty," Robin said, a grin twitching about his lips.

"All three of you can stop your grinning," I snapped ruefully, although I could not help but feel a little amused. The three men were desperately attempting to contain their mirth and the sight of their struggling faces made me smile. It was the first time since Kat died that I truly felt like laughing. I scowled, and yet could not stop my lips from cresting upwards. I gave in and laughed. It was so freeing to know joy again. The three lords, seeing my amusement, surrendered. They released their repressed mirth, allowing the happy sound of merriment to ripple through the gardens.

"You are as beautiful when you rise as you are when you meet the court, Majesty," de Silva assured me, reaching out to take my hand and kiss it. "I will thank the Lord in Heaven for this stolen glimpse of you, fresh-faced and natural as the dawn. It was like being a nymph in Diane's forest, seeing the goddess rise."

Zwetkowich looked rather awkward, despite his mirth. "Please tell me that *you* will say nothing to another soul, my lord," I teased. "I cannot trust these two lords to close their mouths."

Zwetkowich smiled. "My good friend Guzman tells the truth, Majesty," he said, kissing my hand. "Seeing you at that window was something I shall never forget. One might call it a parting gift. And it will be prized in my memory for the rest of my life."

We walked on through the gardens, with Robin trying to stop his fool taunting me. I thought lightly that I was glad I had not been *entirely* natural when they saw me. My face had been powdered, and I had been wearing a wig. Had they seen me with my thin hair, and without powder on, I believe they would have thought the sight not so good a gift. It was not that I was old, being thirty-two, but I was more than aware that these days I needed artifice to make up for the dark circles under my eyes, the thinness of my once-glorious hair, and the greyness upon my once fresh and bright skin. Queens are judged on their appearances, I had no need for rumour to spread, calling me old or infirm.

The slide from the first flush of youth is something that comes as a shock to many women. I was still striking, I was still captivating, as much for my mind as for my appearance... but I had not that beauty which the young possess so fleetingly, and never think to appreciate when it is theirs.

Chapter Sixty-Five

Windsor Castle
Summer's End 1565

"If she sends me any more letters, Lettice," I said. "Put them to one side. I cannot read them all." Lettice did as I instructed and took the piles of parchment away; *more* letters from Margaret Lennox protesting her imprisonment. I was not about to answer each one of them, I had better things to do with my time.

I glanced up at Lettice. Recently arrived back at court and welcomed back into my household, Lettice was a mother now and soon to be one again. It had been long since I saw her and her husband, Walter Devereux. Becoming a mother had done something to my younger cousin... it had *transformed* her. When she was a girl, I had thought her beautiful, but now, with the rounded hips and figure of a mother, she was a star fallen to earth. In truth, there had never been many who could have competed with her before, but now, she was most assuredly the premier beauty of my court. And it was not only young gallants who stared. Robin could barely steal his eyes away.

I often wondered if Robin had a passion for women with red hair. His wife, Amy, who he had married as a love-match, had been a red-head. I was, and so was Lettice. And it was clear from the first instant her velvet slipper stepped into court again, that Robin was attracted to Lettice. Unlike all other times when I had only suspected he had a fancy for another woman, this time he did not attempt to hide it. He danced attendance on her at court entertainments and when he came to my chambers, he flowed to her as though he were a river and she the ocean. Perhaps he was seeking to make me jealous, in another effort to get me to wed him. I was certainly made jealous, but it did not make me want to marry him.

At first, I could not quite believe what he was doing. I had so lately lost Kat. Could he not see how fragile I was? *And why*? I asked my traitorous heart as it pined for him. *Why do you continue to love one who thrusts you aside with such ease? Why do you continue to show him favour?* I did not consider how ill I had treated him of late. I saw only *his* ill-behaviour and did not recognise my own. Perhaps I drove him to her for I was not good company. I was mean, vindictive and rough. Was it any wonder he sought the company of a beautiful young woman who was clearly excited by his attentions? Was it any wonder he raced to her, as I drove him from me? But such thoughts did not come to me then. I was hurt, wounded, and furious.

I tried to make myself believe I cared not for him. My retaliation lashed out, hard and brutal. If Robin was setting his love for me aside, I would do the same. I would show him how easily he could be replaced. I started to show affection to other nobles and was often seen in close conversation with Norfolk and Sussex. I called Thomas Heneage to me to walk with me in the gardens when I knew Robin would be there, slathering like a dog over Lettice. Whenever Robin looked up, I was with another man, or with a whole volley of them. They pranced about me, they wrote poetry to me, and vied for my attention. My ruptured heart lapped up their praises as I sought signs that Robin was being made as jealous as he made me. And how swiftly it worked... Robin's face would turn red and purple, mottled with anger when he saw me laughing and joking with Heneage and others; touching their arms and moving stray hair from their eyes. Those were dark days. As I strode out bold as a cock surrounded by my flock of adoring hens, Robin doubled his efforts to woo Lettice. Even though she was married and carrying a child, rumours flew that the two were secret lovers. When I heard this, I wanted to weep. The thought of Robin being so close to another... sharing her bed...

stroking her skin; offering her the comfort of his company that he did not think to grant to me... It was torture. I considered sending Lettice from court, but that would only have shown Robin that he was getting to me. I wanted him to think I cared not. I wanted him to think I had forgotten him, as he seemed to have forgotten me.

Heneage was overjoyed to have become my new, sudden favourite. He had a place in my Privy Chambers now, and I did enjoy his company. He soothed me and I became fond of him. I have no doubt Heneage knew I was using him to retaliate against Robin, but any ladder to favour is welcome to those who wish to climb. Robin started to become obviously worried by my behaviour. Whilst he did not give up flirting with Lettice, he did start to bad-mouth Heneage about court, and was apparently troubled that I might decide to marry Heneage, rather than him. The fact Heneage was *married* meant little to Robin. My efforts had worked, and perhaps a little too well. Robin confronted Heneage in the gardens one day. Ill words turned to shouting, and a fight broke out. My guards had to be called to pull Robin off Heneage. This had gone too far.

"You have no call to start fights with servants of my own Privy Chamber, my lord!" I shouted at Robin. I had already seen Heneage, and let him off with a warning. I had no doubt that Robin's temper, hot and foul, so like my own, was the cause of the fight.

"You have no right to *throw* yourself at other men when you have sworn your heart to me!" he shouted back, his nostrils flaring and his face an unhealthy shade of scarlet-purple.

"Have *you* not found a new love, my lord Earl?" I bristled with jealousy and indignation. "You dance and simper about my young cousin often enough!"

"As you saunter off with other men, to make me jealous!" he screamed. As my eyes opened wide and dangerous, Robin took a step back.

His tone became as ice. "I wish to leave court, Majesty, for I feel I am not wanted or needed here." He turned from me and made for the Presence Chamber, where most of the court were gathered, eagerly listening to our fight behind the closed door to my Privy Chamber.

"You will do no such thing!" I strode after him, caring not that he had opened the door and the whole court could hear me. "You will stay here as you are commanded to, my lord, and do your duty to your Queen!"

"Get out of my way!" Robin shouted at the guard on the door to the Presence Chamber.

The guard turned angrily to me. "Is my Lord of Leicester King, or is it Her Majesty the Queen?" he asked. My temper was ready to blow. I glared at Robin. The whole court was watching. There was silence in the Presence Chamber as everyone waited to see what would happen next.

"God's Death, my lord!" I screamed. "I have long wished you well as my friend, but my favour is not so locked up for you that others shall not partake of it! And if you think to rule here, I will take a course to see you fall."

I drew myself up. "I will have but one mistress here, and no master!"

Robin stared at me, and then looked back at the gathered masses staring at us. Never had I rebuked him so damningly in public before. He hardly knew what to say. His face went pale with anger and fear.

"Remove yourself from my chambers, my lord," I spat. "And think yourself lucky I do not remove you of your posts! Too many times have you overstepped your mark. Remember, those I have raised up can be cast down. You are not the King, my lord Earl. I am."

"Something you never fail to thrust down my throat, *Your Majesty*," he hissed. Robin strode past all those gathered outside as I stood watching him go.

"Well?" I shouted into the chamber. "Get to your business, all of you! Or what do I pay you wages for at all? Any here who have no task to better occupy their time should remove themselves from court, for you are of no use to me!"

The Presence Chamber emptied with remarkable speed.

Robin shut himself in his chambers for three days and refused to come out. I did not send for him. I was too furious. My ladies dodged me, shrinking from my hands which were free and easy with smacks and slaps. Heneage retired from court at Cecil's urging. I felt rather sorry for him. He had become stuck in the middle of this spat, and although he wished for favour and advancement, he hardly wanted to make enemies at the same time. He and Robin had been good friends once. They were no longer.

After three days, I had a rather surprising visit from Cecil accompanied by Sussex. "Your Majesty must meet with the Earl of Leicester and make amends," Cecil said, causing me to stare at him as though he had gone mad.

"What is it to you, Cecil, if Robin has lost my favour?" I asked in a sour tone. "And you, Sussex, what are you doing here? Has not the Earl ever been your enemy?"

"No man who is a friend to my Queen is my enemy in truth, Majesty," Sussex said. "We disagree on many issues, but that does not mean I do not value the Earl."

"Then you should buy him from me, Sussex," I declared. "I will sell him cheap, for I no longer see worth in such an ill-mannered hound."

"Your Majesty is miserable without Lord Dudley," Cecil said. "All who are close to you and love you know it. Make amends, Majesty. The Earl suffers just as you do."

"He has said this?" How much did I want to believe that Robin sorrowed! How much did I want to believe Robin felt the gulf between us and wanted it mended.

"He has been in a black and dark place ever since your quarrel, Majesty," Cecil told me. "He believes he has lost your friendship and your affection forever."

I swallowed a lump in my throat. "There is nothing Robin Dudley could do to make me care for him less," I said softly. "It seems there is no action he could take, or trouble he could cause, that would make me turn my face from him for good."

"May I tell him that, Majesty, and bring him to you?" Cecil's good face was grave and serious. "You have lost much and all of us know the pain you feel. These games the Earl has played, they have wounded you at a time when you were most able to be wounded. He understands his mistake now, and will not do it again."

"Bring him to me." My anger drained from me. I thought on how I had screamed at Robin, about all I had said to him. I felt awful. I had shamed him before the court, laid him open to attack from his enemies... Robin had hurt me too, there was no denying that, but I should have controlled myself. Anger is a bright flash of senselessness, and all too often the ones we unleash it upon are not the ones we are truly angry at. I was angry at Kat for leaving me. Even though I knew she had no choice, I could not set my resentment aside. I needed her, and she was not here. That was why I was so quick and easily spilt into fury. I was angry at Kat... angry at Death. As I understood this, I understood how badly I had treated my friend.

When Robin arrived, looking guarded and bashful, something shattered within me. I put out my hands and started to weep like a lost child. He ran to me and took me in his arms. When I looked up I saw that he, too, was crying.

"Do not weep, my love," I whispered to him.

"I feared I had lost your love," he said into my neck. "That you loved another."

"And I thought the same of you," I admitted. "I am not strong enough for these games, Robin. I am so alone, and when you are not with me, I have nothing."

"I should not have been so selfish, Elizabeth," he whispered. "I should have not fallen to these petty games. From now on, I am your man. In whatever way you need me. I am yours."

"I need you." I sobbed against his chest. "I always need you, Robin."

Later that day, as Robin and I sat playing cards, I took up a book of his from the table, and wrote in it. Handing it to him, I smiled gently. "A reminder for you and for me, Robin," I said gently. Inside, it read,

"No crooked leg, no bleared eye,
No part deformed out of kind,
Nor yet so ugly half can be
As is the inward and suspicious mind."

Your loving mistress, Elizabeth R

Chapter Sixty-Six

Windsor Castle
Autumn 1565

I rode out into Windsor's park often as summer turned to autumn.

In the darkness before dawn, through the hills and dales of England I rode, seeking to lose my thoughts, lose my sorrow, lose my anger. With Robin and Blanche at my side, I galloped hard over fields sodden with rain, up and over hills, through slim, overgrown paths through dripping dark forests. We rode in silence. I did not need to talk. I needed to lose myself. In riding, I could leave all the horrors I had faced behind, and know only the present, even if only for a brief time.

Sometimes, I would stop my horse, slide from my saddle and stand upon a hillside, gazing out over England. I would stretch my arms out to the dark skies above, and tilt my head back, as rain fell on my face. Standing there, with the wind rippling through my hair, I breathed in deep and faced the coming storms. When I stood there, alone under the grey skies of England, I felt as though there was something left within me, after all. As though there was some courage, some light, some scrap of joy which remained; as though I were not made only of rage and sorrow.

Under England's skies, my feet planted on her soil, my hands lifted in benediction, something started to rise inside me; a strand of the old Elizabeth which still lived within my shattered soul. When I felt that thread of hope flutter within me, it was as though I had not lost the girl I had once been; that girl who had endured so much, and yet had never lost sense of herself. As though my soul was not dead and buried with Kat.

Sometimes, I spoke to God as I stood there. I tried not to berate Him for taking Kat into His Kingdom. I asked Him to watch over her. I tried to remember that all men are mortal; that there is a better place waiting for us when we die. I tried to remember these things... Some days I had more success than others.

We would return to the palace and I went about the business of ruling a nation. But I was not at peace within the palace walls. It was within England that I was whole. My daily rides gave me the strength to continue. The constant exercise allowed me to sleep at night. I dropped into dreamless slumber, waking feeling bleary-eyed and restless. I found peace with England. She was my comfort. She was the place where I believed I could find my soul again.

*

Heneage returned to court, and that autumn, my cousin, Thomas Butler, the Earl of Ormonde, Lord Treasurer of Ireland visited court. Both were handsome and keen to impress, and I walked out with Heneage and 'Black Tom' as my Butler cousin was known. Despite this favour shown to others, Robin did not seek to flirt with Lettice as he had done so openly before and I did not flirt with my men. Robin and I were treating each other gently. He understood he had hurt me, and I knew what I had done to him. Robin even intervened when the Archbishop of York criticised me for my friendship with Black Tom, telling the man that it was the Queen's business alone whom she spent time with, and he was to leave me well alone.

At times, I started to feel like myself again. Having Robin back helped. Losing Kat had almost broken me and having him abandon me at the same time had almost made me lose all sense of myself. My appetite improved, and I started to look healthier, although I still found no pleasure in eating. Blanche nodded with approval as I resumed dancing my six galliards of a morning. My laugh was heard about court at times. My ladies sighed with relief to find my temper restored. I was not whole, not yet. I was fragile still. I became more talented at hiding the sorrow within me, but there were moments when I missed Kat so much it was difficult to breathe. Having Robin with me, protecting me, was sweet to my soul and other friends tried to offer me strength as well. My rides through England brought me the solace I so desperately needed and armed me to face the court, as a queen must. I carried a part of England inside me; a breath of her winds, a drop of her rain, a slither of her sunlight. I drew upon her immortal strength to bolster my mortal weakness. Others noted the restoration of my spirits, too, for one afternoon as I strolled with de Silva through the golden-brown avenues of the gardens, my friend decided to play a trick on me.

"Do you think the Archduke will visit soon, my lord?" I asked de Silva. There was a band of his servants behind us. I always tried to make it appear I was interested in the Archduke when others were around us.

"Perhaps sooner than you think, Majesty." I looked sharply at de Silva. He was wearing an impish expression.

"What do you mean, my lord?"

"Have you not noted a *new* face amongst my servants, Majesty?" He spoke teasingly, but I was unsure if he was actually serious. Did he mean the Archduke was in England, and was concealed somewhere in the milling crowd at my back?

I looked behind me, startled and rather worried that the Archduke was actually here! I glanced back and forth between de Silva and his servants, my heart thumping in panic. His twinkling eyes did not reveal his secrets. The crowd behind us stopped, baffled by my darting eyes and horrified expression. Eventually, de Silva burst into gales of laughter. "Fear not, Majesty!" he crowed, delighted to have duped me. "You are safe! My master is safe and sound in his own lands, I promise you!"

His laugh was infectious, and I started to chuckle. Then I started to laugh. Then I could not speak for I was so weak in the chest and knees. Tears rolled down my cheeks. "You are a bad man!" I slapped de Silva with my lace fan. "You had me believing that my suitor was here! At my very elbow! You are a rascal, de Silva!"

De Silva leaned against a marble urn, gasping for breath. "Majesty... you should have seen your face!"

"You know, de Silva, it would not be such a bad way to meet the Archduke after all," I mentioned when we had recovered ourselves and continued walking. "To meet in secret, without knowing each other... then it could be said whether a true attraction was felt."

"I will mention the idea to my master, Majesty, but I fear he would not engage in such secrecy."

"A great shame for him," I said, thinking of the day I had dressed as a servant. "There is something freeing in the notion of no one knowing who you are."

"Only to those who are *known*," de Silva replied. "To those who are of no importance, becoming known is their greatest desire."

"We all want most what we do not have," I agreed. "But you must promise not to play such a trick on me again, my friend... You made my heart stop!"

"Perhaps Your Majesty will concede it was only payment in return for the times you have played tricks yourself," he said cheekily.

"You know all my secrets, ambassador."

"Unlike many others in my position, Majesty," de Silva assured me with genuine warmth. "Your secrets are safe with me."

"Unlike all others in your position, my friend," I said. "I believe you."

Chapter Sixty-Seven

Windsor Castle
Autumn 1565

With the falling leaves of the autumn, storms carried quick and swift over England. Rain fell, hail arrived. The winds keened, wailing about the walls of Windsor, shrieking to waken slumberous minds. As we faced storms in England, my cousin was riding a tempest of her own in Scotland. Moray and the other rebels were still at large, but Mary was ready to face all that came with courage and vivacity.

Whilst waiting for Bothwell to reach her, Mary rode out to meet the threat of Moray. Darnley at her side, and a pistol on her hip, my cousin embarked on what was to become known as the *'Chase-about Raids'* for Mary hunted her brother through Scotland. Mary cut a gallant figure in her determination and guile in those days. She was a force to be reckoned with. Clashes occurred outside of Edinburgh and beyond and my cousin was ever at the heels of the rebels, gnawing at their ankles. When Bothwell arrived he rode out to join her. Restoring him to her Privy Council, Mary put her trust and faith in this adventurer. She relied heavily on Bothwell, much to the disgust of her new husband, for Darnley believed *he* should be the one to lead the raids and take Mary's forces into battle. His complete lack of experience did not worry him, but that is ever the way with people who know nothing; they believe they know everything. For the sake of peace, Mary made Darnley's father one of her commanders and talked with her new husband often on tactics and plans. By the 8th of October, Mary's army had swelled to twelve thousand men, and they marched out of Edinburgh. Mary petitioned for English forces to come and support hers. I dallied with the idea, but none on my Privy Council would support it. Believing our intervention would only lead to us being sucked into Scottish affairs, and still bristling with resentment about Mary's marriage, the request was denied. But it stopped her not. She went out to meet Moray, with the might of Scotland at her back.

Then, in one of those great anti-climaxes of history, the battle did not happen. Hearing of Mary's superior force, Moray and his allies fled and headed across the border, to Newcastle-upon-Tyne. With Moray and his followers on the run, Mary emerged victorious, and without spilling a drop of blood. She had never been as powerful, or as popular as she was then. Even the presence of her detestable husband could not prevent her people from turning to her with love and adoration.

I was proud of her and sent a message asking that we set aside our old quarrels. Although I did not mention her husband, I suggested we talk anew of friendship and peace. But Mary, in her triumph, was careless. She sent a strongly worded letter back, saying that whilst she would be pleased to be my friend, she would suffer no further "interference" from foreign monarchs. Mary was riding high and thought she had no further need of my support or friendship. I read her letter with great annoyance, and found myself fuming on her words for days. "So she has a husband now and needs no more a cousin and *good sister*!" I exclaimed to Blanche as she and Katherine Knollys dressed me. "My cousin will regret that she did not choose to open talks anew with me, of that you may be assured!"

But if she had prevailed over the rebels in her country, Mary had problems of a more domestic nature rising swiftly take their place. Marital bliss for my Mary fell along with the last leaves of the trees. As expected, her marriage was a disaster. The rift over command of her armies intensified and the couple were seen sparring in public. Randolph reported that Darnley was perpetually drunk and often abusive to his wife, even in front of her court. There were stories of explosive rows behind bedchamber doors. Tales spread of

Darnley's arrogance, his constant demands to be made King, and his blatant disrespect for Mary's lords. He was possessive and jealous, easily roused to rage, and when drunk, he was a demon. Randolph told us that Mary was low in spirits, despite her recent triumph. She floated about her court, a wraith of her former self. And every night, Darnley came to her bedchamber, demanding his rights as a husband.

Even though she was a queen, even though she was powerful, even though she despised him, Mary had sworn oaths in marriage and Darnley forced his rights upon her. There were times we heard of when her *Maries* stepped in, or when Bothwell was called to remove the drunken, swearing, staggering oaf from Mary's chambers by force. I am sure there were many more occasions when she was forced to suffer his desires. Having limited power over her as Queen, he sought to impress his power over her as a husband. Darnley was becoming universally despised. No one in Scotland wanted him named King and princes of other nations tried to distance themselves from any association with him. Darnley was gaining enemies fast. I pitied Mary, despite my irritation at her. Cecil felt quite differently. He was disgustingly merry.

"Now she has only to make him King, and Scotland will be in a fine mess," he gloated, making my lip curl.

"If she was going to make him King, Cecil, she would have done so already. My cousin is no dullard, Cecil, unlike that parasite she is married to. She will not give him more power. All she needs from him now is his seed. Mary will keep him as powerless as possible, and she will win through, I am sure of it."

"I believed you to be altered in your good opinion of Mary of Scots," he said, looking surprised. "Have you changed your mind?"

"I judge her to be more shrewd and quick than you do, Cecil, that is all. Mary has *Tudor* blood in her veins. She will not lie down and allow Darnley to rule her country. The only thing she will lie down for now is for his seed, and as soon as she has what she requires, she needs him no longer."

I had no idea how prophetic my words would later seem.

*

We were distracted from events in Scotland by the arrival of a most remarkable woman. Princess Cecilia of Sweden, sister of King Erik, came to further her brother's suit for my hand. I, however, wondered if her true reason for visiting England *was* to get me to marry her brother. Cecilia thirsted for adventure, and this voyage, made when she was heavily pregnant, was certainly an exciting exploit.

"I have heard so much about you, Your Majesty," she said as we were introduced. "From both my beloved brothers. I just *had* to see you for myself."

Cecilia giggled prettily, tossing her frizzed fair hair. She was an attractive woman. She wore her hair in an odd style; fluffed up with combs and hot irons, it was laid over her head in a tall, swaying pile. But she wore it with such grace that only a day passed before maids at court arrived with their hair done in "Sweden style". Some attempts to ape Cecilia were more successful than others. It was not an easy effect to achieve; many women arrived at court looking like they wished to emulate haystacks. But fashion keeps no company with sense. Soon everyone was wearing their hair "Sweden style". I had a few wigs made in that style myself.

Cecilia was not merely pretty, but merry too. Her gowns were glorious, plumped with rich cloth and smothered with glittering jewels, but it was her adventurous spirit I enjoyed the most. She reminded me of her brother. "How is your brother, Duke Johan, Your Highness?" I asked as we walked through the gardens together on the first day of her visit. "He was a great favourite of mine. You must tell him to write more often, for I miss his companionship."

"He speaks most highly of you, Your Majesty," she told me, stopping to run her hands over a perfumed bush of rosemary. She rubbed the leaves into her hands and inhaled the fragrance. "He always says there is no woman to compare to you, both for your spirit and wit. I will admonish him sharply for not writing to you, Majesty, but you know how men are..."

I smiled, thinking that Cecilia *would* know how men were, indeed. She had caused many scandals at her brother's court. At the wedding of her older sister, Catherine, for example, a man had been spotted scaling the palace walls and entering Cecilia's rooms. When her brother's guards investigated, the brother of the bridegroom was found in Cecilia's chambers, half-naked and grasping at a bed sheet to cover his modesty. The man was thrown in gaol, and rumour had it her brother had taken his manhood for seeking to make love to Cecilia, but even this did not stop her. There had been rumours of other lovers until she was married to Christopher II, Margrave of Baden-Rodemachern. She and her husband had journeyed for more than a year, passing through many countries and apparently happily adventuring along the way. When she arrived, Cecilia was in the last stages of pregnancy. Her first babe would be born on English soil.

I envied her freedom and wildness of spirit. Her husband clearly adored her, and would do anything to please her. I gave her Bedford House in London for her stay and furnished it for her. Four days after her arrival, she went into labour and produced a baby boy, who she named Edward, after my brother, to please me. We held his christening at Westminster Abbey, and the whole court turned out to see this utterly remarkable woman. Cecilia became a regular visitor at court, spent her money with undisciplined abandon, and made many friends. Amongst her ladies was a rare beauty named Mistress Helena Snakenborg. Born to an ancient, and noble yet impoverished family, Helena was about sixteen when she came to England. It quickly became apparent that whilst Cecilia was exciting, Helena was the true new star of the court.

Helena was tall, willowy, with a fair bosom and a complexion of pink rose petals and white silk. Her hair was as red as mine and curled naturally. Helena's eyes were large, brown and warm and if you looked closely, you could see flecks of gold within them. And many did seek to get close. She gained a horde of admirers who hung on her every word, and yet, unlike many other beautiful women of my acquaintance, Helena had made up her mind to be useful and capable, rather than solely relying on her looks to make her way in life.

The poorly-concealed, simmering rage of my cousin Lettice only added to my enjoyment of Helena. Lettice had been the greatest beauty of my court, and now there was a girl of at least equal loveliness, and with a gentle, beguiling temper, who had come to take her place. And since Helena was new to court, and people tend to value the new over the old, Lettice rapidly found her admirers draining away, heading for Helena. Since I had not forgiven Lettice for flirting with Robin, I found ways to make Helena prominent in entertainments and dances. It was ever so satisfying to see Lettice boiling away in her own skin. She was bad at hiding her jealousy.

William Parr suddenly became a *most* regular attendant at court. Although Helena had many admirers, my good uncle was clearly besotted with the girl. He had thirty-five years to her sixteen, but think not that he was the one with the power in this attraction, oh no! He would have done anything for her. Luckily for him, Helena was not one to use the affections of men for ill-purpose.

"That is good to see, do you not think, Blanche?" I asked as we watched Parr and Helena walking down another path in the gardens, deep in conversation.

"It is pleasing to see his broken heart mending under the affection of a good woman," Blanche said, narrowing her eyes, which were growing weak with age. "Bess would have approved of this lady, Majesty. She would not have wanted William to be as sorrowful and lost as he has been since her death."

"I think you speak the truth, Blanche," I agreed. "Bess was always concerned for the happiness of my uncle. She would be pleased to know he has found love again." I sighed, thinking of Bess. Thinking of Parry, Jane Seymour, St Loe and Kat, of course. For a moment, I struggled with sorrow, but watching Helena and Parr made me feel better. Kat had said the only way to thwart Death was to live fully, and when is a person more alive than when they dare to love? Love is the greatest enemy of Death. We forget Death exists, when we give ourselves up to love.

Blanche linked her arm with mine, and we walked along the paths in silence. It was often this way with my new Chief Lady of the Bedchamber. Blanche had never attempted to take Kat's place. She was simply herself. She offered herself to me, heart and soul, and was a gentle presence in my often turbulent life. I leaned on Blanche. She was my crutch.

""Will they marry, do you think?" I asked Blanche after some time.

"I hear Helena's family has no wealth for a dowry," she told me. "Although her father is a baron, he has no more coin than a pauper."

"My uncle is rich enough for the both of them," I said. "And perhaps he cares not for her money, if he is enough in love with her."

"That is the best kind of marriage," Blanche nodded. "One that is made on a foundation of love, rather than commerce and trade, as so many are."

"Is that why you have never married, Blanche?" I asked. "You have been in my service since you rocked my cradle. Did you never think to wed?"

Blanche smiled softly. "Perhaps my heart was too like that of my mistress," she murmured. "I never wanted a husband. I enjoy my position with you, Majesty, and the liberty it gives me. Although I have seen many happy marriages, I believe marriage can be a shackle and I never wished for such a chain. I am like you… I want to be free. That liberty is, to me, more important than finding a man to share my life with. We each of us decide on what is most important in life. I may have missed out on some comforts my married friends have, but then I reason *they* have missed out on much I enjoy, too. No one can have everything they want. I am happy with the path I have taken."

She looked up at the skies. "My grandmother had a saying about happiness," she said. "In order to find happiness one must find *y man lle rydw i mewn heddwch a mi fy hun.*"

"The place where I find peace?" I asked. Blanche had taught me some Welsh, but it was not a language in which I was fluent.

"Almost," she said. "It means, 'The place where I am at peace with myself'." She nodded to the skies. "That is what I found, my lady, with you."

Chapter Sixty-Eight

Whitehall Palace
Winter 1565

As the chill of winter settled over England, we heard of the death of Pope Pius IV. Pius had been a rather genial Pope, who had done much to attempt reconciliation between England and Rome. I was troubled to hear of his death. The missives from Rome during his rule had been conciliatory and piled with overtures of friendship. He had made no effort to start war on England for its Protestantism. His replacement, Pius V, was not made of the same mettle.

A former Dominican friar, who had the motto, *Utinam dirigantur viae meae ad custodiendas justificationes tuas, O that my ways may be directed to keep thy justifications,* Brother Woodenshoe, as he was known before his elevation, spelled trouble for England. As a Cardinal he had prosecuted bishops for heresy. As a Pope he was likely to become a danger to me.

"Just keep him at bay, Cecil, as we did with the last Bishop of Rome," I said upon reading the dispatches.

"This one may be harder to divert than the last, Majesty. He is firm against heresy of any kind, and obviously includes the Protestant faith in his deliberations. He has already made moves to finish the tradition of nepotism in the Vatican; a radical move and one that shows his militant nature." Cecil sighed. "Pius was ineffectual and moderate," he mourned. "I fear his replacement will move against England. He is sympathetic to Phillip of Spain. That can bring no good for us."

"That I understand, *Spirit,* so let us find many new and various methods to confound the Pope."

"There is another matter, Majesty, although I hesitate to raise it with you."

"Then it must be about a cousin, Cecil, for you would not otherwise hesitate."

He inclined his head. "Mary Grey, Majesty. She has been writing to me to beg that I petition you for forgiveness. She says she would rather die than incur your displeasure again, and promises never to wound you again." He sniffed. Cecil did not believe Mary Grey was sorry for what she had done. Neither did I. "She seems quite confused that you have not already forgiven her," he finished.

"She can go on wondering, *Spirit*," I said grimly. "And she will not be forgiven. Mary Grey has a mind inside her skull, even if she chooses not to make use of it. She saw what happened to her sister when she defied me, and yet chose to do the exact same thing. She will stay where she is; under house arrest in the prison room at Chequers and Keyes can stay in the Fleet."

I was in no mood to be generous to traitors. I had quite enough to think upon with the new, energetic Bishop of Rome stomping about the Vatican.

We worried about the new Pope, but we had a good event to distract us when Anne Russell, one of my maids of honour, married Ambrose Dudley. The couple were wed in the chapel at Whitehall and I promoted Anne to the position of Gentlewoman of the Privy Chamber, in honour of her new rank as Countess of Warwick. Ambrose was twenty years older than his sixteen-year-old bride, but that mattered not to them. He walked happily through the wedding party, his cane clipping on the ground, providing an accompaniment to the music that played as we danced through the night. Anne was delighted with her new husband and I was pleased to see her so happy.

As we came to the end of these celebrations, I had word from my cousin Lettice. She had been delivered in November of a fine and healthy boy. What pleased me less was the name she had chosen for her son. Skirting over the name Walter, which would have honoured her husband, the boy was instead named *Robert*. This led to many supposing that this child was not, in fact, the son of her legally wedded husband at all, but that of Robin! I knew this was false, since Lettice had already been pregnant when she came to court, but the rumours persisted. I wondered what her husband thought of it, since he was often far away from his wife, sorting out strife in Ireland. There was no talk of rift between the couple, however, and they both seemed delighted with their son.

Love was in the air at the English Court, but hate had taken love's place in Scotland.

"Randolph writes that he believes the Queen to be depressed in spirit," I said to Cecil one afternoon as hail showers pelted the window panes. "She is often sick he says, and much of it with worry."

"Mary of Scots chose her bed," Cecil replied absently.

"And now must lie with Darnley in it?" I shuddered. "To think of any woman having to lie with that pompous, pox-ridden cumberwold is hideous to me, Cecil. And you and all my lords would have had me jump into matrimony when she did. Do you not see now that no husband is better than a bad one?"

"Your Majesty would not have to choose one like Darnley," Cecil reminded me. "Although there is much evidence to the contrary, there *are* good men, Majesty, many of them. Not all of us are given to lying with whores, humiliating our wives, or pissing out what little sense God gave us along with our wine."

"Indeed, Cecil," I agreed. "I pity my cousin. She has saddled herself with a poor partner."

"Perhaps he will die young, Majesty, and relieve her of this burden."

"And send England into endless fretting over her next choice of husband? Come, *Spirit*, you do not wish for that. At least with Darnley, we know where we stand. Wish not for uncertainty."

When my cousin pardoned Arran, a conspirer in the troubles with Moray, tensions between her and her new family increased. Arran, who also held the French Dukedom of Chatelherault, and his family were old foes of the Lennoxes. His pardon was taken as an insult, seeing as his family had been involved in the assassination of Lennox's father. As Christmas drew near, the royal couple had a series of blazing, public rows. This tension spurred Mary into action. Previously, Mary's state papers had referred to Darnley along with Mary as "the King and Queen," now they omitted Darnley entirely, placed his title second to Mary's, or referred to him as *"The husband of the Queen"*, sure signs that Mary had no intention of naming him King or increasing his influence. Mary also altered the mottos on her coinage from *"Those whom God hath joined together, let no man put asunder"* which had clearly been a message to me, to *"Let God arise and let His enemies be scattered,"* which, to me, suggested Mary might well be considering her husband one of her enemies…

Randolph wrote, saying *"I know now that this Queen repents her marriage; she hates him and all his kin."* Darnley's drinking, too, was getting out of hand, so much so that one of Mary's lords, hosting an entertainment for the couple, asked Mary to moderate her husband's consumption of wine. Mary tried, but only got a snarl from her husband in reply. In response, Mary refused Darnley the right to bear royal arms, and denied him the crown matrimonial, as well as the title of King. Mary was ensuring she would always be of higher rank than he. It also meant he could not claim the throne, should Mary die without issue.

Rather than rely on her husband, Mary was increasingly turning to her newly promoted French Secretary, David Rizzio. *"Seigneur Davie"*, as he was disparagingly called at court, was a mere court musician no longer and had the Queen's ear. Mary's affection for Rizzio caused Darnley to fall out with his once-friend, and rumoured lover. According to Randolph, Rizzio was *"he that works all"* at Mary's court. The fact that Mary gave precedence to this young man, of no title or noble blood, enraged Darnley. As Rizzio's influence at court grew, so Darnley's hatred of him intensified. It is ever the way with those of little talent, to place the blame for their failures upon others. Darnley did not see that Mary elevated Rizzio because he was not only a friend to her, but was *useful*. Had Darnley ever entertained a thought in his head, he might have tried to alter himself to be more like this talented Italian, but Darnley could not see past the end of his syphilitic nostrils. He blamed Rizzio for stealing the love of the Queen, and for all his problems in life. Rumours began, and I have no doubt they originated from Darnley, that Mary and Rizzio were lovers. In his jealousy and anger, Darnley did not recognise he was alienating the only person who had the right and the power to make him, or break him. Her other lords despised Rizzio too. They believed he was influencing their Queen, and might call upon her to restore Catholicism.

As the weeks went on, however, Mary's mood improved. She talked about pardoning the rebel lords if they would offer her loyalty, and she even considered pardoning Moray, who by this point she loathed almost as much as her husband... What was the reason for this alteration in mood? It was simple really.

My cousin was pregnant.

No official word was given yet, but Randolph suspected that her illness, the vomiting especially, was due to a babe in her belly. He made sure we understood this was only speculation, but the news was still hard to hear. I frowned as I read his missive, knowing Cecil would have already seen it. This would lead to renewed insistence that I marry. Another cousin, another babe! The production of an heir could only strengthen Mary's reputation and position, no matter what idiot had sired it.

*

That winter, Norfolk and Robin fell out again, and this time their hatred of each other was reaching epic proportions. Each of their factions of followers wore different colours to identify their loyalties, and the youngest members began to have public quarrels and fights. Brawls broke out in inns about London. In an effort to stop the tensions before something serious occurred, I called Robin to my Presence Chamber, and publicly upbraided him.

"You will keep the peace in my country, my lord, or suffer the consequences!" I said loudly, wanting to reach out and slap Norfolk who was smirking at the edge of the crowds. "I will not have my nobles, those who should be leaders of my people, behaving like aggravated apes!"

"I will talk to my men, Majesty," Robin said. His cheeks kindled to be scolded before the court. "And I hope that others will do the same."

"I hope so too, my lord." I frowned at Norfolk, who had the good sense to cease smiling.

When we left the chambers, Robin asked for a private audience. "I am sorry to have had to do that, Robin," I apologised. "But Norfolk despises you. If he thinks you are out of favour it may bring these tensions down from the boil."

"I understand, Majesty." Robin bowed. "Of course I do."

I started with astonishment. "I thought you had come to upbraid me," I admitted. "What now... This pleasant tone and humble manner? Are you quite yourself, Robin?"

Robin chuckled. "I have something to speak of you with, Majesty, and I would like you to hear my arguments without irritation."

"Is the talk of marriage?"

"It is, but I hope you will listen to me seriously, and not take offence."

I sniffed. "That, I cannot promise, Robin. *You* must make sure you do not offend *me*. You are the one who is speaking, after all."

"You should marry Archduke Charles," he said.

I almost fell off the chair I was in the process of sitting upon. "What?" The word snapped from my mouth.

"I think you should marry Archduke Charles," he repeated. "Your most influential subjects desire it, and if any have offered support to the idea of you and me marrying, it was only because they believed your heart lay with me." His eyes were sad as he continued to speak. "This admission causes me pain, Majesty, but you have always believed you should marry where it was best for England, not for you. If you are to marry, to give us an heir, then you should accept this match. You cannot put aside the thought that I am not worthy for you, or for England. This being the case, you should marry where it is best for England," Robin paused. "And yet know, Elizabeth, I will love you for the rest of my days. No other will ever have my heart."

"I do not want to marry the Archduke," I said, frankly astonished by Robin's speech.

"Then give in to the wishes of your heart, Majesty, and marry me." Robin's swift turn of argument boggled my mind. His eyes pleaded. "Cease to play this game neither of us can win. Make me your consort. Reduce my power and influence as you wish, but allow us to have the life that we were destined for, Elizabeth. Marry *me*."

I stared at him. Had he come to argue for the Archduke only to make me sad, and then throw himself at me? He was trying to play with my emotions. It was another trick. "Will you give me an answer?" he asked after several moments passed in silence.

"At Candlemas, I will give you an answer," I promised. I wanted him gone. I could not stand to look on him. The hateful stranger had returned. Had he ever left? Which man was my Robin? I felt I knew him not at all anymore, so shifting, so changeable, so duplicitous was this soul before me.

Robin left in high spirits, blithely unaware of my feelings towards him, and quickly aggravated everyone at court with his new belief that I would marry him. I had no intention of doing so. All my old suspicions flared into life. I could trust nothing Robin said or did. Robin thought he was clever, no doubt, but when February came and went, he would find himself still single, and I in the same state.

*

As Christmas came my cousin of Scots sent official word that she was with child. Although it came as no surprise to me, since Randolph had written of his suspicions, the rest of my court was afire with the news. It led, of course, to my Privy Council attacking me for not being a *good girl*, like my cousin of Scots. I tried to remind them that no husband was better than a bad one. It did no good, they lectured, protested and pleaded with me. To confuse them, I put great vigour into talks of marriage with my old friend the Archduke, made comments at court about reconsidering a match with France, and pandered to Robin's every whim. Let the court continue to be confused, not knowing which man I meant to choose! I would play them as I always had. I just wished Kat was here to help me bamboozle them. She had been talented at such games.

Charles of France, happy to hear I was thinking of marrying him, sent word that he wished to bestow the Order of St Michael on two of my men. I chose Norfolk and Robin, and the ceremony was set for the end of January. Norfolk, however, did not want to share his honour with the likes of Robin, and came to me in high dudgeon, refusing to attend.

What a child this man is, I thought as he grumbled.

"You would give up this honour all for spite, Your Grace?" I asked Norfolk, viewing his enraged face with cold disdain.

"I wish to share nothing with a man who spreads only discord and disharmony, Your Majesty," he replied stiffly.

"I don't believe the Earl is the *only* one with a talent for discord, Your Grace," I said and then breathed in, looking away from him. "Well, if you do not wish for the honour, I will grant it to Heneage or Cecil instead... They will be sensible of the honour."

Norfolk started. He had expected me to knight him and set Robin aside, and my mention of offering the honour to other men, of considerably lower title and blood, was an affront to everything he believed in.

"If you have no more to say, Your Grace, then you can leave," I continued, inspecting one of my nails. "It is a shame that this *prestigious* title will not grace your noble house, but if this is the way you feel, I will not attempt to persuade you otherwise. The Earl will have his title, and I will choose another to be elevated in your place."

"I will attend the ceremony." Norfolk's teeth squeaked against each other as he spoke. I wanted to laugh, but I contained my amusement.

"Pardon, Your Grace... I did not hear you? What did you say?"

"I will attend the ceremony and take the honour." Norfolk looked as though he might explode, so tense had he become.

"I am glad to hear it, Your Grace," I purred. Norfolk strode off, muttering about the duplicitous nature of his Queen. I sat back and chuckled.

Chapter Sixty-Nine

Westminster Palace
Winter 1566

Frost sparkled on the bare tree branches and the air was filled with snow. London was white. Deep drifts of snow blanketed the houses, shops and markets. Smoke plumed through the icy air, meeting soft falling snowflakes, drifting lazily down to join their friends settled upon the earth. Ponds sparkled like diamonds, and the River Thames froze solid. As frosty as it was outside, it had become even more so inside court.

Robin was losing hope. Although he was pleased I had chosen him to take the Order of St Michael, his true ambition was still far away. When he and Norfolk passed each other at court, ice could have formed in the space between them. Their supporters were equally cold with each other.

The ceremony of investment came at the end of January. Norfolk and Robin stood side by side, dressed in robes of white and russet velvet, decorated with lace and tassels of gold and silver. The heated chamber was chilled by their mutual resentment. After the ceremony, Norfolk sought Robin out and berated him for continuing to try to become my husband. He asked Robin to give up ideas of marriage with me, and support the suit of the Archduke. "Believe me, Your Grace," Robin replied within clear hearing distance of me. "I *have* tried to convince the Queen to wed the Archduke for the good of England, and you can ask her that yourself. But I will admit I believe myself to be the better match for the good of her own happiness."

Not an answer that Norfolk wanted to hear…

This gave Robin another opportunity to inform me I should marry soon, for the good of my country. He pestered me about my promise. "It is not yet Candlemas, my lord," I reminded him sharply. "And I do not like to hear the same words spoken over and over as though I am stood in a cave, hearing the echo of that which I already know." Robin went to his chambers, downcast.

"He has asked me to marry for the good of my country," I said to de Silva later in the cold gardens. I was riddled with guilt, and sought to praise Robin more than he deserved because of it. "This, surely, is a sign of the greatness of which he is capable."

"My master is unwilling to conform to the stipulations on his faith," de Silva admitted. "And so a further delay is caused in any case, Majesty."

"Are our faiths so different?" I asked my friend. Lately I had asked if the Archduke would be willing to become a Protestant as many of my Privy Council were uncomfortable with the notion of a Catholic King. I knew this would not be well-received by Charles, for he was adamant in his faith. It bought me time, but still, I wanted to press the point. There was so much grief, strife and bloodshed in the world, and much of it because men would not admit that they worshipped the same God. "We believe in the same God, my lord, do we not? There *is* only one."

"I will relay your words, as always, madam," de Silva promised. "Although I believe this will be a stumbling post for us in negotiations… as I am sure your Majesty is aware." He flashed a quick, amused look at me, knowing, of course, I had no wish to marry his master. I slipped my hand through his arm.

"Keep my secrets safe, my friend," I murmured as we walked on.

In response to our latest argument, Robin turned to Lettice again and made a grand show of fawning upon her. I could see what Robin was up to, but it still hurt. Not about to let him get away with this, I paid Robin back by flirting outrageously with Heneage and my cousin Black Tom. Gentleness was no more our companion. We lashed each other with spite, jealousy and agony.

At Twelfth Night, I made Heneage King of the Bean, a position Robin had always taken before. Able to order the court around as a king for the night, Heneage organised games and dances, riddles and jests. Robin was vastly unhappy to be set aside. Noting his sour face, Heneage called upon Robin to ask me a riddle. "You will ask the Queen, which is the more difficult to erase from the mind, my lord? Jealousy, or an evil opinion implanted by a wicked gossip?" Robin glared at Heneage, aware he was toying with him, but asked the question all the same.

"I would say they were both difficult to get rid of, my lord Earl," I replied coolly. "But in my opinion, jealousy is the harder to remove, for it festers in the soul and causes noble men to become errant boys."

Robin bowed, and removed himself early from the entertainment. I missed him, despite my anger and hurt. Later, Robin sent Heneage a message saying he *"would castigate him with a stick"* for his impertinence. Heneage responded by saying "this was not punishment for equals, but if my lord came to insult him, he will discover whether his sword could cut and thrust."

"The Earl of Leicester claimed I was not his equal, Majesty," Heneage said, his cheeks on fire and his form looking set to leap into war with Robin. Messages between Robin and Heneage had continued, each more insulting than the last. From once-friends they had become firm enemies. Further conflict at my court was not to my liking. "And that he would save his chastisement of me for a point in the near future," Heneage went on, itching to be allowed to duel with Robin.

"I will deal with the Earl, my lord," I promised Heneage. "You did no wrong in your duties on Twelfth Night. But do not promise your sword against any of my men again. I will have no duels at my court."

Heneage reluctantly promised not to duel with Robin. As he left my Privy Chamber, Robin entered. When they crossed each other in the doorway, a hot vapour rose between them as their glowering eyes met. I shook my head. This was getting out of hand.

"If by my favour you have become insolent, my lord Earl," I said to Robin. "You should reform your character."

"Heneage *insulted* me, Majesty," Robin said stiffly. "And I called him to account."

"Heneage did nothing other than play the part for which he was chosen by *me*." My tone was bitter. "And you should remember, my lord, that just as I have raised you up, I can cast you down. You have disgraced yourself yet again with this foolishness and jealousy."

"Just as you have done the same," Robin retorted.

"Leave my chambers *now*, my lord," I commanded. "And do not return until you have learnt some manners."

Robin spent the next four days sulking in his chambers, until my anger abated and I sent for him, but our friendship was frosty, and awkward. Candlemas came and went, and I gave him no answer. I did not see why I should. Robin continued to court Lettice, and I paid him back by showing favour to others. We had found a new game, but it was more hurtful than even his past intrigues with de Quadra and Spain had been. Each time he paid attentions to Lettice, a part of my heart curled up and withered within me. And each time I was hurt, I went out of my way to wound him back in return. Robin and I scrapped and sliced at each other with spiteful claws.

There were times I hated him.

I began to believe our love had truly died.

Chapter Seventy

Greenwich Palace
Winter's End 1566

Hate spawns hate, as discord breeds discord, or so the old gossips say. In the last days of winter, Mary of Scots held a feast at her court in Holyrood Palace. When all were gathered, she stood before a portrait of me, and announced "there is no Queen in England but myself".

Pregnancy had made her bold and confident. That statement could easily have been taken as a declaration of war. Was that what Mary wanted? Did she think England would fall to her as easily as her rebels had?

"The child has stolen her wits, *Spirit*," I said. "My cousin Katherine Knollys has told me that during pregnancy her mind tends to wander and she forgets much. It would seem the Queen of Scots has forgotten *who she is* as her pregnancy progresses. She thinks she is me."

"Randolph had to leave the feast," Cecil told me. "He said there was a great ruckus caused by the Queen's affirmation, but he could not stay to witness it. He could hardly sit with Mary after she made that statement."

"Poor Randolph." I shook my head. "What is the girl thinking? Is she so secure in her belly that she thinks to goad me to war?"

"There is word, too, that she is intent now on bringing Catholicism back into her realm," Cecil added. "She is mad with the power of this babe. She thinks it can work miracles."

"I have seen many babes, Cecil, and found none miraculous. Mary will not convince her nobles, and is going against the agreements put in place when first she came to Scotland. Knox will eat her alive, if Moray does not get there first."

"Randolph asks that we burn all further letters from him," Cecil said. "He fears that should his news become gossip at court then he will find himself imprisoned as Throckmorton was."

"We burn nothing, Cecil. We have means to keep the missives from Scotland safe."

"I am in agreement, Majesty, but how should we respond?"

"We will ignore her, for now, *Spirit*. They say pride comes before a fall. Let us watch to see if she stumbles."

"I will ask the border guards to keep watch for any developments, and alert Randolph to be vigilant. I'm afraid there is trouble here too, Majesty. Princess Cecilia has announced she is leaving."

"Cecilia is going *nowhere* until she pays her debts, Cecil," I said with a sharp edge to my voice. Cecilia had been living a most extravagant lifestyle in London, and owed money everywhere.

"And what debts they are!" Cecil exclaimed. "She owes thousands, Majesty, and I am told she went to Cornelius Lannoy to ask that he loan her funds as well."

"What has Cecilia to do with my alchemist?" Lannoy was still working to produce the Philosopher's Stone. I little wanted him distracted. The venture was taking enough time as it was.

"He served at her brother's court, and so they know each other. Cecilia believes that since the man is working on the production of gold, he must have plenty to loan to her."

"Precious little of this fabled gold have we seen, *Spirit*," I noted glumly. "Keep an eye on them, will you? I don't want Lannoy distracted from producing my gold by worrying about Cecilia's."

"I will intercept their messages and place someone in her household," Cecil said and I smiled. "What is it, Majesty?"

"It was just... for a moment, Cecil, you sounded like Parry." The admission brought pain, but it was mingled with pleasure. The pain of Parry's death was seeping from me, and even though I would always miss him, I found now I could remember him with joy as well as grief in my soul. I only wished the same could be true about Kat.

"I will admit, there was much I learned from Parry on the intricacies of watching and infiltrating a house," Cecil said with a sad smile. "I only wish he were still here to check on my work."

"You do well enough on your own, *Spirit*. I have faith in you."

Cecilia's efforts to gain further loans to pay her debts were watched carefully by Cecil. Her husband, believing himself to be in a great deal of trouble for his wife's reckless spending, tried to escape England and was arrested at Rochester. There were rumours that Cecilia and Lannoy also meant to try to flee. "What a fool!" I exclaimed to Cecil when he told me about Christopher. "You will forbid Lannoy to have further dealings with Cecilia or her husband. I want him concentrating on what wealth he should be bringing to me, not on what he will give to Cecilia!"

There was another problem with Cecilia leaving, as William Parr came to tell me. If Cecilia left, then she would take Helena with her. "I cannot do without her now that I have found her, Majesty," said my smitten uncle. "I beg you. There must be a way to keep her in England."

I gazed on Parr with gentle eyes. Poor Parr! He had lost his Bess, and now just as he found another to love, was set to lose her too. How hard life can be. "Think not that I do not feel for you, uncle," I said. "And I, too, enjoy the company of Helena. She is a bright young woman... But what you ask is impossible. She has no family connections in England, and since you have said that you cannot marry her whilst Mistress Bourchier is alive, she has no offer of marriage either. She has no honourable reason to remain in England."

Anne Bourchier had been my uncle's first wife, whom he had divorced many years ago. When he had married Bess they had undergone many years where their marriage was not recognised and had been slandered by many and separated by my sister. It was only when I allowed the marriage to be recognised that this had come to an end, although there were still those who did not recognise it even now. Bess had understood her position, and had been willing to risk her reputation for love of him. But Parr did not wish to subject Helena to the same slander, especially since she was so young, and would be far from home, in a foreign country.

"Please, Majesty, for all the love and loyalty I have shown for you... For the affection you bore for my beloved sister... Please think of a way to aid us."

"I promise to think on it, uncle. That is all I can do for now."

Parr left, and I felt terrible for his sad face and slumped shoulders. Bess would have wanted him to be happy. I wanted to do as my friend would have wished, to aid him, but I could not think how. I asked Helena to come to my chambers, so I could speak with her about it. I was increasingly fond of this quiet, calm and self-assured young woman. Her beauty and grace were magical, but her mind was also sharp, her humour merry, and she had a sweet soul. I understood why Parr loved her. I believe I was a little in love with her myself.

"Majesty," she said as she made a pretty curtsey. "You asked for me?" Helena was wearing a very good copy of one of my gowns, and her hair was done in a similar style to mine, too. She had taken to copying me, and although many did so thinking to win my favour, she appeared to be aping me out of genuine veneration. I had been informed Helena was often heard praising me. She said to Blanche that she had long admired me, and had only found me more splendid when she finally met me. I was susceptible to flattery. There were many who would say such just to gain advancement, but it did not feel like that with Helena. She was young and the young are easily impressed; they make heroes out of ordinary people... But, I confess I found her admiration almost as intoxicating as her beauty.

"Your mistress has announced she is ready to leave my country," I informed her. "I am sure you have heard?"

"I have, Majesty, to my great sorrow," Helena said, her face falling. "I would it were not so."

"If I could find a way to keep you, would you stay?" I astonished myself. I had wanted to sound Helena out and find out what she thought of leaving or staying, not rush into making her an offer! What was wrong with me? I must have been as smitten as my uncle...

"If there was any honourable way to stay, Majesty, I would take it," she breathed, her glorious eyes opening wide. "It is my greatest wish, to remain in England, which I love more than my own homeland. To remain near to you, Majesty, and learn all that I can from you, would be a high honour."

"And the Marquis?" I asked with a smile. "He is in your heart, is he not? As you are within his."

Helena flushed becomingly. "He has asked me to marry him," she confessed. "And there is no other man I would rather take as a husband. But he cannot marry me whilst his first wife lives. We love each other, Majesty, and yet cannot be together."

"I could recognise a union between the two of you."

"William has said as much, Majesty… But there would still be uncertainty and speculation on the honesty of such a marriage in many quarters. I do not think my family would agree to the idea."

"What if you were to take a place in my household?" I asked. "And become a maid of honour to me? That would give you an honourable reason to remain in England, and if my uncle became free, the two of you could marry. Would your family agree to that plan?"

I had not thought about this much before I made this offer. Most unlike me. It was a dangerous idea in many ways. As the Queen of England, I had sovereignty over my own subjects, not those of other countries. I was interfering in international politics and might well offend Cecilia. But I liked Helena. Perhaps I *was* a little infatuated. I wanted her to stay and I wanted Parr to be happy. If life and love were what thwarted Death, then Death would I defy by acting for this couple. It was about time I paid Him back. Enough had He stolen from me already.

"If your Majesty could do this for me, I would be so happy." She stared up with those large brown eyes, making my heart feel like butter left out on a warm day. "You are so generous, so warm… so loving, Majesty. No one has ever understood me as you do. And none have ever offered me so much."

I chuckled. "Keep this quiet for now, Mistress Snakenborg," I commanded. "Tell Parr, and write to your father to ask his opinion, but say nothing to the Princess. She will not be pleased to hear I am plotting to steal her ladies. I would prefer to have your father's permission before we inform Cecilia."

"I will tell none but William and my parents," Helena promised.

"Good," I said, suddenly pleased with myself. "And tell your father I will pay you a salary, and give you your own apartments. I will be your chaperone when my uncle comes to call, so your father may rest assured no scandal will attach itself to your name." The girl was a little overcome. Thanking me, she walked from my chambers in a daze.

"It is good to see love prevail for once," Blanche said as we climbed into bed together that night.

"Kat once said to me that the best way to thwart death is to live, Blanche," I murmured as we pulled the covers close. "And to love is to live in the best way there is. If I can restore Parr's happiness, then I have won at least one victory over Death."

Chapter Seventy-One

Richmond Palace
February 1603

The attack came late on the night of March 9th, 1566.

Mary did not expect it.

Sure in his festering mind that his wife carried not his child but that of her Secretary, David Rizzio, and unhappier still that this child would remove all chance of his gaining the throne of Scotland should Mary die, Darnley made a pact with rebellious nobles. Disturbed by Mary's new resolution to alter the religion of her country, and some even more uneasy with her marriage, the rebel lords sought Darnley out. The fact that many of them despised him did not matter. What mattered was removing David Rizzio, who the rebels saw as responsible for many of Mary's late actions. They would remove his influence, and gain control of power in Scotland by capturing their Queen. They would decide how Scotland would be ruled. The Queen would become their puppet. Playing on Darnley's paranoia, his suspicions and fears, lords such as Ruthven and the Earl of Morton took Darnley up and used him as a weapon against his wife.

For better or for worse…

The hour was late. Mary and her intimates were dining at Holyrood Palace. Lady Argyll and David Rizzio kept the pregnant Queen enthralled with their talk as they supped on venison, roast pheasant and quail. Later, as Mary and Lady Argyll sat talking, Rizzio played for them. The soft light of tallow candles danced over the faces of Mary's ancestors whose portraits lined the walls. My portrait hung there too, watching her, and through my painted eyes will you see what unfolded.

The fire leapt and pranced in the hearth. With her belly filled with fine food, and spirits warmed by good company, Mary was content. One hand on her swelling belly, she stroked its contours lovingly. She was six months into her pregnancy. In three months her child would be born and her influence and power would be assured. Even if her child was a girl, she would still be in a stronger position than her cousin over the border. And if it was a boy? Then she would have all the power she required to bargain for her rightful place on the throne of England once her cousin died, and perhaps even the influence to rally Scotland to rise and fight for England's crown here and now.

Mary had become confident. This child had already brought her great benefit, no matter if she and the father were not happy. But the political power of the child was secondary to her love for it. She had hardly expected such powerful emotions. Long had she yearned for a child. She had wanted to bear François's child, but God had not allowed it. Now, God had heard her. She loved the child already. She was eager to become a mother, to have another to lavish care upon, and to know the love of her child in return.

Mary listened to Rizzio play. The late hour and the weight of her babe made Mary drowsy. She rubbed her eyes; they were gritty and sore. She had faced much of late. She had forced rebel leaders from her country, she had proved herself a strong and capable Queen, but she was still human, and soon to be a mother. She was weary, ready for her bed, but she had no wish to insult her gentle friend, Davey, by leaving before his last piece was finished. She would wait until the end of the song.

Good Davey... In a country where she ever seemed to find problems, strife and rebellion, she still had her friend. Her husband, as she now understood, was not the man she had believed him to be. His charms ran as shallow as his intelligence. But even if they were not fated for a happy marriage, as she had so desperately hoped, he had done the one task she required of him for her political survival. No matter that he was a fool, his child would become heir to Scotland, and very possibly, to England, too.

Davey was strumming his last notes, and Mary roused herself from her happy, half-slumberous state, making ready to applaud him. He gazed up at her as he sang of love and hope; virtues she wanted so much to believe in. She knew people whispered about their relationship, but there was nothing more to it than friendship. She loved Davey, but she did not desire him. He felt the same for her. His admiration and respect, his constant desire to put her needs first, these were qualities she valued and was grateful to possess. He smiled at her, as he held the last note of the song, well and true; sweet and beautiful.

She would hear that sound echoing in her mind, in her dreams, for the rest of her life.

Just as Mary made to applaud, in through the doors burst a shouting gaggle of armed men. Their swords were drawn; daggers flashed in the candlelight. Their faces were hard, desperate. Rising from her chair, thinking there must have been an attack on the palace, and these men had come to defend her, Mary stood up, swift but ungainly, with one hand on her swollen belly.

"What..." she went to ask. Mary got no further.

The men surrounded her and the others, herding them into a corner. The table was overturned, sending plates and candlesticks crashing to the floor. Amongst the men who surrounded her, Mary could see faces she knew only too well. Lord Ruthven... and her husband.

"What are you doing?" Mary cried, her eyes wide with terror. She looked at Darnley who sneered at her. Making straight for Rizzio, the men tried to pull him from the group. Rizzio knew at once what Mary was still struggling to understand; these men were here to kill him.

Screaming, "justice! Save me, sweet lady!" Rizzio tried to resist. They grasped hold of him, yanking and pulling him away from Mary. Rizzio fell to the floor, grasped hold of Mary's skirts, and screeched for mercy. Mary, realising the murderous intent of her lords, tried to hold on to her friend, but the others were too strong. They tore Mary's hands from her friend. As the men pulled Rizzio out, his hands clawed at the floor. They dragged him, screaming, into the next room. Mary tried to stop them, but her lords shoved her roughly back against the wall. Mary cried out, calling Davey's name and shouting at the men to stop. Lady Argyll tried to keep the men away from their Queen, batting at them with her hands and shouting at them.

It did not stop them.

Mary could only listen in helpless horror as, in the adjoining room, Rizzio was stabbed, over and over. Every lord present drove their daggers into his flesh. Mary could hear his choking screams, the burbling blood rising in his throat and mouth. He screamed for her as he died. She stood helpless, her hands pinned behind her back, the large lump of her child sticking out before her. What could she do against so many? Did they think to murder her and her baby, too? In those dreadful moments, Mary believed them capable of anything. As Rizzio spluttered, slipping to the floor upon matted rushes thick and sticky with his own blood, Mary let out a sob of terror and sorrow. But Mary was not lost in her fear. She was made furious by it.

"Why have you done this wicked deed?" Mary screamed at her husband. His face was curious. Where many of the men looked hard, their faces set with determination, Darnley looked as though he had lost his nerve. As was ever the way with him, his fantasy, his imaginings, of this moment had brought him more pleasure than the reality. Now that he was actually here, embroiled deep in treason, he was unsure and afraid. But as Mary yelled at him, poison floating in his mind rose to the surface. His fear made him defiant, for a moment.

"Rizzio has had more company of your body than I have for the past two months!" he squealed. Mary stared at her husband with unbelieving eyes.

"I have ever been true to my vows," she said. "The man you have murdered, my lord, was my friend and once yours. There was nothing more between us." Darnley was about to fire back an answer when Ruthven stepped from the other room. Mary stared at his bloody hands. That was Davey's blood. Her friend's blood.

"Your time has come, my lord." Ruthven thrust a dagger into Darnley's hands. For a moment, Mary drew back, terrified, thinking they meant to kill her and her baby. But Ruthven wanted Darnley to strike Rizzio. That way, Darnley would not be able to wriggle out of his part in this treason. Darnley hesitated. Mary had given him reason to doubt the lies he had been told. He swallowed. Perhaps the child *was* his. Perhaps Rizzio had not been his wife's lover. Perhaps he had been tricked into treason.

He did not want to take part. "The man is already dead, is he not?" Darnley lamely protested. "What need is there to desecrate a corpse?" Ruthven would not hear him. Darnley was all but dragged into the next room. Rizzio was not dead, but Death was close. His body was riddled with wounds and the floor was awash with blood. As Darnley approached the body, pushed forward by the men behind him, he slipped. His hand landed in a pool of Rizzio's blood. It trickled down his arm as he tried to right himself, staining his fine shirt.

Shaking, afraid, unsure of what was true anymore, Darnley stabbed his sharp dagger into Rizzio's gut. A small whimper emerged from Rizzio's lips. Darnley walked back to the other chamber in a daze. Mary stood, staring at him with eyes filled with hate. She was led off to her chambers. Her women were allowed to accompany her, but she was under no illusions; she was a prisoner. Her life and that of her child were in danger. Although she was sure that, for now, the conspirators would simply hold her, and take control of Scotland, she was in no good position. She had to escape. She had to get word to her allies… to Bothwell.

Mary was in a desperate situation. She was a captive, and her survival and that of her child had to come first. She began to hatch a plan of escape. Playing on her pregnant state, her women told their jailors that Mary was taken sick. The day after the attack, they told her captors that Mary was suffering a miscarriage. The Queen's sudden frail health gave the plotters cause for concern. They had no intention of killing their Queen for they needed her alive to exercise control over Scotland. Should Mary die, and her child with her, the next best blood claimant was Elizabeth of England. Whilst they had taken the English Queen's support before, they were not about to allow Scotland to become annexed by England. Mary asked that her husband be allowed to visit her, for in her weakened state, she protested, she was unsure how long she had to live. Darnley was brought in, and Mary embarked on the first part of her plan to escape.

Mary greeted him with warmth and sympathy. She despised her husband, but it was important he should not know that now. She played on his pride, his fears, on his vanity and shallow nature. She told Darnley he was not to blame for what had happened to Rizzio for others had duped him. Rizzio had only been her good friend, she said, and the babe inside her was indeed Darnley's. She told him that the child was still safe, but she feared she would lose their baby if she stayed here… And even if it were born safe and hale, what then? These traitors would take their child captive. With the heir to Scotland in their hands, they could murder her and Darnley, and rule through their child.

Mary was clever and she was convincing. Persuading Darnley that the true intent of these rebels was to kill her and Darnley as well, she unnerved him. She told him he had been made so jealous by their evil lies that he had not known what he was doing. She told him she loved him. She wept, she cajoled... And she won the feeble, easily changeable, trust of her husband.

Just as word reached England of this fell deed, and the Privy Council met to talk over what was to be done, Mary escaped.

At midnight on the 11th of March, Mary, her *Maries*, and Darnley sped on swift and quiet feet down the back stairs of the palace. Darnley knew the rotation of the guards on her door, and managed to produce a gap by pretending he would take that hour's watch. They did not have long, but Mary was determined. They quickly made their way through the servants' quarters, where many were loyal still to their Queen, and happy to help her in her hour of need. The attack on their Queen had shocked them, and even those who wavered were pushed into action by wives and sisters who were horrified a pregnant woman had been so abused. Mary did not need a great deal from them, in any case. She just needed them to pretend they had not seen her, as she sped through their halls.

Horses were waiting. Her *Maries* had been busy. Thought unimportant by the conspirators, and therefore allowed to leave Mary's chambers on small errands during her days of capture, they had used their time well. They had roused the sympathy of the stable lads, who had agreed to prepare fast horses. Mary and her party climbed into the saddles of their mounts and rode out. They tore through the night, covering twenty-five miles, and reaching Dunbar by dawn. Mary wasted no time. She raised an army and marched back to Edinburgh to take her revenge on Rizzio's killers. A week later, she had control of the city. The conspirators fled, cursing Darnley.

Darnley soon discovered that his wife's feelings were not as she had protested to him during her capture. She made it clear now how much she despised him. He had betrayed her, sold her to her enemies and endangered the life of their child. He had helped others to murder her friend. Darnley was a traitor, and had proved he was dangerous. He had helped her to escape, and that alone prevented her from having him arrested, but she would never trust him again. The vestiges of any love she had known for him were gone. There was a snake in her bed. She had to find ways to keep him under guard, and neutralize the threat he posed to her. Mary kept him at her side, wanting Darnley where she could keep a close watch on him for he had shown how easily influenced he was. For the first time, she understood what peril she had put herself in, put her country in, by taking him as her husband, but even with this complication, even with a foolish, hazardous husband to watch, she had prevailed.

Standing before her armies, her country once more her own, her foes fleeing Scotland, Mary was victorious. She spoke of her great fear, of the danger she had been placed in, and the peril posed to her child.

Her people went wild for her; their brave, warrior queen. This astounding woman, who had engineered escape from almost certain death, and stood with the future of Scotland still safe inside her.

It would not be long before her people would cease to cheer her. Not long before all that was offered to my cousin was censure and abuse. She knew that not, then. Then, she stood proud, tall and powerful. She had risen from horror, into grace.

Chapter Seventy-Two

Greenwich Palace
Spring 1566

"Had I been in Queen Mary's place, I would have taken my husband's dagger and stabbed him with it!" I exclaimed to de Silva, enraged. Then, remembering to whom I was speaking, I added, "of course, I would *never* do such a thing to the Archduke, but he would not do such to me either, would he, ambassador?"

De Silva replied with all assurances that his master would certainly never act in such a barbaric fashion. "It is the way of the Scots, so I hear, Majesty," he replied smoothly. "To behave little better than beasts recently removed from their caves."

I arched an eyebrow. "Much as I would love to agree with you, my lord ambassador, and save my countrymen the dishonour of being associated with such vile treason, Lord Darnley *is* an Englishman. It seems to me the dark heart of the barbarian is sometimes covered by only the slimmest film of a gentleman's veneer."

I was horrified by this attack. Not only because it was treason, not only because Mary's lords and her husband had murdered her favourite, but because they had treated their Queen with such disdain. It was a frightening event, which rattled many in power; to come so close to such danger and death, and at the hands of one's own lords… It was enough to strike terror into any royal heart. Hearing of Mary's valiant escape, her bravery and her courage, affection for her grew anew in my heart.

Mary, however, appeared to suspect me of involvement, or that I would aid the rebels who had assaulted her, and who had fled to England. I had no intention of aiding such men, but they could not be found. I ordered they were to leave England when discovered, but Cecil persuaded me that if we made little effort to find them, and kept them in England, they might be of better use to us in the future, if they could be used to bargain with Mary. I did not want Mary to hear of this, and even though I could see Cecil's point, was uncomfortable about it, for I had no wish to reward rebels, or make more enemies, but there was trouble brewing in Ireland. The Earl of Tyrone, Shane O'Neill, was inciting rebellion, and our intervention in France had not made us any friends. I did not need Mary turning from me as well. Besides, I admired her; she had faced danger, treason and death, and survived. But as was ever the way, I had to think of England first. Cecil was right when he said these rebels, if found, could be valuable to us.

Randolph had suspected there might be an attempt on Rizzio's life, but he had not believed for a moment that Mary herself might be put in danger. I found out then that he had written to Cecil, asking that he try to warn the Queen her favouritism was putting her friend in danger, for she would not listen to Randolph's warnings. Cecil said he had not had time to even bring the dispatch to me before the attack came. Without realising it, Randolph had made the rebels take swifter action than intended. Fearing his letter might cause English intervention, the conspirators had acted fast so no warning or aid could be given to the Queen.

I did linger over the possibility that Cecil had known, and perhaps had even engineered the attack on Rizzio. It was not out of the bounds of possibility. Cecil had motive enough for having been involved. Rizzio had been a Catholic, and had exerted great influence over Mary. The attack had also placed my cousin in great peril, and, had the rebel lords managed to hold on to Mary, would have usurped her power in Scotland. Removing Rizzio and making Mary a captive to her Protestant lords would have been beneficial to Cecil, and to England, in some ways. Cecil protested he had had nothing to do with the attack, and I did not press him further. However horrified I was by the attack on my cousin, it would not have been to my benefit to pursue Cecil for it. I needed him, and at times such considerations outweigh even the most pressing of moral objections. Sometimes I had to do what I thought was wrong, for the sake of England. Besides, I had no firm proof Cecil was involved.

I sent Robert Melville, brother of Mary's ambassador, to Scotland, to inform my cousin that she had my sympathy and support. I think, given all that had occurred of late between us, she was surprised. *"You have shown that the magnanimity and good nature of your predecessors surpass every passion in you, and thus placed me under such an obligation that I do not know how I shall ever repay you,"* she wrote. I wasn't sure if Mary was entirely convinced. My predecessors had hardly been magnanimous towards Scotland so I wondered if this was a jibe. But whatever her suspicions, it was a start. And I was determined to show that, no matter our problems, at such a time I stood with my cousin. No man had the right to attack his Queen.

I took to wearing her miniature on a golden chain at my waist. My Council believed this incident might encourage something similar in England, and my security was doubled. I was worried not only about myself, but Robin too. These traitors had slain Mary's favourite for jealousy and fear of his influence. Even hating Robin, as I did at that moment, I did not want him dead.

Cecil urged me to act with caution, especially with regards to supporting Mary, but I would not listen. I had to show unequivocally that such an attack was unacceptable. At that time, I did not even care about Mary's recent affirmation that she was the rightful Queen of England. Solidarity was required. I could not allow anyone to speak well of this incident, even if they saw benefit for England. I had no wish to find myself someday in the same position Mary had faced.

I ordered my court to think on Mary with generosity, admiration and love.

"My cousin hath been abused and put down, and yet risen to show her greatness over those who sought to harm her," I announced to the crowded Presence Chamber. "She has shown that those whom God places on the throne can never be removed by will or greed of man. For a Queen, and one carrying an unborn child, no less, to be treated with such disdain and dishonour is not a mark against *her* name, but against those who sought to harm her!" I narrowed my eyes. "Let all men know that such insults against royalty will never be tolerated. Let all men know that such actions, against one chosen by God, will be met with the strongest force, and deadliest retaliation."

Letters flooded back and forth between us, each one more affectionate than the last. We reclaimed some of our past affection and friendship by avoiding any difficult subjects. I began to think of her with great esteem. Faking a miscarriage, fooling her husband, escaping the palace and taking back her country... It was easy to admire her. *"I pray that you will have an easier confinement than you have had pregnancy,"* I wrote to her. *"I, too, am grown big with the desire for good news. If it were within my power, my good sister, I would name you my heir."*

"Words cannot express my gratitude to you, my beloved sister," Mary wrote. *"Your efforts to promote my claim do not go unnoticed, and your gentle affection for me, at such a time as this, only causes me to think ill on all the times I have heeded those who would tear us apart. I am sure, that in our hearts, we have ever been as sisters to each other."*

As winter faded, my cousin was back in unquestioned control of her country. If you had asked me then, I would have told you I considered Mary my true heir. I would have said that the Queen of Scotland had proved herself.

Chapter Seventy-Three

Whitehall Palace
Winter-Spring 1566

If my relationship with Mary had improved, my friendship with Robin only knew fresh grief. From one day to the next I knew not what my feelings were for him; hatred, anger, agony, misery, love... He ripped my heart to shreds, and I did all I could to wound him in return. Lettice had returned to court, and with her return came only new sorrow for me as Robin used her to rouse my jealousy. When I found Robin and Lettice one day locked in an embrace in a corner of my rooms, I exploded at him. "You seek to break my heart, Robin!" I screamed as Lettice sped away. "You make my ladies into your whores! You play with my affections!"

"As you do to me, with Heneage!" he retorted. "You put him above me! You turn to him where only you came to me before!"

"Why should I come to you?" I bellowed, beside myself. "You have shown time and time again that I cannot trust you, my lord."

I ordered him out. Robin later claimed he was ill, and could not perform his duties. I knew it was a lie. I sent Lettice to her husband's estates in disgrace and berated her unfortunate mother, Katherine Knollys, for her daughter's behaviour. When Robin eventually showed up for his duties, he was sullen. We managed a few words before he asked to leave court. "I would rather be away from court at this time, Majesty," he hissed. "I feel I am not welcome here."

"And what of your duties to me, my lord?" I countered waspishly.

"Give my post as Master of Horse to your Carey cousin, Lord Hudson, Majesty, if you wish to be rid of me for good. The man wants the title, and has done so for years."

"You seek to instruct me, do you, Robin?" I asked coldly. "You forget again, my lord, who is sovereign of England."

"I forget nothing."

"Neither do I, my lord Earl." My tone was dark, dripping with hatred. Even Robin stared to hear me talk so. "Leave my presence, but not the court if you value your head, my lord Earl," I said. "Your Queen will decide when your usefulness has ended, not you!"

I watched him go and believed I hated him. He was draining me of all goodness. I had grown so thin that bones could be clearly seen under the delicate veneer of my skin. My skin dried and flaked; I could count every one of my ribs just by looking in a mirror. I was falling apart. Robin sent word by letter that he wanted to leave court. Thrusting his missive at Blanche, I shouted at her "tell the Earl of Leicester that he can go from court, and the Devil may take him for all I care!"

Robin left and what was left of my heart went with him.

Even though he had hurt me, even though he had done me so much wrong, I was lost without him. I had lost too much already. I became despondent and pensive. Soon, I had not energy to rise from my bed, and lay within its covers staring out at the Thames, watching the birds as they came and went, free, as I would never be. I had lost everything. My friends fell from my grasp like sand and I was alone and unloved. Prophesies and gossip that I would die scrambled about court like cats with burning tapers tied to their tails. Cecil grew so worried that he sent for Robin, but when Robin returned, he was in no mood to make friends.

"You look thin, Your Majesty," he noted when he was brought to me.

"As you look angry still," I retorted, gaining a burning look of darkness and flame from my once-friend. "Are you in a mood to apologise to me, my lord? Or have you only come to tell me you may do as you wish, and flaunt your lust for other women in my face?"

"If I am to apologise, you must too," he demanded. "You have done as much harm to us as I have, and all for retribution for envy and jealousy."

"Are you not guilty of the same?" I shouted. "Spending your time with others, flirting with them, *throwing* them in my face? And for what, my lord? To goad me into marriage? Will there be no end to this, Robin? We twist in circles, like cats about a dead fish."

"There can be an end if you marry me." He glared at me.

It was the least enticing proposal I had ever received.

"You may leave court again, my lord Earl," I said, suddenly weary and downcast. "You are not welcome here." Robin left for his estates. And once more I was left to my misery.

"He will not ever be simply a friend to me, Blanche," I said to her later that night.

"He cannot set aside his love, either," she noted, pouring ale for me and adding boiled water. "All men believe they know what is best for the women they love. It is in their nature to seek to dominate and control, for that is what they are taught is their natural role. You confuse this idea in him, Majesty, with your independence and your wish to remain free, and so he knows not what to do. That is why he keeps on trying the same thing. He has no other model to turn to."

"Then he is more a fool than ever I took him for."

"Are we not all fools, when we love?" Blanche's words, so like those of Kat so many years ago, made me ponder. But I could not call Robin back. I was too hurt, too proud… and yet I had no strength, no courage, without him.

*

In April, Princess Cecilia left for Sweden. The shine had been wiped from her presence at court like a cheap spoon washed too many times. As she left she declared she was "glad to get out of this country" just as all those who had loaned her money and goods were glad to find their coin back in their pockets, since I had insisted her brother pay her debts.

Helena remained in England, and entered my service as a maid of honour. Immediately proving useful in my chambers, she was hard-working and infinitely charming when visitors came to call. She made fast friends with Blanche, who was delighted with her. "She is a sweet and modest girl," Blanche said with genuine, high approval. "And yet there is a spirit within her which is strong and true. If I did not know better, I would say there was Welsh blood in those Swedish veins."

"Is every person with goodness in them of Welsh descent, then?" I teased.

"You and I are Welsh, my Queen, are we not?" Blanche asked with a grin. "Cecil has Welsh blood, and Parry was a true son of the valleys. Think as you will, but I find the valour and nobility of my ancient race brings much that is good into the English Court."

At the same time Cecilia left, Lannoy attempted to leave England in secret. Failing to produce a potion of everlasting life, or endless gold, he was found trying to sneak away, after having used up all the money I had granted him. Unable to prove his innocence, Lannoy was confined to the

Tower accused of "greatly abusing" my patience and generosity. He sent a message that if allowed to continue his studies, he could have a return on my investment in weeks, perhaps a month, but I was losing patience with him as swift as I was losing faith in his promises.

"Allow him to continue his work, inside the Tower, Cecil," I said, staring from the window with a furrowed brow. "But I hold little hope of success."

"There are others we might employ who claim to have success in the same venture, Majesty," Cecil informed me.

"I am weary of these alchemists," I told him. "Promises are worth nothing if nothing is what is produced. Allow Lannoy to attempt to save his reputation and my faith in him, but if you promote more alchemists, Cecil, do so with your own money."

To me, the idea of everlasting life was growing only more unpleasing. I had once said I thought it must be a lonesome existence, and in my present state of depression, I believed it all the more so. Was there anything worth living eternally for?

"I am not made to be immortal," I said to the air about me as Cecil left. "I am a creature of blood and bone, of love and pain. I am not made to last for all time."

Blanche was deeply concerned and wrote to Robin, telling him I was hurt by his late behaviour, but only more so by his refusal to write to try to make amends. By the end of May, Blanche had convinced him to return to court, but our friendship was not easy. Neither of us talked about what had driven us apart. I was too hurt, too raw, to make such an attempt.

When Robin returned I was surprised to see that he had become as gaunt as I, and had dark circles under his eyes.

"Have you found sleeping to be a problem, Robin?" I asked gently as we pulled our horses to walk through the park. "You look as though you have."

"I am fine, Majesty," was his stiff and formal reply.

I sighed and led my horse away. He did not want to be my friend; that much was clear. Having him back like this was almost as bad as having him gone.

*

Cecil decided now was the time to demonstrate to me the ills of choosing Robin as a husband. And, as was ever Cecil's way, he made a list, comparing Robin to the Archduke Charles. In every way Robin, of course, came out the worst: he was of common blood; he would bring nothing of wealth or power to England; his marriage to Amy had been childless, and therefore there was a possibility he was sterile; he was hated by many, and suspected of his wife's murder; if I married him then all would believe I had been complicit in his wife's murder... "And the match would only ever be seen as a carnal union, Majesty," Cecil said, finishing his list. "Such marriages always begin in pleasure, and end in sorrow."

"I am as far as ever I will be, *Spirit*, from considering marrying the Earl of Leicester," I said despondently.

Robin heard of this conversation, and Cecil's list, and removed himself from court yet again. He went to his estates in Norfolk. When he again failed to write to me, I wrote him a terrible letter. Filled with rage and hatred, my spite sparkled from the pages.

"You think yourself so above all others that you no longer believe you have need to respect or glory in me as your ruler," I wrote. *"You have become vain, proud, and arrogant. You force your will upon me and value my friendship and love no more. You have become a stranger, Robin, a face I*

no longer recognise and a heart I no longer love. You have no respect for me, for my position, or for the love which was once strong between us. God help me if I ever showed you affection so deep it could turn all that was once good within you to evil. You have altered and changed. You have brought me low. You have turned the love within me to hatred. And yet, I grieve without you. I know not now whether I grieve so long and dark because my friend is absent from my side, or if sorrow assails me because the friend who was once more dear to my heart than any other, has truly been destroyed."

Robin received my letter, and was amazed at the outpouring of grief, malevolence and rage. He sent a letter to Throckmorton, not daring to send it directly to me. "I have received your missive, my lord, and another from one whom it has always been my great comfort to hear from, but in such sort that I know not what to impute the difference to… I never wilfully offended. Foul faults have been found in some. My hope was that one only might have been forgiven, yet it seems she hath forgotten me. If many days' service, and not a few years' proof have made trial of unremovable fidelity, what shall I think of all past favour, which brings about such an utter casting off of all that was before?" Robin went on for some pages about his confusion, and my unkindness. He finished by saying he was so miserable that "a cave in the corner of oblivion or a sepulchre for perpetual rest are the best homes I could wish to return to."

Throckmorton showed me the letter. Robin had included another for me. It was signed at the end not with the symbol he always used of two eyes, for my pet name for him, but with a heart, coloured black, to show his broken heart. I wept over his letter when I was alone. I wanted so much for all of this to be true, for Robin to truly grieve as I did. I called him home to court. When he arrived, I saw he had lost more weight. "You should have more care for yourself, Robin," I said gently. "I do not like to see you looking unwell."

"You, too, look as though you have suffered, Majesty," he said. There was no pleasure in his voice. He took no pride in seeing me brought low.

"You will resume your duties and no more will be said," I said and then my face crumpled. "Robin..." I breathed, tears in my eyes. "I have missed you so."

He took me in his arms. "I will not leave again," he murmured into my hair. "I cannot be without you."

"I cannot do without you," I sobbed into his doublet. "No matter what you do to me, Robin... No matter how much you hurt me. Your absence stings more keenly than any wound you inflict."

I had never understood the slavery of love until then. I could not stop my heart from loving Robin.

Chapter Seventy-Four

Windsor Castle
Spring - Summer 1566

"Move them to another house, then." I responded to Cecil's pleas without any great enthusiasm. He wanted to move Katherine Grey and her sons from house arrest in Essex because her gaoler was sick. There were rumours of plague already abroad in England. I could see that allowing Katherine and her sons to die of pestilence would be ill advised, but I suffered no great alarm for her welfare.

"Gosford Hall is close by, Majesty," Cecil said. "Sir John Wentworth can act as her new guardian."

"Guardian? Jailer, you mean?"

Cecil lifted his shoulders. "One word is as good as another."

"Not when they imply vastly different situations, Cecil." I glared at him. I had no wish for him to start acting as though Katherine was merely being protected by my men. She was under arrest; that was the truth, no matter how Cecil tried to spin it. "Have them kept as they were before, Cecil. No visitors and I want them isolated. I will not have her lover sneak through the cracks in the plaster to plant yet another bastard in her belly!"

"Hertford is at Wulfhall, and under close watch there."

"And there he can stay! He is fortunate I did not decide to add him to my family's collection of dead Seymours in the Tower."

Our plans did not go ahead with ease. Wentworth wrote to the Council to protest that he and his wife were too old to be adequate jailors, and his house was not secure enough for such an important prisoner. Fearful that failure would bring swift punishment upon his family, Wentworth wrote often to Cecil. The Council did not heed him, neither did I. He was told to make the best of what he had.

But my cousin was a quiet prisoner, much to Wentworth's relief. She requested to be allowed to send letters to Hertford, which I grudgingly allowed, and he wrote back. Hertford's mother wrote many missives to Cecil, praising the couple's young, lively son who was in her charge, and protesting that I kept his parents separated. *"How unmeet it is that this young couple should thus wax old in prison,"* the Duchess of Somerset wrote, but I was unmoved. Cecil wrote back that he had already incurred my wrath for speaking out for Katherine and her sons in the past, and had no wish to do so again.

Soon there would be another child who could claim the right to be my heir. Mary of Scots was growing larger every day, and when her child was born, be it girl or boy, it would have a claim to my throne; one which I believed was stronger and purer than any Katherine Grey or her children possessed. Others saw Mary's babe as a threat to me, and to England, but I did not, or at least, I did not see it *only* as a threat. Mary believed that with the birth of her child, I would have to resolve the succession upon her. Cecil was fearful of the same. I would wait and I would watch, as had ever been my way. Ill as I had been of late, I was not yet willing to give up on life and hand my throne to another. Mary would have to wait, as all heirs must.

*

As I walked into the Bedchamber that night, I unthinkingly called for Kat to attend upon me. As my other ladies stared at me, and Blanche's eyes swam with quick tears, I realised my mistake. Before they could see my face crumple, I ran to my Privy Gardens. Dusk was falling. A guard hastily trotted after me to ensure I was not left alone. As he hovered at the edge of the gardens, I looked up at the darkening skies. "Kat…" I whispered. "Why are you not here? Why did you leave me?"

There was no answer from the skies. There was no voice carried soft and gentle on the gathering wind. There were no arms to tuck themselves about me, to tell me all would be well, with England, with Mary, with Robin… Those times were the hardest; times when I would forget that she was gone, and then remember. You would think that one would never forget such a loss, and I had not forgotten it, not really. It was simply that Kat had been a part of my life for so long I had grown used to her always being there. My mind forgot, even if my heart did not. I stood there for some time, trying to gather my emotions. Eventually Blanche came out and took my arm. "It is time for bed, Majesty," she said.

I allowed myself to be taken inside, to be put to bed. That night, I dreamed of Kat. Of the first day I had met her. I dreamed that she told me she would never leave me, that I would never have to do without her. I awoke the next morning to find my dreams had been naught but pretty lies. It was almost a year now, since her death. At times, my sorrow was as fresh as the first moment of loss. At others, it was a dull ache. I missed her so much. I yearned for her advice and company. At the worst of times, I believed a part of me had died with her.

Chapter Seventy-Five

Greenwich Palace
Summer 1566

That summer, Bess St Loe returned to court, finally having handled most of the troubles resulting from William's death. She was restored to my Bedchamber, serving beside her friends, Frances Cobham, Blanche and Dorothy Stafford. Almost immediately she attracted the attention of Henry Cobham, brother-in-law of Frances, and the two were often in each other's company. There were rumours they would marry, but Bess said it was too soon for her to think of another husband, if she wanted one at all. "Three husbands have I buried now, Majesty," she said as we sat in the gardens at Greenwich under a bower of honeysuckle. "I know not that I have the strength to bury another."

"Consider, Bess, that the next might bury you, and draw comfort from that," I jested and she laughed.

"It is true, I grow old," she said. What a lie! She was a mature woman, but by no means old. Then she sighed. "But I miss William. It is not the same as it was when I lost my other husbands, Majesty. I loved them all, in different ways, but I felt as though William and I were intended for one another. When I was with him, no matter where we were, I felt as though I was home."

"*Y man lle rydw i mewn heddwch a mi fy hun,*" I said, thinking of Blanche.

"Majesty?"

"It is a Welsh saying. It means the place where I am at peace with myself." I smiled sadly at her. "I know how you feel, Bess. Kat was my home. She was the place where I found peace. William was yours." I looked about at the glorious gardens and inhaled the fresh, sweet air. It was warm and sunny, but a hard wind blew, gusting through the garden paths. In this bower, we were protected from the worst of its power. "Perhaps you will find another place," I said.

"As will you, Majesty."

"Perhaps," I said. "Perhaps we should just be grateful that we found such grace once, even if it never comes to us again. Before Kat died, Bess, she said that she had lived well and full; that she had known love. She said that must be enough for anyone. I think I agree with her. Perhaps we should be content to have known such souls, even if they could not remain with us. Perhaps we should be grateful just to have touched them, touched their lives, even for a moment. There are many who never have the joy of knowing love as we have."

We spoke little more, but sat thinking of those we had loved. That evening, I held a small party in my chambers to welcome Bess back to court. Cecil arrived just after we had finished eating. The dance had started. My ladies, partnering each other, were lively with giggling and prancing, practising the steps we learnt each night, so that when we performed for the court, we were spectacular. It was unusual to see Cecil at such an hour, and when he came over as I stood, my chest heaving from the effort of the dance, he whispered into my ear that Mary of Scots had been delivered of a healthy baby boy.

My face dropped. "The Queen of Scots is delivered of a fine son," I said, sinking into a chair. "And I am but barren stock." Cecil did not answer; there was no need. How many times had he said I needed to marry, only for me to defy him time and time again? My ladies gathered about me, reassuring me I was yet young, and could have *many* babes if I wanted. I listened to their chatter, wondering on my choice to remain unwed and childless. I will confess to you that never in all the time I was alive did I feel more troubled for the course I had taken, then, for England and for myself.

The next morning, I rallied my spirits. It would hardly do for me to be seen sorrowing for my choices. I welcomed Melville, the ambassador who had brought this news, with a show of dancing. I wanted him to see that I was healthy and fit, especially seeing as many would now compare Mary to me.

"It is joyful news you have brought of our royal nephew," I said to him. "This news has restored me from the sickness I recently suffered. It was as though a tonic had been brought to me last night, lord ambassador. As I heard of the delivery of my good sister's son, I was brought back to full health and vigour, as you see today." It was a lie. I felt awful, but I was not about to let that show.

Melville decided to relay to me, in gruesome and lengthy detail, the process of my cousin's labour. Perhaps thinking that since I was a woman, I would naturally *love* to hear all about the blood, gore, pain and strife of bringing a child into the world, he told me all he had gleaned from the midwives who had attended my cousin. To own the truth, that *did* make me feel better, but only because it made me all the more determined never to face such an ordeal.

The boy was christened James Charles Stuart, the second name given to him to honour the French King, his uncle by marriage, and the first for Mary's father and grandfather. I am not surprised my cousin chose to skirt over the name 'Henry', which would have honoured her repulsive husband. I spoke to Melville often and warmly about this new Prince of Scotland. "I am now resolved to satisfy the Queen on the matter of the succession," I told him. "I esteem the position of my heir to belong most justly to my good sister, and I wish with all my heart that this will be the way it will come to be decided. The Prince's birth will be a spur to the lawyers to resolve the matter, and I will ask it to be discussed at the next meeting of Parliament."

I was not alone in my support for Mary. Much to Cecil's disgust, Norfolk, Pembroke and Sussex all agreed with me, seeing potential for England's future in this Prince. To my surprise, Robin also added his voice to theirs. "The new Prince of Scotland is not only of Tudor blood," he said to the Council. "But will be raised in the Protestant faith, since that is the faith of his country. Our Queen is not at present disposed to marry, and therefore it seems only right that we respect her wishes for the succession, as well as seeing this Prince as the natural, and royal, heir."

"And yet his mother is still dubious and suspect," Cecil complained.

"Did you not once say to me the same of Katherine Grey, Cecil?" I asked. "And said that were her boys to be raised properly, they could be named heirs to England's throne, despite whatever ills their mother had done?"

"I did," Cecil reluctantly admitted.

"Then your own argument has foiled this latest attempt to remove my cousin from consideration," I replied, pleased to have caught him out. Cecil was unhappy. He had cause to hate my good memory. "And this child has more claim to my throne than any other, because he is of royal, undiluted blood. His mother is no slattern, set on bedding the first handsome man to pass her way. His mother is a Queen. And whilst I disapprove mightily of her fool of a husband, Mary Stuart is my nearest relative." I looked about me. "You have said, oftentimes, my lords that you wanted an answer on the succession. This is my present resolve."

Of course this was not the end. Cecil uncovered a plot which Mary was possibly involved in; to contact Catholic nobles in England, and have them support her claim. If this was true it would have been to her advantage. Cecil brought this up as a way of trying to put me off Mary, but even he admitted that he believed Mary was focussed now on the succession rather than interested in taking my throne by force.

"When Sir Henry Killigrew delivers my gift for Mary's son," I said. "I will ask him to counsel the Queen on the importance of not soliciting my subjects for support. But I do not believe she is planning an invasion, Cecil. If she is seeking support for her claim, no matter how ill-advised, it does not hold that she is planning to storm England with her troops. Despite the birth of her son, she has troubles of her own to deal with."

Mary had vanquished the late threat to her life and throne, but her country was not entirely stable as yet, and there were her ongoing problems with Darnley. They were rarely seen together, and when they were, the coldness between them made her courtiers shiver. Darnley had finally remembered his mother was my prisoner and had asked me to release her. I refused. And it was not only in my court where the name of Lennox was dust and dirt. Mary had lately said she would make the Lennoxes as poor as ever they had been in Scotland. Later that summer, the Earl of Bedford sent a report to the Council wherein he apologised for not being able to repeat what the Queen had said about her husband. *"It cannot, for modesty, nor for the honour of the Queen, be reported what she said of him,"* the man wrote. I could almost sense his blushes resonating from the parchment.

Darnley was also boasting that he would invade England and make himself King here. Obviously, since his wife would not grant him a crown, he thought to take mine. Rumours came to us that he was considering a Spanish-backed invasion of the Scilly Isles off Cornwall, and there were further indications that Margaret Lennox had tried to aid him in escaping to Flanders, from where he could rouse support from Phillip of Spain. Margaret immediately lost all her privileges in the Tower, and everything entering and leaving her apartments were searched. Mary got wind of Darnley's plotting and questioned him, but he denied everything. His wife did not believe him, and had no wish to see him voyage out to wreak destruction elsewhere, or bring war upon her country. As I tightened security about Margaret, my cousin did the same about Darnley.

But no matter what dilemmas there were to come for my cousin, I was resolved to show her my support. I rejoiced publicly about Prince James and ordered a golden font to be made as a gift for the baptism, but I was right to think that Mary's delivery would only bring trouble to my gate. Within days a petition arrived, begging me to marry and produce an heir. I was thirty-three now, a mature age for a woman. If once, ten years ago, I had thought and pondered on marriage and children, I believed now it was impossible. I did not believe I had the capacity to bring forth hale children from my body, and to try and fail would only expose me to the same humiliation my sister had suffered.

"My physician, Huick, has told me that childbirth would be fatal, or at the least would bring harm to the present delicate state of my body as to put England in danger," I informed my lords, grateful for this fresh excuse. They could hardly dispute it for they could all see how wan and thin I was.

Poor Huick was accused of having scared me off marriage, and many of my Council wanted him dismissed, but I refused to send him away. He had only spoken the truth as he had seen it, after all.

The magnificent font I had ordered was sent to Mary with Killigrew for the baptism of her child. The Earl of Bedford was also sent with reassurances for Mary that I would not do anything prejudicial to her right to be named heir of England. As time passed, I no longer felt ill as I thought about this babe, this new contender for my throne. In truth, just as I considered Mary to be my true heir, so this son of hers was too. I felt, in some ways, as though this boy was *my* child...

A son of the Tudor line forged from royal blood. It mattered not who his father was, as long as Darnley was kept from exerting power over the child. James Stuart, Prince of Scotland, became my hope for the future. If a male heir was what was wanted, then there was a legitimate, royal one now living and breathing in the world. I would have always preferred Mary's child to that of Katherine.

That summer, I left for progress with a heart which felt both lightened and strange. James of Scotland was often on my mind. I could not help but feel as though fate had shown me a strand of the future, and one which could satisfy all the wants of my people, and me.

Chapter Seventy-Six

Woodstock Palace
Summer 1566

We travelled through England that summer in high spirits. Through Northamptonshire we went, staying at Stamford. We were due to spend a night with Cecil, but were forced to seek shelter elsewhere because his daughter had come down with smallpox. Remembering my brush with the terrible sickness and what it had done to poor Mary Sidney, I sent my doctors to help Cecil, and was relieved to hear that his daughter was swiftly on the mend, and had suffered only slight scarring. From there, we moved on to Oxfordshire. We were to stay at Woodstock.

As I rode up towards that old palace, I stopped my horse on the road. Dust flew up, circling in the air. A thousand memories came flooding back to haunt me. Here, I had been a prisoner. Here my sister had kept me locked away after she released me from the Tower. Here had Parry come, and set himself up in the local inn, making Bedingfield, my gaoler, more nervous every day by sending me messengers and keeping me in contact with the world.

"Do you remember how cold the gatehouse was, Blanche, when we lived in it?" I asked.

She shivered even to recall those days. "And how small it was, Majesty!" she said. "Why, I could scarce turn about without hitting my elbow on a wall!"

"Why were you housed in the gatehouse?" Robin asked, drawing his horse close to mine.

"The palace was then in a sorry state," I said, pointing at the new repairs. I was not overly fond of Woodstock, since it had been my prison, but I had ordered some work so it did not crumble to the ground. "When I came here, as a prisoner, the roof leaked and the walls were crumbling. Bedingfield was terrified to keep me here. Parry and others had come to meet me when we left London, and they tailed us all the way here. Bedingfield could not send them away, for he knew he had not the skill to care for my financial affairs, and there were only three locks in the whole house that worked. Two of them in the gatehouse." I chuckled. "That is why he kept us there." I pointed to the old, small gatehouse. "But locks meant nothing to Parry. Even had there been a thousand, he would have found ways to reach me."

I paused, feeling sadness creep over me. "Parry kept me a part of the world, then," I said softly. "He was my eyes, he was my ears. There was nothing that went on I did not hear of, nothing of import which was kept from me, despite my sister's best efforts." I smiled sadly. "How I wish that good man was still here. I have much cause to despise Death for stealing him, and so many others, from me." Robin was a little quiet as we entered the courtyard. He seemed lost in thought.

"Will you come to your rooms to wash, my lady?" Blanche asked as we dismounted.

"I will be there shortly, Blanche, you and the others go ahead." I looked at Robin. "Would you come with me, to see my old prison, Robin?"

"If you wish me to," he replied. His face was gentle, thoughts I could not read swimming in his mind. I put my hand into his and nodded to my guardsmen to follow me.

"I do wish you to," I said as we walked to the gatehouse. "There is something I would show you."

We climbed the old, creaking stairs. As we passed through each small room, and there were only four, I told Robin of the days, nights, weeks and months I had been imprisoned here. Of how Parry and I had driven Bedingfield mad with suspicion; how Parry had got his men to steal Bedingfield's diary from his room so I could read it. "Bedingfield called me *this great lady*," I said, affecting a pompous tone and making Robin laugh. "And he believed I was the Devil in a damask gown." I stopped, looking about the chamber where I had spent most of my days. "I felt cut off here, Robin. I felt as though the world might forget me. Parry made me believe this was not the truth. He kept me a part of the world. I can never thank him for all he did for me."

"Did you not have Blanche and Kat, too, though?" Robin asked, gazing with disapproval at the fireplace which was full of mouldy leaves. "They must have been of comfort to you?"

Kat's name struck a dart into my belly. I shook my head. "Kat was not with me here," I said. "One of the few places, perhaps, left to me where there are no memories of her to haunt me. She was under house arrest with her kin. My sister did not want her near me for she believed Kat was an ill influence." I sighed, tracing a hand over one of the broken shutters. "And yet, perhaps here I feel there is a link, too, to the past... to Kat. When I was here, without her, I missed her so much. And I am here again, and I miss her now. Where then, I knew she was safe and alive, now I know she is lost to me."

I swallowed hard and glanced out of the window. My eyes filled with tears. My God, how I missed her! I looked up as I felt a hand near my face. I blinked, and Robin took a tear from my cheek. Lifting it to his lips, he kissed it. He reached out and stroked my face. "You grieve for her still, do you not?" he asked gently.

"I don't believe I will ever stop grieving for her," I confessed. "There was a part of me which died in that room with her, Robin. She was as my own mother, and I knew her better than any soul. There is none who could ever take her place."

Even as the words left my mouth, I feared this would bring that stranger back; that hearing me speak of my love for another would make him react with jealousy and selfishness. But it did not. He put his arm about my shoulder and drew me to him. "I have had much cause of late," he said. "To consider my actions over these years that have passed since Amy died." He heaved a sigh. "And to think ill of them in so many ways... I know that you lied to me, Elizabeth. You told me there was hope we might marry, but you did not believe it. You were lying to me, were you not?"

I swallowed. "I could not bear to lose you," I said quietly. "I thought that if I told you the truth, then you would find another to love, that you would forget me."

He turned me to face him. "There could never be another for me," he said. "You are all I have wanted, for so long now, that it sometimes feels as though you are a part of my own self."

"I never meant to hurt you," I said. "But if we were to marry, Robin, it would confirm to all our enemies that you killed Amy, and I helped you do so. I could never place you in such danger. And yet, I was too selfish to let you go."

"Where would I go?" he asked, and smiled. "My place is with you."

I put my hands over his, on my shoulders, savouring their warmth. "I cannot do without you, Robin," I whispered. "When you left court, when you were with others... I lost all the fire I had left, all the courage left within me."

"I felt the same," he said. "I did not eat, I could not sleep. I was lost, Elizabeth, alone in a barren and empty world."

"And I the same," I murmured.

"I have not been a good friend to you, these years past," he said. "And whilst I know that some measure of the fault was yours too, I did you much ill. I think I have begun to understand what you meant when you said I was not being a true friend. At the time, I could only see that you were putting obstacles in the way of us marrying. I thought you were afraid, or at times, that you no longer loved me. And then I would hope anew, and lose that hope again..." He shook his head. "But I should have been a better friend. That will not happen again. I love you too much to see you in such pain. And if I can never replace the likes of Thomas Parry, or Kat Ashley, I can at least be at your side, when you have need of me." He paused. "When Kat died... I was jealous, Elizabeth. It is hard for me to admit now. It sounds so petty, so stupid, but seeing you then... seeing how much you loved her, fearing you loved me no more... I was jealous. I wanted to strike out at you, and so I did."

I choked on my tears. "You had no need to be envious of Kat, Robin. You have no need to try to take their place," I said. "I loved Kat. I will never stop missing her, but there will never be another who I love, as I love you."

"Then let that be enough for me," he said. For a moment, I heard his words as a ghostly echo of Kat's. *That must be enough for anyone*, she had said.

"So you give up, my lord, in trying to force me to marry you?" I smiled through my tears.

"I will never give up trying to convince you to be my wife, Elizabeth," he said. "But I will wait. If you wish to marry me, then I am yours. If you never do, I will satisfy my heart's jealousy and pleading by reminding it of all you have said this day. I love you, and I know I am loved by you. I will try to make peace with that, whatever may come."

I nodded. Too overcome to find words to speak, for I believed him. There was a naked honesty in his words.

Robin had never been good at lying, and I knew he was now, finally, telling the truth... Just as I was.

"Now," he said, his voice catching. "What was it you wanted me to see?"

I squeezed his hands and he released me. I led him to the window and pointed at the broken shutter where, as a captive princess, I had scribbled a poem, and then at the window where I had etched it into the pane with a diamond. "Much suspected of me, nothing proved can be," he read and turned to me with a grin. "Typically Elizabeth."

"In what way, Robin?" I asked.

"Saying much yet revealing nothing." He chuckled as I swiped a hand at him. "It is naught but the truth, my lady!" he protested, pointing at the poem. "See? Nothing proved can be? This is no clear statement of innocence. It is a message of *defiance*. It is not a protestation of blamelessness; it is a taunt."

"See it however you wish, Robin," I said, grinning mischievously and turning for the door. He ran to my side.

"Come now," he protested, "you must tell me the truth. Were you involved with Wyatt and the other rebels?"

"You seem to have made up your mind to believe I was," I said evasively. "And so what can be done to protest otherwise?"

We walked to the palace with Robin capering at my side, trying to get me to reveal my secrets. I chuckled at him. I had not actually been much involved with Wyatt, of course, but this new game we were playing was so much more enjoyable than all the other, so much more painful ones, that I did not want to give it up.

It was a merry night. We danced in the great hall, and feasted with the court. My feet were as light as my heart. We had found honesty, at last, and after so many years. Robin and I had emerged from a terrible darkness. We had been lost in the fog, and had found each other. I hoped, hoped with all my soul, this was indeed the truth.

Chapter Seventy-Seven

Oxford
Summer 1566

We left Woodstock and made for Oxford. I rode in a silver litter draped with the Tudor colours of green and white as we went to meet the dons. The whole city turned out to meet us. The cries of *"God Save the Queen!"* and *"Bless our Bess!"* were thunderous. There were welcome speeches, in Greek and Latin, which I responded to in those same ancient languages, much to the delight of the scholars, and we undertook a packed schedule, visiting all the colleges. I delighted in it for seeing England's universities so full of eager minds was a great joy.

We went to talks, lectures and debates held by the students, scholars and masters. Then there were plays and lighter entertainments. I was enjoying one piece in particular when a part of the temporary stage collapsed, injuring several people and killing three. I sent my doctors to aid them. Despite the terrible accident, the organisers wanted to go ahead with the rest of the performance, but I had them postpone until the next day. Their eagerness to please me was clear, but I had no wish for more people to die or become injured, simply for my pleasure. I sent bags of coin to those who suffered injury and to the families who had lost loved ones, and asked Robin to help with repairs. It was a sad event in an otherwise lovely visit.

We visited St John's College, where Robin was Chancellor, and Master Edmund Campion gave a talk where he told me "there is a God who serves Your Majesty, in all you do, in all you advise."

I turned to Robin. "He means you, my lord," I whispered. Robin was barely able to keep a straight face. Campion was less pleased with me.

On the last public event of the visit, I gave a speech where I talked of the glories of learning and education. "It is my great wish that learning should prosper in my realm," I said in Latin. "For there is no greater grace that the accumulation of knowledge and the pursuit of wisdom. I see you here, gentlemen, and my heart is warmed to know you do God's work. If I have one sliver of advice, it would be to make the most of every moment you have here; immerse yourselves in learning, drown in books, glory in the grace you have been offered and never forget, that no matter how old, how accomplished, or how wise we believe ourselves to be, we are always students, we are always scholars. The wisest amongst you will never sorrow for this state; for to be a scholar, to be a student, means you are always open to wisdom. Seek the truth. Embrace your role, and be glad of it. Keep your minds, your ears and eyes ever open. God will give you more and more to learn, for that is His gift to us, and one that should never be set aside."

The hall erupted into cheering. Even the stoical, usually calm dons and masters threw their hats into the air. As we left the hall, many of them gathered about us, trying to force their ways through the crowds to kiss the train of my gown, or shout their blessings. When we left Oxford, the scholars and officials of the colleges ran beside my litter for two miles, to give me a grand send-off.

"These wonderful, masterful, silly men," I laughed as I leaned out of my litter watching them. Seeing my face appear, many of them redoubled their efforts, panting and puffing, but never giving up the chase.

"Fools for love, Majesty," said Robin from his horse which rode beside my litter. "You made quite an impression."

"As they did on me," I noted. "Had I not been intended for the throne, I would have wished myself a man, so I could go to one of these great universities, and lose myself in the pursuit of knowledge."

"I am sure, although they do not admit women, a concession would have been made for you, Majesty," Robin said.

"Even had it not, Rob, I would have shaved my head, bound my breasts and donned britches and a tunic to possess such a life as they have."

*

We were supposed to visit Robin's new seat of Kenilworth Castle next, but news of this intended visit sparked off fresh rumour I was to marry him, making me pause to think better of it. I had only just reconciled with Robin, I did not want him tempted into becoming that other man I hated so. But when he heard I was thinking of bypassing his house, he was downcast. "I have made so many improvements, Majesty," he said. "I wanted to show them to you."

I gazed at him with wary eyes, but I allowed the visit. Robin's castle was still undergoing a great deal of work, but the sections which were habitable were glorious. I was housed in a set of apartments which were supposed to be Robin's. He took me to see the work going on to transform other parts of the castle into permanent royal rooms. "These will be yours, Majesty," he said as he showed me his plans. "Held for you, and only for you, so you will always have somewhere to stay in my house." He gazed about him with a critical eye. "I just wish they were ready now."

"The chambers you have given me are more then adequate, my *Eyes*," I said. "And Cecil is delighted with his. Could you have stuffed any more maps in his rooms? I believe we will not see him for days, for he will be lost in his imagination, traversing the hills of Africa, or plodding through the forests of China!"

Robin smiled slowly, a naughty expression emerging on his face. "You did it on purpose!" I exclaimed, laughing. "Robin, you cunning imp! You gave Cecil all those maps to keep him occupied!"

"Whenever you and your Secretary come here, Majesty, you may be assured that state business will be set to one side so you can enjoy yourself. Cecil will be happy, lost in his maps, and you and I can take to the parks."

"Sly sprite!" I batted him with my fan, feeling more pleased than I could say.

*

As we were travelling back to London, Thomas Dannett caught up with our party, with news from Vienna and the Archduke. Ambassador Dannett was at a loss to know what to do about the Hapsburg negotiations, which had reached an impasse. The Archduke would not change his religion and he had no wish to come to England if I would not pay for his stay. Dannett also said there were many rumours that my reluctance to marry was because I loved Robin.

"This is not the case, ambassador," I said to Dannett. "No other of my court is as addicted to this match as the Earl of Leicester is. He solicits me often to take the match. The problems you have described are between the Archduke and me alone. I have said I will have him come to England, so we may finally meet, but for a lady to have to *pay* a man to come a-wooing her…? Surely he can see what a grievous insult this would be? And the terms on religion are not my concerns, but those of my men… If the Archduke will make no concessions to my requests, then we are indeed stuck."

Seeing Norfolk and Sussex were disgruntled, I beckoned Sussex forward. "Master Dannett, when you return to Vienna, tell the Emperor that Lord Sussex will be close on your heel. I will invest the Emperor with the Order of the

Garter, our most prestigious English knighthood, and my lord Sussex will be my envoy to grant him this honour. Let it be seen, then, by the Emperor and by all others, that I only wish to bring honour to his country and to the Archduke. I would ask he takes this honour, sees the friendship in my heart, and may come to reconsider his thoughts on the match."

This mollified Norfolk and Sussex, but did nothing to convince Cecil I was at all serious. "Your demands about the 'dowry' of the Archduke are upsetting the Emperor, Majesty," Cecil informed me. "He says it is outlandish for you to expect the Archduke to provide a dowry, as though he were the bride and you the groom."

"*I* am the greater prince, Cecil," I said to him. "Am I not? I am a queen. The Archduke is not a king, nor emperor. If he wishes to be raised up in title, by marriage to me, then he must play the part of the female here, and I the male."

"The Emperor will never understand that, Majesty." Cecil looked faintly amused at my reasoning, but he was not about to dispute it. England was ever in need of money. If I decided to ever marry, *I* was not about to hand a dowry over to a husband and impoverish England. England was a great prize, of strategic importance. Any man who wanted to become king consort would have to pay for the honour.

"Well he will just have to change the manner of his thinking, won't he, Cecil? The way I see it, the Archduke would be gaining a great deal from such a marriage, and I see no reason he should not think that worth an investment."

"I will… speak to Dannett on how to explain your reasoning to the Emperor," Cecil said, frowning at the paper.

"Tell him to remind the Emperor that I am not only a queen, Cecil, but a prince. I am the only Prince of England. The Archduke will be my consort. I am the King, and he the Queen."

"I will attempt to find words to express such ideas, Majesty."

Chapter Seventy-Eight

Whitehall Palace
Autumn 1566

"Money is surely the greatest curse," I muttered to myself. "For the more one has, the more one needs." I had to summon Parliament into session that autumn, for lack of funds. I had no wish to call them. I knew that the Houses would only lecture me on the succession and I was so very tired of hearing about my own death! Could they not talk of some other matter for just a while before nailing me in my coffin?

Pamphlets had circulated recently, anonymously written, but clearly penned by those who supported Katherine Grey and her sister. There were supporters for Mary of Scots as well, but they were fewer, and many were reluctant to speak out lest they be accused of having Catholic sympathies. Marriage and the succession; two ghosts ever set on haunting my steps. I needed money, and so I had to call Parliament to session, but I knew, far ahead of time, this would bring divisive talk. True to my suspicions, Cecil informed me he had information that both Houses intended to petition me to marry and settle the succession. Hoping to lay this to rest before it came to debate, I sent word to Parliament, saying *"by the word of a prince, I will marry,"* but for the present *"the perils to my own life are such that I cannot suffer to hear of it."* I sent them the findings of my doctor, Huick, who believed that to risk pregnancy was to risk my life.

Both Houses seemed not to care for the opinions of my doctors, however, and pressed ahead. The Commons refused to sanction any release of funds until the matter was discussed and settled. This angered me, for I had already said I would marry, when I was able to. The fact that I never intended to be able to did not curtail my wrath. My Parliament should take the word of their prince and be satisfied with it!

"If you were to simply marry, Majesty," de Silva said as I raged. "Then all of this aggravation would be set aside."

"Have you turned against me, too, de Silva?" I asked and then tossed my head. "In any case, I have decided to write to the Emperor this week and agree to the match with Charles of Austria."

"I see," he said with a grin. "And will this letter be a real one, Majesty, or one which disappears with the coming of the dawn?" I did not answer, but I did chuckle. De Silva knew me too well to believe me. I could only hope my men did not know me as well as him.

A gathering of representatives from the House of Lords came to press the issue. I had not wanted them near me, but Robin urged me to listen to them, at the very least.

"The Lords should not be supporting the Commons in this insubordinate behaviour!" I exclaimed to the lords when they had put forth their case. "The Commons would never have been so dissident in the time of my father. They take advantage of my natural generosity, my lords, and you are helping them to rise in a revolt of words against me!" Many voices broke out in protest, but I held up a firm hand. "You, as lords of England, may do as you will in your lives, my lords, within the sanctions of law, and I will therefore do the same. I am a lord, a prince, a queen and the monarch of this realm. I have given my word to embark upon the voyage of marriage when I am fit and able to, that should be enough for all the men of England, common and noble!"

The delegation of lords did not leave in a clement mood. Three days later, the Lords united formally with the Commons, apparently taking me at my word that they, as lords, could do as they wished. The nobles of the House of Lords returned to pressure me again, and I abused them for their defiance. "You would have me marry, when my doctors say that pregnancy would endanger my life?" I asked them. Many had the good sense to begin an intense study of their shoes as I spoke. "You value my life not at all, then, my lords? You cherish not your Queen?"

"We cherish our Queen, *and* wish to secure the future of England." Norfolk was the only one who dared speak up.

"You are little better than a traitor, Your Grace." His eyes widened with shock. "You and all who sit in there with you! For you plot now to end my life, by harrying me into a union which will steal my life... What is that if not high treason?"

Norfolk stared at me as though I were a stranger he had found under his bed, and his friend Pembroke leapt in to defend him. "Majesty, all your people want are assurances of a safe and stable future," he started. I did not let him finish.

"And you!" I snarled, turning on Pembroke. "Are little more than a swaggering soldier to talk to me in such a manner!" I spun about and attacked Robin. "And you here, too, my lord!" I exclaimed. "If all others in the world abandoned me, I would have thought that you would never have done so! This petition, coming at such a time when I have been unwell, when all my doctors say that to risk marriage risks too my own death... and you would still force me to the wedding bed! Mean I so little to you, then, that you would risk my life for that of a babe? Is your Queen so unimportant to you that you care not for her own life?"

To be entirely fair to Robin, I do not think he had wanted to be a part of this party of protest. No doubt pressured to attend by the other lords, he had actually been standing at the edge of the crowd, therefore fulfilling any promise made to them, but had not been a part of badgering me to submit to the demands of my Parliament.

"I would die at your feet," Robin swore, looking wounded.

"What has *that* to do with the matter?" I retorted, scowling at him. I lashed out at Northampton who looked ready to open his mouth. "And before *you* come, my lord, mincing words about marriage," I spat. "You had better talk of the arguments which got you your scandalous divorce, my lord, aye, and a new wife into the bargain!" Glaring at all of them, I stalked from the chamber. "Bring de Silva to me," I shouted to Mary Radcliffe as I strode out into the garden. "For if I wish for a friend in this country, it seems I must turn to a Spaniard rather than to the men of England!"

They all heard me, of course they did. I had meant for them to hear me. De Silva found me sitting by one of the ponds in the gardens, close to tears. "They would have me marry even if it meant I would die," I said before he had even bowed. "Even Robin, even my greatest friend, to whom I have granted so much wealth and favour, would rather have an heir to the throne than be secure in the knowledge of my well-being. I have suffered much ruin to my reputation, for the honours I have granted him, my lord, and what I get in return is ingratitude!"

Seeing Robin there, surrounded by those who would pressure me to marry, tore old wounds. I thought this was a sign Robin was drifting from me again. It was not, actually, the case. But I did not know that then.

De Silva sat at my side and took my hand in his. "Robin Dudley *loves* you, Majesty, as well as any man who ever loved a woman and was desperate to have her as his own."

"And to plant a child in my belly, a child who will murder me. Perhaps then they will have all they want, de Silva, for they will be rid of me and they will have a babe to mould into the King they really want."

"They want another like *you* to follow your reign, Highness," de Silva said. "They fear to be left uncertain about the future, and they know, Majesty, that like all other men and women, your time upon this earth is limited, just as theirs is. It is the uncertainty which gives them cause to fear. They love you well, and would have you as their Queen always."

I wiped my eyes. "I do not think what you say is true, my friend," I said. "But thank you for saying it, all the same. Sometimes a lie is prettier than the truth."

"Sometimes it is easier for us to believe the worst of others, and ourselves, even when that is not the truth," de Silva counselled. "Your men are loyal, and they love and admire you, Majesty. Look at the so recent troubles of Mary of Scots. Your men would never do such to you. They would die for you, if that was what was asked of them."

I did think on that. I had not actually considered that my cousin's men, so set on taking her power, had obviously not fallen under the spell she seemed to cast over so many. My men were truly more loyal than hers. Perhaps I had magic of my own, and could not see it. "I will see none of them when I return to the palace," I said to de Silva. "I want you to make sure they have gone, my friend, and know not to come unless called."

"Including the Earl of Leicester?"

"*Most* especially the Earl."

*

I had Robin and Pembroke barred from the Presence Chamber and when the Commons refused to see to any other business until I had answered on their requests, I was enraged. "What do the devils want of me, de Silva?" I cried.

"Do not give in, Majesty," he advised. "To do so would be an affront to your dignity. The House of Lords is one thing, the

Commons quite another. It is not fit for the Commons to make demands of you. You have told them you are not hale enough to risk a child of your body, to this, they must accede."

I allowed them to bring a delegation of thirty members of each House to me, and stood before them quivering with indignation. I did not allow the Speaker of either House to attend. They were going to listen to me. I went over all the old arguments against naming a successor, and impressed upon them the issue of my frail health, and then I continued, admonishing the Lords who had supported the Commons against me.

"Was I not born in this realm?" I cried. "Were not my parents? Is not my kingdom here? Whom have I oppressed? Whom have I enriched to others' harm? How have I governed since my reign began? I will not be tried by envy itself. I need not use many words, for my deeds do try me. I have sent word that I will marry, and I will never break the word of a prince said in a public place, for my honour's sake. And therefore I say again, I will marry as soon as I may do conveniently, without risk to my own health and life, and I hope too to have children, otherwise I would never marry."

I gazed around me and saw many had dropped their gaze at the mention of my life being in peril. Clearly some Lords and members had been ushered here against their better judgement. There was much uncomfortable muttering, too, for supporting the Commons in outright defiance of me, their Queen, was not something to be taken lightly. If the Commons could defy their Queen, what was to stop the common man defying their noble masters?

"And on the matter of the succession, my lords, I will tell you that none of you have been the second person in the realm as I have, or tasted of the practices against my sister when she was alive. I would to God Queen Mary were alive again so that you could think yourselves fortunate to have me!

There are some in the Commons now who, in my sister's reign, tried to involve me in their conspiracies. Were it not for my honour, their knavery *would* be known."

More eyes refused to meet mine. All of those who had conspired against me when I was a princess knew how fortunate they were I had not moved against them with vindictiveness. I was seeking to remind them that they owed much to me, and should be grateful for my willingness to forgive their past sins.

I narrowed my eyes at them. "I would never place my successor in that same fragile position, and never risk England to the plots and plans of men who would seek to replace me with another before my natural death, acting solely on the whims and feelings of their secret desires. The issue of the succession is one fraught with peril for my realm, and not for the *uncertainty* which you all so often speak of, but in naming one, in raising up one person, who could then be used against me and against England, as a figurehead, a banner, to call men to war against me and the peace of our beloved country. Therein lies the greatest peril and uncertainty for my realm and my beloved people. The succession is a matter for me to decide, not you. I find it monstrous that the feet should try to direct the head in this country! *I* shall be the one to resolve the succession, and I will do so in good time, and in a manner that will not imperil me *or* the people of England, who are my first and greatest care.

I turned a steely eye on the men about me, watching their faces fall, watching their downcast eyes. They had dared to attempt to treat me as though I were their subject, and they my masters. Such a thing would never have occurred in my father's time, and I was not about to let them get away with it.

"As for my own part," I went on. "I care not for death, for all men are mortal, and though I be a woman, yet I have as good a courage, answerable to my place, as ever my father had. I am your anointed Queen. I will never be by violence constrained to do anything. I thank God I am endued with such qualities that if I were ever turned out of the realm in my petticoat, I were able to live in any place in Christendom."

They left me in silence. The Lords were admonished, but the Commons were not. Three days later and there were calls for a further petition. I sent Francis Knollys to the House, with a statement which declared I had already promised to marry at a time convenient and safe for me, and they were to therefore desist from their suit. It was not received with humility or grace. Protesting this was an infringement on their liberties, the Commons refused to talk on the subject of the money I required until I was more obliging in the matter of matrimony. The dispute about the succession was sliding dangerously into the realm of a war between the privileges of a sovereign and her Parliament; a battle I had no wish to fight. I sent word allowing them to talk about the succession and my marriage. The fools were so happy at this sign of appeasement that they straight away debated on the money I required and issued it!

Not that I wanted them to... but did they never learn?

I dissolved Parliament some time later, giving them some last words to chew upon. "Beware, however, how you prove your prince's patience, as you have tested mine! Let this, my discipline, stand you in stead of sorer strokes, and let my comfort pluck up your dismayed spirits. A more loving prince towards you, you shall never have."

I was overjoyed to have won, and to have the money I needed. Cecil was less pleased. "There is no answer on the succession, no answer on marriage, and all there is, is bewilderment, as ever, Majesty," he said.

"It is not bewildering to me, Cecil," I told him. "I am your Queen, here and now. The future is yet to be seen, and is always uncertain. Be content to live in the present and to know yourself fortunate to have a Queen who knows what is best for her people, and for her country."

Chapter Seventy-Nine

Hampton Court
Autumn - Winter 1566

Although they had attempted reconciliation at the end of the summer, as autumn arrived, Mary and Darnley were back to knowing only misery in their marriage.

"Perhaps they are trapped together indoors more, *Spirit*," I said as I put the missive from Randolph on the table. "The summer gave them time to be outdoors, to feel space about them. Being forced inside due to the weather, and in close confinement with each other, they were bound to discover anew all the irritating habits they hated in each other before. Who would marry, and know such a fate?"

"Majesty, many who are married *are* happy in the companionship of another and all the comforts it brings."

"All you speak of are not royal, Cecil. I have come to think that royalty never breeds a happy marriage. There are too many factors set to bring all to ruin. I saw as much with my father. Although he would have said he only had two wives, Jane Seymour and Katherine Parr, the others he left in the wake of his destruction would likely agree with me, rather than you."

"Randolph says Darnley has announced he will leave Mary and live abroad," Cecil continued, ignoring me. He took up a ring of dried apple from the platter before him and chewed thoughtfully on it.

"The lords will not let him leave, even if my cousin wished to face the mingled shame and relief of being released from his odious presence," I replied. "Darnley will make mischief for Scotland abroad. They will want to keep an eye on him."

"There are rumours that he physically pushed the Queen at a public assembly as they argued," Cecil went on. "And that their battles in private have ended with him striking her."

"For my cousin's sake, I hope such is not true." I could believe it of Darnley though. He was just the type of vindictive, petty, little creature to resort to hitting his wife if he thought it might help him master her. "He insults the sanctity of the throne, as well as her, if this is true."

"As long as she refuses to crown him, he will continue to abuse her," Cecil said. "And their fights are increasing with the passage of time."

"My cousin is right not to set a crown on that boy's head," I replied. "She shows more wisdom now than she did in agreeing to marry him."

Darnley, however, had no wisdom, none at all. Arriving at Holyrood, and demanding that Mary dismiss her councillors before he would deign to enter, he was dragged inside by Mary's guards. Mary spent some time attempting to make him see that he was alienating everyone with his ill behaviour, but Darnley would not listen. With continued gossip that he meant to go to France and set up a court there, Mary's Council wrote to Catherine de Medici, telling her Darnley was suffering from temporary insanity, and asking her to offer no French support to his wild plans.

Mary was due to go on progress, but Darnley refused to go with her. He was, by now, attempting to gain support from Catholic rulers in France and Spain by saying he would have the Mass restored in Scotland. Mary had distanced herself from the resurrection of the Catholic faith ever since the attack on Rizzio, and knew Darnley was putting her in danger from nobles who would not welcome such an idea. My cousin was becoming downcast and feeble in health as her husband brought nothing but strife to her court.

After going to see her general, Bothwell, when he was attacked and almost slain when a rival clan raided his lands, Mary was visiting Jedburgh when she became perilously ill. She complained of a pain in the spleen, and vomited blood. Her body fell to convulsions, and she lost her power of sight. At one point, as she lay unconscious and barely breathing, her men believed she was dead. Her doctor, Charles Nau, saved her life, bandaging her limbs, forcing her to drink wine and administering an enema. Mary vomited and released noxious substances from her bowels, but within three hours she had her sight back. Darnley did not visit his wife as she lay close to death, but stayed away, sulking.

Mary recovered and returned to Edinburgh, but her horse threw her into a bog on the way, and when she arrived at the palace she was in the first stages of a virulent fever. This time Darnley visited her, but he took no pains to comfort her. He took her sickness as an opportunity to berate her, and demanded again to be named King. Weakened by illness, and further depressed by her husband, Mary was brought low, so low she said to many she wished for Death to come, to release her from her pains. Believing she was dying, she said to Randolph that she wished me to become the protector of her child if she died. Clearly not trusting her husband, who had barely seen the boy, to care for his interests, she turned to me.

"Ask the Queen, my good sister, to receive his life into her hands as though he were her own child," Mary said to my ambassador. "And if my good sister never embarks on marriage, let my son be her son, and her heir, in Scotland and in England."

When I received this letter, I admit I was as touched as I was surprised. Whatever the problems over the years between Mary and me, she knew that I respected the right of royal blood and dynastic inheritance. Mary was not offering me the regency of Scotland. She was not offering that I take

Scotland as mine in the event of her death. She was asking me to protect her son and his rights. It was the request of a loving mother, from one woman to another.

That she would offer her child to me, that she would trust me to protect him, was not something I took lightly. I knew well enough that what she was doing was open to much interpretation, for to be the child's 'protector' could be taken many ways, but still, it showed that she considered me a worthy guardian. It was clever really, for she was ensuring her child's future by flattering me. But I believed there was also a real desire within my cousin for me to start looking on her child, as my child. I wrote to her, agreeing that in the event of her death, I would become her son's guardian. *"All that you have decided on here, I promise to bring to pass,"* I wrote. *"And know that I am touched beyond measure that you would put such trust and love in me. I will not fail you, my good sister, nor our son."*

I sent word that in light of her new trust in me, I would respond in kind. Still rather annoyed at my Parliament's interference and defiance, I decided to conduct these negotiations alone. I wrote to Mary saying I would no longer expect her to ratify the Treaty of Edinburgh. We would instead negotiate a new treaty, one of perpetual amity and peace. I also wrote I was willing to acknowledge her as my heir, as long as I did not marry and have children of my own. We would sign a treaty which demonstrated we were both lawfully ruling Queens, and neither would do harm to the other. This would remove any possibility of either invading or usurping the other's throne. *"The manner of proceeding is the way to avoid all jealousies and difficulties betwixt us,"* I wrote.

It was a guarantee of my safety, and an assurance of her future and her son's. We would still encounter difficulties, I knew, one being my father's will, which ruled Mary out of the succession and was likely to be used by others to thwart this plan, but I was confident of success. I was as close as ever I had been to naming an heir. And more than that, I was hopeful for the future.

My cousin asked me to be her son's godmother, and I accepted. Mary postponed christening James until such a time when she could call all the dignitaries and officials she wanted to Scotland. But even as she prepared to celebrate her son's christening in style, there were rumours she was seeking to separate from his father. Being told that a divorce or annulment would endanger the legitimacy of her son, Mary's lords advised her in secret to arrest Darnley for treason, for his involvement in the attack on Rizzio. But Mary was reluctant to do so. Arresting her husband for treason just as foreign envoys and dignitaries were flooding into the Court of Scotland would be highly embarrassing.

The Earl of Bedford was sent to represent me at the christening, since I could not attend in person. He presented the golden font, carved with beautiful flowing leaves and cherub faces, and inlaid with gorgeous enamel. It was a little small, for which I told Bedford to make apology. *"I did not realise how well and fine my godson, the Prince, would have grown since I ordered it made!"* I wrote to Mary. The Queen sent back word that she minded not, for the font was a work of such beauty that all who came before it were struck dumb, dazzled by it, and she had every intention of using it in the ceremony. In addition to the great font, Bedford took promises to Mary. I told her that I would allow an inquiry into the will of my father, which had barred the Stewart line from the throne, and that I hoped this would show there was no cause for this clause to exist. Since there was disparity of opinion on whether my father had actually signed this will, given his fail state of health at the time of writing it, there was room to manoeuvre should I wish the clause to be rejected. Mary was delighted, and although she saw no need for the investigation into my father's will, seeing it as obsolete, she was overjoyed to hear of my support for her and her son.

Darnley did not attend the christening of his own son. He was not missed.

A few days after the ceremony, for the sake of peace, Mary pardoned the murderers of her friend, David Rizzio. All in Scotland seemed to indicate a time of peace was upon us, but as it turned out, it would not last for long.

Chapter Eighty

Whitehall Palace
January 1567

"They say the boy is sick with syphilis," I said to Robin as he lounged by the fire, drinking wine and devouring a plate of walnut comfits with great relish.

"I can affect little surprise at that news, Majesty, having seen the state of Darnley some mornings when he lived at your court… stumbling to his duties with the scent of drink and whores rising from his body."

I wrinkled my nose. "What a husband for my cousin to have been lumbered with!" I mourned. "I pity her, Robin, in honesty I do. I wish now there had been another method to use to stop my cousin marrying into Spain." I paused. "But at least she has her son. That thought gives me peace."

I stared off, watching my new chamberer, Mary Shelton, make her quiet way about the chamber, tidying as she went. Mistress Shelton was quite a mature lady to have entered my service, being close to fifty years old, but I had reasons for allowing her employment. One reason was that she was kin. Her mother, Anne Shelton, had been the sister of my grandfather, Thomas Boleyn, making her a cousin of my mother. But the motive that had prompted me to accept her above all others was that once she had served my mother, and if rumour was to be believed, had served her in many ways other than simple fetching, dressing and carrying.

When my mother had been in peril as my father's love for her waned, a woman who supported Imperial interests had become his lover. In response to this, my mother had gone to her loyal kinswoman and asked her to take her rival's place in his bed, promoting Boleyn interests in an effort to save her from harm. The lady had done as she was asked, and managed to bring about a temporary reconciliation between my ill-fated parents. Long ago, Kat had told me this, and I had retained an interest in Mary Shelton ever since. Although some, whose memories were confused after so many years, said that it was her sister, Margaret Shelton, who had been my father's mistress, it was not so. Mary had been the more beautiful of the two sisters and was a woman much admired for her intelligence; just the type of lady to attract my father's interests, and that of others. She had once been promised to the unfortunate Henry Norris, who had cut short their engagement by dying along with my mother, and had also attracted the poet, Thomas Wyatt, with whom she was a contributor to a book of poetry, riddle and verse which was still being copied, added to and read at court even to this day. Her background, and the fact that she had attended upon my poor mother in the last days of her life in the Tower of London, made Mary interesting to me. I had had no chance, as yet, to speak to her about the past, and was wavering in my mind as to whether to bring up the subject at all, but no matter if we spoke of the past, or of my mother or father, I was glad to have her there in my chambers.

Sometimes we need a reminder of the past about us. Sometimes we need to remember all that has gone before, and learn from it.

"You admire her, in many ways, do you not?" Robin asked, drawing my thoughts from the past back to the present. For a moment I thought he was speaking of Mistress Shelton, and turned to him with a confused face. But then I realised that Rob was not privy to my thoughts, and was speaking of Mary of Scots.

"I admit I do, Rob." I came to warm myself at the fire. Outside the wind was howling, fresh and wild, as it tossed sleet and rain through the winter skies. "Sometimes she is naïve and childlike, but often enough she has proved her strength and her courage. She has shown she can set aside her own wishes and act for the good of her country."

"As you have so often done," Robin noted. I looked at him to see if that old grimace of disappointment was on his face. It was not.

Lately, since our latest talk at Woodstock, Robin and I had entered a new stage in our friendship, and in our love. He had assured me that he had intended to play no part in the rebellion of the Commons and the Lords, and, when I looked back, I had to admit he had not been in the eager detachments of those assaulting me. Norfolk, in fact, had publicly admonished him for not taking a larger part, and Robin had retorted that he was first *my* servant, and his loyalties lay with me.

Truly, my friend was restored.

We understood each other now. Bound together, in our love for one another, we yet understood that we would ever be apart. He had become as my best friend, as a *Kat* at my side. We had found peace together, at last, and that was worth more to me than all the gems on my gowns, or coins in my coffers.

"Aye, Robin, I have put aside my own wants often for the good of England, and I believe Mary is capable of the same sacrifice. Has she not shown it when she married Darnley? I thought little of her at the time, but now I recognise that she understood before she married him that he was a fool. It did not take long for his mask to slip. She put aside her own feelings of disgust which were left when her illusions of love faded, and she married him for political gain. And now she has a son, and the future of Scotland, and perhaps England too, is secured in him. Were I to die this day, I would hope that my men would see the same. I would hope they would set aside their fears on her sex and her religion, and see her as I do."

"Would you make a proclamation of this?"

I shook my head. "I would trust her, if this treaty goes ahead. Although I admit the idea still fill me with dread, but there is a part of me that yearns to trust her."

I paused and smiled at him. "It is a most disturbing thing, Robin, to have the strands of your winding cloth gathering about you whilst you still live. To have all men think about your death, whilst you are alive. I never appreciated this until I came to the throne. I came to look on Katherine Grey, Mary Grey, on the Countess of Lennox and on Mary herself, with fear... because I knew that men would look to them as an alternative to me. And it is not far, from deliberating on the natural demise of a monarch, to considering plotting to end her life." I shook my head. "No, not so far at all. Is it any wonder, therefore, that I would have all men think on the present, rather than the future? That I would have them think on what I may do with my life, rather than deliberate about my death?"

I breathed in and gazed at the flames. "My sister felt the same about me; she became suspicious of me, dangerous towards me, for in me she could see her own death. How can anyone look into the gaping maw of mortality and not know terror? I am asked to name the one who will come after me. I am asked to look on my own death and fear it not. But how can anyone live, and live well, with Death at their elbow? And how can any love the one who is to follow them, when their future depends on your own demise?"

"I do not believe we are to lose you soon, Majesty," he grinned at me. "You look hale and bonny to me."

Taking hold of my skirts, I curtseyed playfully at the compliment, making him chortle. "I plan to be here for many years yet, my *Eyes*," I informed him. "And I have had enough of Death. If I had Him here, I would tell Him that He hath stolen enough of our happiness, and should leave for another court. He has grown greedy, and has eaten too much at this feast."

"Command Death, then," Robin said, setting his cup down and rising to kiss me on the cheek. "Only you could do so."

"I doubt such a spirit would listen to a mere Queen," I said, putting my hands on his arms. There was a gentle warmth and affection between us, without the feeling that anything more was required other than us just standing here, together, as close in our hearts as we were in our bodies.

"Perhaps Death will go to Scotland, on a winter progress," Robin said. "And remove Darnley from his poor wife."

"Then Death would serve a useful purpose, for once," I agreed.

I wondered, later on, if Death had been there, listening.

*

I was distracted from thinking on Mary that month as my cousin, Margaret, Lady Strange, came to me with a problem. Lately separated from her husband, who she described as boorish and cruel, she had run into financial problems. Her husband owned and controlled all of their wealth, and since divorce would be a problem, seeing as Margaret was a Catholic and a dispensation would have to be granted by the Pope, which would not find favour with me, she was left with no money and remained bound to a husband she despised.

"I will find a way to support you, cousin," I said, looking on her worried face. Margaret resembled my aunt, Mary Tudor, so strongly that to order her to stand beside a portrait of my long-dead aunt was like seeing double. Her beautiful brow was furrowed with worry, and she twisted her hands into each other as she stood before me. In truth, I felt most sorry for my kinswoman. She was a good servant, my official trainbearer for ceremonies and events. She had served me loyally, and had never attempted, as my more odious cousins often did, to rise above her station. Clearly mortified to have to come to me for help in such a personal matter, Margaret was relieved to hear that I intended to help her.

I entered into a financial agreement with the Stranges, allowing an income to Lord Strange and ordering that part of it was to be released to his wife. It had to be done this awkward way, since he was still her legal husband and master. Later that year, I presented Margaret with her own lodgings at court to further relieve her financial difficulties, and gave her permanent rights to be fed by my kitchens. I also paid her servant's wages. There were many who said that I was cruel and unfair to all my cousins, but it was not so. If I was treated with respect and due deference, then I was kind and magnanimous in return. It was the same attitude with which I approached all my courtiers and subjects; if they were fair with me, I was fair with them. At least most of the time…

And as I dealt with the unfortunate marital issues of one cousin, it seemed that another was doing all she could to heal the rift in her marriage.

Visiting her husband in Glasgow, Mary persuaded him to return to her side at court. Darnley was sick and weak, and his friends and family had deserted him. When she promised him he would live with her again when he was well, and that she wished to mend the hurt between them, Darnley was mollified. Bothwell was waiting for them at Edinburgh and took the royal couple to a house in the Kirk O'Field, which Darnley himself chose for his recovery. The Old Provost's Lodge stood on a small hill, and was surrounded by lovely gardens, although the air was reported to be unhealthy.

Mary was true to her word, sitting with her sick husband and tending to him with care which surprised many, seeing as she had so lately been set on separating from him. To all who saw the Queen, it seemed that she had set aside such ideas, and was determined to reconcile with him. Many praised this gentle forgiveness, but later, when people had cause to look back and remember this time, they would come to gaze with suspicion on the actions of their Queen, and wonder what truly lay in her heart towards her husband at that time.

Chapter Eighty-One

Greenwich Palace
February 1567

"Papists are becoming increasingly outspoken in the north of England," Pembroke noted as reports were read to the Council. "Religious matters are heading backwards there, rather than forwards."

"We will continue with our policy of gentle progress in matters of religion," I said, wondering if there would ever be a time when there were not stirrings of rebellion in matters of religion. "Slow and steady, my lords; that is the way of things in England."

"Priests are being harboured in many houses, Majesty, and the Catholic Mass is being said by them for rebellious subjects." Cecil's brow furrowed as he spoke. "William Allen is named as responsible for much of this discord."

Allen. A name I was hearing more and more these days. Although much good had come from my insistence on leniency towards Catholics in my realm, there were still divisions and troubles. The old faith had been sent to live underground, and as is the way of the creatures that live beneath us, it had found ways to survive. There were zealots who could not reconcile themselves to the idea of a Protestant state, or with the daughter of Anne Boleyn on the English throne, and they caused the most problems. There were, however, many who were willing to accept the public face of the English Church, who attended Mass publicly, and also kept Catholic priests in their houses to hear the Mass said. These moderates did not trouble me, and I was not about to set forth an order to ferret out every Catholic priest hiding in England... but the zealots were another matter.

Allen was one of them. A scholar and a doctor of Oxford University, Allen hailed from an ancient family of Catholic blood. He had resigned his post at St Mary's Hall seven years ago, when asked to take the Oath of Supremacy, and then left the country a year later, to head for Flanders where many Catholics had gone, unable to reconcile their faith to the new order in England.

In Flanders, Allen had continued his studies, but had also taken to writing tracts against my religious settlement. He had returned in secret to England only to apparently find himself reinvented as the saviour of the Catholic faith. Visiting friends, family and neighbours, Allen had done his best to create resistance. Cecil's spies had noted his activities as he travelled up and down the country, spreading discord. Although such actions were unlawful, I had instructed Cecil not to move on Allen, for I always believed that to make martyrs out of mere mortals was bad policy. I did not arrest him, as many of my forbears would have done. I let him travel, watched closely by Cecil.

Perhaps three years ago, feeling himself under surveillance, Allen had left for the Low Countries. There he had been ordained a Catholic priest, and taught at a Benedictine college in Malines. From there, Allen wrote many inflammatory papers which were smuggled into England. And now, his name was linked to many of those causing trouble in the north of England.

"We should have arrested him years ago," Cecil mourned. "He was only ever going to cause more trouble for us, Majesty."

"Send word to the Sheriff of Lancaster that he is to investigate and question any who are openly causing trouble in the north, Cecil," I said. "Particularly any who have been removed of their offices, and therefore have cause to think ill of us, but there will be no harsh measures taken against them. Let them know that they are seen by us in London, and let them have a chance to think better of their actions before they do more ill."

"Shall I put Allen on this list, Majesty?" asked Cecil.

"If he has not the wit to remain in the Low Countries," I replied. "But yes, add him to the list of those wanted for questioning. *That* one has had enough generosity from me."

My Council wanted me to be harder on Catholics in England. They wanted me to order arrests, to deal out fines and other punishments, but I resisted. They saw each problem that arose as an insurmountable stumbling block, to be triumphed over by shedding blood and stealing life. I did not think so bluntly. To my mind, the religious settlement *was* working. Just as we had had resistance at the beginning, it was only natural there would be more as time went on. But gradually we would wear them down. Eventually, people would see that there was much gentleness in the Protestant faith, and think better of it because of my generosity and lenience. If there was one thing I had learnt in my sister's reign, it was that to murder or hunt people in the name of religion only makes that which you are seeking to destroy all the stronger. People resist, they rise up; they multiply underground. What I wanted was to slowly ease the Catholic faith from my country, and to those who remained in its grip, I still offered a home in their own country, as long as they kept their practices secret, and concealed from public view.

But it was also true that leniency was getting harder to maintain. Each time there was a plot by fanatics, or an arrest made when someone preached against the Protestant faith, or was obvious in their attempts to hide a priest, my men grew fearful. There is nothing like fear to make men do foolish things.

"The Queen of Scotland sends word that she is ready to ratify the Treaty of Edinburgh." Cecil moved on, sensing that I had had enough of the talk of persecuting Catholics.

My eyebrows shot up. "After all this time... She wishes to go ahead with that treaty rather than the new one I proposed... Why?"

"She says that since the birth of her son, and your promise to act as his guardian, she has re-read the terms and decided they are acceptable," Cecil informed me. "The Queen appears to have had a complete change of heart and mind on the subject, Majesty."

"Children are indeed a blessing if they can so alter the perceptions of their parents!" I exclaimed, feeling merry. "And you see, Cecil, once more my cousin surprises us all. I would wager that other than me, there has never been a queen so surprising."

"She also writes she will accept a trial of the will of your father, King Henry VIII, as you suggest, Majesty," Cecil went on. "To ascertain her right to be named heir to England."

"Another surprise," I noted and smiled. "You see, Cecil, what friendship can bring between two monarchs?"

My cousin's talent for surprise, however, was about to take us all aback...

Just after two in the morning, on the 10th of February 1567, the Provost's Lodge in the garden of Kirk O'Field exploded.

Mary was at Holyrood Palace, far away from the blast, attending the wedding of two of her servants. The body of her husband was discovered as local people searched the grounds. Leaning against a tree, and sitting beside the body of his servant, Darnley was dead, but without a mark on his body to show how he had died. He had obviously escaped the explosion, for there were no burn or ash marks on his nightshirt, but he was still dead.

Many who searched the grounds that night believed this was an English plot to kill Mary and her husband. Why I would try to assassinate my cousin, at this time when we were so lately reconciled in sisterly affection, was beyond me. As talks of English plots died down, so discussion of others rose. Darnley had been murdered, that much was clear. The explosion, which had taken most of the house with it, seemed to have been put into place to cover this foul deed, and when the dust settled over the broken house the next morning, Scotland was on fire with talk of treason. There were many who had reason to hate Darnley enough to remove him, but none more so than his wife. From almost the first moment, my cousin was in peril from rumours which cast themselves into the skies above her, and crawled on their bellies below.

When I received word of Darnley's death, I was shocked, but I did not mourn. He had been a contemptible creature, a man of no worth. But I saw the danger inherent for my cousin. I also could not allow Darnley's murder to go un-noted by England. However much I had despised the fool, he had been an English subject; one of my people. His murder had to be investigated, and those responsible brought to justice. This was just as important for my cousin and her reputation as it was for the path of justice.

I could not help but remember the death of Amy Dudley on the day I received the news of Darnley's murder. In so many ways, Mary and I had lived lives that echoed one another's... not in all ways of course... but still, there were shared shadows of experiences. When Amy had died, the finger of suspicion had pointed at Robin and me, just as now it pointed at Mary and Bothwell. There were rumours that Bothwell wanted to marry the Queen. I knew not if this was true, at the time, but it brought memories of the terrible days after Amy's death back to me. I had chosen, in those dark days, to keep Robin in my favour, but to refuse to marry him, and I knew now I had chosen well. My cousin was faced with a situation only too similar. She had to do as I had. She needed to investigate the matter fully, otherwise she would experience the same horrors I had in feeling my own people turn against me, suspecting I was a party to unlawful murder.

I wrote to Mary. "*Madam,*" I wrote, *"my ears have been so astounded and my heart so frightened to hear of the horrible and abominable murder of your former husband, our mutual cousin, that I scarcely have spirit to write. Yet I cannot conceal that I grieve more for you than him. I should not do the office of a faithful cousin and friend if I did not urge you to preserve your honour, rather than look through your fingers at revenge on those who have done you that pleasure, as most people say. I exhort you, I counsel you, I beg you, to take this event so to heart that you will not fear to proceed even against your nearest. I write thus vehemently, not that I doubt, but for affection."*

I sent Lady Cecil to the Tower to tell Margaret Lennox that her son was dead. We had been told, erroneously, as it transpired, that the Count of Lennox had been killed along with his son. Margaret collapsed when she heard that both her son and husband were dead.

I felt genuine pity for Margaret. True, we had never been friends, but I could not help but feel for her. I, too, knew what it was to lose a person most precious. When we received word that Lennox had not been at Kirk O'Field when Darnley was slain, and had in fact been sent to Glasgow that night, I sent Cecil to the Tower to inform Margaret that we believed Lennox was alive. When he returned to me, it was in a sombre mood.

"I honestly believe you should release her from the Tower, Majesty," he said. "She has suffered an almost complete collapse. I do not believe she will be a danger to you."

I agreed. I had her removed from the Tower and taken to Sackville Place. She was still under house arrest, but I would not compound her misery by keeping her in the Tower. I permitted her visitors, and brought her son Charles to her to bring her comfort. It was not long before Margaret heard all that had occurred in Scotland, and decided that Mary was guilty of murder. Margaret wrote to me in blazing, grieving fury, demanding justice for her slain son. Lennox, when he was found, was no less hungry for vengeance, and was determined to stay in Scotland until he found the murder, or murders of his son.

I was not the only one urging Mary to move with all speed to discover the murderers. In France, Catherine de Medici said that Mary was fortunate to be rid of the fool, but also sent word that those responsible would need to be found and swiftly punished, or France would become her enemy. The murder of a consort, no matter how universally despised, was taken most seriously by all ruling houses. Mary ordered an inquiry, but there were immediate reports that statements had been extracted under torture, making all who heard them believe them less. Darnley's parents started to protest the Queen was not doing enough to investigate and suspected her involvement. A pamphlet, naming Bothwell as the chief conspirator, was published anonymously in Edinburgh, and many believed Lennox was behind it. By the end of March, everyone suspected my cousin of having murdered her husband, with the aid of Bothwell. My cousin was in grave peril, and yet she was moving like a snail to do anything about it.

Our spies in Scotland were quicker to investigate than the Queen was. Alarming reports arrived in Cecil's hands, all implicating Bothwell, and by association, Mary. Bothwell had been seen watching the Provost's Lodge after Mary had left, and one of his men had taken a large consignment of gunpowder the week before. Cecil's men believed the gunpowder had been hidden in the basement on the night of the murder, which also explained why Mary had cause to note that one of her men was 'begrimed'.

"All this only means that Bothwell was involved, Cecil, it does not mean my cousin was."

"Majesty... the Earl of Bothwell is Mary's right hand. He does all for her at court and she leans on him. There are rumours that they are lovers."

"Just as there were rumours about me and Robin, if you remember, Cecil. A rumour does not mean something is true." I paused. "There were many who believed ill of me, Cecil, when Amy Dudley died, and yet I had no hand in her death. Many people had cause to hate Darnley... not only Scottish nobles, but Catholic princes who did not want his lewd behaviour staining their names, and Protestant ones who would have viewed him as a threat. Even if Bothwell is involved, it does not mean my cousin is... And why, Cecil, if she were involved, would she call attention to the begrimed face of her servant that night? Surely, if Mary was party to all this, she would have known the reason for his dirty face, and would not have called attention to it."

"I admit, there is a possibility the Queen was not aware of what her men had planned," he said. "But there are others, Majesty, many others, who will not be so generous in their evaluation."

"As I am well aware, having lived the same events myself," I answered ruefully. "I have heard rumour too, Cecil, that the Douglas clan, Darnley's own kin, had a hand in this for they had good reason to despise the lad." I rolled my eyes. "If only Mary would act faster! I know she has been ill, but she needs to order a full investigation, and to act against those involved."

"If Bothwell was involved, Majesty, it may be impossible for her to act against him."

"Could it not be possible that the explosion was meant to target Mary, but she left and something went awry?" I asked. "Darnley could, himself, have plotted to take her life and make himself regent for their son."

"Then how did he end up half-naked and suffocated in the gardens?"

I breathed out sharply through my nose. "I know not, Cecil, but if all others have decided to abandon my cousin, I will not. I know well the pain of suspicion. I know what it costs. I will show my support for her. I will not allow mere suspicion and rumour to stain her name."

"And if she is found to be involved?"

I stared out of the window. "I pray to God that will never happen."

I sent word to Scotland that I supported Mary and believed in her innocence. "We assure you that whatsoever we can imagine meet for your honour and safety that shall lie within our power, we will perform... It shall well appear that you have a good neighbour, a dear sister and a faithful friend, and so you shall undoubtedly always find us to be towards you."

I was alone in my support of my cousin. Phillip of Spain, Catherine de Medici, even her brother-in-law King Charles, all expressed cold disapproval. I defied my Council, who wanted me to set aside Mary's right to be named my heir. I admit I also told Mary that we could not talk of the treaty of perpetual peace until this matter was resolved. But I added if she did right by her slain husband, then I would be in a better position to continue to support her.

Darnley was not given a state funeral. He was laid to rest quickly, during the night, a bare week after his death in a private ceremony without the trappings of a royal funeral. The strange hour and swiftness of the funeral helped Mary not at all for many decided she must have something to hide. Finally, Mary responded to the rumours and to Lennox's demands for justice and allowed Bothwell to be tried in a private court for the murder of her husband.

I rejoiced to hear this, but it was not the end of my cousin's troubles.

Chapter Eighty-Two

Greenwich Palace
Spring-Summer 1567

"She believes he can protect her against the factions that surround her," Cecil said as we looked over the latest reports from Scotland with amazement. "That is why she will not move against him."

In a travesty of a trial, Bothwell had been acquitted of the murder of Darnley. Within days, he and Mary had been seen walking and talking together as intimates. Her brother, Moray, had left court, refusing to become involved in this scandal. Lennox had sent me a letter comparing his son to an innocent lamb, and Mary to Judas. Clearly the Count of Lennox believed his daughter-in-law was guilty.

Mary was losing friends fast.

Pamphlets were circulating in Scotland and England, blaming Mary for Darnley's murder. Seeing her feeble efforts to bring the guilty to justice, her people were turning against her. Lewd images of a mermaid and a hare were distributed. The mermaid, a symbol of sexual abandon, was crowned and was clearly meant to be Mary. The figure also held a sea anemone in her hand, meant to represent female genitalia. The suggestion was that Mary was a marauding whore, bent on capturing men, and bewitching them with sex. The hare was the heraldic symbol of Bothwell's family, indicating the two were intimately involved.

"Bothwell is slowly taking control of Mary's household and military," Cecil said. "There are rumours he means to marry her, and become King."

"He is married already, to Jane Gordon. He cannot wed Mary."

"Marriages can be set aside, if there is enough to gain," said Cecil.

"My father would certainly agree." I tapped my fingers on the table. "She will not marry him, Cecil. I know it. She is not so foolish. Mary has no need to marry again when she can live as an independent queen and raise her son."

Cecil lifted his eyebrows, but I believed I was right. Over the next days, we had many ill reports of Bothwell: he had beaten a man in Mary's household and killed him by accident; after his trial he rode about challenging all who opposed him to duel; he held supper parties and entertainments, vastly inappropriate behaviour under the circumstances, trying to win men to him. Cecil's spies also discovered he had sounded his wife out about a divorce, and that he was trying to get other lords to sign a paper saying they would support him as Mary's next husband.

"He is after her," I said to Robin. "He will chase her, but he will not catch her. She cannot fail to see his rashness, can she?"

When Robin was silent, I glanced up to see him looking uncomfortable. "Do you compare yourself with Bothwell?" I asked.

"Perhaps," he said. "I can understand his desire to wed her, if he loves her."

"Cecil's men say he shows little attempt to woo her," I noted. "He woos her men but does not seek to pay court to Mary."

"Then I do not compare myself, for I wanted you and not your crown."

I slipped my hand into his. "I know, Robin."

I believed my cousin would resist Bothwell's attempts to gain her hand, and was confident in this. What I did not foresee, however, was what that man was willing to do in order to claim his crown. At the end of April, Mary kissed her ten-month-old son goodbye as she left for Linlithgow. She would never see James again.

On the ninth anniversary of her marriage to François, her party was intercepted on the road to Holyrood by Bothwell and hundreds of his men. Riding to her side as she was surrounded, Bothwell ripped her reins from her hands. Mary screamed to her servants to ride for Edinburgh and get help. They tried, but Bothwell's men were too many. He took her captive at Dunbar and surrounded her with his guards. He kept her under lock and key.

And then he raped her.

It was treason and it was sacrilege, but Bothwell knew it was a good method to make Mary marry him. There is a hideous belief that if a woman is raped then marrying her rapist will wipe the stain of that act from her abused honour. Because, as we all know, another, an equally repulsive myth exists that if a woman is raped then it must in some way be her fault. Mary was held at Dunbar for twelve days. Bothwell was only there some of the time. For the rest he was arranging his divorce from his wife. His wife filed for divorce on the grounds Bothwell was an adulterer. Something he admitted to keenly.

Mary and Bothwell appeared in Edinburgh together at the beginning of May. They rode into the city, and were surrounded by sullen, displeased masses. The same day, their banns of marriage were read to Mary's country. Mary stated she had never been held captive by Bothwell, nor raped, but only wanted to be joined to him for love.

This was the worst thing she could have said.

All suspicion that she and Bothwell had long been lovers and had murdered Darnley to remove him from their path was now confirmed. There were others who did not believe it, and knew their Queen had been forced into this match, and was now attempting to save what little there was of her reputation by marrying her attacker. They urged her to make this known, and abandon Bothwell. Mary did not seem to hear their pleas. Bothwell was made Duke of Orkney and Lord of Shetland. On the 15th of May, they were married.

After the wedding there was no banqueting, there was no dancing. On the night of her marriage, a placard was nailed to Holyrood Palace gates. It read

"As the common people say,
Only harlots marry in May."

But three months had passed since the death of Darnley. Mary's people now either believed their Queen to be a murderous whore, or a pawn to the power of Bothwell. Her lords were all vastly opposed to her marriage. Mary and Bothwell were seen arguing only days after their wedding. He refused to allow her to hold power over him. She was depressed, and so listless that at times she did not rise from her bed.

And all the while, her men were gathering arms against her.

War was stirring in Scotland.

*

"I can no longer offer my full and unquestioned support for the Queen of Scotland," I said without pleasure to my Council. "In the matter of her marriage, I find much to be suspicious about. I still believe her innocent of the murder of Lord Darnley, and I believe she is the chosen ruler of Scotland. I will not abandon her request that I become protector of her son in the event of her death, but I cannot support her actions after the death of her husband, nor her marriage to the Duke of Orkney. I must therefore inform you that I have set aside the talks of Mary of Scots becoming named as my heir, and will do so until her innocence is proven."

There were rumbles of approval. They sounded like a death dirge in my heart.

"The Earl of Lennox has arrived back in England, Majesty, and wishes us to take up the case for his dead son," Cecil said. "He does not trust the findings of Mary's men and wishes us to investigate instead."

"And I suppose next he will claim he was ever a good and loyal subject to England, Cecil."

"He indeed protests such is true."

I grimaced. "I cannot say I have much faith in such an assertion."

"We should request that Prince James is brought to England to be raised by you and Lady Lennox, Your Majesty," Robin added. "There is clearly much peril for him in Scotland since it is in such disarray, and the boy is the heir to your throne and to that of Scotland."

I nodded, but I knew even then that the Scottish lords would not release their Prince. Should I even put forth such a request, seeing as my cousin, his mother, was still the Queen? Margaret Lennox had already visited me, asking for Prince James to be brought to England, and for justice for her son. I had received her at Richmond and looked upon her with no small amount of horror. Margaret had always been a handsome woman, but her son's death had aged her. Shadows hung under her eyes and her shoulders seemed slumped. She looked smaller; wizened by her grief.

"Cousin," I had said as she approached me. "Know that I sorrow with you for the untimely passing of your son."

"Your generosity and clemency have been great comforts to me, Your Majesty," she had said in a meeker tone than ever I had heard emerge from her lips.

"We will do all we can to bring about justice for my cousin, Henry," I had continued on. As I spoke, I saw vengeful fire leap into her eyes.

Margaret had left with my assurances that I would aid her and her husband, but I wondered what I could do. I had told her she could visit me whenever she wished, and her son, Charles, and her husband were greeted at court and shown favour. I had told the bitter Lennox that I would help with money, men and all he needed, but I could not act against Mary herself. Mary was the Queen in Scotland. Were I to act directly against her it could put my own position in jeopardy. But it seemed my intervention would little be needed, for Mary's lords were determined to remove her themselves.

But a month had passed since the marriage of Mary and Bothwell and Scotland was in turmoil. Mary's lords had risen against her and she had fought for control of her country. She had been captured at Borthwick Castle, but escaped in the guise of a man, and ran straight back to join with Bothwell, who was, by then, her sole ally. She had mustered an army of perhaps three thousand, but this was nothing to the forces her nobles were bringing together. They had offered twenty shillings a month to all who would join, a staggering sum, and one which bought many a man's loyalty. Their armies met at Carberry Hill, but hesitated to fight. It was one thing to attack Bothwell, quite another to face their Queen. Mary was called upon to set Bothwell aside for good, and yet she did not. She had the chance then, to make peace honourably, and yet she chose to remain with her husband. There was a good reason for this.

Mary was pregnant with Bothwell's child.

Their armies had met in battle, but many were unhappy to be fighting their Queen and so single combat was proposed under a flag of truce; Bothwell against a lord named Kirkcaldy. Bothwell had rejected the duel, saying his opponent was not worthy of him. He demanded to face Lord Morton, who had been suspected of playing a part in Darnley's murder. But Morton was fifteen years older than Bothwell and knew he would not survive. Lord Lindsay, a relative of Darnley, volunteered in his stead, but as the combatants made to fight, Mary intervened. She knew that whatever happened, she would become the prisoner of one side or the other. She offered to surrender if Bothwell was allowed to escape. When this was refused, she had given the order for her army to attack.

Did she want to save the father of her child? Had she truly fallen for this man who had so abused her? Was she seeking to protect the only man still allied to her? How can we ever know?

Her army lost the battle. Bothwell fled. Mary parted from him in tears, and became a prisoner of her own lords. She rode towards them with her head held high. At first, they were respectful, but cries of "Burn the adulteress!" and "Burn the whore!" soon erupted. Mary was stunned. She looked to her lords to discipline their men. They looked away from her.

As she was led to Market Cross in Edinburgh, her people turned out to add their insults to those of her lords. Mary was taken in the dead of night to the island castle of Lochleven in the Firth of Forth as her men worked to depose her.

She was their prisoner, and soon they would take her crown.

Chapter Eighty-Three

Richmond Palace
February 1603

How could it be, that we, two women so unlike in character, and yet so alike in fortune, could suffer an experience so similar, and yet emerge with such different fates?

I do not deny I was the more fortunate. I had never been subject to the violence Mary's lords had showed to her. She had lived an easier youth than mine, and perhaps that was her downfall, in the end, for she did not have the skill I had when I came to the throne.

Mary had little choice but to marry Bothwell, and when she stepped in to save him? He was her only ally, and she was carrying his child. Was she to leave herself friendless and unsupported? I like to think that if I had been treated as she was, I would have resisted marriage with him. I like to think thus, but I know not if it is the truth. No one can know, until we are put in the same situation.

But now, my cousin had chosen her path. It was opposite to what mine had been in a situation so similar. It steals my breath to consider how close-linked our fates were. Mary married the man suspected of killing her husband, where I had refused Robin, suspected of murdering his wife. However much she had been forced, the deed was done, and she lost her throne for it.

For me, it was as though when I looked on Mary's life, I looked into a glass which showed what my own life might have been. Had I married Robin, when his wife was found at the bottom of those stairs, would my people have called me a whore too? Would they have screamed for me to be burned? Would they have taken my throne, as they took my cousin's?

Fate, like history, likes circles.

Strands of stories never resolved touch ends and play out their tale. Perhaps, like Death, stories do not like to be cheated of their endings. Perhaps, like Death, when they cannot resolve themselves in one life, they steal from another.

Circles upon circles. Never-ending threads of fate dipping in the darkness and dancing through the light. I felt as though these strands had fallen from my fate, and bound themselves instead to Mary. As though the destiny I might have had, had not wished to be so easily set aside.

From my path, that strand of fate fluttered out, hanging in the breeze, until it found Mary.

Where it failed to steal from me, it took instead from her.

Sometimes we do not control the stories. Sometimes the stories control us.

Chapter Eighty-Four

Windsor Castle
July 1567

"Do you not think there are strange echoes, here, Robin?" I asked him as we rode out into the summer sunshine. Dog roses bloomed at the edge of woodlands and the fields were bright and lush. Sparrows chattered over our heads and the air was fresh, warm, sweet. The scent of my horse, earthy and deep, mingled with the smell of flowers opening their buds to the sun, washing against the scent of rain, recently fallen, seeping into the earth.

"Of Amy, you mean?" he asked and then sighed. "I do feel them."

"My cousin chose to marry the man who all suspected of having killed her husband," I said, ducking my head under a low branch as we rode past some trees. "She has lost her people's love, and her nobles have taken her crown. Now perhaps I will see what might have been in my own life, in the path hers will take in the future."

"Do you regret that we did not marry?"

"At times… but Mary was put in a different situation, was she not? Kidnapped, carried off to some low castle and abused." I shook my head. "She would never have married Bothwell had he not raped her. I was not handed such an ill fate."

I breathed in as our horses walked over the field. "More and more, Robin, I see what I have made of my life and I bless it. I am fortunate. I offered my heart to you, and for all we have done to one another, I rest safe in the knowledge you would never have acted as Bothwell did."

"It is not in my nature to do so," Robin said. "And his actions disgrace the name of all men, all decent men. No man of honour would ever do as that man has done. Although many now say that the Queen must have loved him, for choosing to marry him."

"What other choice did she have?" I asked, pulling my horse to stand as we rose to the crest of a hill. "Once her honour was so abused, the only remedy was to try to make the act itself honourable, and marry her rapist. Although I do not understand the idea, many seem to think that an act of honour outweighs one of dishonour." I sniffed. "It is not true of course. It punishes the woman for the act done against her. It takes the victim and says they were to blame for the actions of the criminal. It is another part of that evil we maintain; that a woman is always to blame for any ill done to her. Bothwell did not love her, he loved the crown she wore, and cared not for the woman underneath. Mary acted as she believed was right, and she was wrong. But all the same, he was the one who brought about her destruction; for ambition."

Mary had been taken to Lochleven where she had delivered still-born twin girls. Lying in her bed, grieving and weak from loss of blood, she had been forced to abdicate her throne in favour of her thirteen-month-old son. James VI had been crowned five days later. Her brother, James Stewart, Earl of Moray, had been made Regent of Scotland. I had refused to recognise King James, as he was now known, and had demanded the Prince be brought to England to be raised by me, his protector and godmother. I wanted to aid Mary in escaping her prison and recovering her throne, but I had few supporters. It was not only for Mary's sake that I wanted her restored, but for mine. I little wanted my enemies getting any more notions into their heads about replacing me.

Robin sat for a moment without saying anything. His eyes moved over the hills and dales, over the pockets of woodland and the fields bursting into new life below us. "I will not push you anymore, Elizabeth," he said softly, looking ahead. "Perhaps now, more than ever before, I understand why you were so distraught when I sought to make you marry me through subterfuge and trickery. You thought that I was seeking to force my will upon you, just as Bothwell has done to your cousin. And perhaps that evil was within me, although I swear to you that I recognised it not. I did not see what I was doing. I did not see I was killing the love between us with my wish to make you mine. Now that I have had the chance to look my actions in the face, as they are done to full and evil effect by another, I see the sin in them. And I am sorry for all that has come between us."

"As I am too, Robin," I said. "And you were not solely to blame. I, too, acted wrongly, seeking to punish you. I acted out of spite and jealousy. I, too, ceased to talk of our troubles, and drove a hard wedge between us. I was not brave enough to tell you that I did not believe we could marry after the death of your wife. That first confusion and all that came with it was my error, not yours. Had I been more courageous, we might have saved ourselves all the troubles we have had, over these years."

I breathed in. "But if you look on Bothwell and compare yourself to him, then you should desist," I continued. "For he is no man, when compared to you, and he has no heart when his is brought against yours. Never would you have done to me as he did to her, I know that. The thought would not have crossed your mind, and for all the ambition in your heart, Robin Dudley, I know now, more than ever I did before, that your love for me is more important to you than a crown. The same was not true of Bothwell."

He gazed at me evenly, and then I was surprised to see tears in his eyes. "I do love you," he said. "I have never loved another. In whatever way you wish me, Elizabeth, I am yours until the end of my days."

I smiled and reached across to take his hand. He pulled it from his carved leather glove and took hold of my fingers. "Let us talk no more of the end of days, Robin," I said to him gently. "Let us speak no more of death. There has been enough loss. For once, I would that we could think only of the present, and enjoy all that we have together. For what use is the present, if we cannot live and love within its hours? If we do not live as we are supposed to... fully and well, our friends gathered about us, and our hearts made merry by their love?"

"Then race me to the next hillock, Majesty," Robin said, releasing my hand. "And let the feel of the wind on our cheeks steal us from resting on sorrows."

I turned my face to my England and breathed in her air. The sunshine was warm and pleasant. The scent of new leaves and flowers was on the breeze. There would be matters to worry on, my cousin not least of them, when I returned to the palace, but here, lost in England, I was a free soul riding at the side of the man I loved. And more than loved. He had become my soft comfort and my steady friend. My place of peace; my place to come when I was tired and sickened by the world. We had found a new way to be with each other... No longer fired by restless desire and unsated dreams, but bound by a deeper tie, in friendship, in honesty, and in love.

I clicked my tongue at my horse and sped down the hill with Robin's horse thundering at my side. "Ride on," I shouted over the rushing winds. "Ride on and let Death feel grief at our pleasure!"

For the first time in years, I felt free of the shroud that had covered me. Katherine Grey, Mary Grey, Margaret Lennox, Mary of Scots... the strands of my winding cloth would be set aside as I ceased to feel their fluttering threads against my cheek, and found joy in living, in loving, in the present day. Life was not perfect, and never would it be so. But I had much for which to be thankful. I had Robin. I was in control of my country, and my people loved me. I had lost much, and the loss of those I loved would never cease to hurt me, but there was much in life to make up for the grief I carried inside.

Those I had loved would never leave me. They were within me, every hour and every day that I lived. And when I spoke their names, they lived on anew, breathing life from the life within me; living in my memories of them. Time does not lessen grief, we do; by accepting that death is a part of life, by understanding the grace of having known great souls and in remembering to be grateful that they touched our lives. In these ways, do we lessen grief. In knowing them, in having had the honour of knowing them, I could not grieve. My life had been blessed by them. And in knowing love for them, for Robin, I was only more alive.

This is how we thwart Death... To know however imperfect we may be, that we are loved. To never spite the love we are offered, and to give love in return to those who deserve it. Then, even when Death comes, He has not won over us. If we have lived our lives well, and full, then He takes not a reluctant soul desperate to cling to life, but a friend, whom He may take hands with and but lead on, to the next adventure.

"You were right, Kat," I whispered as we stopped at the next hill. "This is the way to beat Death..."

"Shall we ride on, Majesty?" Robin asked, not hearing my soft words. I inclined my head and we started down the hill.

The scent of lavender rose from a cottage nearby where it grew by the garden gate. Kat's scent. It flew in the air, upon the breeze, as free and sweet as her soul. I lifted my nose and breathed it in. I feared the memory of her no longer. I welcomed it. I had a sense, then, that Kat had heard me. That she had heard my words and come to me to let me know she approved of my resolve.

Kat was keeping her promise. She would never leave me. She never had left me, for she lived within my soul.

Chapter Eighty-Five

Richmond Palace
February 1603

Death does not look pleased. It makes me want to chuckle.

He has listened to my tale. He had thought it would be one about His victory over me, as the last one was. Now He finds that I was not broken by His work, was not vanquished by His thievery. He is disappointed.

He has no cause to feel this though, not when I will join Him soon enough. But fear Him, I no longer do. With age they say wisdom comes. I know not if this is truth, or if the old simply have lived long enough to have experienced that which others have not. The appearance of wisdom is easy enough to create. With age, with Death drawing near, though, I feel I have learned something. I have learned to look on Him and know that this is not the end. I have learned to see Him as a welcome friend, who will lead me out of pain, and take me to join those I have loved.

From behind Him there steps a figure. One I know only too well. How many times have I believed her to be at my side over the years since she left? I would know her form anywhere.

Kat stands, with Parry, Bess and St Loe behind her. Death does not seek to take her hand and make her dance; He knows better than to dare such a thing. She does not come to prance about me, to dance as Amy's ghost did. Kat just looks on me with her warm brown eyes. She smiles and holds out her hand.

I cannot take it yet and perhaps she knows this, for she smiles wider and brushes down her skirts, nodding at me. There are still words to be said, tales to be told.

We are creatures of stories, we humans. Bound since the first days of our existence to tell tales, to bring heroes to life, and life to our words. Over the years, the stories have grown, and there will never be enough to sate our appetite. We grow strong with their telling, just as the stories draw life from us.

There is much left to be told, as the hours go on, as the shadows and shades of my past come to gather about me. But I fear not to see them, not now. I am reminded of all that I lost, and yet here I find them all… not lost, not gone, simply waiting for me to join them when I am ready.

Death spreads His hands, and waits for me to continue.

Epilogue

Workington
The Mouth of the River Derwent
Cumberland
16th May 1568

It was seven of the evening.

Walkers taking the evening air of the Sabbath noted a small craft bobbing on the horizon of the water that lapped at the shores of their small fishing village of Workington. It was unusual to see such a craft on this day, when all work was meant to be set aside, for it was a small boat made for fishing from the shore, or transporting coal and lime across the Solway Firth. As the craft drew near, travelling through the light summer mist that hovered over the small port, it became clear that the people in this boat, sixteen in all, were not fishermen, nor were they traders, but people of consequence and wealth.

Bedraggled, they were; stained with splattered mud and sticking soil which spoke of travelling in haste. Weary, both in their eyes and in their movements, they came ashore. Amongst their numbers was a woman, taller than any that the people of Workington had ever seen. Full as high as a man, she stood with a dark velvet cowl covering chestnut hair which held a trace of red in its tresses. Although the common people gained only glimpses of her face, it was said widely that she was the most beautiful creature any had beheld. As she stepped ashore, this tall beauty stumbled, and all who travelled with her rushed to aid her, speaking words of love and comfort as they lifted her to her feet. The people who saw her said she seemed sadder than any woman they had ever seen, and yet was gracious to all who spoke to her and offered aid. There was something fragile about this lady. A ghost of sadness drifted from her, spilling out like the mist over the waters, speaking of the sorrow and hardness that she had endured.

The party who arrived that day sought beds for the night in Workington Hall, home of a man who travelled with them, and spoke for them, John Maxwell, Lord Herries. Herries said to any who enquired that he had carried off an heiress whom he hoped to marry to a friend of his son's... but by the time twilight fell, many had guessed at the truth.

Rumour spread through the village, and women gossiped in the streets. Whispers grew. The local inns and ale houses were full of those trading stories of the mysterious beauty that had emerged from the foggy waters. A retainer of Lord Herries, a native of France, recognised the woman as soon as he saw her. And why should he not? He asked the men who whispered with him in the ale house later... For once she had been a Dauphine of his own beloved France... Once, she had been his Queen.

The events which had brought her there were not secret. All had heard of the troubles in her land. All knew of the mysterious death of her husband, the revolt which had risen when she married her husband's suspected killer. She had fought to keep her throne, and she had failed. She had been held captive... But what she was doing here, upon the shores of England, was another question.

Had she come for aid, from her cousin, the Queen? Had she come to seek sanctuary from the evils which chased her? The troubles which travelled in her wake, haunting her steps? None knew, but many suspected.

But one truth was certain, on the lips and tongues of all who had seen this tall beauty arrive. This was no kidnapped heiress. This was no ordinary traveller.

Mary, Dowager Queen of France, deposed Queen of Scotland, had landed in England.

This is the end of *Strands of My Winding Cloth*.
In the next book of the Elizabeth of England Chronicles,
Treason in Trust, Elizabeth struggles with troubles from
without her realm, as well as from within…

Author's Thanks

This book is dedicated to two women, without whom, I often consider, I would never have become a writer; Terry Tyler and Sue Cooper-Bridgewater. When I first started writing and publishing on Wattpad, it was Sue who read my stories and encouraged me to continue writing. At the time I was rather lacking in confidence, but with her encouragement and that of others, I began to have a little faith. Terry, I had the good fortune to meet on Twitter. When I first started to send out sample chapters to agents, and was politely rejected, I talked to Terry on Twitter. It was she who encouraged me to turn to independent publishing rather than traditional. Without both of these fine ladies cheering me on, I might still be in my previous job, and might never have published a single book. In addition then, to the thanks I must give to my editor, Brook Aldrich, and my proof-reader, Julia Gibbs, and all that I owe to my family, my patient partner, Matthew Nott and to all my friends, I offer up my thanks to these two women. Both marvellous authors themselves, they allowed me to keep my laptop and my imagination open, and begin a career as an author.

I have never met either, in person, but via email, Twitter and Wattpad, have found two great souls, and am fortunate to have them in my life.

My thanks, ladies, for all you have done for me.

Gemma Lawrence
2017

About The Author

I find people talking about themselves in the third person to be entirely unsettling, so, since this section is written by me, I will use my own voice rather than try to make you believe that another person is writing about me to make me sound terribly important.

I am an independent author, publishing my books by myself, with the help of my lovely editor. I left my day job last year (2016) and am now a fully-fledged, full time author, and very proud to be so!

My passion for history, in particular perhaps the era of the Tudors, began early in life. As a child I lived in Croydon, near London, and my schools were lucky enough to be close to such glorious places as Hampton Court and the Tower of London to mean that field trips often took us to those castles. I think it's hard not to find characters from history infectious when you hear their stories, especially when surrounded by the bricks and mortar they built their reigns and legends within. There is heroism and scandal, betrayal and belief, politics and passion and a seemingly never-ending cast list of truly fascinating people. So when I sat down to start writing, I could think of no better place to start than a time and place I loved and was slightly obsessed with.

Expect *many* books from me, but do not necessarily expect them all to be of one era. I write as many of you read, I suspect; in many genres. My own bookshelves are weighted down with historical volumes and biographies, but they also contain dystopias, sci-fi, horror, humour, children's books, fairy tales, romance and adventure. I can't promise I'll manage to write in *all* the areas I've mentioned there, but I'd love to give it a go. If anything I've published isn't your thing, that's fine, I just hope you like the ones I write which *are* your thing!

The majority of my books *are* historical fiction, however, so I hope that if you liked this volume you will give the others in this series (and perhaps not in this series), a look. I want to divert you as readers, to please you with my writing and to have you join me on these adventures.

A book is nothing without a reader.

As to the rest of me; I am in my thirties and live in Cornwall with a rescued dog, a rescued cat and my partner (who wasn't rescued, but may well have rescued me). I studied Literature at University after I fell in love with books as a small child. When I was little I could often be found nestled halfway up the stairs with a pile of books in my lap and my head lost in another world. There is nothing more satisfying to me than finding a new book I adore, to place next to the multitudes I own and love... and nothing more disappointing to me to find a book I am willing to never open again. I do hope that this book was not a disappointment to you; I loved writing it and I hope that showed through the pages.

This is only one of a large selection of titles coming to you on Amazon. I hope you will try the others.

If you would like to contact me, please do so.

On Twitter, I am @TudorTweep and am more than happy to follow back and reply to any and all messages. I may avoid you if you decide to say anything worrying or anything abusive, but I figure that's acceptable.

Via email, I am tudortweep@gmail.com a dedicated email account for my readers to reach me on. I'll try and reply within a few days.

I publish some first drafts and short stories on Wattpad where I can be found at www.wattpad.com/user/GemmaLawrence31 . Wattpad was the first place I ever showed my stories, *to anyone*, and in many ways its readers and their response to my works were the influence which pushed me into self-publishing. If you have never been on the site I recommend you try it out. It's free, it's fun and it's chock-full of real emerging talent. I love Wattpad because its members and their encouragement gave me the boost I needed as a fearful waif to get some confidence in myself and make a go of a life as a real, published writer.

Thank you for taking a risk with an unknown author and reading my book. I do hope now that you've read one you'll want to read more. If you'd like to leave me a review, that would be very much appreciated also!

Gemma Lawrence
Cornwall
2017